SOME OTHER NOW

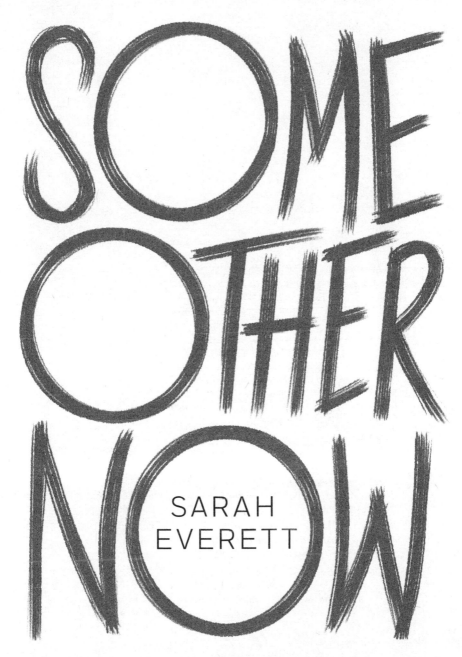

SOME
OTHER
NOW

SARAH
EVERETT

HOUGHTON MIFFLIN HARCOURT

BOSTON NEW YORK

hmhbooks.com

The text was set in Perpetua.

Library of Congress Cataloging-in-Publication Data
Names: Everett, Sarah, author.
Title: Some other now / by Sarah Everett.
Description: Boston : Houghton Mifflin Harcourt, [2021] | Audience: Ages 14
and up. | Audience: Grades 10–12. | Summary: Jessi is caught between
two brothers as the three navigate family, loss, and love over the course
of her seventeenth and eighteenth summers.
Identifiers: LCCN 2019042911 (print) | LCCN 2019042912 (ebook) |
ISBN 9780358251866 (hardcover) | ISBN 9780358359043 (ebook)
Subjects: CYAC: Family — Fiction. | Sick — Fiction. | Friendship — Fiction.
Dating (Social customs) — Fiction. | Depression, Mental — Fiction.
Racially mixed people — Fiction.
Classification: LCC PZ7.1.E96 Som 2021 (print) | LCC PZ7.1.E96 (ebook)
DDC [Fic] — dc23
LC record available at https://lccn.loc.gov/2019042911
LC ebook record available at https://lccn.loc.gov/2019042912

Manufactured in the United States of America
DOC 10 9 8 7 6 5 4 3 2 1
4500817383

SOME OTHER NOW

1

THEN

If you had asked me before the night when everything changed, I'd have said that I was family. That the Cohens were flesh and blood, as ingrained in me as every cell in my body. Not because I was as clueless about genetics as my bio teacher, Mr. Waters, seemed to think I was, but because we shared things that mattered: history, memories, secrets, and time.

So the evening we sat around the dining table waiting to hear Mel's news, it didn't even occur to me that I could be somewhere else. That it was summer and the lake was glistening and I had my own home across town.

I was sitting in my usual spot, across from Rowan and beside Luke, the same spot I'd occupied since Ro and I met at tennis camp when we were seven and became best friends.

"Pass me the salad." Naomi, Mel's best friend, was sitting on my right, and she tapped my wrist to get my attention.

Mel had gotten home from the doctor less than an hour earlier and, instead of answering the barrage of questions we threw at her, immediately insisted that we sit down to "a nice dinner." She said we would talk after we'd eaten. One of the things I'd always loved about Mel was that she never treated me, Luke, and Ro like kids. She told us the truth and spoke to us like we were her equals. Which made the way she was acting now all the more unsettling. She was talking and laughing with Naomi, as if everything was completely normal, as if everything was fine. But it couldn't be, could it?

If the doctors had given her good news, she would have just said so.

She had to know that the way she was dragging this out meant that there was only one conclusion we could reach: Mel was sick.

The kind of sick you couldn't get over with chicken noodle soup and a warm water bottle and a couple of days spent watching Netflix in bed.

My stomach lurched at the thought.

"I need some guinea pigs for this new cupcake recipe I'm trying for the bakery," Mel said, trying to engage us, but Ro just kept vigorously chewing, violently scraping his fork against his plate. I didn't know it was possible to eat angrily, but he was doing it. Apparently he had even less patience for Mel's stalling than I did.

Beside me, Luke was staring down at his plate, moving the food around but not really eating anything. Ever the opportunist, Sydney, the dog, was sitting primly beside Luke's chair, and I caught him sneaking her a cooked baby carrot when he thought no one was looking. Ordinarily, the sight would have made me smile, but Luke looked so miserable it made me feel like crying.

Oblivious, Mel kept chattering about her new cheesecake cupcakes, her voice as raspy and as calm as ever.

She talks the way Billie Holiday sings.

I'd written those words in my journal once, many years ago, after one of the afternoons I'd spent at the Cohens', lounging around in the living room with Mel and listening to the old jazzy songs she liked. I'd doodled hearts around the words. Honestly, most days I wasn't sure whom I loved more: Mel or her sons. I was a little bit in love with each of them, in slightly different ways.

"Jessi." Ro's voice suddenly cut through my thoughts. "Can you come help me in the kitchen for a sec?"

His voice had an edge to it, but I stood and followed him out of the dining room. I wondered whether he'd come to the same conclusion I had—that something was very wrong. As soon as we were in the kitchen, I couldn't help it, I threw my arms around him. Ro hugged me, then patted my back like *he* was the one comforting me.

His voice was a whisper when he finally spoke. "You have to go."

I froze, then stepped back. "Go where?"

His arms dropped to his sides. "Home," he said almost sulkily, staring at the ground.

It took me a moment to understand what he meant.

Home. As in, *my* home.

"What? Why?" I asked.

"Because you shouldn't be here."

I started to laugh, but then I realized Rowan wasn't smiling. "Ro. There's no way I'm going home before Mel tells—"

He didn't let me finish.

"Jesus, Jessi. Do you think you *live* here?" he spat. "Because you don't. This is family shit."

I was speechless. I'd known the Cohens for ten years. I'd spent birthdays and Thanksgivings and Christmases with them. I was there when Buzz, their old cocker spaniel, died when we were nine. A few weeks later, when Mel brought home a box with a shivering Labrador retriever, I'd been the first to peek inside. I helped them choose the name Sydney. I was at their house the day Dr. Cohen packed his things into his SUV and backed out of the driveway, never to return. Never —not once—had any of the Cohens insinuated that I belonged anywhere other than with them.

"Are you serious?" I asked, my voice small.

He nodded, his jaw still set. He made to run his hand through his hair but stopped halfway through the motion, as if just remembering the buzz cut he'd gotten at the start of summer.

"Rowan, I don't get it," I said, starting to feel less indignant and more hurt. I felt breathless, like we'd been sparring and someone had suddenly thrust something sharp and lethal between my ribs. Had I done something wrong? This had to be Ro's way of lashing out because of everything that was happening with his mom. Right?

"There's nothing to get," Rowan said, his voice a whisper. "Just like . . . imagine if this was your mom."

He walked out of the kitchen, leaving me standing there, stunned. The last thing he said was the worst.

Imagine if this was your mom.

Was he fucking serious?

I didn't need to imagine anything. I didn't love Mel any less because she hadn't given birth to me. I didn't *need* to be a six-foot-one prick named Rowan Cohen to feel how devastating even the thought of a world without Mel would be.

I stormed back into the dining room and sat down. Beside me, Naomi was refilling her glass of water. I stole a glance at her, at the white-blond hair she wore in a stylish bob. She and Mel had been friends for twenty years. She didn't need to pass a freaking 23andMe test, and no one was asking her to leave. Who the hell did Rowan think he was?

As I scooped more pasta onto my plate, I felt Ro's glare bouncing off the top of my head, but I kept going until I had enough food for two people.

Even though my stomach still felt unsettled, I shoveled a forkful of pasta into my mouth.

"This is really good. Thanks, Mel," I said.

For the next few minutes I ate in silence while Naomi and Mel kept the small talk going.

When I felt Rowan's gaze on me again, I met his eyes, expecting to see the same annoyed look he'd been giving me for the last five minutes, but instead there was something I couldn't place. Something like desperation.

Pleading.

His eyes were pleading.

I shot him my own look, one I hoped conveyed my hurt and anger at everything he'd said to me in the kitchen. *I can't believe you asked me to leave.*

He lowered his gaze then, as if he could no longer meet my eye.

I couldn't understand it. Was he ashamed? That made no sense—what did he have to be ashamed of? This was about Mel; it had nothing to do with him.

I kept staring at Ro's bowed head, imploring him to look at me. This wordless conversation wasn't over yet. But his eyes stayed fixed on the table, and in that moment, all his anger and bravado and Ro-ness was gone. He was just . . . sad.

And something else I couldn't explain.

Shit.

I could deal with Rowan if he was just being a bully, hurting me because something bad was happening with his mom and he needed somebody to take it out on. But this wasn't that.

I didn't understand what was happening. I'd never seen him like this. He seemed desperate for me to do this for him.

For me to go.

My instinct was to stay and make him tell me what was wrong, to stay and hear what Mel had to say after dinner, but Rowan's sad eyes kept avoiding mine.

Until I heard myself standing, pushing my plate away.

"Oh God, Mel," I said. "I'm so sorry. I just remembered I have this really big assignment due . . . and also a quiz . . . and my dad will kill me if I fail."

I heard myself mumbling a string of excuses.

In the end, I couldn't even remember everything I said.

I just knew that Ro still wouldn't meet my eye as I packed up and that Luke stared at me, confused, the whole time.

I remembered feeling that I was making a mistake, that this wasn't how any of this was supposed to go. Mel wasn't supposed to be sick. But if she was, then I was supposed to stay at the Cohen house until after dinner. I was supposed to sit on the slightly lopsided living room couch, wedged between Luke and Ro, while Mel told us her news. Ro and I were supposed to find ourselves in the dark of the backyard shed afterward, the place we always went after big moments to collect our thoughts. We were supposed to lean back against the metal walls, whispering truths too heavy for a bright summer evening in July. We would talk and cry and hurt, and it would suck, but we would do it together. Because we were family, and that was what families did.

I remembered hugging Mel before I got on my bike to ride home, tears streaming down my face the entire time because I couldn't shake the feeling that I was going the wrong way.

And I didn't even know why.

THEN

In the end, my mother had been the one to tell me.

As soon as I got home, I'd taken the stairs two at a time to my parents' bedroom, where I knew my mom would be if she wasn't at work.

Everything was blurry through my tears, but I saw her right away.

She was a lump in the bed, a blade of light slipping through the crack in the curtains just enough for me to make out her form.

I padded over to where she was, touched what I thought was her shoulder. I'd spent seventeen years trying not to disturb her when she wanted to be alone, but tonight was an exception. Tonight I actually needed her, and for once Mel couldn't take her place.

"Mom," I said to the mound of blanket that still hadn't moved.

She pulled the covers away from her face and squinted at me like she was staring directly into the sun.

"What's wrong?" she asked.

"Mel's home from the doctor," I said. "Can you call her and find out what they told her?"

She blinked up at me, probably wondering why I couldn't call myself or where I'd come from, if not the Cohens'.

"Okay," she said finally, slowly pulling herself into a sitting position.

I grabbed the phone on her nightstand and held it out to her.

Her fingers brushed mine as she took the phone, and I wondered how her hands could feel that cold in the middle of summer.

"Melanie, hi." Her voice was bright and breezy, as if she hadn't been lying in a dark room for what was probably hours. "Oh, me too. I meant to call and congratulate you on Luke's graduation."

I sat at the foot of her bed, hugged my knees to my chest, and listened to my mother's side of the conversation. To her laughter and easy banter. She couldn't always pull it off, but sometimes, for short spells, she could pretend to be okay. She somehow managed to pull it together for the things that were really important to her. Like work or the occasional parent-teacher meeting, though those were more Dad's territory.

But I wondered for the hundredth time why Mom bothered pretending for Mel, who easily knew more about me than either of my parents did. Mel, who knew about the days my mother spent in bed, the medication she wouldn't take, the therapists she wouldn't see. You wouldn't think my mother would be opposed to medicine; she was an optometrist, for God's sake. But she was one of those people who believed it was okay for everybody else, but not for her. *She* was just tired, overworked or under the weather, or in need of some alone time. So we lived with it, this nameless, shapeless thing that had hollowed out my mother.

Mom got quiet now as Mel talked on the other end of the line.

I was far enough away that I couldn't make out distinct words, but Mel's voice sounded somber, like the melody of something in a minor key.

While she was talking, my own phone vibrated in the pocket of my cutoffs.

It was a text from Luke.

Why'd you leave like that?

He didn't text me very often, and when he did, he did so frustratingly. In complete sentences, with punctuation and zero emojis. It was so aggressive.

Usually, though, I knew him well enough to know he wasn't mad.

But tonight he sounded like he *could* be mad. At the very least, he was confused.

I considered telling him the truth — that his brother had told me to leave — but I couldn't bring myself to do it. Something was going on with Rowan, and even though I wasn't sure he deserved it right then, I felt like I had to protect him. If I told Luke what had happened, he would confront Ro, and Ro would . . . well, no one ever knew what Ro would do.

There was something I forgot to do, I texted back. I knew how lame it sounded, but I couldn't think of anything better.

It couldn't wait? Luke texted back immediately, and despite myself, I felt vindicated. *He* didn't think I didn't belong there.

I wasn't an idiot. I had brown skin and a thick, curly mane of hair, courtesy of my black father and white mother. Mel's parents were from the Philippines, and maybe that was what drew us together — that we both stood out in our mostly white town. But still, it meant I looked nothing like her. I looked nothing like Luke and Ro either,

Mel's raven-haired boys who loomed over everyone. Nobody would look at the four of us and think we went together, but I'd always known — or I *thought* I knew — that inside, we were all the same. That we'd chosen one another, Luke and Ro and Mel and me, and that made us family.

Whatever Ro was going through didn't change that.

A wave of anger mixed with regret washed over me.

I should have stood my ground tonight. I shouldn't have left.

And honestly, I hadn't needed Luke to tell me that. I'd known it in my bones that I belonged with the Cohens on the worst night of all our lives so far.

My mom was finishing up her phone call with Mel, so I didn't respond to Luke's text.

I shoved my phone back into my pocket and walked over to the side of the bed again.

"Take care of yourself, Melanie." Mom's voice had gone all somber now, and a lump formed in my throat.

When she hung up, she told me. She said it quickly, like she thought it was kinder to just rip the Band-Aid off, and if I was capable of thinking at that point, I would have appreciated it.

As I buried my face in my hands, blubbering like I was all water, my mother did something she'd never done before.

She slid over into the middle of the bed so I could slip in next to her.

Lying there in my parents' room, I cried as if I'd never see Mel again. Mom said nothing, running her hand through my hair while I snotted all over her sheets.

As I was growing up, there would be days on end when I didn't see my mother. She would be just a lump in a bed or a figure hunched in the dark of her room. She needed time, my father would say. She needed space.

Sometimes he'd make her bundle up and go for a walk in the fading sun. She'd look gaunt and pale and hollow-eyed. *She needed fresh air.*

There was never a time when she needed me, but every time he had the chance, my father told me that she loved me.

She just needed to get better, but she loved me.

I don't know if I ever really believed it. But if I hadn't, tonight would have shown me that he was right. My mother hugged me and listened to me cry about the woman I would have—and always had —picked over her, time and time again.

NOW

Summer in Winchester is a bitch.

This time last year, I was taking calculus at summer school and dealing with the kind of news that rocks the foundation of your life. But at least it was air-conditioned.

Sweat makes a lazy trail down the back of my neck as I feed tennis balls over the net and try to avoid getting whacked by a bunch of hyper nine-year-olds. Maybe the time would pass faster if I hadn't emptied my water bottle within the first half-hour of lessons. Or maybe the time would pass faster if I got paid for what I was doing.

There are a lot of reasons why I'm probably not the ideal teacher, but when the tennis club was down an instructor last year, I volunteered to help out, and I don't intend to break my promise.

"Looking good, Madison!" I call out to the newest girl in my group, a toothy kid dressed in all-pink everything.

"Nice! Make sure you bring your racket back all the way, Lewis," I tell the next kid.

I reach into my cart and toss another ball over the net. It comes whooshing back with interest, and I don't have enough time to jump out of the way before it pelts my right knee.

"Oof. You okay, Jessi?" Derek winces in sympathy from the ad side of the court, where he is also feeding balls to a lineup of kids.

"Yeah. I'm good." I rub at my knee, trying to erase the pain.

Derek walks over and holds a tennis ball to his mouth to hide what he's saying. "That kid's got a forehand. If only he'd tone it down a little and occasionally try to get it *in* the court."

"No kidding," I agree.

Derek is in his forties, a former college player with a massive serve. He started at Tennis Win only a couple of months ago, but he's already a far more dedicated head coach than the string of coaches the club has hired in the last year, since it's been under new management. If he didn't keep a running commentary throughout the day, he wouldn't be half bad. I miss the husband-wife duo who taught us when Ro and I were kids, but they retired and moved to Florida two years ago.

I manage not to get hit again for the rest of the morning lessons. After cleaning up the courts, Derek and I head back to the club building. My knee is throbbing at this point, so I grab an ice pack from the freezer in the kitchen and fall into a chair in the mercifully air-conditioned lounge room.

As soon as I sit, I am hit with all the reasons I tend to avoid the lounge room like the plague. A grinning fifteen-year-old Rowan stares at me from one of the portraits in Tennis Win's Hall of Fame. He sports an identical smile in three other pictures that are interspersed among the photographs of past "Winchester stars." There's even one of both of us at a tournament we won when we were about ten and playing mixed doubles together, beaming at the camera as if it's the best day of our lives.

A lump forms in my throat, and I pack up my stuff and quickly leave the lounge, dumping the ice pack in the freezer on the way out. I'm in the parking lot of the tennis club, back out in the scorching sun, when my phone vibrates with a text.

Come to the lake with me and Brett this afternoon! It's from Willow Hastings, whose dad owns the tennis club. She usually hangs around Tennis Win on Saturday mornings, watching lessons, and I feel relieved that I missed her today. I'm not in the mood for her cheeriness and relentless optimism. Frankly, it's a miracle that we're friends — for me, anyway. Because of everything that happened last year, I was basically friendless my senior year, until Willow came to Winchester. Thanks to the brutal luck of having to move just before the last semester of her senior year, Willow and I were the only two untethered planets in the Winchester High galaxy, and we soon found our way into each other's orbits. I doubt we would be friends if she'd grown up here like everyone else.

I text and walk at the same time.

Can't. I have to work. I add a sad face emoji, as if this pains me greatly.

With the grandpa you babysit?? she writes back.

I smile, but don't dignify her text with a response.

I climb into the car my parents bought me at the start of the year.

All Saints Assisted Living is only a couple of miles away from the tennis club, and I arrive fifteen minutes before my shift starts at one. I make my way inside anyway, swiping my badge over the door and going up the elevator and down the hallway to Ernie's room.

When I knock, he calls for me to come in. I open the door and step into the kitchen of his small apartment, the lights on even though it's the middle of the afternoon.

"Hey, Ernie. Are you decent?"

"Enough," he retorts, his usual answer, and I smile.

I find him in the living room, sitting in front of the TV, watching a curling match with no volume.

"How are you doing?" I plop down on the couch next to his beloved rocking chair.

"Better than the alternative," he says.

"Which is what?" I ask, knowing I'm walking right into the trap of a carefully orchestrated joke. I know he spends all of the days before I come thinking of jokes he can try out on me, so I always play along.

"Six feet under, like my brother Gareth Richard Solomon IV, the unlucky son of a bitch."

"Ernie!" I say in mock horror. "Don't make me call your mother."

"Why not? I haven't been to a good seance in some years."

I laugh. "I can't, when you're like this," I say, even though he is always like this and that's what keeps me coming back. That, and the

14

fact that I get paid for it, which honestly feels like a con, since most times he is easily the best part of my week. I was nervous to apply when I first saw the ad Ernie's family posted online late last year, looking for someone to keep him company a few times a week. I didn't have a lot of experience with older people. We live far from Dad's parents, and I've never even met Mom's. Thankfully, it has turned out to be the perfect job for me. I literally get to sit and exchange barbs with the funniest old man I've ever met, and I make money from it.

"Want to go for a walk?" I ask while I tidy up his small table.

Ernie scoffs. "I didn't do all that exercise when I was young just to get old and do even more. When do I reap the benefits of what I sowed?"

"The fresh air will be good for you," I insist.

He shakes his head.

"Put on some music," he says, "and then I want to ask you something."

I've been here enough times that I can hook up my phone to the wireless speaker Ernie's kids bought him last Christmas, and within seconds Ella Fitzgerald's voice comes spilling out into the room.

I let myself listen to the old jazz classics only when I'm with Ernie. First, because he's old enough to appreciate them. Second, because with him as my audience, I can usually manage to keep my tears back.

Today the ache in my chest is dull but bearable.

"What's up?" I ask when I'm back on the couch.

"I'm always wondering, but I've never asked," he says. "What's a girl like you doing hanging around all afternoon, three days a week, with an old fart like me?"

"First of all, you're not—"

"Save it. I know what I am. A goddamned piece of flatulence," Ernie insists. "Well?"

"Well, what?" I ask.

He is quiet a minute, and then he speaks, his eyes serious, "Why do I get the feeling that I'm replacing something for you?"

I swallow hard.

"You're not replacing anything," I say when I manage to speak. But the truth is, we both know he's right. He's replacing the family I thought I'd never lose, just the way Willow is replacing the friends I thought I'd always have.

"Hmph," he says, clearly dissatisfied with my answer, but we go back to listening to the music and not speaking.

As I'm leaving Ernie's place just after three, my phone vibrates in my pocket and I answer it.

"Hi, honey!" The cheeriness in my mom's voice is even more unexpected than the call itself. It really shouldn't surprise me, because that's a thing my mom does these days. Call me.

"Just wondering when you're coming home," she says.

"I'm just leaving All Saints. I had to work, remember?" I probably should have texted to remind her, but I'm still not used to checking in with anyone about where I am.

"Are you sure you're not working too hard, Jessi? Two jobs *and* volunteering at the club?"

"I'm fine, Mom," I say.

"All right." There's a short, awkward silence; then she sighs. "Well, I just wanted to see where you were. Drive safe, okay?"

I tell her I will and hang up.

My mother has changed so much this past year that I still have trouble believing that this new version of her, Mom 2.0, is here to stay. The memories of our quiet house and the dark of my parents' bedroom gives me whiplash, and it's easier to focus on my conversation with Ernie than to remember how things used to be.

So I go back to what Ernie said about the people he's replacing, and soon I'm in a sinkhole made of the past. I'm drowning in thoughts of Mel and Ro and Luke, and even Sydney.

I'm usually good about not acting on my impulses, but on my drive home, I break.

I let myself do the thing I rarely ever do.

I drive by the Cohen house on the far east side of town. Slow down to get a good look at the car I don't recognize and let myself wonder, for just a minute, what my life would be like if last summer never happened.

2

THEN

For the whole week after we found out she was sick, I could hardly look at Mel without bursting into tears. Not quiet, dainty ones either, but loud, jerky hiccups. Sometimes I swore I could feel Ro's eyes on me, and I thought about what he'd said that night.

Imagine if this was your mom.

Did he feel as if I were hijacking Mel, binding myself to their family, to their pain, when it wasn't mine?

And how could he possibly think that? That it wasn't mine, too?

I'd grown up following the same rules Ro and Luke did, hearing the same bedtime stories, being hugged and chastised and loved the same way they were. I had more memories of Mel tucking me in than I did of my mother doing so. In all the ways that mattered, Mel was family to me.

How did Ro not see that?

Things had been weird with me and him ever since that night at his house. He still wouldn't tell me the real reason he'd asked me to leave, and I still hated him a little for it. Or I tried to hate him, anyway. Mostly, I was just sad. Ro and I didn't keep secrets from each other. We sometimes fought, but we never purposely hurt each other.

It made me wonder if something had changed in our friendship, if somehow we were drifting apart.

On Saturday, just a couple of days after Mel's news, Ro and I were sitting in Rosas, the bakery Mel owned, stuffing our faces with red velvet cupcakes. *Rosas* is Tagalog for "rose," but people always assumed it was Rosa's, and that Mel was Rosa.

Now, temporarily abandoned in front of me, was my calc textbook and a pile of papers documenting my failed attempts to figure out derivatives. I'd jumped at Rowan's offer to help me, glad we could spend some time together, but his "help" was turning out to be of no use. He was nearly as bad as I was at calculus.

I could hear Mel's voice in the back as she was training the lady who would be managing the store over the next few months while Mel started treatment.

"I love her accent," I whispered to Rowan, who was scrolling through his phone, probably watching tennis highlights, as Wimbledon was on at this time of year.

When he didn't answer, I tapped his foot under the table and repeated what I'd said. The woman, Beverley, had this prim British accent that mixed unexpectedly with a Midwestern drawl on certain words. I'd heard her telling Mel that she was from Brighton but had lived in Ohio for more than fifteen years. As a rule, Winchester didn't get a lot of new blood, and we always got excited when it did.

"Hmm," Rowan said absently.

I stood and walked around to his side of the table. I leaned down, pretending to get a napkin, when what I really wanted was to see what held his attention so tightly. If he was looking at anything gross, I was going to round kick him.

I stiffened when I saw the logo of the hospital where Mel's treatment was supposed to start the next Monday.

Rowan finally noticed me, and he quickly turned off his phone screen, saying, "Do you mind?" That his impulse was to shut me out stung. It was like the night Mel had been diagnosed all over again.

"Why did you make me leave?" I asked, still leaning over him. "That night, why did you want me to go?"

"I already told you," he muttered. "It was a family thing."

"Naomi was there."

"She's *Mom's* friend. Mom clearly felt comfortable enough to share the news in front of her."

The implication was that I had been at Mel's house as Ro's friend and had no other reason to be there that night. I blanched. "Are you fucking kidding me?"

He shrugged.

I glanced into the back of the bakery, where I could make out a sliver of Mel's green shirt, and wondered if there was any truth to what he was implying.

Could *Mel* have wanted me to go that night?

Why wouldn't she have told me that herself?

Until that night, I'd felt so confident in my place with the Cohens. But now, thanks to Rowan, I was starting to question every assumption I'd ever made.

Like, how *did* I know Mel saw me the way I thought she did? Had she ever actually said I was the daughter she'd never had?

A voice in my head told me she didn't have to say it. She had always been super affectionate with me, she'd always included me in her family's plans, right from that day, years ago, when seven-year-old me was left standing outside Tennis Win because my dad was late picking me up again.

Maybe it's because she felt sorry for you. That wasn't much of a stretch. I was the girl with the absent mother, the girl whose tennis whites had been dyed purple by a dad who didn't know the first thing about doing laundry. Pity was the most logical explanation for the way I'd been embraced by the Cohens all those years ago, but was it the truth?

I turned on Rowan.

"You're such an asshole. You know that?"

"Whatever," Rowan said, standing. "I have to get to practice. You need a ride or what?"

"I'll walk, but thanks."

He rolled his eyes. "Let's go."

"*I said*, I'll walk but thanks."

"Fine," he said, and stalked off. He'd made it all the way to the door before he stopped again. We both knew my house was all the way across town and that walking would take a good hour and a half. "Are you for real right now?" he asked, raising his hands in exasperation.

I ignored him and sat down at our table, my back to him. I heard the door slam shut a few seconds later.

"What was that?" Mel asked, appearing again behind the counter.

"Just Ro, being a jackass. Can you give me a ride home when you're done? I mean, if that's okay."

Mel was wiping the counter now, but she looked up at me with a frown. "Of course it's okay. Why would you think it wasn't?"

Ro's acting like he's sick of me, I wanted to say, but I didn't want to throw him under the bus. So I kept my mouth shut and simply shrugged.

"I'm giving you a ride home," Mel said, letting me know there were no *ands* or *buts* about it. When I nodded, she turned and disappeared into the kitchen.

It was intensely inconvenient, being newly seventeen and still not having a car. Ro had managed to land a cheap secondhand Ford, even though money was much more of an issue for the Cohens than it was for my parents. Correction: money was much more of an issue for Mel and the boys. Dr. Cohen and the ER nurse he'd left Mel for definitely had no money issues, going by the lavish gifts Luke and Ro normally got for birthdays and Christmases.

Even though I'd gotten my license last year, my father still felt I wasn't "ready" to have my own car. I think, in his mind, my having a car meant one more thing he had to worry about. He already had Mom and EyeCon, the eye clinic my parents owned. The way I saw it, it was one *less* thing he had to worry about, because I would no longer be bumming rides off my friends or taking buses or walking, but as far as Dad was concerned, a car meant ample opportunity for accidents and mischief, and I had yet to convince him otherwise.

Over the next few weeks I continued to ask Rowan about that night. He would probably have used the word *harass,* but I wouldn't let it go. He had done this to me — making me question how the Cohens really saw me after all these years. I just couldn't accept that any of what he'd said was true. Mel did not seem to act, in any way, like I was the pest Ro had made me feel I was. She was never short with me, never distant or annoyed or anything less than what she'd always been: kind.

I was used to feeling unsteady in other ways. For my whole life, my mother had been the biggest question mark in my world. I used to spend hours staring at the photographs lining the living room walls, pictures from when my parents were newlyweds, traveling through South Africa and France and the UK. I'd park in front of those framed photos, asking the pictures questions they couldn't answer. Why the two people in them looked like strangers. Why my mother seemed happy and vibrant and round-faced in those early pictures, but haunted and gaunt and faraway in all the pictures taken after I was born. I'd ask the old Polaroids they took in grad school when that ever-present crease between Dad's brows first appeared and what caused it — and why, if he turned away from looking at my mother for even a second now, it seemed she would break.

I was used to questioning so many things about my life, and now, in addition to the other things I could never figure out, I had questions about my place with the Cohens.

THEN

I went from spending every night at the Cohen house to every second or third night, even though, while Mel was undergoing treatment, I kind of wanted to be there all the time. I wanted to know when she was having a bad day. I wanted to be the one to watch scary movies with her and paint her toenails when she wanted to forget about being sick. I wanted her to know how much I cared.

Once, when I was nine, my mom had been in bed all day and I was hungry and cranky and tired of being quiet, so I kept inventing excuses to go into her room and talk to her. First I told her I was hungry. Then I asked if I could have a Popsicle. Then I asked if she knew

It was raining. The fourth time I went in there, my dad, who had just gotten home from work, stopped me before I could say anything. He pulled me out into the hallway, shut Mom's door, and leaned down to talk to me.

"Mommy's really tired today. Let's let her rest for a little while, okay?"

He tried to get me to follow him to the kitchen, but I refused to budge.

"Jessi," he said with a sigh.

"Can I go to Rowan's house for dinner?" I asked.

"Not tonight."

"But why?"

Dad sighed again, this time through his nose. "You know, honey, sometimes people just need to be on their own."

I knew what he meant — that the Cohens were their own family and we were ours. But it was also true of my mom, that most times she didn't need or want me around.

I was remembering those words alone in my room one Friday night, the second week after Mel's treatment started, when my phone rang.

I lunged for it, panic setting in when I saw the name on the screen.

"Luke," I said as soon as I answered. "Is she okay? Do I need to come over?"

"Mom's good," Luke said, knowing right away who "she" was. "It's not that. It's Ro."

I sat up straighter in bed. "What's wrong with Ro?"

"He went to practice this morning and never came home. I told Mom he was with you, so she wouldn't worry. He's . . . not, is he?"

24

"No," I said, shaking my head as if he could see me. A sick feeling flooded my body. It wasn't like Rowan to disappear without telling anyone. I wasn't used to this distance between us—my best friend not confiding in me.

"Do you have any idea where he could be?" Luke asked.

I racked my brain and threw out some names. Luke had either already checked with those people or they were people we didn't have numbers for. Like that Saul kid Ro co-taught with at the tennis club. Or Claudia, a sophomore last year, who Rowan had dated for, like, half a minute.

"Shit," Luke muttered low, under his breath. It wasn't that often he swore or that often he was worried, really worried, but I'd seen it twice just this summer. Tonight, and the night Mel got her results.

It unnerved me.

Luke was saying something about calling him if I heard anything, when it suddenly hit me.

"Celia!" I shouted into the phone. "It's Friday night!"

Celia famously had a blowout bash every Friday night in the summer. She lived on the edge of town, and her parents were always spending weekends at some lake house upstate. It didn't make sense that Ro would be there. He could be impulsive and stupid, and from the time we were little, he had always been the life of the party, but the last thing Ro would do was risk losing a tennis scholarship by being busted for underage drinking. Also, Mel would kick his ass. Still, I couldn't think of any other place to try.

"Celia?" Luke repeated. Sometimes, with the year between Luke and Ro and me, I forgot that there was a small but significant group of people we knew at school who he didn't know, and vice versa.

"Ophelia Murphy. I can show you where she lives."

Luke was in front of my house in fifteen minutes. When I climbed into the passenger seat of his car, the moonlight cut a jagged line across his face, but it was clear how stressed-out he'd been. His hair was all messy, like he'd been running his hands through it, and his eyes were wide and tired.

"Thanks for coming with me. Are you good with your parents?" he asked, and I waved off his question.

"It's okay. They won't care." It wasn't true. Dad was most likely to notice my absence, and he would certainly care, but I was counting on my parents not waking up until the next morning, when I would be fast asleep in my own bed. Just in case, though, I'd scribbled a quick note on the kitchen counter before I left, telling them Ro was missing and I'd gone to help Mel look for him.

We didn't speak much as we drove. It was only after the sound began to aggravate me that I realized I was responsible for the tapping noise, my nails rapping repeatedly against the door of the car. If it annoyed Luke, he didn't show it.

It was rare for it to be just us two, driving somewhere this late at night, and the fact that my best friend was missing made it even stranger. Still, I felt a quiet comfort that Luke and I were in this together. That wherever Rowan was, we would find him. Everything would be okay.

I was glad I was the person Luke had thought to call when he needed help.

"He better have a damn good reason for disappearing like this," Luke said, annoyance temporarily overtaking his worry.

"I'm sure he will," I said, even though I wasn't quite sure it was the truth.

I leaned back in my seat as a trace of mint tickled my nose. I wondered whether Luke had been eating something minty or whether the small leaf air freshener around the rearview mirror was new.

Stealing a glance at his profile, I wondered where he'd been before he'd started looking for Rowan. Had he worked at the computer store today? Was he packing for college already?

The thought of him being six hours away in just a couple of months made my stomach lurch. I would probably only see him over the holidays and in the summer from now on. Mel kept reminding Luke that she had Mom Rights, as far as communication went, so he'd definitely have to call home at least once a week. I was another story. Would he even think about me when he was surrounded by a bunch of new friends in a new town in a new life? I could barely get him to drop punctuation in our sporadic text messages; a phone call would be downright earthshattering.

"What?" he suddenly asked, touching his chin. My cheeks warmed as I realized I'd been caught staring. "Do I have something on my face?"

"Yep. Skin," I said, the best I could do to save face.

Luke grimaced at my lame joke.

"I'm thinking of staying," he said all of a sudden.

"Staying—" I repeated dumbly.

"In Winchester. Not leaving Mom and Ro when she's so . . ." He cleared his throat.

A pang went through my chest.

"And not going to college?"

Luke nodded and glanced over at me.

"But . . . Mel would kill you. And what about your scholarship? She said she just bought you a laundry basket."

Luke's laugh filled the car. He laughed so rarely that it felt like a badge of honor when I was the one responsible for it.

"I called student financing at State, and they said my scholarship would still be there if I deferred for a year. I know I won't be able to concentrate on anything while I'm there. As for the laundry basket, I'm pretty sure it can be returned."

"I wouldn't be so sure. Walmart's return policy is ironclad these days."

He laughed again, and I bit my lip to hide my smile.

"So what do you think?" he asked. "Seriously?"

I thought about it for a minute. "I mean, it's your decision. Yeah, Mel will have a Mel-tdown, but it's your life, you know?"

Luke sighed. "That's it? I know it's my decision. I want to hear what *you* think."

Don't go, I thought.

I shrugged, we drove in silence for another minute, and then I told the truth. Or half of it, anyway.

"If it was me, I'd stay."

The "if it was me" part reminded me of Ro's *imagine if it was your mom* comment, and that felt gross, but I was being honest. If I had been Mel's daughter, there was no way in hell I'd have been able to go to college and leave her.

Luke smiled over at me. "I knew you'd say that."

"Why'd you ask, if you knew?" I said, exasperated.

"I wanted to hear it," he said. Then, after a moment, "Thanks."

Another couple of minutes passed before we pulled up in front of Celia's sprawling circular driveway. Cars were littered all along it and all the way down the street. It would be a shitshow trying to get out of here when this party got busted. And that was a matter of when, not if, judging by the sheer volume of noise spilling out of the house.

Luckily, I spotted Macy, who Rowan and I were friends with, almost as soon as we walked in. "Have you seen Ro?" I asked, feeling a flicker of anxiety. If she hadn't, there was no plan B.

"Mmmmm." She frowned, like she was thinking hard about it.

Today would be nice, I thought.

"Actually, yes!" she said, as if she'd just had a revelation. It was clear she had been drinking. Her voice was all watery and high-pitched. "Yes! And he was getting his ass beat at beer pong."

Relief shot through me.

"Thanks, Mace," I said, and turned to follow Luke, who was already headed to the next room.

We found Rowan in the dining room, breakdancing. Like, he was literally on his head when we walked in.

I felt Luke stiffen beside me. So much for Ro having a good excuse for disappearing.

Still, I pulled out my phone and took a picture of him balancing on his head. I had to.

As disconcerting as it was seeing Ro drunk off his face, it was too good an opportunity to pass up. Ro and I had a policy that if you were stupid enough to do something, pictures were more than fair game. He had a picture of me wailing after downing two packets of hot sauce on a dare, I had dozens of pictures of him with his hair dyed green for Spirit Day.

"Did you just take a picture?" Luke asked as I stuffed my phone back into my pocket. He shook his head, still annoyed, when I grinned. If he wasn't used to our antics by now, he never would be.

We walked over to Ro, and he stopped mid-spin and stared at us.

"You're taking up my space," he complained.

"You're upside down!" I shot back, but as Luke and I helped him to his feet, he didn't seem too embarrassed. He held his head, as if the room were spinning.

"What the hell is your problem?" Luke asked him in a low voice.

"What's yours?" Ro spat back, glaring down at Luke. He had about an inch on his older brother, and he wouldn't let anyone forget it.

"Okay, settle down," I said, getting between them. I hadn't seen Ro and Luke fight since they were like ten and eleven, and though I doubted Luke would indulge him, a keyed-up Rowan had to be stopped before he got going. The motto of Ro's life was to act first, think later, unless it directly affected his ability to play tennis. His scholarship and spot on the team were pretty much the most important things to him. Which was why it was so unsettling finding him drunk.

"Grab your shoes. We're leaving," Luke hissed, and I noticed for the first time that Ro was, in fact, barefoot.

Surprisingly obedient, he crossed the room and picked up a pair of Vans that may or may not have belonged to him, and then we followed him out of the house.

As we crossed the driveway and walked back to where we'd parked on the side of the road, Ro stumbling between us, Luke and I discussed the logistics of one of us driving Ro's car home, but the parking situation being what it was, we decided not to deal with it.

"He can take the bus and come and pick it up tomorrow," Luke said. He used one hand to steady Rowan while his other held his phone up to his ear.

"Don't tell me you're fucking calling Mom!" Ro suddenly snapped, and I swear he had never sounded more petulant in his life.

"Rowan, shut up!" I said. I was pretty sure Luke had been listening to a voice mail.

"Calm the hell down, or you can walk," Luke told him.

"Asswipe," Ro murmured, but it was significantly below his breath, so I took it to mean that he knew Luke was serious.

After we'd gotten him into the car, I climbed into the passenger seat and we drove back to my house. About an hour had passed since I'd left, and I had no missed calls or messages, so I felt pretty confident that my parents were still asleep.

By now, Rowan was snoring softly in the back seat.

Luke cut the engine in my driveway and looked at me as I climbed out of the car. "Thanks, J.J.," he said quietly, not wanting to wake his brother.

My stomach flipped at the nickname. When I was a kid, I hated my name. Jessi Rumfield.

I hated that my parents hadn't even gone as far as to commit to "Jessica." They'd been so busy living their best lives, and then I'd come along. And maybe I was still such an afterthought to them that abbreviating one of the most overused names of all time was the best they could do. They hadn't even bothered to give me a middle name. In elementary school I started trying to convince people to call me J.J.

Right around the time it caught on, though, common sense kicked in. I realized how immature the whole thing had been and forbade anyone to call me anything but Jessi. All the people who had obliged me (basically everyone but my parents) went back to my given name. Everyone except Luke.

Sometimes.

Rarely, but sometimes.

With my newfound maturity and, with it, my newfound disdain for tryhards who went by initials, I don't know how I didn't manage to beat it out of him. Or maybe I didn't really want to.

"Anytime," I said now, and I meant it.

Luke smiled—he knew I did mean it—and then I shut the door and walked back into my house.

As expected, I was safe on the parental front, but my heart was doing this weird leapy thing it sometimes did where Luke was involved. Like when he'd wiped his ancient iPod and filled it with a bunch of Mel's jazz songs for me one Christmas. Or the time when I got braces and he said my smile was "still a ten."

I flopped into bed, thinking of Luke, but it was Ro's words I woke up to the next morning.

Sorry bout last night ... if it's any consolation, head fucking hurts, Mom yelled at me for like an hour and Luke says there's a picture of me breakdancing???

I kept scrolling and saw another text.

Wake up wake up

I'm up. What? I asked.

U pissed? He wrote back within seconds.

He sent a GIF of a kitten belching out neon letters that spelled out SORRY.

Am I forgiven?

Oh sure, I wrote. **I mean, you've only been a jackass all summer but kitten gifs so I guess all is forgiven.**

I'd set my phone down beside me, and it pinged with his response now. **Are you being sarcastic?**

What do you think? I wrote.

I thought you might say that.

Before I could ask what he meant, there were two quick raps on my window.

I pulled open the blinds to see Ro's face pressed up against the glass. He was standing precariously on the tall ladder my father used for cleaning the gutters.

"Ro!" I cried. "Have you lost your mind?"

"I'm about to lose my fucking brains if you don't open up and let me in," he said.

I quickly slid my window open, and Ro thrust a small white box at me, then tumbled in after it. He fell hard on the floor and stayed there, staring up at the ceiling and breathing hard.

"Shh," I said. "My parents are downstairs."

"Holy shit," he panted. "Remind me never to do that again."

I sat on the floor beside him and burst into laughter. "Oh my God. You're such an idiot."

"I was trying to make a grand gesture!" Ro said.

"Dying's a pretty grand gesture."

I opened the box Ro had handed me to find two of Mel's mini cinnamon rolls.

"A peace offering," he said. "For being a jerk lately."

"Aw, Ro," I said, a warm feeling rushing through me. I handed him a cinnamon roll, then took one myself. It was sticky-sweet and so delicious I found myself licking my fingers even after it was finished. I leaned back until we were shoulder to shoulder on the floor, our eyes fixed on the ceiling.

"Tell me something good," Rowan whispered. I knew he was thinking of Mel's illness and the way it had cast a film of sadness over absolutely everything, and I knew he was asking for a distraction.

I thought about it for a second, grinned, then said, "I *do* have a picture of you breakdancing. Wanna see?" I reached for the phone on my bed, found the picture, and shoved it in Ro's face. He groaned and pushed the phone away, but he turned on his side so he was facing me.

"*You* tell *me* something good," I said.

"When I go pro," he said. "I'm going to buy Mom the biggest fucking house in Winchester. She'll travel everywhere to see me play on tour, stay in the best hotels, and then come back home to a mansion. She'll only have to work if she wants to. She can hire people to permanently run Rosas."

I spoke over the lump in my throat. "That sounds perfect."

This was classic Ro. My bighearted, big-dreaming best friend.

"I guess I'd have to buy Luke something. Maybe like a lifetime supply of comic books and whatever video games he wants." Then he turned to me. "What do you want?"

He nudged my toes with his sneakers. "Come on, I'm giving away pipe dreams here."

"I want . . ." I said, trailing off, feeling stupid.

"Say it," Ro prompted. "I'd give you anything."

"I just want my best friend."

He stared at me then, his brown eyes intense on mine. "You've got him."

It all felt so perfect, this moment where we were sharing everything and nothing at all. Ro had apologized for the way he'd been acting the past few weeks. And all this — climbing up to my window, the cinnamon roll — was a nice gesture, but none of it answered the questions I had for him.

"Ro?" I said. We were so close, our foreheads almost touching. "Why did you kick me out that night?"

Rowan heaved a loud sigh. "You really wanna know?"

I nodded, bracing myself for something about how I was annoying and overbearing and they all needed a break from me. It would destroy me to hear those words, but at least I would know.

"I didn't want you to see me cry."

I sat up, confused. "That makes no sense. I've seen you cry."

He shrugged. "I wasn't thinking, okay?" His entire face had gone red, and he wouldn't meet my gaze. "That whole night just sucked, and I needed to fucking fall apart and . . ."

And he hadn't wanted me there for it.

It was the explanation I'd been waiting for, and I knew he was telling the truth, but it still felt like something was splintering between us.

Everything had shaken him that night, but for the first time in our lives, my best friend hadn't wanted me there.

NOW

On Sunday, the second weekend after graduation, the rare day when I don't have anything else on, my mother places a line of fabric swatches in front of me while I'm halfway through breakfast. Mom 2.0 is always busy, grappling with important choices such as whether we need a whole new dinner set or whether the one we've had for the past decade is fine. I've learned that if there are any household items I'm particularly attached to, I have to tell her in advance, or I might come home and find them gone. It's been one of the weirdest things to get used to, suddenly having to keep up with her.

"Thoughts? Complaints? Recommendations?" she asks, watching me eye the line of patterns in front of me.

"Nice. Super nice. All of them."

She sighs. "Jessi! I need you to help me narrow it down. Even if you just close your eyes and point to something."

I feel bad for not sharing her enthusiasm about our new couch set, and I feel even worse that she can tell.

I don't close my eyes, but I do randomly pick something, a grayish cloth material.

Mom's face lights up. "Really? That was the one I was leaning toward!"

"Great minds," I say, and tap my temple.

"Will you go with me to the furniture store to place the order?" she asks. With Mom 2.0, one errand usually turns into five or six, so I quickly try to shoot down the idea.

"Um, I can't. I'm . . . listening to a podcast. That Ernie recommended." It's a terrible excuse, and not just because Ernie can't tell the difference between a phone and "one of those music recording devices," despite his grandkids' efforts to make him the most tech-savvy octogenarian there ever was.

"We can listen in the car while we drive," she offers.

I concede.

First, with an excuse that lame, I deserve what I get. Second, I really don't have anything else to do, and I've learned that the days when I have the chance to think — those are the worst. Third, my mom is trying really hard. It still catches me by surprise, seeing her bustling around the house and stepping out for groceries and going out for coffee or anywhere that isn't work. This time last summer, like all the summers in my life before it, Mom was basically catatonic. Now she's picking out fabrics for a new living room set.

It's part of her therapy, changing up her environment and getting rid of any reminders of the "hole" in which she spent the last eighteen years of her life. I guess the sofa was particularly offensive to her.

"I'll just go get dressed," I tell her as I get up from the table.

"What's wrong with how you're dressed?" she asks.

I'm wearing a pair of cutoffs and a tank top I'm pretty sure I slept in. But if it passes Mom 2.0's test of approval, it's good enough for me.

"Okay, let's go," I say.

We pass Dad in the living room, where he's watching TV and

getting in as much time with the old furniture as he can. It's almost as jarring to see my father stretched out across the couch on a Sunday morning, doing nothing. Before, if he wasn't working, he was getting groceries or mowing the lawn or trying to talk Mom into eating something.

"Don't have too much fun," he calls out as we go.

"Right backatcha," Mom says, shutting the front door behind us and slipping an arm around my shoulders, and it's almost more than I can take. This sudden change in the universe, where my life now consists of my parents shooting cheery comments at each other and furniture shopping and wanting to do things with me.

It makes me feel both hopeful and like crying, realizing this is what I've missed out on all my life. As soon as I think it, though, I feel guilty. It's not like I never had a family.

I did.

It wasn't anyone I was related to, but they were still family. Even if, near the end, I sometimes doubted the way they saw me.

We drive by the spot downtown where Rosas used to be, and I'm suddenly desperate for red velvet cupcakes and mini cinnamon rolls and choc-chip cookie dough. I'm desperate for Mel's voice and her laugh and the way she hugged people with absolute abandon, as if for one glorious minute we were merging into one being.

"I haven't told your father," Mom says, "but I'm thinking about us switching the dining room chairs too. Maybe we can look at those as well?"

The first time I heard my father joke that Mom's was the most expensive recovery plan he'd ever seen—that was the first time I let myself even consider it. The thought that she might be healed. Or not even healed, but better. The fact that *recovery* was a word that could apply to her.

"Sure," I say. As strange and as fragile as it feels, dealing with this new version of my mother, it also feels nice to have her care about my opinion. For her to *want* to spend time with me. In a messed-up way, it feels a little like having Mel back. It was from Mel that I learned what it was supposed to feel like to have a mother. The Cohens taught me what it felt like to have a home.

We spend the next hour perusing Sofa!Sofa!, debating the merits of leather versus cloth and stripes versus solid and wood versus glass. After that, we drive to the grocery store to pick up some stuff for dinner.

We're headed for self-checkout when Mom realizes she forgot the waffles. I volunteer to get them and leave her in line, nervously standing behind some biker dude who is covered in tattoos on every visible patch of skin. My phone vibrates in my pocket as I walk back to the frozen food aisle.

It's a text from Willow.

Pool party at Bailey Marvin's tonite! You in?

The impulse to think of an excuse is instant, and I'm already typing my response — **oh, I wish I could but helping my mom out all day!** — when I find the aisle I need.

Let me know if you need a ride home though, I quickly add before hitting Send.

I'm a walking hazard, thumbing away at my phone as I go, but it's not until I see him that I stop. In a microsecond, I take in every inch of him. His curly black hair, his broad shoulders, his jeans frayed at the hem like he's been living in them. He looks older, tired.

Everything freezes when our eyes meet. The deep brown eyes that belong to the three people I loved the most in this world. They look different from here, full of grief and anger and something else I can't name. He's at the far end of the aisle, no longer walking this way. I open my mouth to say something, but nothing comes out.

I try again and fail again.

Finally, without permission from my brain, my legs start to move. Carrying me back out of the aisle, empty-handed.

When I reach Mom at the self-checkout, she looks confused.

"Where are the waffles?"

"I . . ."

"Jessi, what's wrong?" she asks, following my gaze in the direction I just came from.

"They're out," I manage to croak after another second.

"Well, that's okay," Mom says uncertainly, like she's not sure why she needs to reassure me about the fact that there are no frozen waffles in Wally's. "We can check Safeway on the way home."

I glance over my shoulder one more time, like there's something on my heel.

I'm not expecting him to follow me, and he doesn't.

Of course he doesn't.

I help Mom carry the bags out to the car, and the whole time she's chatting about the avocados we found on sale. I'm trying to pay attention to her words, but the biggest part of myself is still standing there in the frozen food aisle with a boy who was family, but never my brother and not really my friend.

I know he comes back to Winchester all the time, but this is the first time I've seen him here since the funeral.

I think stupid things: *I'm dressed like a hobo.*

Mundane things: *He's growing a beard.*

I fight to concentrate on this moment, in the car with my mother, but my ears are swimming with too many sounds.

My mind just keeps replaying it. Luke Cohen, in the middle of Wally's, looking at me like I'm a complete stranger.

3

THEN

Mel called being sick her Big Bad. She had this theory that we all had one, whether we knew it or not. She also believed it could change over time, that the most pertinent issue in your life could go from having a bad temper to being bankrupt or something.

My mother's Big Bad was that she was a barely functioning depressive. My father's was that he didn't know how to help her or how to be two parents, so he buried himself in running EyeCon. Luke's, Mel said, was how determined he was that he would never end up like his father. And Rowan's, I knew even without Mel's telling me, was how desperately he wanted things. To play tennis in college, to perfect his already near-perfect forehand, to make his mother well. It oozed out of him, a desperation that made his skin glisten and his eyes blaze.

"What's mine?" I asked her multiple times, afraid it was something like I didn't belong anywhere or that everyone I loved was destined to eventually grow tired of me. Knowing Ro's reason for kicking me out of their house that night helped, but in the days before he told me, an awful seed of doubt had taken root inside me. And it still made me wonder if there was something horrible at my core. Something that meant home would always be a fantasy for me, something I could experience only by proxy.

But Mel refused to tell me what my Big Bad was. "You'll know when you know," she insisted. I could never figure out whether she knew what it was and didn't want to say, or whether she had yet to figure it out. Probably the former. Mel had this way of looking in your eyes and seeing your soul, of listening to your small talk and hearing the dreams you'd never said out loud. She read people the way some people read tea leaves. She knew me, the way no one else did.

So, of course, she knew about Luke.

The first time I suspected this was the day of the fair, during the summer between seventh and eighth grades. The Dog Days Fair always took place during the last days of summer in Winchester. The fair was downtown, just a couple of blocks away from the bakery, so Ro, Luke, and I walked over to it that morning while Mel stayed back at the store. The day passed slowly, the air sticky with sweat and humidity and the smell of roasting hot dogs. At thirteen, the prospect of endless rides and caramel popcorn had lost some of its appeal for me, but Luke took his boredom to a whole other level, trailing behind Ro and me and playing on his phone for most of the afternoon, as if it were a special kind of torture being forced away from his equations and scientific formulas for even one day. Not that I blamed him. I too wanted nothing more than to go back to the air-conditioned peace of Rosas and see if we could weasel any baked goods from Mel. But Rowan had a list of rides he wanted to go on and Mel said we'd all been spending too much time indoors over the summer, so we soldiered on.

By the time we were ready to head back to Rosas, I was ready to write the day off as completely unremarkable. Until Luke disappeared for a few minutes and reappeared with a small stuffed white polar bear.

"Here," he said, holding it out to me.

"Where's mine?" Ro said, trying to grab it out of his brother's hands, but Luke swung the bear out of his reach.

"You won this?" I asked, stunned as I took it from him.

"I bought it." Luke said it like it was nothing, like it was every day he bought me a stuffed animal at a fair, but it was absolutely a big deal to me. It was a gift. The first non–special occasion gift he'd ever given me, and I was convinced it meant something.

Ro made to grab it out of my hands again, but I held it behind my back. I was never letting it out of my grasp, if I could help it. To Luke, I whispered a shy "Thanks."

He shrugged and went back to playing on his phone.

I was still on cloud nine when we walked into the bakery a few minutes later.

"How was it?" Mel asked.

Ro gave her a recap of the day, all the rides we'd gone on and all the games we failed to win. I contributed here and there, but I was still flipping out over this new development.

Luke had given me a freaking stuffed animal.

That's what couples did on dates.

And then, as Mel was closing up the store, I'd seen it. Luke reaching into his pocket and handing her the change. She whispered something to him, and when he nodded, she patted his back. I knew right then and there what an idiot I'd been.

Mel had told him to buy me the bear. The gesture hadn't been spontaneous or romantic or any of the things I'd thought just seconds ago. It was an act of charity, something his mother had made him do.

"Ready to go?" Mel asked, looking over at me and Ro. I nodded and followed them out of the store, feeling small.

I suspected then that Mel knew how I felt about Luke.

I knew it for sure when I strode into the Cohen house four years later, and Mel and Naomi were sitting in the living room, watching TV and laughing at something I hadn't heard. Sydney was curled up at Mel's feet, sleeping.

I hadn't seen Mel since she had completed her first month of treatment two days earlier, so I'd taken the bus from summer school and brought snacks to celebrate. Boring snacks like rice cakes and saltine crackers, as they were the only things that didn't set off her nausea.

Ever since Ro had told me the truth about that night, I was back to visiting Mel whenever I could. Not *all* the time, because I was still a little afraid to overstep, but I came over often enough that Mel knew I cared.

"Jessi-girl! Please tell me there is food in that bag," Mel said, staring longingly at the plastic bag in my hand.

I pulled out the rice cakes, and she squealed.

She actually squealed.

I frowned, looking between Mel and Naomi. Naomi, who was famous for being in a perpetually bad mood, was actually beaming.

"Are you drunk?" I asked.

"Drunk?" Naomi repeated, offended. "What kind of question is that?"

I took a step closer to them, and that's when I smelled it. I gasped.

"You're high?"

"On life!" Mel said, then giggled. "And a wee bit of medical marijuana. No biggie."

"No biggie," Naomi echoed, and they burst into laughter again.

I couldn't believe it. I shook my head, then went to the kitchen to grab some plates and peanut butter. While I was in there, Sydney scampered into the kitchen, and I set down everything I was carrying to play with her. Sydney and I had our little games. One of our favorites was when she stood on her hind legs and I took her front legs and pretended we were waltzing. Another was when I lay flat on the ground, playing dead, and she ran around me frantically, licking me back to life. I always tried to stay in character, but within seconds I'd be giggling at the ticklish wet feel of her tongue. That day, I knelt so we were eye to eye, and she slobbered all over my face.

"Hi, pretty girl," I said in the baby voice I reserved just for her. "Is it just me, or have Nay and Mel completely lost it? I know! They're freaking me out too!"

As I spoke, she licked my top lip and I backed away, laughing. Maybe it was because of how often we played dead, but Sydney seemed to believe that mouth-to-mouth resuscitation was her life's calling. One of Mel's (bad) jokes was that Sydney had taught us three kids how to French kiss.

"I love you too, girlie," I said, still laughing. "But not like that."

I wiped my lips on the collar of my shirt, washed my hands, and picked up the things I'd come into the kitchen to collect.

"So, which of my sons are you here to see?" Mel called as Sydney and I reentered the living room.

"I'm here to see you!"

"I thought for sure she'd say Luke," Naomi said in a fake whisper.

"That's what *I* was gonna say!" Mel cried. She scooched over on the couch so I could sit.

"Ugh," I groaned, sitting beside her and trying my best to keep my expression even. "What's that supposed to mean? Don't be weird."

"Oh, I'm sorry," Mel said. "I thought we were talking about three teenagers. I love y'all fiercely, but it's already weird."

I stared between her and Naomi as they kiki-ed all over themselves and dug into the rice cakes. What the hell did she mean?

If Naomi hadn't been there, I would probably have forced Mel to tell me, but right then I couldn't face the possibility of either of them saying out loud the words I'd never admitted to anyone—that I had a crush on Luke—and giving them more to cackle over.

I liked Naomi, but sometimes she brought out a side of Mel that I liked far less than all the other sides of her.

The good news was that I knew for sure that Luke and Ro were both at their jobs and not at home. The key was to not make a big deal out of it, not to draw unnecessary attention to myself by freaking out about what they'd implied. But for the rest of the afternoon I felt like a bottle that had been shaken up and was close to exploding. It took me a while to figure out what exactly it was about Mel's and Naomi's behavior that bothered me so much, and it wasn't until I was on the bus back home that I figured it out: they had made my feelings for Luke seem like a joke, like some childish crush. I didn't think they intended to be malicious, but it had still hurt. And maybe they were right and I had no clue what it was like to be in love, but I desperately wished I'd defended myself, told them that nothing about the way I felt was silly or trite.

I had never told anyone that I liked Luke, and it suddenly felt vital that I got it off my chest, that I got to express exactly what it felt like to secretly love someone you've known nearly your whole life. Normally the ideal candidate to tell would have been Mel, and if I thought she would be alone or any less high by the time I got there, I would have gotten off the bus and turned around and walked back to her house. As it was, for one of the first times ever, talking to Mel wasn't an option.

So I did something I'd never done before.

When I got home that evening, I passed my dad, where he sat at the dining table doing paperwork for the clinic, and made my way upstairs to my parents' bedroom. I knocked once, and when I didn't hear a response, I pushed the door open and crept inside. For once, the curtains in the room were open — definitely Dad's doing — but Mom was fast asleep anyway, a satin sleep mask over her eyes to block out the light.

I sat down on the carpet at the foot of her bed and pulled my knees up to my chest, listening to the steady rhythm of her breathing, and then I spoke.

I told her what I'd kept buried for so many years. I told her all about the boy who was my first real crush: Luke Cohen.

NOW

I can't erase his face from my brain.

Deep cleaning my room doesn't help. Going for a run in the scorching midafternoon sun doesn't help. If anything, it makes me hallucinate. Seeing him in cars and behind trees and everywhere else I look.

My thoughts are no better than my eyes; they are loud and anxious and sad.

Finally, figuring there's no other way to shut my mind off, I call Willow and agree to go with her to Bailey's party. It's kind of a gamble, because people I might not want to see could be there. People like Eric Lerner.

But I also know who's not likely to be there, since he's a year older and this isn't really his crowd: Luke. And that's good enough for me.

"Yay, you're going to have so much fun!" Willow says that evening as she climbs into the passenger seat. Willow is a tall brunette with bright eyes and an even brighter future. She lives in this massive, Old English style house, but it's only a couple of minutes from my house, so we're carpooling and meeting her boyfriend, Brett, there.

"Seat belt," I say, waiting to start the car.

"One sec," she says, holding her phone to the roof of the car and aiming the camera at her face. At this point Willow knows me well enough not to even ask if I'll be in the picture with her, but I scoot closer to the door anyway, out of her camera's line of sight.

She taps away on her phone, and it vibrates immediately. The first of hundreds of likes she's going to get. Willow is what people call "internet famous." Her videos accumulate hundreds of thousands of views, companies send her all sorts of products clamoring for a feature in one of her posts, and a couple of her followers recently started selling T-shirts with quintessential Willow sayings. A favorite is "Hold hands, not grudges." Budding social media empire aside, she manages to be one of the nicest people alive.

"I'm so happy you're coming," Willow says now, finally pulling her seat belt across her chest. "What changed your mind?"

I start the car. "Just super bored."

"Right," she says, unconvinced.

"I'm serious."

"No, I believe you. I would be too if I spent most of my days with a grandpa I'm not even related to."

Spending time with people I'm not related to is kind of my specialty, but since we rarely discuss what my life was like before she got here, she doesn't know that.

"He's really sweet, you know," I say in Ernie's defense. Willow may be a good person, but like most eighteen-year-olds, I guess she prefers spending time with people her own age. Which is probably why she hates our job at the community center, where we work with kids. Her dad, who has no clue about her thriving online life and the money she earns from views, made her work there because, millionaire dad or not, he wants her to learn the value of hard work.

"Like, it's not a bad job if they took out all the sports and science classes and let me teach something I actually have a clue about," she muses when the topic of work comes up. "Like makeup tips or confidence advice. We could call it a life skills class or something! If I had access to experts at that crucial stage, I'd have turned out completely different." She says the last part so wistfully, I have to laugh.

"Um, it seems to me like you turned out just fine."

"Omigosh, Jessi. You don't even know who I used to be," she says, giving her lip-gloss a once-over in the mirror.

You don't know who I used to be, I think.

"One day I'll tell you all about the glow-up," she promises. Considering that she isn't even in the vicinity of ugly, I'm skeptical that Willow's "glow-up" involves the usual ugly duckling to swan tale, but I say nothing.

We pull up to Bailey's house, which is nestled in a cul-de-sac. I've been here a couple of times before. Once, for her all-girls eleventh birthday party. Another time to work on a group project with Bailey and Rowan.

My heart pinches with a familiar pain, but I force my brain to think of something else. *No Cohens tonight,* I tell myself.

We park and make our way around Bailey's house to the backyard pool, where the party is taking place. There are a bunch of people already in the pool, another few lounging around in swimsuits and drinking.

"Wills, you made it!" Bailey says, grabbing Willow by the hand. They hug, like long-lost friends, even though I've known Bailey longer than Willow has been in the state.

"Hey, Jessi," Bailey says. She looks a little surprised to see me, but she gives me a genuine smile and leads us over to a cooler full of cans and bottles on a small foldout table.

"What do you want?" Willow asks me, digging into the cooler.

"Is there soda?"

"Oh, yeah," Bailey says. "There's some in the fridge. I can go grab a couple of cans."

"Do you want me to come and help?" I offer.

"No, I've got it," Bailey says, then disappears into the house.

When she's gone, Willow turns on me. "You're not drinking? I thought you said you were ready to let loose and get crazy!"

"Not my exact words," I say.

"Close enough."

"I'm driving," I point out.

"In like *maybe* three hours. One drink won't kill you," she says. "Or I can make Brett stay sober and be DD."

"Soda's fine," I insist, starting to wonder how I ever thought that coming out tonight was a good idea. Thankfully, at exactly that moment, Brett appears, snaking his arm around Willow's waist.

"I heard my name," he says. When he gives her a slobbery kiss on the cheek, she giggles.

"Ew, you're all wet."

"You're all dry," he says.

"On account of how I haven't been in the pool yet, yeah," she deadpans.

"Hey, Jessi," Brett says. Brett is one year younger than we are, a senior next year. He's a little self-obsessed for my taste, but he's always been nice to me. His sport of choice is also soccer, which helps. I may teach tennis to little kids, but avoiding the tennis team this last year has basically been my full-time job.

"Hey," I say back.

"Ooh, I promised I'd post from the party," Willow says now, and draws Brett closer for a selfie.

"Hell, yeah," Brett says. "My hot girlfriend's dress deserves to be seen."

"Aww." Willow plants a kiss on his cheek.

"I'll take it," I offer. Willow hands me her phone and I back up to take the picture. They lean in close, their bodies facing each other, and they're so cute it's a little nauseating.

As parties go, this one is fairly tame. The music isn't crazy loud, and everyone is only mildly drunk and it's both a good and a bad thing. A good thing because wild parties really aren't my scene, and a bad thing because it isn't doing quite enough to quiet my thoughts. Still, it's nice to hang out with Brett and Willow, and both of them are nice enough to not complain about my third wheeling.

And then everything changes.

They arrive in a pack, like most jocks, and they're almost all already wasted. My stomach drops as soon as I see Eric Lerner. I knew I was taking a chance, hoping he wouldn't be here. But he'd been off work all this week, so I thought the odds were in my favor.

"Bails!" Eric says, lifting her off the ground as soon as he sees her. "Orange looks good on you."

"Shut up, Eric," Bailey says, but she's smiling.

After Eric puts Bailey down, he and a couple of other players make a beeline for Brett and Willow. They're instantly all talking over one another and laughing. I feel stupid for trying to sink into the shadows. Brett, Willow, Eric, and I all work together. You'd think I'd have developed a better strategy than camouflaging into the scenery and hoping for the best.

Thankfully, I'm the furthest thing from Eric's mind.

He pulls out his go-to party trick, holding his forearms out and getting everyone to see how much bigger and stronger his right arm, his dominant arm, is. Then he moves on to his other favorite, showing off the calluses on his hand from his racket.

Eric is going to the University of Illinois on a tennis scholarship, and he never lets anyone forget it. All through high school, he and Ro were competing for the same scholarships and titles. When they weren't commiserating about how much of a hard-ass their coach was, they were embroiled in an intense (mostly friendly) rivalry. Other than me and his family, I think Ro spent most of his time with Eric.

Andrew, another guy on the tennis team, starts chatting up Willow. "Wills, how come you're not in the pool right now? I heard you can hold your breath underwater for, like, a minute. Do you have any —what are they called—hacks?"

Willow rolls her eyes and ignores him, but a flash of annoyance crosses Brett's face.

Undeterred, Andrew tries again. "You can teach me your tricks."

"I'm not teaching you anything," Willow says.

"Dude, you're barking up the wrong tree—" Some guy I recognize as a junior smacks Andrew on the back, but he is too drunk to be embarrassed, so he just laughs, and everyone laughs with (or at) him.

"You'd have better luck with Jessi," Eric says. I freeze at the sound of my name and try not to react to the words that follow. "Everyone knows she's easy."

I give him what he wants anyway. I flinch.

You can hear a pin drop in our group, until Willow whacks his shoulder. "What the hell, Eric?"

Even after all these months, she still manages to be shocked at his comments.

"Yeah, not cool, bro," Brett says.

"Fuck off, Eric," I say. Embarrassment snakes its way around my body, but I force myself to look him in the eye. It's nice of Brett and Willow to stand up for me, but I am more than capable of telling Eric which cliff to jump off.

Not that it helps.

"Great suggestion, Rumfield, but I don't think I will."

You can slice the tension in our group with a knife.

"How can you drink that?" Andrew asks out of nowhere, pointing to my club soda. "It tastes like piss." His comment is meant to be a diversion, an easy out of the friction all around us. I'm supposed to say something funny and smile, but I don't play along. As it turns out, I'm also more than capable of making myself feel like shit. I don't need Eric to do it for me.

So I turn around and walk off, empty my half-finished soda in the garbage can near the drinks table. I hear Willow telling somebody off, and then she's running across the yard to meet me.

"Hey, are you okay? We can leave if you want."

"I'm fine." I roll my eyes to make it seem like Eric's comment was only slightly annoying. "I was just going to wait in the car until you're ready. I don't want to make you leave."

Willow hooks her elbow in mine. "As if I'm going to stay and hang out with these jerks."

"Wills—" I start to argue, but she doesn't let me finish. She's steering me toward the backyard gate and around the house again to the place where we parked.

"I'm really sorry," I tell Willow for the third time when I pull up in front of her house.

"Can I ask you something?" she asks, quirking her head to the side.

"Yeah, of course."

"Why does he do that? All these comments . . ."

I look out through the windshield at her house. "We've just never gotten along. We've known each other since we were kids."

"Yeah, but it seems so personal. And, like, so *mean*."

I shrug. "That's just Eric." I attempt a smile, but she doesn't buy it. If she knew everything that happened last summer, she'd probably hate me too. Now she leans over and hugs me.

"Just think, once this summer is over, you never have to see him again."

"Yeah, I know," I say, though it's not really true. We live in the same small town, and though everyone thinks they're leaving and never coming back, they do. Even if it's just for visits or holidays or whatever.

In my case, I'm not even leaving.

Willow climbs out of the car then and waves at me.

As I drive home, I'm trying not to dwell on Eric's asshole comment, but I can't help it. It's not even that he said it in front of everyone, or that he's been making these digs for months and clearly doesn't intend on stopping. It's that I know in my heart that he's right about me.

That I'm not a good person, no matter how hard I've tried to make everything right.

There's so much I can't undo.

As I'm pulling into my driveway, I notice a car on the side of the street in front of my house. It's silver and looks vaguely familiar.

When I get out of the car, I realize it's the same one I saw outside the Cohen house days ago. And climbing out of it now is Luke.

I stay frozen as he crosses my driveway, walking toward me.

My heart beats a frantic rhythm in my chest the closer he comes, and then he's standing right in front of me, the moonlight making his hair look shiny in the dark.

"I tried to call you" is the first thing he says. "Didn't know if you were home."

After a second, I manage to stutter, "I didn't—haven't checked my phone."

I stare at him, and all the ways he is different stare back at me. The edge in his eyes, the coldness in his voice, the thin layer of scruff along his jaw.

"Luke—" I start to say, but he talks over me.

"She wants to see you," he says.

And I know right away who he means.

Mel.

Mel wants to see me.

A million questions race through my mind, but all I manage to say is, "When?"

"Tomorrow?" Luke asks, and I nod.

He looks at me for one more second, then turns and walks back to his car.

He drives off, leaving me standing in my driveway, wanting to call after him, to drive after him, to go with him to the place that used to feel like home.

4

THEN

If you counted all the secrets I'd spilled in the Cohen house over the past ten years, you would think I lived there. We were cleaning out the garage when I told Mel I'd gotten my period when I was in fifth grade, and we were dancing to Amy Winehouse in the living room when I told her about Callum Turner, the first boy I kissed when I was thirteen. Ro, Luke, and I were in the backyard running through the sprinklers when I told them I'd seen my dad smoking in the driveway, and Ro and I were in the shed when I told him that having me was what made my mother so sad.

We were in the kitchen during the fourth week of summer school, when I finally admitted to myself and to Mel that I was failing calculus.

"Oh, no! Is it because you're spending so much time over here?" Mel asked. "I told you to stop trying to look after me. I'm fine!"

"No, it's not that. I just suck at it," I said, defeated, as I sifted flour into a mixing bowl.

"Do you know what sucks? Babies and climate change," Mel said. "You do *not* suck."

"Maybe I'll just retake it in the fall and drop one of my electives."

Mel took a break from whisking her sugar and butter mix and

frowned thoughtfully. There was a line of sweat on her upper lip and her face was paler than normal. I'd tried to suggest that we spend the day lounging in front of the TV, but she'd refused. These days it was like she was on a personal mission to prove she was the lone human who responded to radiation with renewed energy and zest for life rather than the nausea and fatigue she'd been told to expect. Between me and her sons, though, she was fooling absolutely no one.

"Should we take a break?" I asked, but she ignored me.

"You *could* retake it in the fall," she said now. "Or maybe you could find someone who excels in math, has the time to tutor, and won't make you pay an arm and a leg for it."

I knew right away where she was going with this and immediately regretted not keeping my academic woes to myself. I was so used to divulging all the details of my life to Mel; it never occurred to me to keep my mouth shut.

"I probably just need to study more," I said, trying to course-correct.

"You probably do," she agreed, nodding. "Then again," she continued, "a tutor could have its benefits. Someone who lives in the area, has experience tutoring, probably wants to be paid in comic books, and is around six feet tall. But we shouldn't be too specific."

"Mel," I sighed. "He won't want to tutor me."

"He personally told you that?"

"Well, no," I said. "But like he has his job and everything. Also, I'm not just a little bad at this. I'm pretty bad."

"Sounds like you need a tutor," she said smugly.

"Not *that* tutor."

"And why not?" she asked, a challenge in her voice. She started to beat her egg mixture again. I stared at her for a second, trying to figure out what she was doing.

Clearly, my feelings for Luke were one of the few things we never spoke outright about, and after that weird afternoon when Mel and Naomi were high, I didn't see this changing. Mel had never done anything to discourage my crush, but she had also never done anything to *en*courage it. Unless that stuffed polar bear from the Dog Days Fair counted. Did it?

That one moment of distraction resulted in flour blowing in my face, and I used my hand to fan it away.

"Why does it have to be Luke?" I asked now, using his name for the first time in our conversation.

"Oh! That's who you meant? Luke? *My* Luke?" She was in a theatrical mood today.

When I rolled my eyes, Mel cackled. "Why does it have to *not* be Luke?"

Because he was easily the smartest person I knew. Right from the moment I'd met him, a then-bespectacled eight-year-old, I'd always been so aware of how much he knew that I didn't. About the water cycle and grubs and why thunder always came with lightning.

"I'm not trying to look stupid," I admitted.

Mel's expression got serious then. She took my chin and forced me to look at her. Her thumb brushed something I assumed was flour off the tip of my nose. "Not being the best at something doesn't make you stupid. It makes you human."

Growing up, Mel would let us get away with saying almost any word, but *stupid* had always been off-limits.

"Fine, then I'm not trying to look *unintelligent*."

Mel sighed. "Anybody who thinks you're unintelligent is stupid."

Done with the flour now, I hopped on the counter and watched her continue to work. "Moms have to say that, even if it's not true," I said.

"Only to their own kids," Mel argued. "So when I say it to you, I mean it."

I laughed. "But not when you say it to Ro and Luke?"

One of the things I loved best about Mel when I first met her was the way she rarely distinguished between me and the boys. We were "you kids" or "the gang." Little reminders that I wasn't one of them used to feel like a punch in the chest, and as if she knew it, Mel made sure to steer clear of them. She made nothing of the fact that our skin colors were different. She didn't even acknowledge some of the odd looks we got in Winchester, which wasn't the most diverse of towns. It didn't matter that we didn't share the same genes. If anything, I was special *because* I wasn't Mel's child. She'd chosen me. Ro would sometimes even jokingly call me just that—"the chosen one."

Now Mel smiled. "Pleading the Fifth on that. So, Luke will tutor you, okay?"

I sighed. "What if he says no?"

"Who said anything about asking him?" Mel said. "If I ask, it'll be a Thing. Mom made me do this, blah blah blah." Her deep barrel-voiced imitation of Teenage Boy sounded nothing like Luke, and I burst out laughing.

"It's better to just put it out in the universe and see what happens," she said.

I didn't understand what she meant until a few minutes later, when Luke got home. I thought he'd been at work, so I expected him to be in his blue polo and black slacks, but he was in a pair of jogging shorts and a T-shirt that clung to his chest, his curls wet with sweat.

He raised his hand to us in greeting, went to the sink, and gulped down a glass of water. His Adam's apple bobbed as he swallowed, and I tried to act indifferent under Mel's watchful eye.

I shouldn't have worried, though. She was preoccupied with her own plans.

"So, what's the thing you're struggling with the most right now?" she asked me out of nowhere. We hadn't talked about math for several minutes, but by the look she gave me, I knew what she was referring to. "Derogatory units? Derivements?"

"Derivatives?" I offered, confused. Like Mel didn't know the word *derivative*.

"That's the one," she said, snapping her fingers. "I think we used to do that one with protractors when I was in school. I'd be happy to take a look tomorrow, but I can't promise anything."

As though he were an actor in a script, Luke set down his glass and looked at us, playing right into Mel's hands.

"Oh, um, thanks, Mel," I said. I couldn't tell if this was going well or not.

"Of course, Jessi-girl," she said.

"Luke, do you have one of those math sets Jessi and I can borrow for tomorrow?"

Now Luke was frowning. "A math set?"

"Yeah, you know those small silver cases?"

He was looking at me now. "You need help with derivatives?"

Despite all the buildup, my face still warmed. "Yeah, kind of."

"I'm a little rusty," Mel said. "But I was great at geometry. I should actually go and see if I can find that old calculator of mine." She took off for the stairs. I had to bite my lip to keep from laughing. Her rickety old woman spiel had officially entered the vicinity of the ridiculous.

Luke had turned his back to fill another glass of water, but he spoke now.

"I'll tutor you."

I couldn't believe Mel had been right. He was actually offering.

"If you want," he added, turning around to face me.

"That would be amazing," I said quickly. "Are you sure?"

He shrugged. "Why not?"

He gulped down the rest of his water, crossed the kitchen, and stopped at the counter, inches from me. I was eyeing him as he reached for an apple in the fruit bowl behind me, so I barely had time to notice when his other hand touched my chin.

"Tomorrow?" he asked.

Both our eyes followed his index finger as the flour he'd brushed off my face left a white smudge on his black shorts.

"Tomorrow," I whispered.

THEN

Derivatives.

Given how distracted I was, I'd managed to learn a lot more about them than I expected. Luke and I were sitting next to each other at the dining table, where we always sat during dinner at the Cohen house. Except this time it was just the two of us.

Our bodies were angled toward each other, our heads had almost touched twice, and I realized that the whisper of mint I'd smelled in his car the night we picked Rowan up from Celia's party was from Luke. When I leaned in even closer, a clean, soapy scent emanated from his skin. I stumbled through all sorts of olfactory equations in my mind. Mint gum + the ocean breeze detergent Mel used = Luke's indelible scent? Or was it breath mints + some as-yet undiscovered shower gel that was making me want to bury my head in his chest?

Rowan didn't smell like this. He smelled like Old Spice and sweat, which, to be fair, usually lacked that offensive sting that BO had, unless he'd just come from the court. Did they have their separate soaps even though they shared the same shower?

I felt I should know them well enough to answer this question, but it was also creepy as hell — grounds for Mel to throw me out of her house for good if she ever found out how badly I wanted to know.

"You know what you're doing," Luke said suddenly, and I knew it was all over. I was caught. He'd read my mind.

"What?" I said, tucking my hair behind my ear and retreating into my chair, as my attempts at sniffing him had sent me almost into his lap. I didn't know what was wrong with me. Mel was in the next room, for God's sake.

"You know what you're doing," he said. "Don't overthink it."

"Oh, thanks," I said, my face warming. Whether it was from the encouragement or the crazy thoughts I'd been having, I couldn't tell. "You're too nice."

It was true. I knew that Luke rarely lost his temper and was obviously supersmart, but I hadn't been prepared for how patient he was, how willing he was to go at my pace and compliment me.

"Should I not be nice?" he asked, and his gaze on my face from just inches away was like a physical touch.

"No, nice is good. I like nice." When I realized what I'd said, I scribbled hard and fast on my paper. Even if I got the problem wrong, at least the sound of our quiet breaths and my loud, traitorous heart would be drowned out by our voices again as we went over it.

I managed to avoid doing anything really embarrassing for the rest of the lesson, and then we were done and packing up.

"You've got this," Luke said. "We can meet a couple nights a week until your final, if that works for you."

"That would be so great. What do I owe you? I can pay you, you know."

He shook his head. "You don't owe me anything."

"Wow, okay — thanks," I said before bounding away like an excitable puppy. Later, I wondered if I should have hugged him. I could probably have gotten away with it, right? He was doing me an enormous favor after all.

Thankfully, the next time we met was significantly less awkward. Mel was in her room taking a nap and Rowan was at work, so it was just us, with Sydney by our feet. We seemed to always schedule our tutoring sessions while Rowan was at work, and since we worked around Luke's schedule, I wondered if that was intentional on his part. Maybe he thought Ro would be a distraction. He probably would, but I found myself missing him all the same. He'd gone back to being MIA ever since that morning he'd snuck into my room. He was hardly ever at home when I was at the Cohen house, and he barely answered my texts. I told myself that he was just busy, or he was just struggling with Mel's illness, but I couldn't help wondering once again why Rowan had become so distant.

I ignored the ache in my chest and focused on the present, this moment, with Luke.

That second time, while I worked on problems, we chatted about a bunch of things — Mel's treatment. Senior year. College.

"Mom really wants me to go," Luke said, watching as I scribbled out a problem from the textbook. "She says it feels better for her to see us living our lives instead of putting them on hold for . . . however long."

However long, we both knew, meant as long as Mel had left. The one thing about Mel's Big Bad was that it had never given us any hope. There was no good outcome; it was only a matter of when.

"That maybe this way, she might even get to see me graduate college," he continued, his voice dry.

"So maybe you'll go?" I asked now.

"I . . . I think so." He raked his hand through his hair, and I could feel his conflict. "Is that what you . . . You still wouldn't?"

It was a weird question for him to ask. Did he care that much about my opinion? What I would do if Mel was my mom?

"I won't judge you for going, if that's what you mean," I said at last, because it was the truest thing I could think of to say. It was easy for me to make declarations about what I would and wouldn't do if I were Mel's daughter, but as Ro had painfully pointed out all those weeks ago, I wasn't. I got to love her in that selfish, uncomplicated way people who weren't related got to love each other. And, like I'd come to see over the years, maybe that was why Mel meant so much to me. Her love for me was optional and totally unwarranted, not forced upon her by blood or relation or any sort of obligation, making it all the more special and unusual. In the same way, I got to love her with as much bias as I wanted. I didn't have to know whether she was bad with money. I didn't have to care if she had been as unfair to Dr. Cohen as he had been to her. I got to blindly choose her side. All her suggestions to me were just that—suggestions—but to Ro and Luke, they were directives.

Maybe I loved her just as much as they did, but I loved her differently.

I could admit that.

At my next tutoring session, Luke seemed distracted and didn't offer many directions, corrections, or compliments as I worked. He didn't say much of anything.

"Is everything okay?" I asked at last, worried as I always was that something had happened with Mel that no one had told me. As privileged as I was to have our uncomplicated love, I was also at a disadvantage: I didn't live with them. They weren't obligated to tell me everything.

Luke rubbed the back of his neck. "You know how I said you didn't owe me anything? You still don't," he said quickly. "But I could use your help with something."

"Okay, shoot," I said, sitting up straighter.

Minutes later, Luke was opening the door of his bedroom and leading me in. He had revealed the reason for his distraction, and it led us on a mission, of all things, to find him something to wear. Sydney, who had trailed us up the stairs, weaved around me and settled in a spot at the foot of his bed. I followed her, knelt, and stroked her fur, pretending not to be the least bit affected by being in Luke Cohen's room.

"Sorry about the mess," Luke said, as if the state of his living space even registered on my radar. Of all the rooms in the Cohen house, Luke's was by far the place where I spent the least amount of time. I'd been in it a bunch when we were younger, playing games on his computer or spreading out a board game on his carpet because his room had more space than Ro's. But it had been a couple of years since I had seen more than glimpses through an open door.

His room was nowhere as neat as mine. He had piles of books everywhere — on his table, in stacks on the floor, and spilling over off his two shelves. There were a bunch of weights in one corner and shoes in another. His bed was unmade, but clean-looking.

"Hey, Sydney," Luke said now. "Should we show Jessi our little trick?"

Sydney jumped up obediently at the sound of her name and ran over to him.

"Ready?" Luke asked, and I grinned, not sure whether he was talking to me or the dog.

"Shoes!" he said.

At the command, Sydney ran over to the corner that was full of Luke's shoes, found one gray house slipper, and brought it back to him.

"Other foot," Luke said, and Sydney trotted back to the shoe pile and retrieved the matching slipper, dropping it in front of him.

"No way," I said. "How did she know which pair —"

"Secret," Luke said with a grin.

"Good girl, Syd," he said, bending to set the slippers next to each other in front of Sydney, who stood patiently wagging her tail. "And now for the grand finale . . . okay!"

At that command, Sydney slid one paw into each slipper.

"Oh my God," I cheered, bending down to pet her again. "You're so good, Sydney. Such a clever girl. Yes, you are."

Luke and I both loved on her for a few seconds, and she beamed up at us, letting us pet her.

"Think we should take our show on the road?" Luke asked.

"Um, heck yes," I said. "I'd pay good money to see that. You need to put it on YouTube or something."

Luke just laughed, standing again, and I remembered that he'd brought me up to his room for something other than watching the tricks he'd taught Sydney.

I stood too, then sat on the edge of his bed, trying but failing not to wonder how many other girls had sat on it. Luke walked over to his closet, pulled it open, and rifled through a bunch of shirts hanging there, and my attention veered back to the fact that I was in his room. In the place where he spent most of his time. Where he slept and dressed and undressed. Based on the number of times he'd come down for breakfast, hair disheveled and in pajama bottoms that hung low on his hips, I knew he didn't sleep with a shirt on. But were the bottoms only for the sake of modesty, something he pulled on before rubbing the sleep from his eyes and trudging downstairs?

"So, clothes—" he said now, and my body felt warm all over.

"Yep, clothes. A definite necessity," I squeaked, squirming.

Luke gave me a weird look, but all he said was, "Thanks for doing this. I'd have asked for Mom's take, but you know how she gets."

I smiled. "You mean, *Forces of the Universe, is it possible my firstborn has somewhere to go on a Friday night?*"

"Pretty much," he said. I thought my impersonation had been pretty spot-on, but from the way he rubbed at his neck, I could tell I'd embarrassed him.

He held out a bunch of shirts.

"Um, so you'd wear them with dark jeans?" I asked, absently inspecting each shirt. They were all so soft. If I had a moment alone with them, I'd bury my face in them.

Luke nodded.

I wondered if he was interested in patenting his smell so girls like me (mostly me) didn't have to reduce ourselves to sniffing him or his clothes.

"And you said it's karaoke night?" I said, trying to remember what he'd told me downstairs. If he wasn't doubting my brain capacity at this point, he soon would be. I pulled out a dark blue T-shirt and a gray Henley that was one of my favorites. And, okay, I was a creep for having favorites from his wardrobe, but it was what it was. I hadn't claimed to be any kind of saint.

"I have to be honest," I said. "I wouldn't have thought karaoke was your thing."

"It's not," Luke said. "It's *really* not. But I got invited, and I'm trying to step out of my comfort zone more so college isn't a complete culture shock. I figure I should start changing."

I glanced up at him, surprised. "You don't have to change."

"Yeah, I do. College is a whole different ballgame," he said. A moment later he added, "And you know what I'm like."

"What you're like?" I repeated, not bothering to hide my

confusion. He'd already seen me do calculus; there was no way he held my IQ in high regard.

"You know," Luke said, looking at the shirts hanging off his arm and not at me. "I'm not Ro."

I did know. Luke wasn't gutsy and expressive and spontaneous like his younger brother. He never had been.

"That's not a bad thing . . ."

He shrugged in response.

Silence stretched all around us, and I took a breath, determined to mine as much information as possible from whatever this interaction was turning out to be.

"So, am I to take it that you're trying to impress a girl?" I said in a teasing way, making my voice as light as possible.

"That's . . . uh, I can't answer that."

I placed both hands on my hips. "How am I supposed to help you if you're withholding information?"

Luke laughed. "I didn't realize your advice was so specific."

"It absolutely is," I insisted. After a moment I said, "Okay, let's try it this way. The person who invited you . . . is it a girl?"

When he nodded, my heart sank, but I forced myself to maintain an unbothered expression. "Okay, so definitely go with the gray," I said, pointing to the Henley. "That's the one."

"You sure?" he asked, and I nodded.

We went over a couple more details—I approved the Keds he planned on wearing and told him to pick a song everyone knew, like by ABBA—and then he said, "Thanks, J.J."

"No problem," I said, still feeling stung by the whole thing but also a little bit delighted that he'd trusted me enough to ask. Even though he seemed reluctant to talk about it, I had some seemingly innocuous questions up my sleeve that I intended to ask about this girl who invited him. For example, did she work with him? Had she invited other people?

But I never got the chance to get those answers because right at that second, Ro burst into Luke's room.

"There you are!" he said, as breathless as if he'd run a marathon. "What the fuck? I've been looking all over for you."

"I've been right here," I shrugged, as if this were a normal occurrence.

Ro looked between me and Luke, started to say something, but then shook his head and said, "Nine nine nine. Major emergency. In the shed."

"Right now?" I asked, catching Luke's eye. I had intended to stay right there on his bed until he kicked me out.

"Right now," Rowan said. He repeated, "Nine nine nine," as if I hadn't heard him the first time.

I sighed and stood, wanting to stay and talk to Luke, but knowing that Rowan needed me. If he wanted to go to the shed, if he was using our not-so-secret code, it was serious.

No matter how I felt about Luke, Rowan was still my best friend. I hated how different everything felt between us lately. Tentative and fragile. I wondered now if this was why he'd come to find me, if he was missing me as much as I missed him, if he was as desperate to talk —really talk—as I was.

So I said goodbye to Luke and followed Ro outside to find out what the emergency was.

NOW

I know this is not a matter of life and death.

Everything will be okay, I tell myself, but it doesn't help.

It doesn't help, either, knowing that Mel doesn't care. That she won't be looking at the way my hair is styled or the clothes I'm wearing or how much mascara I have on. If she's asked to see me, it means she's finally ready to say everything she hasn't said since last fall. Everything she hasn't said since Rowan's death.

I think about not going.

I can't stand the thought of looking in her eyes and seeing the same anger that was in Luke's eyes. Can't stand the thought of her not calling me Jessi-girl, of her yelling in my face or, worse, crying. But in the end, I force myself to climb into the car and go.

It's the least I can do.

The very least.

I feel unsteady as I walk up the Cohens' driveway, and my fingers have developed a sudden tremor. I push the doorbell and then clasp my hands inside each other, trying to force the shaking to stop.

About a minute passes before the door swings open, and I don't know why I'm so surprised to see Luke.

He barely looks at me as he nods for me to come inside.

One step in, and I'm hit with a deluge of memories. Ro and I sliding down the railing from the top of the stairs. Helping Mel bake or cook. Lying on the ground and playing dead while Sydney sniffed me up and down and tried to lick me awake.

Luke watches as I unbuckle my sandals and slip them off in the foyer. I feel stupid the whole time, like we're playing at something. I'm pretending to be polite, a stranger who takes her shoes off at the door and has never climbed into his mother's bed fully clothed.

The silence is heavy and thick, so I try to think of something to say.

"Where's Sydney?"

"We gave her away."

I was just making small talk, but his response is like a punch in the gut. Sydney's gone?

Luke is looking off to the side, impatient and bored. Like he just told me the sky was blue, not that they gave away the dog whose fur I cried and laughed into routinely during the last nine years.

"Oh," I say belatedly, and try to get myself under control. This visit is going to be a nightmare if I'm already crying and I haven't even seen Mel yet.

Once I'm finally out of my shoes, I follow Luke past the living room to the small guest room off the dining room. The last five or so years, it was where I'd sleep when I spent the night at their house. Mel had this rule that as soon as I was old enough for training bras, there were no more sleepovers in Rowan's room. Even if we were both in separate sleeping bags.

Luke knocks twice on the guest room door. "Mom?"

A voice I'd recognize anywhere calls back, "Come in!"

He pushes the door open, and then I'm standing in what is obviously Mel's new bedroom. A hospital bed is the centerpiece, but the same IKEA table I spent far too little time doing homework on is pushed against one wall.

It takes me a second to spot Mel, another second to realize she's in a wheelchair. A lump so big lodges itself in my throat, making speaking an impossibility.

Mel, too, seems speechless.

She blinks at me a few times, and in the silence that passes, I notice how small and frail she looks. The old Mel used to try out diets every once in a while (starting them, but never finishing), claiming sabotage over the fact that she worked in a bakery and had two sons who ate like bears, but now she's the kind of skinny that no diet could cause. Her skin is pale, and I can't stop looking at her wrists. There's so little flesh there.

"Jessi," she breathes finally

I shuffle closer, wanting to touch her but so afraid.

"Baby, hi," she says, and that's the thing that finally undoes me. I burst into tears and kneel in front of her, hugging her legs.

She laughs and runs her hand over my hair. "Oh God, that's so not the response I'm looking for. Making people cry with just one look."

I'm sniffing and shaking and gasping for breath all at the same time. Why is she hugging me? Why is she comforting me right now?

"What are you doing here?" she says, as if she didn't know I was coming.

"Told you, Mom. She's your surprise." It's the first moment I remember that Luke is still in the room. It's also when I realize that she *didn't* know I was coming. I turn around and look up at Luke, confused, but he's just leaning against the wall, watching us.

I'm her surprise?

But he said . . .

He told me . . .

Luke is the reason I'm here?

"I'm so mad at you," Mel says now, cupping my face in her hands. My heart drops, and I lower my gaze.

Here it goes.

This is the reaction I expected.

This is the reaction I deserve. Maybe she's only holding my face so she can slap it.

"So, so mad at you," she continues. "Except you win, because I'm so fucking happy about you two that I'm willing to overlook your disappearing on me."

Us two?

She points at me and then at Luke as she speaks.

Confused, I back away from her and get into a standing position.

"I don't know what you mean," I say.

Luke is suddenly beside me, saying, "She means about us."

I jump when I feel his arm snake around my waist, and I look down at it to make sure I'm not hallucinating.

"I . . ."

"I know we were going to keep it on the down low, but I told her. I couldn't help it," Luke says.

I turn and gape at him, and that's when he brings his hand up to my face and softly brushes the tears off my cheeks.

My heart stops at the feel of his skin on mine after so long.

"I hope that's okay," he adds.

Luke's gaze is like a magnet, and there's a message in his eyes. A challenge? No, a plea.

But a plea for what? What exactly is he asking me to do?

The silence stretches out so long that Mel's curious stare is starting to burn a hole through the side of my face.

Finally, I croak out, "Oh, yeah . . . it's . . . fine."

Whatever else may have changed about her, Mel's intuition remains unrivaled. "Okay, I wasn't born yesterday. There's something you're not telling me."

"What . . . what do you mean?" At this point, I'm practically squeaking.

Mel narrows her eyes at us, and then Luke laughs.

I haven't heard his laugh in so long. Up close, it's like standing too close to the epicenter of an earthquake. I flinch.

"We might as well tell her," he tells me conspiratorially, tugging me closer with the arm around my waist. "Mom, trust me, you don't wanna hear how it happened. Us getting back together."

She still seems skeptical, but she leans forward. "Tell me."

"It's kind of . . . personal," he says, and I'm just looking from him to her, entranced by this show, in which I have absolutely no idea who any of the characters are, not to mention what the plot is.

"All the better. Have you ever known me to have boundaries?" Mel says.

"Mom," Luke groans.

"Don't Mom me. You want to deny a dying woman one of her few pleasures in life?"

The atmosphere in the room turns at that, Luke's expression becoming sober. The Mel I remember didn't call it dying. She called it surviving her Big Bad.

"Another day," he says quietly. "Marilyn should be here any minute."

"Marilyn's my nurse," Mel explains to me, and I nod like it's normal that she's telling me this. Like it's normal that she's telling me anything or acting thrilled about the lies spewing out of Luke's mouth. I have no idea what is happening.

"I . . . have to get to work," I say, seeing my quickest exit out of this conversation.

"Oh, right, I forgot about that," Luke says, and scratches his head. My bullshit radar is so broken at this point that I wonder for a semi-second when the hell I told him anything about my having to work. When I realize that I didn't, a cloud of anger temporarily overtakes my confusion.

"Well, give me a hug before you go," Mel says, and I step forward, out of Luke's embrace and into Mel's.

"I love you," Mel whispers in my ear. "Always have, always will."

Which is the exact moment that I realize she doesn't know.

How?

How does she not know? After all these months?

"I love you, too," I manage to choke out over the tears forming again.

She squeezes me tight, her patented Mel hug, and then I step back and leave the room.

Luke tells his mother he'll be right back, and he follows after, his hand on the small of my back. My head is spinning as we walk all the way down the hall, confusion quickly turning into a wave of hot red anger.

As soon as I'm certain we're out of Mel's earshot, I turn on him, shrugging his hand off my back. "What the hell was that?"

He looks over his shoulder and signals for me to keep walking until we're in the living room. Once we're there, he grabs a half-finished bottle of water from the table and takes a swig.

"Why did you do that?" I ask again, and his look of total disinterest makes my blood boil even more. "You told me she wanted to see me."

"She did," he says.

"Bullshit! She didn't even know I was coming. You lied to me!" My voice is escalating by the minute.

"Calm the fuck down," he says, finally looking less impassive.

"Don't tell me what to do!" I spit back, and for a second, it's a standoff. I can't believe Luke and I are speaking this way to each other. Me and Ro, maybe. But never Luke and me.

"She's sick."

"You think I don't know that?"

"It made her happy."

"So you just made up a lie? Because it made her happy?"

"Yeah, I did," he says. "And you know what, it's more than you've ever done. Where the fuck have you been? All this year, where the fuck were you?"

I step back at his words, my voice quiet. "I thought she didn't want me here."

"She was fucking ecstatic to see you just now, so no, that doesn't work," Luke says. "Try again."

"I thought *you* didn't want me here."

He runs a hand through his hair, but he doesn't deny it. "This isn't about me."

"I'm not lying to her," I say after a long moment. "You want to make her happy? Fine. But leave me out of it."

"Jessi, she's sick." His voice is quiet, and he's not looking at me.

"I know she is!" I say, exasperated.

"Then think about someone other than yourself for once!"

I flinch. "I'm leaving," I say, turning for the door.

"You owe me!" he calls just before I reach it. I bend down to slip on my shoes, not even bothering with the straps.

"You know you do," he says in a quieter voice, and I stop.

I turn around to look him straight in the eye. "Screw you," I say, and run out of the house. In my car, I'm shaking so hard, I can barely grip the steering wheel.

His words haunt me all throughout the drive.

You owe me.

You know you do.

I turn on the radio and try to let the music drown my thoughts. When that doesn't work, I go back to that positive affirmations thing Mom's therapist taught her to do.

I know me.

I'm allowed to make mistakes.

The past is past.

But I can't outthink or outdrive it—

I know he's right.

5

THEN

I had made a terrible mistake.

As soon as Ro opened the door of the shed, a line of sunlight illuminating the entire space, I saw the old sleeping bag and the cans of beer on it.

This is why he'd dragged me from Luke's room?

My heart plunged, and with it, all my hope that we were going to have a heart-to-heart, that we would finally connect again.

He just wanted to drink.

"You said it was an emergency," I said flatly.

"It is," he insisted, walking inside and flopping down on the makeshift mat. "It's a fucking disaster."

He patted the space on the sleeping bag beside him.

I hesitated, looked back at the house, and followed after him. Whether there was alcohol involved or not, Ro was asking to talk. That had to count for something.

He handed me a can of beer, and I shook my head. "Where'd you get it?"

"It's not Mel's," he said defensively.

"I know it's not," I said. Mel didn't drink cheap beer.

A couple of years ago, Ro and I had gotten into Mel's liquor, getting completely wasted on vodka while Luke and Mel were out of state for some Mathlete competition of Luke's. It was the first real hangover I'd ever had, and still the worst to date, but it paled in comparison with the crippling amount of guilt I felt when Mel got home. It had taken no more than fifteen minutes for me to break and confess the entire ugly truth. Since then, none of us knew where she kept the keys to her cabinet, and I wasn't interested in finding out. Since then, Ro also (rightly) considered me the biggest stick-in-the-mud of all time, second only to his brother, who didn't drink at all.

"So, what's the emergency?" I asked.

Ro sighed, tried to run his hand through his hair, and gave up mid-motion, remembering it was mostly gone.

"I kissed Cassie Clairburne," he said.

I blinked at him.

"Cassie Clairburne?" I repeated.

"I know," Ro said miserably. He fell back in surprise as I shoved him.

"An emergency, you said! Nine nine nine, you said!"

We'd adopted the code after watching some British TV series and realizing it was their equivalent to 911.

"Plus, flipped, it's the devil's number," Rowan had added at the time. "Anytime one of us uses it, we'll know they mean serious business."

Serious business like a medical emergency or a breakup or — hell — even discussing his mother's illness, which Rowan still wouldn't talk about. When I knew more of Luke's thoughts than Ro's on something that big, there was a major issue.

"It is both those things," Rowan said, unyielding. He pulled the tab off his can of beer and took a big gulp, as if he were drinking water. One of my eyebrows skirted up, but I said nothing.

Ro was finally confiding in me again about something, and maybe it wasn't what I wanted him to tell me, but that didn't matter. At least he was here. "So," he went on, "you know Cassie and Eric are now paired up for mixed doubles, right?"

I nodded and got comfortable.

Honestly, Ro had called enough emergency shed meetings centered solely around his love life that it shouldn't have surprised me. The difference was that those *had* actually been game changers, even if they were a little on the frivolous side.

The first time he'd called a shed meeting, we were ten and Jenna R. had just agreed to be his girlfriend. A secret so big, he couldn't say it in the house for fear that his mom, brother, or dad — who still lived there at the time — would hear.

When we were fifteen, he'd asked me to ride over and meet him in the shed. "Don't even go into the house," he'd said, and I'd known it was really big. He told me he had lost his virginity to Ashley Paul.

I'd called my own shed meetings in the past, of course. When I'd overheard Dad on the phone one night, talking to someone I didn't know about possibly hospitalizing my mother. When I was fourteen and it seemed for a while that we might be moving to Massachusetts, where Dad's family lived. We needed more family support, Dad said, and Mom's family weren't an option because she hadn't spoken to them since right before she married my father. In that shed I had told Ro about my first kiss, even though it was cheating because I'd technically spilled the beans to Mel first. I'd told him that I wanted to stop being his mixed doubles partner after four years of him being

the standout and me being average, not to mention bored of tennis.
(Watching it was fine; playing was an entirely different story.)

The shed was for those hard, awkward truths that were too fragile for sunlight or a space without cobwebs and old garden tools. I didn't always like his reasons for dragging me in here, but I always tried to hear what he was and wasn't saying.

"Eric had been making all these comments that he had the hottest partner, and he might give up the singles life entirely and just take up mixed doubles. All this stuff," Ro continued. "So I thought, whatever, he can have her. Cassie is high-maintenance as hell anyway."

"Ro—" I said with a roll of my eyes.

"Don't *Ro* me. If you've never had to share a court with her, you can't even judge." He drank from his beer again. "Don't get me wrong, her backhand is sick. I'm talking that old-school Henin one-hander."

"Are you saying that because Cassie's short?" When I was a kid, I used to get the Justine Henin comparison too. What I lacked in height, I made up for in tenacity. She was many a short girl's tennis idol, and if I'd ever gotten passionate about tennis, I'd have been obsessed with Henin.

"No," he said. "She's just that good."

I nodded and waved for Ro to go on. "Continue."

"Anyway, so we're at Cody's party last night, right? And I'm waiting in line for the bathroom when Cassie taps me on the shoulder and tells me there's another bathroom in the pool house, but she's scared to go by herself.

"So, I'm like, I'm down, let's go, 'cause I'm getting really desperate." Ro slurped on his beer. "We get there. She goes in first . . ."

"Gentleman," I remarked, and he rolled his eyes.

"Then I go in. When I come back out, she's waiting for me at the door, and she just like grabs my face and kisses me. Did I mention I was super wasted?"

"No, you did not." I spoke calmly, but I felt a pinprick of worry. First the party where Luke and I picked Rowan up, then a party last night, and now he was drinking again today?

"Okay, I'm super wasted. So I kiss her back. We mess around, whatever, then go back to the party. I get to practice this morning before work, and Eric is like, 'Dude, I'm going to ask her out. She's been giving me all these hints.' How am I supposed to tell him?"

"Maybe you don't have to," I offered. "If she's giving him hints, maybe she's into him and last night was just a series of bad decisions. On both your parts." I couldn't help voicing my disapproval. Cassie Clairburne was known for dating guys and dumping them the moment she got bored. Ro could do way better.

"Jessi, he thinks *everyone* is giving him hints. I swear to you, when he stayed over last weekend, Mom asked if he wanted pancakes and he thought she was hitting on him."

I laughed. I could see Eric doing that.

"Maybe you should text him and say you have something to tell him, then just rip it off like a Band-Aid."

Ro sighed. "I guess."

We talked idly for a while, about what I'd do when summer school was done the next week. We talked about the tournament Ro had won last week and how he was now going to be ranked third for his age division in our state.

"Mom wants to celebrate. She's planning some kind of fancy dinner," he said. "If she had her way, she'd probably do high tea or some shit."

"That could be fun," I said.

"For who? The count and countess of Notre Dame?"

I laughed. "Well, if they're coming, tell them to RSVP so Mel knows."

Ro laid back so his bottom half was on the sleeping bag and his top half was on the grimy floor of the shed, a hygienic risk that I personally was not willing to take, so I stayed sitting, my legs stretched out in front of me.

I was trying to think of how to bring it up, this wedge forming between us that I had been feeling for weeks. But before I could speak, Ro spoke.

"What were you doing in Luke's room?"

"Helping him pick out an outfit for a special occasion."

"Is he having vision problems or something?" Ro had been in a state of perpetual annoyance with his brother ever since the night we picked him up from the party. It had been weeks, and he was still making passive-aggressive comments about people not staying out of his shit.

I wouldn't dignify his question with an answer, but I asked what I'd been gearing up to.

"Are we okay?" I asked, signaling between us.

"Why wouldn't we be?" Ro asked, sitting up again. He sounded genuinely surprised. "Is this about that night I asked you to leave?"

"It's about . . . everything," I said, struggling to voice my thoughts. "You never text me back lately. We barely see each other."

"I was busy getting to third in the state!" Ro protested. "And you know I suck at texting."

"You're sucking extra hard lately."

"I just have a lot going on, okay?" He seemed so indignant, I wondered now if the distance — the weirdness — had all been in my head. Worse, I wondered if I was being selfish, making this all about me and our friendship when it had nothing to do with me.

"How are you doing with Mel's . . . stuff?" It was a clumsy way to ask, but it was all I had.

I heard Rowan shrug in the dark. "How should I be doing? I'm not the one doing treatment and whatever."

"You're just being so weird. So secretive," I finally admitted, exasperated.

I expected him to get annoyed and bite back about how it was none of my business, or something to that effect, but he didn't.

"I don't know how else to be."

"You could tell me what you're thinking," I said.

"I can't," he said, and it was the quickness of his response that stung more than what he said.

"You don't think you can tell me what you're thinking?" I repeated, hurt slipping through my words. This — *this* — was exactly what I'd been trying to articulate. I'd noticed the change the night Mel was diagnosed, but it might have started before that. Clearly, something had changed in the way Rowan saw me, and I couldn't figure out what it was or why.

"I know I can't," he said. "Because you'll just run it back to Mom or Luke or someone."

"Ro, that is so unfair. I'd never tell them something you told me in confidence."

"Sorry," he said with a sigh. "I shouldn't have said that."

I wasn't so quick to accept his apology. How many times was he going to take out whatever he was feeling on me? I wasn't his punching bag. "You're a jackass."

"Sorry," he repeated. He picked up my hand and put it on his lap, running his finger over my lifelines the way we used to do when we were little and telling each other's fortunes. It tickled, but I didn't pull away. "I just mean, like, it sucks because Luke is Mr. Perfect. He never does anything wrong. And you—you're, like, Mel's best friend. The chosen one. I'm the shit son, who never knows the right thing to do or say."

"There's no right thing with this, Ro," I said, feeling my throat closing up again the way it did whenever I was about to cry. I rested my head on his shoulder. "This is the worst thing that has ever happened to us. This is the worst-case scenario."

Ro didn't say anything, and when his fingers stopped moving over my hand, I returned the favor, pulling his hand onto my lap so I could tell his future. His palm felt dry and, thanks to his racket, more callused than I remembered. Once upon a time, I could trace the lines on his palm in the dark. Now there were more and more parts of him that were unfamiliar.

"I wish you'd talk to me, even if everything you say is the wrong thing."

"It's not that simple anymore," Ro said at last.

I didn't know what he meant by that last word. *Anymore.*

If he could admit that it had once been simple to tell each other everything, why wasn't it any longer? What had changed?

NOW

I can't figure it out.

I'm standing in the rec room of the Winchester Community Center, in the middle of calling roll for my group of squirmy nine- to twelve-year-olds, when I see Luke Cohen standing at the other end of the room, watching me.

At first I try to ignore him.

Keep calling names, look anywhere but at him, and he will disappear.

But when I steal another glance at the west doors of the massive room, he's still there.

"Willow!" I call, and like the amazing cocaptain she is, she appears.

"Mmhmm?" Her long brown hair is in a perfect fishtail braid and her makeup is flawless, completely out of place for a Tuesday morning at Camp MORE. Especially before eight a.m.

"Can you finish?" I ask, handing her the clipboard and already moving toward the other side of the room.

"Uh, sure," she says, following my gaze to the figure standing near the doors, watching us.

I brace myself for the staccato beats of my heart, the butterflies in my stomach that always come when I'm in Luke's presence, but being prepared makes no difference. He runs a hand along his jaw as I reach him, and I notice he's shaved since yesterday. He looks closer to nineteen today and slightly less intimidating, but neither of those things is to my advantage.

"What are you doing here?" I ask, coming to a stop in front of him. I fold my arms over my chest, trying to seem as confident and in control as I normally am at work.

"What are *you?*" He lobs the question back at me.

"I work here," I say. "And it's obvious you knew that, or you wouldn't be here."

He glances over my head, like I'm barely keeping his attention. "Obvious how?"

"I don't see you in months, but you show up three times in the last forty-eight hours? You're clearly stalking me."

That brings his attention back to me. "Or you're stalking me."

"Bullshit," I counter. "You were lying in wait at my house."

"That was not what I was doing."

I push my hair off my face, exasperated. "I don't want to fight, Luke. Please just go."

"I can't just go. I work here."

"Hilarious," I say. Then, a second later, a wave of fear crashes over me. "Is it . . . is Mel okay? Is that why you're here?"

"She was, as of twenty minutes ago," Luke says, and he's back to not looking at me. "But she does want to see you again."

I'm too confused to feel relieved. "Did you tell her the truth?"

"Which part?" he asks.

I take a moment to answer, try to keep my expression even when

I say, "All of it." It'd make her hate me, but she deserves to know the truth. I deserve her fury.

"I'm not going to do that to her," Luke says. "At least not while she thinks we're together."

"But we're not together," I point out.

"She thinks we are," he says. "And I'm not telling her anything different."

My mouth drops open. "You're just going to keep lying to her?"

"She's happy." He repeats his words from yesterday morning.

"It doesn't matter if she's happy. It's a fucking lie."

I can't believe how long Luke managed to fool everyone into thinking he was some kind of saint.

His eyes narrow, and he looks down at my T-shirt. "Don't you work with children?"

"So?" Self-conscious, I try to cover more of the unflattering shirt and the embarrassing ALL WE DO IS WIN, WIN, WIN NO MATTER WHAT logo emblazoned on it. On the back, it says WIN-CHESTER SUMMER CAMP MORE, which you'd think would be the more pertinent information, but apparently not.

"So you shouldn't curse." He stands up straighter and looks around. "Who's in charge, anyway?"

"If you hang on a moment, I'll go get the manager." It's meant to be a threat, but that apparently goes over Luke's head.

"Thanks. That'd be great," he says.

I disappear into one of the offices tucked into the back of the rec room. "Can I get your help with something?" I ask Diana, and she pops up from her desk.

"Sure. What is it?"

I'm genuinely surprised to see Luke still there, leaning against the wall and scrolling away on his phone. I point him out to her.

"Luke!" Diana says as we approach him. "Nice to see you again."

I gape as she and Luke shake hands.

"Jessi, this is our new science coordinator, Luke Cohen. He's a biochem major at State."

Shit.

"Luke, Jessi's one of our best team captains. She's been here since the start of the summer."

Shit, shit, shit.

Luke doesn't extend his hand, and neither do I.

"Let me just grab my phone," she says, "and then I'll take you to your cabin . . . classroom . . . whatever you want to call it. We like to call them stations."

"Got it," Luke says, following her back to her office. As I watch them go, Luke pulls out the green fabric hanging from his back pocket. The same green T-shirt I'm wearing, matching logo and all.

My heart drops.

NOW

The next time I see Luke is just before lunch when Willow and I and our eleven campers file into one of the classrooms on the second floor of the Community Center. Our previous science coordinator was a retired schoolteacher who missed days in a row because her MS was acting up. Her real name was Sunny, but she went by Sunshine in front of the kids.

As all the kids file in, Willow and I help them get settled and then retreat to the back of the room.

Luke claps his hands once to get their attention. "Hey, everyone." He settles on the wooden desk that Sunny used to sit behind and introduces himself. "I'm Duke. I'm the new guy here, so I'm counting on you guys to tell me what's what."

"Duke," Willow repeats so only I can hear. "He's cute."

He's asking the kids what they think of when they hear the word *science*.

I mumble something noncommittal to Willow, but the truth is that I'm kind of mesmerized by Luke. The least surprising thing obviously is his affinity for STEM. I'm used to bookish, quiet, thoughtful Luke. *My* Luke. But the boy in front of me is the same only on the surface. This boy is animated and lively and charming. He talks with his hands and holds the attention of every kid in the room.

He gets a volunteer to hand out sticky notes, asks the kids to write down their three favorite scientific facts, and makes his way to the back of the room, where Willow and I are leaning against the wall.

"Hey," Luke says, his eyes finding mine for half a second before totally focusing on Willow. "I'm Luke."

"Ohh," Willow says as she shakes his hand. "I was wondering about that. I'm Willow, but I go by Oak."

"Like the tree," Luke says.

"Yes. Oh my God, you're like the only one who has gotten and appreciated that."

Luke grins, and his smile makes something turn in my stomach.

Of course Willow would love him on sight. My Luke, but with different eyes. My Luke, but different.

So not my Luke at all.

"This is Jessi," Willow says, introducing us for the second time in the space of four hours. "But she goes by J.J."

Luke's eyes dart back to me. Neither of us makes a move to shake hands.

"It's like this thing where they want leaders to be relatable and fun and all that," Willow explains to Luke, "but still be authority figures, you know? So kids can't use our first names. But sometimes one of us will slip up and use somebody's real name."

He nods in understanding, tells us he'll be right back, and resumes his role as teacher. I'm mesmerized by his energy, his easy rapport with the students. I wonder what other sides of Luke I've never seen.

Thankfully, the science lesson passes uneventfully, and then it's lunchtime. All the camp leaders eat together in the cafeteria, at one table when we can all fit. Two, when we can't.

I spend the whole forty-five minutes with my eyes peeled to the cafeteria door, waiting to see him stride in wearing the T-shirt that is way more flattering on him than it is on most of us. Brett and Willow are sitting on my left side, practically spoon-feeding each other. A college-age student I don't know very well is on my right side, the only person between me and Eric, who is the sports coordinator here, so overall, it's a pretty uncomfortable lunch.

I breathe a sigh of relief after the period passes, relieved to get back into the swing of things for the rest of the day and not have to worry about seeing Luke again. The day does pass quickly, and before I know it, I'm saying goodbye to Willow and making my way into the staff parking lot. I stop when I see Luke leaning against the back of my car, his head down as he reads something on his phone.

He doesn't see me coming, and it takes everything I have to keep walking. I'm wondering if I can just get in and drive away without saying anything. Sure, it might surprise him a little, but I doubt there will be too much damage.

"Hi," I say, coming to a stop in front of him against my better judgment.

"Hi." He tucks his phone away in his back pocket. It's a total one-eighty from this morning, when he wouldn't give me the satisfaction of his full attention.

"I went about it all wrong," he says now. "The other day. Today."

"So, we *are* going to acknowledge that your getting a job here just to mess with me was going a bit too far?" I ask.

"I didn't get a job here to mess with you. I swear, it was a coincidence. Meant to be, I guess," he says, and I flinch at the idea that anything about us was ever meant to be.

The art coordinator, a girl in her early twenties with more piercings on her left ear than on my whole body, walks by us and waves. "See you later, J.J."

"Bye, Rouge," I call back.

One of Luke's eyebrows goes up. I start to explain that her name is Ruby, so she goes by Rouge, but then I catch myself and shut my mouth.

"Look," he says, leaning against my taillights again. "Mom stopped treatment a couple of months ago. She doesn't have that much longer. She misses having you around, and she's never gotten why we didn't end up together."

Heat floods my face, and I have to look away.

"It made sense . . ." he said. "I *thought* it made sense, to just act like we were back on. She'd have something to be happy about. You'd be there. And then things could go back to the way they were."

Things will never go back to the way they were.

"At least until she's . . . not here," he amends.

I swallow.

He holds my gaze, and it feels like a stranglehold. I can't look away.

"Please," he says now. For one awful, desperate moment, he looks like he might cry. But he doesn't.

He waits for me to respond.

I open my mouth to say no. I can't — won't — have never been good at lying to Mel. I miss her, yes, but it's not fair. Not after everything that's happened.

I can't say anything . . . we both know that I would sooner set myself on fire than to disappoint any of the Cohens.

I will always have a hard time saying no to Luke, but I would never forgive myself for doing it to Mel.

I don't know what he sees, but Luke's face relaxes after a moment.

I think he knows before I say it, even before I admit to myself what my answer will be.

He knows I will say yes.

6

THEN

Mel always got her way.

Correction: Mel almost always got her way.

It wasn't fair to say *always*, when her Big Bad went from being that she was a sugar fiend to something that was going to kill her eventually and leave her sons motherless.

So, Mel mostly got her way. But as far as Ro was concerned, "mostly" was still entirely too much.

"Rowan says I'm acting like a dictator," Mel said with a laugh as I changed lanes. "Because I'm making us celebrate that he's now in the top three in the state! The top *three*. I told him, if you're not careful, I'm going to up the ante and we'll start celebrating everything. Every win, every tournament, half birthdays, and half Christmases too."

I giggled and looked over at Mel in the passenger seat. She'd been letting me drive more and more since she'd started her treatment. She was probably too sick to get behind the wheel most days, but she'd never in a million years admit it.

"I thought it would help," I said, "that we were calling it a joint celebration for his ranking, plus Luke's going away to college and my passing calculus."

Naomi, who was in the back, harrumphed. "You think boys his age are programmed to care about anything but their own——"

"Nay!" Mel shouted before Naomi could finish her thought.

"Interests. I was going to say *interests*," Naomi said.

Mel and I laughed.

"Sure you were," I said. I didn't want to think about anything else she might have said, any more than Mel wanted to. Rowan was too . . . Rowan.

We pulled up at the Continental Hotel, piled into the restaurant, and settled in the waiting area until our reserved table was free.

"Those boys better not be late," Mel said as we watched the hostess escort a party that had arrived before us. "I told them about three times this morning alone."

"They won't," I assured her. Well, *Luke* wouldn't. "It's still five to six."

Two minutes later Luke jogged in from the parking lot. He was fixing the collar of his dress shirt, the sleeves already rolled up to his elbows.

"Sorry. Am I late?" he asked.

"No," the three of us said at once.

I shifted closer to Naomi so Luke could sit next to me. His gaze flittered over me, over the sparkly emerald-green top I was wearing with my favorite white skinny jeans, and I pretended to be distracted with something outside. It was too awkward watching someone watch you.

When I glanced back at him a second later, he was still staring at me, adjusting his collar again, and I wondered if he just needed something to do with his hands. He opened his mouth to say something, but it was swallowed up as Mel spoke over him.

"Honey, do you need help with that collar?"

"No, thanks," he said quickly.

"Well, you look spiffy," she said, and smiled at him.

Finally, Luke sat beside me. "Thanks for driving Mom," he said to me in a low voice. "I couldn't get out of work earlier."

"No problem," I said. As I spoke, I got my first inhale of the Luke scent for the night. I tried hard to hang on to my train of thought. "Plus, if I hadn't, Naomi would have anyway."

"What do you want? I heard my name," Naomi said grouchily.

"We were talking about you, not *to* you," I said.

"Carry on, then," she said, and I turned back to Luke.

He grinned at me. "Congrats, by the way. Mom told me you crushed your final."

"Oh, yeah," I said, feeling my face warm. "Like a B is crushing it to you."

He frowned. "B is amazing. You get A's in English and art, and basically anything that isn't calculus. I wish I could do that."

I started to argue that he already *did* gets A's in all those subjects, but then his knee was knocking mine lightly, and he said, "Just say thanks."

"Thanks," I said lamely.

He smiled. "So, anyway, I was going to say—"

"We're here! Let the party officially commence!" Ro said, pushing through the restaurant doors in a bright red polo and khaki pants. Eric hung back awkwardly, wearing a dress shirt instead of his usual athleisure style.

"Uh hey Mrs. Cohen," he said, nodding at Mel.

Mel stood and walked over to Rowan. "Are you *drunk?*" she whispered, horrified.

"What? No," Rowan said entirely too quickly. Beside me, I heard Luke murmur something.

"That's it. Get in the car," Mel said, grabbing Rowan's arm and beginning to drag him back outside. Mel was cool in every way, but she did not approve of underage drinking. That, coupled with the fact that she detested nothing as much as lying, meant Ro was in for a rough night. "Jessi, give me my keys."

I stood, but Luke said, "Mom, wait. Why should he ruin everybody's night?"

"He's *drunk*," Mel repeated, dismayed. "Eric, please tell me you drove."

"I drove," Eric confirmed.

"Luke's right," Naomi said, and now we were all standing. "We have things to celebrate. Isn't that what you said? So let's celebrate."

Mel looked unsurely at our faces. "This is just . . ."

"Not what you planned, I know," Naomi said. "We'll make the best of it. I mean, we'd have to anyway. How many stars is this place?" She looked around critically.

Mel's face broke into the smallest smile, and then she turned back to Ro. "I'm so upset with you."

"I—just had two drinks, Mom," Ro slurred.

"Are you actually brainless or just acting like it?" Luke hissed as he steered Rowan toward the waiting area where we'd been sitting.

Mel, Ro, and Naomi had just sat down when our hostess appeared and led us to a table.

I somehow found myself wedged between Naomi and Ro. Luke was on his brother's other side, and Eric was next to Luke and Mel.

After our drinks arrived, Mel held up her cup to make a toast (she had pointedly ordered a coffee and an extra glass of water for Ro). "Despite the untoward start to this evening," she said, and we all looked at Rowan, who shifted in his seat, "I want to say that I'm really happy we're all here. Here tonight, and here at all."

She swallowed, and I imagined Ro and Luke stiffening the same way I had.

"It's been a rough couple of months, as you all know. I'm not gonna lie, it sucks being sick. But one thing the Big Bad has taught me is that every day—every moment—counts. I want to spend it as happy and grateful and well-dressed and brave as I possibly can. It's hard, but you lot make it easier."

She blew a kiss around the table and took a sip of her water.

I stood up and went around the table to hug her.

"Love you, Jessi-girl," she said into my hair, and I blinked hard. As I settled back into my seat, I noticed Ro giving me a strange look.

"What?" I asked.

"Why do you look like that?" he asked me.

"Look like what? This is how I always look," I said, feeling self-conscious as everyone looked over at us. It wasn't how I always looked. I had curled my hair and was wearing more makeup than I normally did. I'd felt pretty when I looked in the mirror, when Mel had complimented me, and when I'd caught Luke looking at me, but now I felt like the biggest idiot. Like an imposter.

"Rowan, can we not hear from you for the rest of the night?" Mel snapped.

Ro shut his mouth and guzzled down his water.

The rest of the evening was better. The food was delicious (Naomi said she was going to write a review saying their food managed to "overcome their stars") and I laughed more than I had in ages. Being with the Cohens always made me feel good, and tonight, with the added relief of summer school being over, I was close to giddy.

I kept thinking of Mel's words from her toast.

I want to spend it as happy and grateful and well-dressed and brave as I possibly can.

I wanted a tattoo of those words somewhere on my body, but I knew I'd settle for scribbling it in my journal tonight, along with all the other Mel-isms and Cohen memories I had.

I was still thinking of it when I stepped out of the restroom after dinner. I'd gotten up while Mel was asking for the bill, and I was absent-mindedly walking back to the dining room when I heard my name.

I spun around to find Luke coming out of the men's room across the hall.

"Hey," I said, slowing down so he could catch up with me. After a couple of steps, he stopped walking completely, so I stopped too. "What's up?"

"I hope you know to ignore him," he said.

"Ignore who?" I asked.

"Ro. *Idiot* doesn't begin to cover it."

Ro's comment about how I looked came rushing back, and with it, all the embarrassment I'd felt.

I shrugged. "He's wasted, I guess. But also entitled to his own dumb opinion."

"*Dumb* being the key word," Luke said. He rubbed the back of his neck. "He's . . . whatever. Everybody knows you're beautiful."

My heart stopped at the word. *Beautiful.*

According to Luke Cohen.

When I recovered enough, I figured the only way forward was to make light of it. "That's nice of . . . everybody to say."

A small smile crept across his face. "Everybody says you're welcome."

I grinned at him and then realized, a minute later, that we were standing in a corner of the Continental smiling at each other.

Also, that he thought I was beautiful.

The next few moments were a string of things I should have done—and didn't.

Should have: taken three steps and closed the distance between us.

Should have: taken his hand in mine.

Should have: leaned up and kissed him, because he was leaving for college in a couple of weeks and there would never be a better chance.

I stayed in the same spot.

I clasped and unclasped my hands.

I said, "How was karaoke?"

He seemed dazed for a moment, and then he said, "Oh, yeah. Fine. I took your advice."

"The Henley?"

"That, and the shoes, and singing a song everyone knew. All of it."

"And?"

"Thanks," he said, but did not elaborate on how things had gone for him after that. Was the girl who invited him impressed? Did she kiss him like her life depended on it and convince him to let her keep his shirt, like a normal lovestruck fool would have done?

I didn't ask, and Luke didn't tell.

We walked back to our table in silence.

I drove Mel and Naomi home after that, beating myself up internally the entire way to Naomi's place and then to Mel's.

Why, why, why hadn't I been brave enough to kiss him?

Why was I such an obsessed nut job?

Why was I such an obsessed nut job with no balls to do the thing I most wanted to?

I had said goodbye to everyone and was sitting in the driveway in Mel's car when a light came on in my head.

Mel had told me to drive myself home in her car, return it tomorrow, and get a ride home with one of the boys.

I could do that.

I could pull out of her driveway, go home, and forget this night ever happened.

Or I could do something deserving of Mel's words, the ones I wanted inscribed on my body someday.

I want to spend it as happy and grateful and well-dressed and brave as I possibly can.

I wanted to be brave, and though I was reasonably sure this hadn't been what Mel had in mind when she'd said it, I used her words as motivation.

I dug for my phone in my purse and texted Luke.

Can you come out for a second?

He responded unusually fast.

Sure. Out where?

I bit my lip. **Your driveway?**

Okay, he wrote.

I hopped out of Mel's car and walked back to the front door. A slight breeze had picked up, and I hugged my arms around myself, feeling cold and vulnerable in my halter top and bravado.

A couple of nerve-destroying minutes passed before the front door opened. Luke slipped outside, forcing an unhappy Sydney to stay inside. He had already changed into a pair of pajama bottoms and a hoodie. I could have bet money he hadn't been wearing the hoodie when I'd texted, but I still wasn't sure about the pants.

He looked at me, curious. Maybe he was surprised I was at the front door when I'd told him the driveway. Maybe he thought I'd be home already.

Either way, I took a step toward him.

"I'm sorry. I just needed to do something, or I'd have to figure out a way to physically kick my own butt and keep doing it for all of time," I rambled.

An amused grin lit up Luke's face. "Okay," he said.

"Okay," I said, taking another step toward him, my heart drumming wildly in my chest.

Then I did it.

I stood on my tiptoes and kissed him, saying everything I'd wanted to say for years.

He was caught off-guard, for sure, but he recovered quickly enough and gently pried me off him.

"Jessi," he whispered, still close enough that our foreheads were touching, and he sounded so, so sorry. "I can't."

NOW

I need a time machine.

I need a way to go back to this afternoon and my conversation with Luke, to tell him how batshit crazy the whole thing is. We're going to pretend to be together to make Mel happy?

There is no way we'll be able to pull it off.

Furthermore, there is no way Mel will buy it. We are just too . . . obviously not together.

He can barely even look at me. And honestly, maybe things are better that way.

He doesn't have to be reminded constantly of how much he hates me now, and neither do I.

I knock twice on Ernie's door and call out to him. "Ernie, can I come in?"

"You better. I've been talking to myself for fifty-seven years, and it's getting strange," he shouts back.

I grin and go inside. He's sitting in his favorite rocking chair, his glasses on his nose, as he reads the piece of paper in his hands.

"I talk to myself all the time. That's not strange," I say.

"Well, I wouldn't use you as my barometer for normal," he quips. "Anyway, it's not the talking to myself part I'm worried about. It's the fact that I'm starting to talk back!"

I laugh and settle into the couch beside him. "What are you reading?"

"A letter from the great-grandson." He shakes his head sadly. "Sweet boy, but I don't know how he's going to make it through school with that name. *Eustace.*"

"Maybe he'll go by a nickname," I offer, but Ernie isn't going for it.

"What sort of nickname? Eu? Stace?" He folds the letter and gingerly sets it on the coffee table in front of him. "Ah, well. His mother says she labored with him for two and a half days, so he deserves it."

I smile. "When do I get to meet them all? Over the holidays?"

Ernie shakes his head. "I'm hoping we'll both be out of here by then. Especially you."

I know he's mostly joking, but my heart sinks.

"Don't look at me like that," he says. "Girls your age . . . *boys* your age . . . the things we got up to. Youth is wasted on the young."

"I get up to things," I say defiantly.

"Like what?" he asks, his eyes gleaming with genuine interest.

"I went to a party over the weekend. I went for a run. I work at a day camp on weekdays before I come here."

Ernie looks disappointed. "Sounds like a riot. You could live next door to me in one of these units with everything you have going on."

"That would be lovely. You'd be a great neighbor."

"I think so too, but Clarisse says that when my snoring isn't keeping her up, my pounding around is."

"Your pounding?" I repeat. "That's . . . weird. Do you walk around a lot at night?"

"Not so much walking, but there is a tennis ball I like to throw at that wall," he says, pointing to the wall that divides Ernie's unit from his neighbor's. "Physio says it's good for the bum shoulder."

I sigh, and Ernie does a villain laugh.

"I'm taking that tennis ball when I go."

"If you promise not to come back, you can have all six of them."

My stomach tightens. I've laughed off most of his comments over the eight months I've been coming here, but I'm starting to get worried. "Are you . . . tired of me coming around?"

Even though I met him only late last year, he's one of the few people I spend any time with these days and the thought that he might have had enough of me stings.

Ernie snorts at my question. "No, but we both save face if you stop coming before you get sick of me."

I touch his arm, relieved. "I'm not going to get sick of you."

"Oh, please," he says. "My Mary did sixty-some years with me, so they made her a saint."

"I think that was a different Mary."

"That's not what I heard," he says with a chuckle. His face grows more serious now. "Look, my kids have their lives on the East Coast. I raised them to be independent — they're only doing what I taught them to. Same with the grandkids. Great-grandkids . . . well, one of them is named Eustace, the other Titus, so they have enough problems of their own. Sure, sometimes it gets lonely, but it was six years after my Mary left me before they moved me here, and I managed fine. I *will* manage fine."

"I know you will, Ernie, but I *like* coming to see you."

He stares at me skeptically for a few minutes and sighs. "Well, I suppose they pay you good to say that."

"You're so frustrating, you know that?" I tell him, and with his level of delight, you'd think I just complimented him.

"So I suppose you're just going to keep on coming despite my wishes?"

"I am," I say defiantly. Maybe I don't deserve it, but being around Ernie makes me happy. It also makes me feel like I'm doing some good in the world, which makes me at least a little bit different from who I was last year.

He sighs again. "Well, all right. Next time, bring a bag of those salty chips if you're coming anyway."

"Done," I say.

"And a tub of yogurt, but real. None of that low-fat nonsense."

"Got it."

"And a pack of Marlboros and a lighter."

"Not happening."

"Ah, well. Had to try."

At the end of our two hours, Ernie pats my hand and says, "You're a good girl, Jessi."

Even though I work hard every day for this to be true, the voice in my head is still louder. And it's still right, even though I hate it.

I'm not good.

A good person wouldn't do the things I've done.

A good person would have told Mel the truth when I saw her yesterday and would certainly not go along with some plan to keep lying to her, no matter who suggested it.

I find myself veering off course and driving in the direction of the far east, through neighborhoods as familiar as the back of my own hands. When I'm in front of the Cohen house, I take a breath to steady myself and run through what I plan to say to Luke.

He's going to be disappointed, maybe even angry, but he's the one who started this lie. I don't have to go along with it. No matter how happy it would make Mel, I can't continue to lie to her.

I ring the doorbell and find myself listening for the pitter-patter of dog feet before I remember that Sydney is gone. The realization every time feels like a bruise that I keep pressing on.

When the doorbell swings open, Luke is still in his Camp MORE T-shirt and jeans, half a carrot in his hand.

"Hey." He looks surprised to see me.

"Luke, who is it?" I hear Mel call from somewhere close by, and my eyes widen.

I give two vigorous shakes of my head and put my fingers to my lips.

"Jessi," he calls to her, ignoring my wild gesticulation.

"Is she staying for dinner?" Mel calls.

"I'll ask her," he says, looking right at me.

"We need to talk," I whisper.

He glances over his shoulder, shuts the front door, but stays on the porch. He's standing in the exact spot where I kissed him almost a year ago, and the thought feels like a stab in my chest.

"I changed my mind," I tell him now.

"About?" he asks.

"Us," I say.

He gives me an odd look. "Us?"

Luke has never been accused of being slow, so I suspect he is dragging this out for my benefit.

"You know — what you told Mel," I whisper now, not sure how to say the words out loud. *Us pretending to be together.*

"I can't do it," I say. "First of all, she's never going to buy it. I don't know what you're thinking. Second, it's just wrong, and it's a horrible thing to do."

"What's so horrible about it?" Luke asks, which is the last thing I'm expecting him to say.

"It's a lie," I say, surprised that this is not obvious to him.

"I don't see how it hurts anyone."

"We would have to hang out all the time," I blurt out, and his eyes narrow.

"Is that what's bothering you? Having to be around me?"

"No. I mean, obviously, it's weird, but . . ." My voice trails off.

"She has weeks, Jessi. If that." His eyes get this hard look. "I thought that would mean something to you — that you, of all people, would understand. But I guess I was wrong about you."

The word *again* hangs in the air, but neither of us says it.

I swallow hard. "I want her to be happy, but —"

"But not at the cost of your own comfort? Got it." He starts toward the door, then turns back. "Do you think that I *want* to do this? You think pretending to be *anything* with you is my idea of a good time?"

I open my mouth to speak, then shut it again.

"You think I like hearing all the fucking time about you, and how you were the daughter she never had — what did Ro call it, the chosen one — and how I'm the reason you're gone?"

It's the first time either of us has brought up Rowan, and I feel like I'm going to throw up.

I'm swiping at the tear on my cheek before I even register that I'm crying. "I miss Mel, too," I say, because it's true, and it's easier than talking about his brother.

"She's here," he says, pointing toward the house. "She's waiting to hear if you're staying for dinner. If that's what you want."

Against my better judgment, I'm nodding my head and wiping my eyes with my arm.

That's what I want.

For everything to go back to the way it was.

More than anything in this world, that's what I want.

"Do I look like crap?" I ask, fanning my wet face with my hands. "Don't answer that," I say quickly, because this isn't the Luke Cohen from my childhood, and he's certainly not the Luke Cohen from last summer. This Luke, I know without knowing how, is no longer worried about trying to protect me. This Luke doesn't care about hurting me.

He goes in without saying a word, and I follow.

NOW

Dinner is different. It is sitting in the living room on the loveseat while Mel is sitting out on the sofa, swimming in a sea of blankets. Her food is half the size of mine and much less than Luke's.

It is catching up but not talking about anything that matters, like we're navigating a giant hole in the ground without acknowledging it.

It feels so wrong—the thought of Rowan being a hole, something to navigate around.

I sit on the edge of my seat, watching Mel slurp down her soup, and I try to act like I'm not staring.

It is Luke's arm stretched out behind me on the couch, both of us trying to act normal but ready to jump up at a moment's notice to adjust Mel's blankets or take her bowl away or hand her water.

"Nay is coming over later tonight," Mel tells us. "She's back to teaching full-time in the fall, so she's spending lots of time preparing for that. Oh, and did I tell you she got married?"

"Naomi got married?" I repeat. I'm distracted by the sallow flesh of Mel's shoulders that is exposed by the oversize shirt she is wearing, but I'm trying not to let on. The last thing I want is to embarrass her or to make her feel like the state of her body has changed her for me.

Mel laughs. "I'm going to tell her you sounded that surprised. She never had trouble landing a man, you know."

"She will tell her, too," Luke tells me. "They still gossip like hens." Even though he's sitting right beside me, our bodies inches apart, it's jarring every time he talks to me. If not for Mel's presence, we would have absolutely nothing to say to each other.

"Hurtful, Luke," Mel says with a shake of her head.

"It's not *that*," I amend. "Like, it's not that I ever thought she couldn't find a man or anything, but I guess I just kind of figured she . . . didn't want to?"

"I'm taking this *all* back to Nay," she says.

"For years, we all used to think—" I start and then stop. Luke looks up from cutting his meat to look at me, and Mel looks too. I have no choice but to go on, "We, um, thought that maybe there was something going on with you and her."

Mel throws her head back, and her laugh is bigger than her whole body. "Me and Naomi? Seriously?"

"We literally used to sit around, and I'd ask, do you think Mel and Naomi have ever kissed, and would you be mad if they had? And we all decided we wouldn't." I feel myself walking on a literal land mine, but stopping will set off the explosion.

"Who's we?" Mel asks.

"All of us," I say, not looking at either of them.

Everything is quiet, except for the sound of Luke chewing, and then Mel says, "Well, as nice as it is that it wouldn't have bothered you, we've always been just friends. Romance is great and all, but friendship is every bit as miraculous and special." Another beat passes, and as I'm reaching for my water, she adds, "Advice brought to you by a forty-seven-year-old who hasn't been laid since creation."

"Jesus, Mom," Luke groans, and I spit out my water, laughing.

"Don't worry. Nothing sounds less appealing right now," she says.

"Mom."

"What?" Mel says. "If I can't tell it like it is at this point in my life, I never will."

Luke and I must have matching somber expressions, because Mel says, "Oh, come on! We can laugh about it. The Big Bad can have everything else, but not my laughter."

I give Mel a close-lipped smile, my heart feeling heavy.

She sighs and slowly lowers her body back down from its sitting position.

"Tired?" Luke asks, and she nods.

He stands up, ready to take her back to her room, but she waves him off.

"No, I'm fine. Keep hanging out. Don't let me ruin the fun."

Luke and I look at each other.

"Actually, I probably need to get going," I say, standing.

"So soon?" Mel's eyes are closed, and she winces as if she's in pain. "It feels like you just got here."

"I have to get some stuff done before camp tomorrow."

"You two are sneaky as hell," Mel says now, opening one eye and pointing at both of us. "Luke tells me he's working at the community center camp, and then this afternoon, he's like, 'So when I saw Jessi . . .'"

I steal a look in his direction, but he's just watching his mother with a passive expression.

"I said, 'You saw Jessi?' He goes, 'She works there too.' As if you didn't plan it out like that so you could work together."

"Yeah, uh, sorry," I say lamely when Luke says nothing. "I'm going to go now, Mel," I say, leaning down to hug her. When I was little, I used to squeeze her as if she were oxygen and I was running out of air, but now I'm tentative and cautious, not wanting to hurt her.

"Bye Jessi-girl," she says.

"I'll walk you out," Luke says as I straighten. We head out of the house in silence, and once we're on the porch again, the air feels weighted.

"So we should probably figure out schedules," he says now. "Like, so we're seeing each other as often as . . . *people* would."

"Oh," I say. "Okay."

I realize we're doing this. We're really going to pretend to be together to make Mel happy.

Luke was right, though; it's the least I can do.

He leans back against the side of the house. "What are you doing tomorrow night?"

"Helping out at the club." I'm hoping I don't have to specify which club, but he knows.

"The night after that?"

"Thursday I'm working at All Saints. And Saturday afternoons, too."

He frowns. "Why do you work so much?"

He asks, but we both know he doesn't care what my answer is, so I don't offer one.

"How's Friday night then?" he asks. "We can meet up at eight, act like we did dinner, and then come back here to see her."

I nod. "That works."

"Okay," he says, straightening.

"Well, good night," I say, then turn and walk back to my car. I feel Luke's gaze on me the whole time as I get in, start the car, and pull out onto the road, and it makes my stomach flutter. I'm guessing he waits out there long enough for Mel to think he walked me out, kissed me good night, and waited until I drove home.

Seeing Mel, along with all the pretending tonight, has taken its toll on me, and I feel heavy and sad as I enter my house. The lights are on in the living room, and I'm surprised to see Mom in there, working on her laptop.

"Sweetheart!" she says brightly when she sees me. "How was your day?"

"Good," I say.

"Good?" she repeats skeptically, and I'm surprised that she can see right through me. After all the years of living together but existing in separate universes, I'm used to my mother knowing exactly nothing about me. It catches me off-guard to realize that this new version of her is starting to know me well enough to read me, to recognize my moods. It makes me feel strangely grateful, and I try not to think about it going away again.

Mom looks pleased when I come and sit on the couch beside her. "Not so good," I admit. "I had dinner with Mel today—"

"And?" she prompts.

I tell my mother how weak Mel looked, how guilty I feel for missing so much of the end of her life. My parents think I just drifted away from the other Cohens after Rowan died, and I don't ever intend to tell them otherwise. I also don't mention the added guilt I feel about going along with Luke's plan to lie to his mother. I doubt Mom would approve of us faking a relationship just to make Mel happy.

"No matter how much time you lost the past year, the important thing is that you're back now," Mom says, taking my hand. "You know, I reached out to my parents a while ago, when I started therapy."

"Did they respond?" I ask.

She looks sad when she shakes her head. "I didn't expect them to, to be honest," she says. "We left things in a pretty ugly place. But I remember thinking when I sent that email that I no longer care what happened, or how long it's been, or how much they hurt me with their absence. I just wanted to try again with them. I wanted them to see me now, to know the person I've become. To know my beautiful daughter." She brushes her hand over my cheek. "And I'm sure that's how Mel felt. When you miss someone enough, it doesn't matter how much time has passed."

I swallow. "What ever happened between you and your parents?" When I was really little, I used to think my mom was an orphan. I even invented a story in my head that that was why she was so sad all the time. Then I got older and realized that her parents were alive and that her unhappiness stemmed from something deeper.

"Your father and I never told you?" she asks.

When would you have? I think, but just shake my head.

"They didn't approve of him," she says.

"Of *Dad?*" I ask, thinking of my put-together father with his warm smile. I think of the way he looks at Mom, the way his eyes light up when she's in the room, the way he's stood by her all these years, and I don't get it.

"Because he's black," she says plainly.

It takes a few moments for her words to sink in, and then I balk. "Seriously? What century are they from?"

Mom shakes her head. "It's ridiculous. It was then, and it is now," she says. "But it's why they never supported our marriage. They were willing to lose me before opening up their family to him. I had hoped that things might have changed over the last eighteen years, but apparently not.

"Anyway," she continues. "I won't ever forget the way they treated him, the way they treated us, but I was ready to start a new leaf, if they were willing — if they could accept that they'd been wrong."

Her eyes are watering now, and I reach over and squeeze her hand.

"I guess what I'm trying to say is that even when you're wrong — especially when you're wrong — lots of times, it's not too late to do better. And instead of beating yourself up about not being there for Melanie, you should be glad it's not too late."

When we finish talking and head up the stairs, Mom's words continue to replay in my mind. I can't believe my grandparents are racist jerks, that that's the reason I've never known them. It breaks my heart for my father, knowing how much he loves Mom, how good a person he is, yet all they could see was the color of his skin.

I think about Mom's other words, too, about focusing on the fact that I still have time left with Mel, that it's not too late.

I decide right then that I'm going to take advantage of every moment I have left with her.

Still, I think about Luke's coldness since he's been back, and I'm pretty sure Mom was wrong about one thing: sometimes it is too late. It is definitely too late for me and Luke.

7

THEN

I didn't think Luke and I could have been any clearer about where we stood.

I'd kissed him, he'd pushed me away, and I'd sprinted down the driveway and jumped into Mel's car as quickly as I could.

So why did he keep texting?

He texted me more during those two weeks than he had throughout all the time we'd known each other.

At first he kept apologizing.

I'm sorry, Jessi.

Call me?

Please call me?

I called you and it went to voicemail. Can you call me back?

Come on, J.J. We need to talk.

I'm really, really sorry.

After about a week, his messages took a turn.

Are you coming for dinner at our place tonight? Mom's making lamb chops.

Hey, missed you tonight.

Mom and Ro are getting worried about you. I am, too.

We're watching Say Anything tonight (Mom's choice). Willing to be your footrest.

I almost smiled at that.

Almost.

When we were younger and had movie night at the Cohens', we would all run and try to claim the long couch for ourselves. Whoever got there second got to sit on the loveseat with Mel, and whoever got there last had to sit on the end of the slightly lopsided long couch and serve as a footrest.

Ro and I were almost always competing for the long couch. Luke, who had the toughest time abandoning whatever book or video game he was currently immersed in, pretty much always settled for last. And since I was quick and as sly as a fox, I almost always outwitted Ro and beat him to the long couch.

So Luke's permanent position during movie nights became being my footrest.

Still, I didn't respond to his text.

I couldn't.

I was still too mortified to face him or any of the Cohens. Ordinarily, I wouldn't have been able to keep the truth from Mel or Ro, but Mel was preoccupied with her treatment, and maybe Ro's distance was turning out to be a good thing after all. I had *kissed* Luke, for crap's sake. And he'd peeled me off him.

I didn't even blame him for doing it. Say what you will about Ro's being drunk the night of the celebration dinner, I was the one who had lost my inhibition and was going around kissing people with no advance warning. Luke had clearly been humoring me — when he'd called me beautiful . . . and maybe all my life—and I'd misunderstood and taken it as an excuse to jump his bones. I'd thought I was following Mel's life advice, being brave, but all I'd done was thoroughly embarrass myself and ruin everything.

Thankfully, it was only a few days until Luke went off to State. Then, maybe, I could start showing my face at his house again. Maybe.

The night before he was scheduled to drive to college, I got this text from him.

Jessi, Mom and Naomi cooked this huge dinner in celebration of the fact that I'm heading to school tomorrow. It was amazing. Wish you'd been there.

The next day, late at night: **Arrived at State. Mom bawled pretty much the whole morning and Ro got that quiet way he gets when he's sad. I hope I'm doing the right thing, but I know you will take good care of them. You always do. If it wasn't already clear, I'm sorry and I acknowledge that I am a complete and utter idiot. I hope things can go back to being OK with us soon.**

I'd cried at his words.

I was sad that my stupidity had caused me to miss such a milestone in the Cohen house—Luke was going to college! I felt horrible that I hadn't been there for him, or for Mel and Ro, and it started to sink in with horrible clarity that Luke was gone. He'd probably never live in Winchester again. He would make new friends and go to hundreds of parties and karaoke nights and never think twice about me. He'd kiss heaps of girls, all of whom he'd actually like.

The whole thing was devastating.

Still, I rallied myself enough to compose a response.

Glad you made it safely. I'll look after Mel and Ro. Good luck at State.

I never heard back.

Not that there was anything else for him to say.

The next day, I went over to see Mel and Ro, claiming a crisis with my mother, which was pretty much true. She was basically always in crisis, but all we did was live with it.

Just like that, things went back to a new normal.

Mel's treatment continued.

Ro and I started school again.

Life went on.

And then one day, three weeks into September, my doorbell rang.

"I'll get it!" I called out from the kitchen, where I was elbow-deep in dish-washing soap. It was unnecessary for me to say it, really, because my mom was in bed and my dad had fallen asleep over a table full of papers. He also didn't like to get the door unless we were expecting company. He was convinced that everybody was peddling a product "too useless to be carried in a real store" or were Jehovah's Witnesses.

It was after ten on a Saturday night, and I opened the door, expecting it to be the neighbors, who lost their dog weekly, but it was Luke.

He was standing with his hands in his pockets, wearing a dark blue version of the Henley I loved so much.

I opened my mouth, but no sound came out.

"Hi," he said, and his voice was blanket-soft and familiar.

My heart skipped a beat

"Can we talk?" he asked.

I stole a look behind me to make sure my dad was still at the table, then stepped out the front door and shut it behind me.

"What's up?" I said, finally finding my voice.

"Not much. I'm back in town for the weekend."

"How's school?"

"Different," he said. "Good different. I think."

I nodded.

"How have you been?" he asked, and it was weird making small talk like we were strangers. Sure, Ro had always been my best friend, not Luke, but we'd been such integral parts of each other's lives that there was never nothing to say.

"Good. School's . . . school."

He grinned and then rubbed the back of his neck.

"Why are you here?" I asked finally.

Luke looked down at the ground for a minute and then said, "I miss you."

At first I thought I'd misheard him. "Please don't make fun of me."

He looked surprised. "I'm not. I . . . wouldn't."

"So what do you want?" I said, folding my arms across my chest.

"About that night . . . I'm sorry. It wasn't . . . it's not you."

I cringed. "Please, dear God, don't say it's you."

"It is me," he insisted.

I took a step back. "Okay, good night, Luke."

I opened the door to go back in, but he grabbed my hand, stopping me. "You're making this so complicated."

Luke was basically holding my hand now, but I didn't react.

"It's not that complicated," I said. "I liked you, I kissed you. You didn't like me, you didn't kiss me back."

"That's what you think happened?" He let go of my hand to push his hand through his hair. "Please come out and talk to me."

I hesitated, let go of the door again, and turned to face him.

"I'm trying to be . . ." He shook his head, like he was struggling to find the right word. "I'm trying to be a good guy here."

"No one asked you to be."

"You're supposed to be like my kid sister," he said.

He couldn't be serious.

"Since when? That's bullshit."

"Is Mel like your mother?" he challenged.

"That's irrelevant," I said stubbornly.

"Is Ro like your brother?"

"He's my best friend."

"Okay," Luke said. "So what am I?"

"I don't know, Luke," I said, annoyance starting to fill my every word. "You're Luke. Unattainable, too good to be true, not on my level."

"I'm not *good,* okay?" he said, surprising me with his fervor. "I'm fucked-up just like everyone else, but I'm trying. I'm trying to be better than my dad — than both my parents . . ."

"What did Mel do?" I asked.

"That's not the point."

I sighed. "I really don't know what you're saying, Luke. I'm not sure you do either. It's not supposed to be so freaking hard. You don't have to be Good. I said I like you. If you like me, say it back. I kissed you. If you liked it, kiss me back."

I'd barely gotten the words out before Luke's lips were on mine. He kissed me frantically, as if we were running out of time, his hands threading through my hair.

When he pulled back, his voice was rough and unfamiliar. "Now do you know how fucking much I liked it?"

I opened my mouth to speak, then changed my mind and kissed him instead. I felt feverish as his hand curled around my waist, pushing us closer, and I looped my arms around his neck. We kissed for so long I lost track of time.

"Jessi, who's out there?" Dad's voice sounded like it was coming from close by.

Luke and I stepped back from each other as my father appeared in the doorway.

"It's just Luke, Dad," I said, my voice sounding gravelly.

"Hi, Mr. Rumfield," Luke said, standing up straighter.

"Luke, how's your mother?"

"She's good, thanks," he said. I pressed my lips together, hoping they didn't look quite as swollen and as pink as Luke's did.

"Good. And how's the biochem?" Dad asked. "Are you thinking pharmacy? If you're considering optometry at all, I'd be happy to talk—"

"It's late, Dad," I interrupted, trying to save Luke, but my father shot me a look that said *if it's so late, why is he still here?*

"I better get going. Nice seeing you, Mr. Rumfield. Jessi."

He held my gaze for a second before turning and heading back toward his car.

I followed Dad in and shut the door, trying not to float away.

THEN

I barely slept that night. My mind kept replaying the kiss(es). Luke's soft lips on mine, his arm around my waist, his hand in my hair. I tossed and turned all night and fell asleep just as the sun was starting to sneak out across the sky.

The first thing I did when I woke was to lunge for my phone.

I had no messages, no texts. No voice mails.

Nothing.

Had I imagined the whole thing? Had last night even happened?

Maybe he'd changed his mind.

I didn't know, but I intended to find out.

I focused on one of the tenets of Mel's advice about boys, which was that girls could totally make the first move. I'd definitely made the first with that kiss on his porch step the night of the dinner. It was true that being too forward had resulted in the most miserable five weeks of my life, but it also had resulted in the previous night.

I pulled up Luke's name on my phone.

In the end, all I could think to say was **hey.**

About ten minutes passed before my phone vibrated with his response.

Hey.

It offered exactly zero clues about what he was thinking, whether he'd spent the night regretting coming to see me.

About last night... I texted, letting it hang in the air.

I saw the three dots indicating that he was replying. Then they disappeared.

Then reappeared again.

I wrote **are you having regrets,** but didn't send it when I saw that his three dots had disappeared again.

Ugh. He was the most aggravating person in the world to text with.

I deleted my text and wrote: **you go first.**

I'd had enough embarrassment to last me a lifetime. There was no way I was professing anything until he did first.

No, you, he wrote, and I wanted to throw my phone.

Before I could, though, another text popped up from him.

But if you're going to do that thing where you take it back before I have a chance to tell you that I can't stop thinking about you, then I'm not going to take it well.

My heart stopped.

You can't stop thinking about me? I wrote back.

A couple of minutes passed.

Only for the past three years.

I had to reread the text four times before I allowed myself to believe what it said.

??????? I texted back.

What? He said.

Three years?? I didn't kiss you three years ago.

I know you didn't, he wrote back.

I felt dizzy and hot, as if I might pass out from shock.

But you liked me then? Why didn't you say anything?

He wrote back a couple of seconds later: **You were 14, it was weird.**

You were 15!!!!!

His message came back nearly instantly: :)

My mouth dropped open.

Did you just . . . send one more emoji and I'm going to turn to mush.

:) :) :) :) :), he wrote.

My mouth is literally open right now.

He said: **I didn't know mush could do that.**

I let a couple of minutes pass before I sent anything back, and when I did, I simply said, **So.**

So? He wrote.

I kiss you, you kiss me back (after an unforgivable amount of time), you tell me you've liked me for 3 years and then we just go back to normal? I asked.

I bit my lip as I waited for his response.

Is that what you want? He wrote.

No.

What do you want?

I started to say that I didn't know, but then I changed my mind and decided to be totally honest. **To kiss you again.**

It took ages for him to write back. Glaciers melted, animals went extinct, man touched the sun. Finally, his response: **We could start with frozen yogurt?**

So we did.

I borrowed my mom's car and drove to Cold Rock Café. My palms were slick against the steering wheel, and I wondered the whole way whether I was underdressed in my denim skirt and T-shirt, or was it overdressed? Was it possible to be both?

Luckily, when I pulled up in front of the fro-yo store, I saw Luke waiting outside, his hand in the pocket of his jeans. He, too, was wearing a plain T-shirt. His face relaxed into a grin as soon as he saw me, and I couldn't help but smile.

The butterflies in my stomach were having a riot and my heart was staging a stampede, but neither of those things mattered.

Luke Cohen was looking at me like we shared a secret. *And we did.*

"Hey," he said when I stepped out of the car.

"Hey," I said, feeling shy. We both kind of hesitated, not sure whether to hug or kiss or neither or both.

In the end, we did neither and just walked into the store. "What's your favorite flavor?" Luke asked, holding the door open for me. "I feel like I should know that."

"Mango," I said. "What's yours?"

"I like vanilla. Kind of boring," he said.

"No, I like it, too."

We made small talk as we waited in line and ordered. When it came time to pay, Luke slid a bill across the counter before I could.

"I got it," he said. I flushed. If there had been any doubt that this was a *date* date, this erased it.

"Thanks," I said. "Do you care where we sit?"

"Probably shouldn't sit too close to the window. Mom and Ro think I'm already on my way back to school."

I smiled. "Okay, how's this?" We settled into a table for two near the back of the store.

As we dipped into our respective cups, the awkwardness threatened to engulf us again.

Without permission from my brain, I heard myself speaking. "When did you know?"

Luke didn't pretend not to know what I was talking about. "Honestly? One day you were just different to me."

I narrowed my eyes at him. "So, when I got boobs?"

He laughed. "You didn't get boobs at fourteen."

"Oh my God, does that mean you were looking?"

He gave me a smile that could only be interpreted as devilish, but what he said was, "I mean, just a basic knowledge of human biology and reproductive health tells me you didn't get boobs at fourteen.

"When did *you* know?" he asked me.

We had just spent the last minute discussing my boobs, so I didn't bother trying to hide anything. "Pretty much the day we met."

Luke raised his eyebrows skeptically. "You had a thing for near-sighted eight-year-olds?"

"Your glasses were cute."

He looked at me like he didn't quite believe me, but he didn't argue. We continued talking about random things, and soon I'd forgotten I was on a date with Luke Cohen. I was just hanging out with one of the people I knew and loved best on the planet, and it was easy and comfortable and nice.

When we finished, we stood outside in front of my car.

"So, did you change your mind?" he asked.

"About?"

"Wanting to kiss me."

"Did you?" I asked.

"I wish I did," he said before leaning down and pressing his mouth to mine. This kiss was slow and soft, a complete one-eighty from yesterday's frenzied kisses. When what he'd said registered, I took a small step back.

"Why do you wish you did?"

He pushed his hand through his hair and looked at me. "Mom's going to kill me."

"That's it?" I asked, relief seeping into my body. "That's all you're worried about?"

He shrugged.

I closed the distance between us again and covered his lips with mine. "Let me worry about Mel."

NOW

It's not like I ever stopped worrying about Mel. She's always been a thought lingering in my mind, and I never stopped missing her. Knowing I'd lost the woman who made me so many of the things I am was like having a thin film between me and the world. It changed the way I saw things, the way music sounded, the way good things and bad things and mundane things felt. I was always wondering what Mel would think of this or what Mel would say about that or what Mel would tell me to do. When I really wanted to torture myself, I would go online and read the Winchester obituaries, bracing myself to see her name, her picture, survived by, predeceased by.

But what Mom said was right—Mel's still alive. She's been alive all this time, and now she's back in my life again. My heart feels like bursting at the thought, and my mind is a blur of things I need to catch Mel up on, things she's missed, things *I've* missed.

On Wednesday, the day after I have dinner with her and Luke, and after my talk with Mom, I'm happy to the point of distraction, even as I lead my campers from activity to activity and chat with other leaders and pretend like I'm anywhere in the vicinity of the Winchester Community Center.

"You're in a good mood today," Willow remarks, but I sober when we take our kids to the science station before lunch. Luke is as mesmerizing and as in control as he was on his first day, yesterday. He is funny and silly and passionate, and watching him, my heart pounds in my throat. Thankfully, he does not acknowledge me. When he has a question about the field trip next week, he asks Willow and not me.

At lunchtime, though, he shows up in the cafeteria. He's sitting at the second staff table with Eric, who goes by Ace at camp, and Ruby/Rouge, and a couple other staff members. Unless we're on lunch duty, leaders can go off-campus for lunch, but it's such a short break that most of us stay and eat in the cafeteria anyway.

"J.J. —"

A ten-year-old girl with freckles taps me on the back just as I'm unwrapping the sandwich I've brought from home.

"What's up?"

"Can you help me open my container of yogurt?" Casey is one of the sweetest kids in my group, but one of the least independent. She has me and Willow do everything from tie her shoelaces to put her hair up for her. She'd probably have one of us feed her if she could.

"You can't get it open?" I ask, and she shakes her head.

"Show me," I say. I'm willing to help if she needs it, but I want her to at least attempt it.

She makes a face as she struggles to get the lid off the bottle.

"So close," I say. "Try again?"

She twists and twists, and the top comes off.

"There you go!" I say enthusiastically.

"Most times I can't get it open," she says, trying to justify her coming to me.

"That's okay. Just have to keep trying," I say, giving her shoulder a squeeze.

"Thanks, J.J.!" she calls before running back to her table in the middle of the hall.

I turn back, intending to follow the conversation Willow and Brett are having about pores versus follicles, but someone calls my name.

"Hey, J.J.?" I turn, expecting it to be another student, but it's Eric. Unfortunately, it's too late to pretend I didn't hear him.

"What?" I ask.

"What's the J.J. stand for? Just Jessi? Jessi Junior?" I can tell by the glint in his eyes that he's gearing up for something good.

I turn back to my food.

"Like, are you second in line to some kind of dynasty or throne? A family business?" he muses. "Can you say what y'all do? Or not in front of the children?"

Someone snickers at his table.

I roll my eyes and go back to eating.

The worst part isn't that he's still making these kinds of jokes; it's that today he's doing it in Luke's presence.

"You know, you can tell us. No judgment among friends," Eric continues.

"Ignore him," Willow tells me, and I nod.

"Brett's going to be in my video tonight," Willow continues, clearly trying to distract me. "We're doing some gross *Boyfriend Versus* challenge, where we have to eat nasty stuff."

"Ew, what are you eating?" I ask.

Thankfully, Eric seems to be out of material for the day and I'm able to continue the rest of my lunch without further interruptions.

On Thursday, though, it's the same thing.

"Is J.J. like one of those pseudonym things? Did you get it in the witness protection program?"

His jokes are scraping the bottom of the barrel, so I don't even flinch when he starts.

"Give it a rest, would you?" Willow says, but Eric ignores her.

"I'm just asking a question. Can't I ask a question? Inquiring minds want to know."

On Friday, by the time I sit down and he starts up again, I'm close to snapping. At first I was embarrassed that Eric was doing this in front of everyone, especially Luke, but now it seems as if he's doing it *because* of Luke. As if Luke's presence has emboldened him or something.

"I think I figured it out," he shouts across our two tables. "It's Jessi Job, isn't it? Like a handy with whatever special you decide to include."

Both our tables are quiet, and anger sears the back of my neck. "Fuck you, Eric."

Over the past eight months, my strategy has mostly been to ignore him, but he's getting worse.

"Is there an offer in there somewhere?" Eric asks, looking around comically. I'm so tempted to grab my salad and dump it over his idiotic head, but the last thing I want to do is make a scene and show him how much his words get to me. Instead, I push up from the table, throw my food in the nearest garbage can, and storm across the hall toward the cafeteria doors. I've almost reached them when someone grabs me by the arm.

My first thought is that it's Eric, so I shrug the arm off, but the person catches mine again.

"What the hell do you—" I spin around and find myself face to face with Luke. I don't have the chance to finish asking my question before his lips are on mine. His mouth devours mine in a hungry rush that lasts one second, two seconds, and then the kiss is over and he's gone. Someone wolf whistles, and I watch Luke stalk over to the food line as if nothing happened.

I steal a look at the staff table, and a bunch of shocked faces stare back at me. Willow looks particularly shaken.

I march over to the line, where Luke is laughing with one of the lunch ladies as she scoops a spoon of mashed potatoes onto his plate. I grab his elbow and start to drag him toward the exit. He abandons his plate on an empty table as he follows me.

Once we're outside, I slam my hand against his chest, but he doesn't budge.

"What the hell was that?"

"What?" he asks, as if he just got here.

"Why did you kiss me?"

He blinks at me, then looks away, and for a long moment there is only silence between us. When he speaks, his voice is quiet. "Were you just going to let Eric get away with the shit he was saying about you?"

"Luke . . ." I begin, but I can't make any more words come. My lips are still tingling from the feel and taste of him. It's pretty much the very last thing I expected, to have his mouth on mine again.

He's still not looking at me, but finally he sighs. "Eric thinks he's impressing me by running his mouth. He keeps looking over at me after making his comments, checking for some sign of approval, and I just . . . now he knows he and I are not on the same side."

It takes me a second to understand what he's saying. Luke kissed me to show everyone that he's on my side. Or at least not on the same side as Eric. Some small part of me sees this as a nice gesture, but the larger part of me, which controls my tongue, is suddenly furious at Luke's reasoning. He kissed me to *protect* me? "I can defend myself," I say in a growl.

"Is that what you did in there?" he asks, eyes narrowed. "Defend yourself?"

"Yes, it is," I spit. "Maybe I needed saving when I was seven and didn't have a mother, but I'm none of those things now. I don't need your help."

He starts to say something, but I speak over him.

"Did you see the way everyone was staring at us? Now they'll think there's something going on between us."

"Good," he says. "It should help us keep our story straight."

At this point, my blood is straight-up boiling and I can't tell who I'm more upset at, Luke or Eric.

"Don't *ever* ambush me like that again. I don't need your help," I repeat.

We watch each other for a minute, and then his jaw tightens. "Got it."

He walks off and disappears around the side of the building. I take a deep breath and go the other way, back to the rec room, trying to figure out what I'm going to say to Willow and how the hell I'm supposed to explain what just happened.

NOW

Because Willow is pretty much the sweetest human in the entire world, she's more worried about me than anything.

"I wanted to punch Eric's face in," she says. "Are you sure you don't want to report him to Diana?"

I shake my head. "No, it's fine."

Because Willow is also unequivocally the most inquisitive person in the entire world, she wants to know everything.

"So obviously you know Duke. Luke. Whatever his name is. How do you know him?" she asks as we clean up the rec room while our campers are at art with Rouge.

"How do you know I know him?"

She gives me a disbelieving look. "Because people who just met two days ago do *not* kiss like that. Also, I've been trying to set you up with my cousin since the day we met, and you're like, 'No, are you sure he's a good guy? I don't think you've known him long enough.' "

I laugh. "I did not say that."

"You implied it. You were like, but how do you *know* he's good?"

I wince at her impersonation of me. So maybe I am a little over-zealous about knowing people before dating them, but given the fact that I knew my only boyfriend for ten years before anything happened, can you blame me?

"So how do you know him?" Willow asks again.

I struggle to find the right words.

Do I start with Mel? Ro? Mel and Ro?

"He's my ex," I say, the simplest answer I have.

"Oooh. But you're back on now, right?" she asks. "That kiss was definitely Back On."

"We're, um, figuring it out," I say. As easy as it would be to just deny everything, Luke had a point about keeping our story straight. If we're pretending to be something for the next few months, I better get used to it. I guess I hoped that the only person we'd be pretending for was Mel.

"I wish you'd have told me when I met him. I was like *he's so cute.* I'm such an idiot."

"You're not," I say. "I should have told you. I'm sorry."

Willow stares at me for a second. "It's weird that you didn't, but I forgive you. Relationships are so confusing."

"Is everything okay with Brett?" I ask.

She sighs. "I guess. It's just that he keeps wanting me to introduce him to my parents, and I'm not ready. He's like, 'So what happens if your dad stumbles on one of your videos and I'm in it?' And I'm like,

'Well, if he stumbles on one of my videos, that's problem *numero uno* because xothelodown does not exist as far as he's concerned.'"

"Do you ever think you should just tell your dad?" I ask.

"Every day," she says. "But he's so weird about everything. He thinks my only concerns should be school and getting my business degree and taking over the family business. He thinks makeup is my hobby. And that boyfriends are a waste of time. Where exactly does making fun videos for a living fit into all of that?"

I give her a sympathetic look. "Parents are so weird."

"Agreed," she says. "Well, anyway, if you and Luke ever want to double with me and Brett, we could totally do that."

I wipe at a swatch of marker graffiti on a desk. Someone needs to tell these kids to maybe *not* write their full name when they're defiling city property. "Thanks," I say noncommittally.

I know the last thing Luke and I are going to be doing anytime soon is going on double dates, but I decide this is one more thing I'm going to have to keep to myself.

8

THEN

The truth was, I had been almost bursting from wanting to tell Mel.

Other than the fact that I liked Luke, I had never kept a secret this big from her. In fact, my liking him hadn't even been a secret; she and I had both known it but just never discussed it.

For the week after our fro-yo date, when Luke was back at State, he and I kept in touch, texting and talking every night. A couple of times, we fell asleep talking on the phone. He told me my lips tasted like cherries (probably thanks to my favorite ChapStick), and I told him I couldn't get enough of the way he smelled. I could hear the grin in his voice when he promised to give me one of his shirts when he came home again that weekend.

Six hours was a long way to drive, but Luke liked being able to check in on Mel. Plus, we had to tell her. This was for real now.

I'd wanted him in the house for moral support when I told Mel, so he was upstairs. For some reason, I'd thought it would go over better if I did the actual telling alone. Maybe if I approached it right, she'd just see it as an extension of girl talk and be totally casual about the whole thing.

It's no big deal, I told myself over and over, but my hands were shaking as I walked into the kitchen. I'd talked to Mel many times in the past about boys, of course. And she always gave me advice like "Be yourself" and "Carry breath mints" and "Girls can totally make the first move." But none of those boys had been her son. I had no idea how she was going to react. Would she yell? Laugh in my face? Throw me out of her house and forbid me and Luke to see each other? That afternoon when Nay and Mel were high had made me uncertain of just how Mel felt about my feelings for Luke.

The kitchen had that yeasty bread-baking smell. Ever since her treatment started, Mel had hardly been able to stomach baked goods. But baking had always been what she did when she was anxious or happy or sad, so even though she couldn't eat much, on days when she wasn't wiped out from the Big Bad, she was in the kitchen.

That day, she was sitting at the counter, stirring a bowl of something. A bandanna covered most of her head. Mel had never been a skinny woman, and a lump filled my throat when I saw the way her collarbones were starting to protrude.

"Jessi-girl, did you just get here?" she said, stretching her arm out so I could hug her. I clung to her for a minute, then backed away.

One of her eyebrows skirted up, and I could tell that my body language had already alerted her that something was up. So I blurted it out before she could ask, before I could talk myself out of it.

"Something happened with Luke," I said.

From her lack of reaction, I wasn't entirely sure she'd heard me. In fact, the next thing she did was to hold out the wooden spoon so I could taste the batter.

I did.

Finally she sighed. "Is that why he's home this weekend?"

I nodded, horrified, but not surprised that she'd figured us out that quickly.

"Get Luke," she said. "He's in his room."

A few minutes later the three of us sat in the living room. Luke and I sat on opposite sides of the long couch while Mel sat in the middle of the loveseat.

"Okay, so I guess ground rules?" Mel said, puffing out her cheeks and releasing a breath.

I stole a look in Luke's direction and found he was giving me the same quizzical look.

"No closing the door of your room when you're alone. Actually, no closing the door of any room," she said. As if talking to herself, she continued. "You'd think that would be enough of a deterrent, but contrary to popular belief, I actually *was* both seventeen and eighteen, so I'll say this too: the most important thing is that you are safe."

Luke groaned, and I buried my face in my hands.

Mel soldiered on. "I'm serious . . . There are lots of urges and all kinds of things . . ."

"God, Mom," Luke said. "All we did was kiss." He turned to look at me. "What did you tell her?"

I shrugged helplessly.

"Listen, if you can do it, then you sure as hell better be able to talk about it. Any other way is a cop-out, and we're not doing that."

"Mel . . ." I pleaded.

"I'm only saying this because I love you both and I know you're smart, but this is one of those Mom things that you only get the chance to do once, and that's if you're lucky," Mel said, suddenly

getting choked up. "So I'm not wasting this — one of those opportu-
nities to embarrass you and scar you for the rest of your adult lives."
She dabbed at the corners of her eyes, but she was laughing.

Luke stood up and walked over to her, giving her a side hug. I
went to her other side and did the same.

She held us that way for a while, the two of us pillars by her side.
Or maybe she was the one holding us up; it was hard to say. Finally
she squeezed out from between us. "Well, I might be a downer, but I
know better than to be a third wheel."

"You'll never be a third wheel," I assured her, and she laughed.
She stood up and headed for the kitchen, leaving Luke and me on one
couch again, with less space between us.

The reality of this moment setting in, I felt a wave of embarrassment and brushed some invisible lint off my dress to avoid meeting
Luke's eye. When I did glance up, he was looking at me in this weird
way, like he was trying not to laugh.

"So that went . . . well? I think?" he said.

"It could have been worse," I agreed. "She could have repeated
the banana demo she gave us when we were twelve." I hadn't even
stopped playing with dolls then.

"Don't remind me," Luke said with a shudder. "I got it first."

It dawned on me that we were sitting around talking about sex
ed. Or Mel's version of it anyway.

"Want to watch TV?" Luke asked.

"Sure."

He grabbed the remote, then came back and sat down, and the
awkwardness was making it hard for me to breathe. I started to panic.
Maybe our connection wasn't the earthshattering thing I'd thought it

was when there was six hours of distance between us. Maybe we'd jumped the gun by telling Mel. Maybe . . .

Luke found some random sitcom, plopped the remote down on the ottoman, and patted his lap.

"Feet?" he asked, and it took me a second to understand what he was saying. When I did, I turned on the couch so I was facing him, adjusted my dress, and stretched out my legs over his lap the way I'd been doing for years. Everything might have changed, but he was still my footrest.

His thumb made small circles on the top of my foot. He used to tickle my feet to annoy me when we were younger, but he'd grown out of that a couple of years ago and now it was more like a feather-light foot massage.

Luke's eyes were fixed on the television, and he continued to absently run his hands over my feet. The only difference was, this time he went even higher, gliding his thumb over the swell of my ankle and then over my calves. I wondered whether it was a conscious decision on his part or whether he was just spacing out. Was touching my leg like this something he'd always wanted to do, something he'd wondered about—the way I wondered about the freckle just below his left ear?

I couldn't play it cool, couldn't stop looking at him, until he turned to face me.

"What?" he asked.

"You have a freckle right there," I said, reaching forward to touch it. He leaned closer so I could run my finger over it. It felt like we were on the same page, like he knew that I knew that we were both doing the things we'd always wanted to.

Feeling brave, I asked, "Also, just how soft is your hair?"

He leaned over again, letting me have at it. I dug my fingers into his hair, slowly brushing up from root to tip. I loved that he closed his eyes until I was finished.

"Anything else?" he asked, his voice quiet.

"We'll stop there for now," I said over the lump in my throat. His eyes darted to the kitchen door, then back to me, and I noticed that his neck was getting red, like maybe he could think of other things he wanted to do.

We went back to watching TV in silence.

Rowan walked in the front door about halfway through the second episode of our sitcom marathon. He held a basketball under one arm, had a gym bag over the other shoulder, and was dripping with sweat. My first instinct was to jump away from Luke, to put as much distance between us as possible, but doing so would make it look like we were doing something odd. Which, technically, we weren't. Luke had always been my footrest.

So I stayed exactly as I was. Luke, for his part, didn't react, glancing away from the screen just long enough to throw his brother a casual "Hey," his hand continuing to make small circles on my leg the whole time.

"Hey, Ro," I said, trying to sound normal.

"Jess! Didn't know you were coming over." Ro sounded genuinely happy to see me, which instantly made me feel guilty. I'd purposely come over when he wouldn't be home, so I could have my talk with Mel.

Ro strode over to the other couch and flopped down. "What are we watching?"

While I was answering, Sydney came prancing into the room and Ro became temporarily distracted.

"Hey there, puppers! Did you miss me?" he cooed.

I turned my attention back to the TV.

When Sydney wandered out after a few minutes, a long silence filled the living room. I looked over at Ro on the other couch, but to my surprise, he was already looking at me. Or, more specifically, he was looking at Luke's hand on my leg.

"Did you and Eric have a good game?" I blurted. I knew they'd spent the afternoon playing pickup basketball.

"Yeah," Ro said shortly, then stood. "Going to go take a shower."

"Thank God. I can smell you all the way from here," I said, feeling the need to lighten the mood. Maybe there was no need, but I could have sworn something changed when Ro saw Luke's hand.

Rowan snorted and started toward the stairs.

Before he went up, he turned and looked over at us again, his eyes resting on the hand Luke still had on my leg.

Luke's gaze remained trained on the television, but the feel of Rowan's eyes made me warm and self-conscious. Our eyes caught for a second, and he looked at me as if asking something. If his eyes held a question, I had no idea how to answer it, so I didn't. Just stared back at him.

After a moment he turned and started up the stairs. "Cool story," I heard him mutter to himself, and then he was gone.

For the next few hours I kept expecting Ro to come back down, but he never did.

I didn't see him again the rest of the night.

THEN

Ro knew something was up.

The way he'd looked at me told me he did. Half of me wanted to leave it at that, or leave it to Luke or Mel to tell him, but I couldn't do that to Rowan. No matter how absent he'd been from my life lately, he deserved to hear it from me. And I didn't know why exactly, but I had a feeling he wouldn't like what I had to say.

By the time Luke and I said goodbye that evening, kissing for minutes in the Cohens' driveway, I had decided that I'd tell Ro the next day, after Luke left for State.

I came bounding downstairs on Sunday morning, planning to borrow Mom's car to drive to Ro's house, when an unfamiliar sound stopped me in my tracks.

A laugh.

Deep and short.

My father was laughing.

In general, our house tended to be pretty light on laughter.

When I entered the dining room, my father was sitting at one end of the table, his hand wrapped around a mug of coffee. His iPad was in front of him, and he was grinning. It shouldn't have surprised me so much, finding Rowan in the chair beside my father, eating a blueberry muffin like he lived here, but it had been a while since he'd come over for one of his and Dad's "chats." They happened sporadically. Every once in a while Ro would drop in on Dad and chat his ear off about tennis. Ro claimed he liked doing it, that he *liked* being regaled with optometry school anecdotes and eye horror stories that Dad offered in turn, but I knew he was just being nice. That just the way he'd looked at me years ago and seen a lonely little girl who needed a friend, Ro had looked at Dad and seen someone who could use a distraction, could use some levity, if only for a few minutes at a time.

"Morning, sleepyhead," Dad said now.

"Brought you guys some of the muffins Mom made yesterday," Ro said, talking with his mouth full. He slid a large Tupperware container over to me and patted the chair beside him. "I was just telling Jeff how I got out of a ticket last week."

"Let me guess — all you had to do was blink and show your teeth," I joked, sitting down beside him. I nudged his thigh with mine, and he nudged me back.

"You wound me," Ro said, but he was grinning. He was in a better mood than I'd seen him in weeks. "I also gave Officer Hamilton an autograph."

"Of course," I said, reaching for a muffin and taking a bite.

For the next few minutes the three of us sat around the table talking and laughing. I felt an unfamiliar ache then, and it took me a second to realize what it was: I wished my mother were here, that we were the kind of family that sat around on Sunday mornings, laughing and telling stories.

"I'm just going to go up and check on Jessi's mom," Dad said, excusing himself as if he'd heard my thoughts. "She has this head cold."

Ro gave me a knowing look, but said nothing.

After Dad was gone, I turned to Rowan. "He loves you."

"They all do. Can't say I blame them either," Ro said, and I shoved him.

"Well Luke's gone back to school." He said it in a strange way, like he knew it would mean something to me to know this.

"I know," I said, bracing myself for what was coming next. "I was going to come over today. I need to tell you something."

"What's it about?" From the way he was staring at me, I knew he knew what I was about to say. My cheeks warmed, and I couldn't look up at him.

"Luke and I . . ." I began. "We . . ." Again, the words didn't come. God, why was I being so weird about this? It wasn't a big deal. Luke and I weren't doing anything wrong.

"Me and Luke," I said finally, and looked up to meet his gaze.

Ro kept his eyes on me for a long moment, and then all he said was "Oh." Zero inflection in his voice.

"That's it?" I said, incredulous. "Oh?"

"What do you want me to say?" Ro said. "Ask you what your intentions with him are?"

It sounded like it should have been a joke, but he wasn't smiling. He stared down at the table.

"How long?"

"Last weekend," I said.

"You like him?" Ro asked, finally looking up at me. It was such a weird question, such an *obvious* question. Clearly, if we were together, I liked Luke.

Still, I gave him the simplest answer I could. "A lot," I said.

"Oh," Rowan said again, and then he changed the subject, telling me about the repairs he was getting done on his Ford soon. It was as if he'd gotten what he'd come for, as if the reason he'd come this morning was to hear it with his own ears.

I felt oddly sad, like simply by telling the truth, I'd ripped the gap between us even wider. But I also meant what I said. I liked Luke a lot, and though it might be weird for a while, having his older brother date his best friend, Ro was just going to have to get used to it.

NOW

Everything changes after everyone knows.

Suddenly we're in the cafeteria, and Willow jumps out of her seat when she sees Luke, signals for him to come, and then takes the next seat over, leaving us next to each other.

I shift in my seat, uncomfortable, but Luke thanks Willow and sits down next to me like he's been doing it half his life. Which. Okay, let's say, like he never stopped doing it.

"How's your day going?" he asks, resting his hand on the back of my chair. He looks down at his food as he speaks, so I know he's doing it for the benefit of our audience and not because he really wants to know how I am. This realization stings, but I ignore it.

"Good. Yours?"

"Pretty good. We're making volcanoes next week, so I've just been prepping for that. Been a while since I did a volcano project."

I nod, like he's telling me deeply interesting and romantic things, and I think I'm doing a great job until he leans in and says, "You know you have to pretend to like me, right?"

His hot breath against my ear makes it tickle, and a series of other impulses get sent elsewhere in my body.

"I am," I say back.

"You're not." He tucks a strand of my hair back gently and continues eating.

Willow is telling Brett about the renovations her dad is having done on the courts at Tennis Win, and Luke stiffens beside me. Now, neither of us is acting like we like each other.

The only positive thing about sitting beside Luke all through lunch and enduring this awkwardness is that Eric doesn't speak to me. In fact, he seems to have stood down completely, talking to the group at the other staff table like nothing happened yesterday. It's so infuriating when I think about it. I've asked him to fuck off so many times, and he never listened, but as soon as Luke puts his stamp on me, as soon as it's clear that we're okay, Eric suddenly has nothing else to say. What a piece of crap.

"See — you staring at Eric for the whole hour won't help our cause," Luke whispers. Our cause? Is Luke's whole prerogative in continuing the charade from yesterday to keep protecting me from Eric? Was the whole "keeping our story straight" excuse just bullshit? I thought I made it extremely clear that I didn't need his help.

"I'm trying to think of where I'd hide the body," I whisper back. Also, ew, on the thought that I'd be looking at Eric for any other reason.

"Carry on, then," Luke says, and I find myself fighting the smallest smile.

We somehow make it through to the end of lunch. Before we go our separate ways, Luke kisses me on the temple.

"We still on for tonight?"

I nod, slightly lightheaded from the feel of his lips on my skin.

When it happened yesterday, I was too shocked and wound up to appreciate it. Now it feels . . . I can't think about how it feels.

"Wait—tonight?" I repeat.

"Dinner and then my mom's?"

Oh, right. Today is Friday. "Dinner" which we will pretend to have together before we go back to Mel's.

"Right. Sure," I say.

Willow grabs my arm and walks me across the cafeteria. "Y'all are so cute," she says. "Why did you ever break up again?"

"The whole college long-distance thing took its toll," I lie.

NOW

When Luke picks me up from my house at quarter to eight, there's a bag of takeout on the passenger seat.

"We ate at Dynasty?" I say, peeking into the container.

"Yep. You loved their dumplings. Sweet and sour pork was great as usual. These are our leftovers," Luke says.

"You've put a lot of thought into this."

He doesn't say anything as we come to a stop at a red light.

In the silence that follows, I drum my fingers on the side of the door. At this point I'm not even that anxious about seeing Mel. It's these uncomfortable moments with Luke, when it's just the two of us. A feeling of sadness replaces the awkwardness as I remember the way things used to be with us. I know he can't look at me for real these days, but I wonder if he feels it, too. If it hurts him as much as it hurts me that we've drifted so far apart.

"Luke . . ." I say before knowing what I'm going to say.

He turns to look at me.

"Did you get all my messages?" I ask. "Last year?"

If he got one, he got them all. They were all pretty much variations of the same thing:

I'm sorry I'm sorry I'm so sorry please don't hate me

He had never responded.

"Yeah," he says now, simply, and silence stretches out between us once again. I go back to drumming my fingers in that way I know is annoying, but I can't seem to stop.

Soon we are pulling up in front of his house.

I hop out of the car, the container of food in my hand. Luke starts to reach for it when a loud buzz interrupts us.

He digs his hand into his pocket and stares at his screen. "Have to take this. Door should be unlocked."

"I'll go inside then," I say.

I leave him walking back up the driveway, talking in a low voice. The door is unlocked, and as soon as it swings open, I hear voices and laughter.

Naomi.

I enter the living room and find her on the loveseat, Mel in her wheelchair beside her, and they are watching two men in spandex wrestle.

"Hey, guys," I say.

The TV goes off as soon as they hear my voice.

"Wow, that's not suspicious at all," Mel says.

"I don't care if it's suspicious. It doesn't paint him in the best light."

"Oh, come on." Mel laughs. "Everybody has a past."

Are they talking about Naomi's husband? I've never met Bobby, but Mel described him as a "character."

"She probably already saw it!" Mel says now.

"Saw what?" I ask innocently, and Naomi looks vindicated.

"Absolutely nothing. Hi, Jessi."

"Hi, Naomi." I go around the couch, and she gives me an awkward back-patting hug. I know she doesn't love hugs, but I haven't seen her in so long.

"Where's Luke?"

"Outside taking a phone call." I crouch down, putting the takeout on the floor beside me, and give Mel a hug too.

"Hey, Jessi-girl," she says. "You get prettier every time I see you."

"Stop," I say, embarrassed.

Mel sighs. "What is it with everyone not being able to take the truth today?"

Before I can ask what she means, Naomi points to the takeout on the ground. "You went to Dynasty?"

"Oh, yeah. We just came from there."

"Did you eat there or do takeout?"

"Eat there," I say, feeling uncomfortable about her interrogation. This whole thing was Luke's lie. He should be here to deliver it.

Naomi's eyebrow goes up. "That's weird. I picked up from there just before I came over, and I didn't see you two."

"Oh, we must have just missed each other."

"Hmm." Naomi says, but she doesn't seem convinced. "What did you order?"

Mel looks at her. "Let it go! Maybe they went somewhere they don't want to tell us! They're young and beautiful and in love." When I say nothing, Mel takes it as confirmation of her rightness. "See? She can't even deny it."

My face warms, and I'm thankful for the cover of dark skin. "Has anybody told you that you have an overactive imagination?" I say.

Mel laughs, but Naomi is still giving me an odd look.

Thankfully, Luke comes in then.

"Hey, Mom. Hey, Naomi."

After he greets them, Luke's arms slither around my waist. I jump but recover quickly, letting my hands rest on his.

"So what's the story? You two ran into each other and decided to give things another try?" Naomi asks, looking between the two of us.

"Apparently it's too illicit to share with the class," Mel says, raising her eyebrows.

"Nobody ever used the word *illicit*," Luke insists.

"Well, so what happened then?"

"You want to tell it?" he has the audacity to ask me.

"Nope, you tell it," I insist, shooting daggers up at his face.

"Okay, so I was at Wally's weeks ago," Luke begins.

Wait, is he telling the real story?

"I'm getting milk, and I see someone who looks just like Jessi. But I'm thinking it can't be her. It's been months since I've heard from her, and for all I know, she's no longer even in Winchester—"

"Where else would I be?" I hear myself interrupting.

"Maybe you left early for college. Some people do that. I don't know," he says. If he's annoyed that I'm questioning him in the middle of his story, he doesn't show it. "My whole body freezes up," he says, "and before I know it, I'm following her to the freezer aisle. I have to talk to her."

Okay, now he's definitely making it up.

"So I basically sneak up on her, and we start talking, and all I can think about is how much I miss her." My throat tightens as he speaks. "I ask her for coffee, but we never make it there. We're in the parking lot and . . . one thing leads to another."

What the hell?

First of all, there's no way anyone is going to buy that. Second of all— What. The. Hell.

"I don't want to know what that means," Mel says with a groan, and my face floods with heat.

"We just kissed," I blurt out.

"Mostly," Luke says, grinning at me, and I swear I want to wipe the smirk off his face. Why is he telling them this? Especially when it's complete bullshit.

"Interesting story," Naomi says. She sounds skeptical, but Luke doesn't seem to notice. In fact, he seems pretty damn proud of himself. He pulls me over to the couch, and we both sit.

The next couple of hours pass quickly. I spend the first hour hyperaware of Luke's hand making circles on my back, but by the second hour I find myself starting to relax. As if there's anything normal about having Luke Cohen's hands on my body again. As if there's anything normal about sitting here with Mel and Naomi and Luke when I no longer belong here.

When my body stiffens, Luke seems to sense it, and then he starts gently massaging my shoulders. My impulses war with each other.

Part of me wants to shut my eyes and lean into his touch, the other part wants to jump up as if I've been electrocuted, run out of the house, and never come back.

"I should go," I say, pushing myself to stand.

"Jessi has a busy day on Saturday," Luke says. "Lessons at the club, and then your job at All Saints, right?"

I nod, kind of shocked that he actually remembered.

"Let's get you home," he says, holding his hand out to me. I put my hand in his and watch as he threads our fingers together. All the nerve endings in my palm come alive at his touch, and it's all I can do to act normal.

"Bye, Mel. Bye, Naomi," I say, waving with my free right hand and then following Luke out the front door. I'm expecting him to drop my hand as soon as we're out of their view, but he doesn't let go until we're in front of the passenger door of his car. I guess it's possible that Naomi is looking out the window or something.

"Thanks," I say as he opens it and I slide in.

Neither of us speaks until we've pulled away from the house.

"What was that story?" I ask, trying to get my voice to sound normal.

"The best I could do under pressure, Ms. No, You Tell It."

"You tried to throw me under the bus first!" I point out. His lips twitch with a smile, and I think it's the first time Luke has smiled at anything I've said since the day I saw him at the grocery store.

"What was with we 'mostly' kissed?" I asked.

"I didn't want them to ask questions."

"Well, now they think . . ."

"We're adults. We can do whatever we want," Luke says with a shrug, and I turn to look out the window, my neck hot.

When he adds, "You're not in high school anymore," I face him with a quizzical expression. I hadn't been aware that any of what we'd done and hadn't done when we were together was contingent on my being in high school.

"I don't know what that means," I tell him as we pull up in front of my house, but he shakes his head.

"Never mind," he says.

As I climb out of the car, my mind is a year in the past, flipping through memories I haven't let myself think about in a while. Luke's hands. His hot breath on my skin, his lips slightly parted, and the way his eyes went almost black after every kiss. The helpless way he sometimes looked at me, as if I were in total control, when the truth was, I had been just as breathless and desperate as he was.

"Good night, Luke," I say, unable to meet his eye as I shut the door.

"Night, Jessi."

9

THEN

The hardest thing, with Luke being miles away, was not letting him, not letting *us,* become the single most important thing in my life. When we weren't video chatting or talking on the phone, we were texting. It had become my mission to make him an emoji fiend by the time I was done with him. Which, if I had my way, was going to be never.

School became a simple hurdle to get over before we could get to the weekend, when we would see each other again.

We told Mel and Rowan the last weekend in September. The first weekend of October, Luke drove all the way back to Winchester. It was late on Friday night when I got his text: **I'm outside.**

I jumped out of bed, finger-brushed my hair, and raced down the stairs and out the front door. I waited outside his car door, leaping on him when he opened it. We kissed for what felt like eternity, and then we both slid back into the car, him behind the wheel and me in the passenger seat.

"Your parents are going to hate me," Luke said, running a hand through his hair. It was already messy from me pushing my hands through it while we kissed. I loved seeing Luke, perfect put-together Luke, all disheveled and rumpled, and knowing it was because of me.

"My mom won't notice, and my dad goes to sleep at like nine." It was after ten now. "What will most likely happen is that Mel will start to hate me." Even as I said it, a hint of fear sparked in me. I guess it was natural now to second-guess how each and every one of the Cohens felt about me. After all these years, it turned out that Luke saw me completely differently from the way I'd always thought he had. That was a good thing, but it also meant that the others might have seen me differently, too. Rowan was certainly never in a good mood with me lately. And there was the whole thing the night his mom was diagnosed and the way he'd been after the fact. Maybe even Mel's feelings about me were more complicated than I understood.

Luke grinned now, as if what I'd said was absurd. "Never."

"You skipped your last class to drive all the way out here," I pointed out.

"She doesn't need to know that."

"And you'll get home smelling like Chap Stick and me."

"I hope so," he said, and leaned across the console to kiss me again. "Stop worrying what Mom thinks. She loves you."

Something lit up inside me at his words. Most days, I was ninety-nine percent sure of this, but occasionally, insecurity reared its ugly head.

"All this time we wasted," I said, shaking my head and wanting to get away from the subject. "Being friends. Not kissing. So stupid."

"*So* stupid," Luke agreed, and I kissed the grin off his face.

When we broke apart again, he had a serious look on his face. "How's Ro doing?" he asked.

"Good. I think," I said. Ever since I'd told him about me and Luke, Ro had been even more distant. We had a couple of classes together, but other than that I hadn't seen very much of him. He had a different lunch period than I did and normally sat with his tennis friends anyway.

When I went over to the Cohen house, he usually wasn't there.

"I'm worried about him," Luke said, swiping a hand over his face.

"I don't think he's drinking much anymore, now that school's back on," I said. All the times I'd seen him, at least, Ro had seemed sober. Cranky, but sober.

Luke nodded, but he still had a worried crease in the middle of his forehead.

"My dad's flying out to see me this week," he said then. "He wants me to show him around the campus and my dorm and everything."

"Really?" I knew it had been a couple of years since Dr. Cohen had seen Luke or Ro. "Is that . . . a good thing?"

He shrugged. "I don't know. I mean, on one hand, he's helped with a lot of Mom's bills since she's been sick, so I guess he's not completely heartless—"

"But?"

"But he still cheated on her. He's still *him*."

"I could probably never forgive him," I admitted now. "If he was my dad."

Luke looked at me with a thoughtful expression and reached out to brush some hair off my face. "You'll really ride or die for Mom, won't you?"

I remembered Ro's words over the summer, about how Mel's illness was their business, not mine, and my face warmed.

"It's not a bad thing," Luke said gently. "It's just . . . you know, she's not perfect."

"I don't think she is," I said, though honestly, I couldn't see any reason why I would ever pick anyone else to be my mother.

"I think she's part of why I hate Dad," he said, leaning back against the headrest.

I tried to hide my surprise.

"Maybe she just wanted us to know the truth, but the older I get, the less sure I am. She told us about all the lies, the affairs, the ways he disappointed her even years before those started. I think she needed us to be on her side."

"Mel would never do that. Not purposely."

Luke looked at me for several seconds. "Okay," he said. "Well, intentional or not, it worked, because I can't stand the guy."

"I know he sucks," I said now, "but I think it's a good thing that he's making an effort. Some parents don't even try."

"We still talking about mine?" he asked.

I shrugged.

"Talk to me," he said, tracing circles on my kneecap.

"Okay, well, my mom is sick. I get that."

He nodded.

"But she's been so adamant about not getting help, and I just think that when you love someone, you're willing to try to get well for them. Even if I'm not enough of a reason, you'd think that for my dad she'd at least try."

Luke said nothing, so I kept going. "Also, Dad is always reminding me that she loves me, but everyone knows that the first time things got really bad was right after she had me. How can she love the person responsible for ruining her life?" It was the first time I'd ever allowed myself to say this out loud, though the thought had been there for years, niggling at the back of my mind. How could it not be?

A deep frown was etched between Luke's eyebrows. "Jessi. You don't really think that, do you? That you ruined her life?"

I shrugged. "I mean, having me made her sick."

"Maybe, but maybe not," he said. "Also, she has all this help available to her, and she won't take it. That's not on you. You know that, right?"

I wasn't sure I believed him, but I nodded.

"Have you ever tried talking to her? Telling her how you feel?"

I hadn't — not really. When something is your normal, it doesn't occur to you that it can be any other way.

A lump had filled my throat, and I found it hard to look at Luke. "Can we talk about something else? I'm sick of parents."

"Same," he said, playing with a strand of my hair again. "Have you heard anything back from State yet?"

I shook my head.

"You know where there are no parents? College," he said, leaning in to kiss me.

"That sounds glorious."

"Mhm," he agreed. His lips were moving along my jaw and down my throat now. "And you know who *is* at State?"

"You?" I said distractedly as his breath set fire to my skin.

"You're so fucking smart," he breathed against my neck. I grinned from ear to ear. When Luke had been deciding about schools last year, I'd secretly hoped against all hope that he would pick one in the state. He had his choice of a few, and I'd been over the moon when Mel told me he'd chosen State. I knew it meant I'd get to see him

164

more often, but I hadn't let myself think ahead to going there, too. To being there with him, or even being there as his girlfriend.

"My, my," I said. "It sounds like you've picked up some bad habits from college."

"I say fuck," Luke protested.

"Not like Rowan," I said. It had just slipped out, the comparison between them. I'd spent so many years rehashing all the similarities and differences, all the ways Ro was and wasn't Luke.

"I guess not," Luke said, straightening in his seat again. "I really should go before I get you in trouble."

"You mean before I get *you* in trouble."

He grinned. "That, too."

When I hopped out of the car that night, I couldn't stop smiling. Being with Luke was everything I'd dreamed of and more. The Luke in my head had been, well, the Luke I knew as Ro's brother and Mel's son. But the Luke I was getting to know, the Luke I was dating, was so much more. He was funny and sexy and kind and good. He had told me the night he came to my house weeks ago that he was just as fucked-up as everyone else, but to me, he was turning out to be pretty perfect.

When I entered my house, I was surprised to see the kitchen light on. When I went in, my mother was staring into the open fridge, like she was riveted by something. Scattered around the counters and on the kitchen table were the entire contents of our refrigerator. Milk, condiments, full Tupperware containers, vegetables.

"What's going on?"

"It's stupid," Mom said, her voice weirdly shaky. "I couldn't sleep and I . . . I thought since you and your father do so much around here,

I thought I'd help out and do some cleaning. I had this burst of energy, and I took everything out, and now . . ."

She looked so small standing there, so defeated, that I heard myself saying, "That happens to me too sometimes."

When Mom said nothing, I continued. "The other day I decided to clean out my closet, and I dumped everything out so I could organize from scratch. And then halfway through, I got tired and overwhelmed, but it was too late to stop. It sucked."

The sound of Mom's laughter surprised me. It was short and light, more like a giggle really.

"I guess overambition runs in the family," she said.

I walked over and took the sponge from her. "Here. I'll help."

"Okay," she said, sounding relieved. "That would be great."

As we worked silently, scrubbing and wiping and putting everything back, I thought of Luke's words tonight. *Have you ever tried talking to her? Telling her how you feel?*

I stole a glance at Mom, a strand of hair falling over her pale face as she worked. The topic of her illness felt too big, too delicate to broach without warning, so I decided to start small.

"Why did you name me Jessi?" I asked.

For how much I hated my name, it had never occurred to me to ask my parents where it had come from.

Mom looked surprised at the question, but after a moment she said, "It's silly."

My heart pinched.

So I was right about how little thought they'd put into it.

"I used to have a complex about my name," Mom said now. "Katherine."

"But it's so . . . basic," I said.

Mom smiled. "Exactly. I can't tell you how many girls I went to school with who had the same name. Over the years I was Kate, Katie, Kitkat, Katherine I., and Kathy, all so people could tell us apart. I swore for years that if I ever had a daughter, I'd name her something unique, but not outlandish. Nothing like Tulip or Daffodil." Mom snorted now. "God, I went to college with a girl named Wisteria."

"So basically no flower names?" I said, and Mom laughed again, the sound full and warm. It felt like sitting in the sunshine, feeling the rays of light hit my skin.

"Your father and I took so long to decide when we had you. He really wanted Jessica, but I wouldn't have it. Too common. So we compromised. Went with something simple. Jessi, first of her name, short for nothing."

"I always thought you . . . that you kind of phoned it in," I admitted.

She gave me a weird look. "No, not at all."

We went back to working in silence, and I wondered if I'd angered or hurt her. I was still chiding myself for ruining the moment when she asked, "Who were you with tonight? Melanie?"

"Luke," I said. Then, feeling brave, I added, "We're dating."

Mom turned to me. "Luke? Really?"

"Why are you so surprised?" I sounded defensive, but I couldn't help it.

"I just thought you and Rowan were . . . closer," she said at last. Even though I shouldn't have, I thought then how different Mom was from Mel — Mel who had known for years about my crush on Luke and Mom who knew so little about me. I thought too of that night

167

last summer when I'd snuck into her room and confessed about my crush on Luke. I'd secretly hoped for months after that she'd randomly bring it up, that somehow she'd heard me and remembered everything I told her, but she never did.

"Well, you have to tell me about him," she said as she closed the door of the fridge.

"Okay," I said. She got us glasses and filled them with milk, and we sat at the kitchen table and talked. It was kind of everything I'd dreamed of, everything our first conversation about Luke hadn't been. For one thing, it wasn't one-sided. I told Mom about what Luke was studying in college and how he'd come down last weekend and told me he liked me. She listened and asked questions, and the whole time I was thinking, *So this is what it would have been like to have my mother in my life.*

When we finally went to bed about an hour later, I couldn't believe how well this had gone. I was itching to tell someone.

I picked up my phone to send a text, then hesitated. Should I text Ro or Luke? For the past ten years of my life, it would have been a no-brainer. Ro was my person, but in just a few weeks, everything had changed.

Just had a really good talk with my mom.

It was past midnight, and I wasn't surprised when Luke didn't text back.

Still, I went to bed feeling light and floaty, excited, like things were finally changing.

But when I woke up the next morning, my father was alone at the dining table, looking somber.

"Where's Mom?" I asked.

"Asleep. She had a rough night."

It felt like an arrow to the heart.

"What do you mean?"

"She didn't get to bed till late, so she's exhausted," he said.

"Oh," I said, and went into the kitchen to get breakfast.

I didn't tell my father that we'd been up together, talking. I didn't tell him about the hope I'd felt, that quiet soaring feeling of possibility.

Maybe things were changing. Maybe we were at the start of a million more conversations full of long-held truths and midnight secrets.

I'd connected with Mom last night. Now it felt as if I would never be able to hold on to her for more than just a few seconds.

NOW

She's back in bed.

I feel a physical jolt when I walk past my mother's slightly open door on Sunday morning and see the familiar mound in her bed. Things have been so different the last few months. I thought I'd set my expectations low in terms of her recovery, but it still feels like a punch when I see her dark room again.

I force myself to cross the threshold, force myself not to run out of the house when I see the ghost of the mother I've known all my life.

"Mom," I say gently, coming to the side of her bed. "Do you need anything?"

"No, sweetheart," she says, and her face is smushed against the pillow.

"Where's Dad?"

169

"I think he stepped out to check on something at the clinic."

I try to quiet the voice that says it's all over, that everything is going back to how it was before. I'm alarmed at the way it makes me shaky, the way it makes me want to curl up in a ball and weep.

It was during the worst of everything last fall that Mom started to be more present. On days when I was the one wrapped up in my bed, refusing to budge and unable to stop crying, she'd rubbed my back and brought me water and told me she was so sorry.

Then she'd started meds and started seeing a therapist, and the change in her had been radical. She wasn't healed. The gaunt, faraway look in her eyes didn't disappear overnight, but slowly her body seemed less vacant. I could ask her a question and know she'd heard me. She made dinner sometimes. She went for walks without my father.

Even then, I'd been wary. I'd *known* it was too good to be true. A person doesn't suddenly come back from the dead—which, at the worst times, is what my mother seemed to be. Dead. Now I want to kick myself.

There were times in the past when I almost believed that things had changed. I'd catch glimpses of my mother, happy and healthy, for an hour or a day or the length of a conversation about boys, but it always went back to the way things were.

Why did I let myself believe *this* change would last?

"I'm going out for a while then," I say, desperate to escape this porthole into the past. "Should I get anything for you?"

"No, thank you," she says.

I've almost shut her door when I hear her call me back.

"Jessi . . . I talked to Melanie last night. Is that where you're going?"

"Yeah," I admit, surprised. Mel and Mom are talking now? Since when? My mother's illness meant that Mom and Mel had never gotten to know each other beyond surface-level conversations and platitudes.

"I've been checking in on her from time to time over the past few months," she says, which surprises me even more. But I guess there's a lot I don't know about Mom 2.0. I feel sad that I'll probably never get to know her after all, that it seems like she's gone already. "She told me you and Luke were seeing each other again."

My heart drops.

"It's not that serious," I say quickly.

"Well, we should still have him over for dinner sometime this week. What do you think?"

"Sure, Mom," I say, and shut her door, but I already know the chances of her even remembering this in twenty-four hours are slim to none. When the darkness takes her, it returns her to us wiped clean.

For a long time, I used to think that as soon as I graduated from high school, I would pack up and leave Winchester. Leave my parents and this world where I managed to feel both loved and forgotten, at home and adrift. But the past year has turned my world upside down and crushed it. Instead of leaving, I've decided to take the next year to catch my breath.

Just like Mom guessed, I drive right to Mel's house.

It's like muscle memory being around her again. I push back the thoughts of my parents, forget the fact that Mom 2.0 is gone, and without trying, I am going through the motions, becoming the Jessi

Mel knows and loves again. On one hand, I know I will never be that girl again and that this act can only last so long. On the other hand, it feels so familiar to be in the Cohen house again, to be loved by Mel, and to be with Luke, even if it's all pretend this time.

I'm not sure if Luke is home, but Naomi is there again when I get there.

She's working at the dining table, probably planning lessons for the coming school year, while Mel sits in the living room, surrounded by her mountain of blankets.

"I'm spending more time out of my room now that I get company much more often," Mel says, and I feel a twinge of guilt that I haven't been here for her. That with Luke at school this year, she pretty much had only Naomi.

I can't even imagine how lonely she must have been.

I sit on the couch beside her, and she peppers me with questions the way she used to when I was a kid. At the time, she was the only grownup that even seemed to care what I thought of anything, what I loved and hated and dreamed of doing.

Now she says, "Did you decide to go to State after all?"

"I'm taking a year off," I tell her.

"Oh. How come?" she asks.

I shrug, try to think of what to tell her. "I don't know what I want to do, and I don't want to waste my money and time."

"Lots of people don't know what they want to do," she insists. "You kind of just bluff your way through it the first couple of years until you figure yourself out."

"Maybe I'll bluff in Winchester for a while first," I say.

She looks concerned, but doesn't say anything else.

"I'll go grab you some more water," I say, reaching for her empty cup and disappearing into the kitchen.

The kitchen is eerily the same. The same appliances in all the same places. I swear, even the pile of undone dishes looks the same as the one I saw on the very last day I spent in the Cohen house before everything happened.

"When I take a break from my planning, I'll get to the dishes."

I jump at the sound of Naomi's voice. "Oh, I can totally do them."

"No, it's fine," she says.

"Seriously, Naomi. That's why I'm here — to help out. I'll do it," I insist.

"Thanks," she says. From the way she hesitates, I can tell there's more she wants to say.

I go to the fridge and fill a glass of water for Mel.

"You know, the weird thing is," Naomi continues like we're in the middle of a conversation. "I thought I saw Luke drive past me on Friday on my way here. I must have missed you in the front seat."

It takes me a moment to realize she's still talking about the whole takeout nonsense from two nights ago.

"You must have," I repeat lamely.

"The other weird thing — I keep meaning to ask Luke, but maybe you know. Who is Court?"

"Court?"

Naomi nods. "He's on the phone with her at all hours of the day and night, so I figured you'd know her."

Anybody listening in on our conversation would be wondering how she made the jump from the first weird thing to the second weird thing, but I know exactly what she's saying.

She doesn't believe us.

I swallow.

"Ah well, she's probably just a friend from school," Naomi says, helping herself to a mandarin from the fruit bowl. As she starts to peel it, I smile and say, "Probably," like I'm totally unbothered by what she's just told me.

My façade is breaking, so I turn my back on her and start on the dishes.

When the hell did Naomi, of all people, become so observant?

I'm still filling the sink with soap and water when I hear footsteps, and then Luke walks into the kitchen. He's in his famous pajama bottoms, his chest firm and distracting. He yawns as he walks past Naomi, his hair in bed-induced disarray.

"Morning," he says to both of us.

He's holding a box of cereal, walking toward me to grab a clean bowl, when I do it—I throw myself in front of him and press my lips against his. He freezes for one second, and then he's kissing me back, his tongue wreaking all sorts of havoc on my sanity. I loop my arms around his neck as we kiss for one breathless, frenzied second.

We stop when Naomi clears her throat.

I disentangle myself from Luke, but he just keeps looking at me.

"I'll take Mel's water to her," Naomi says, coming around to grab the glass on the counter where I left it and then leaving the kitchen. If what she saw did anything to assuage her suspicions, I can't tell.

Once she's gone, Luke cocks his head. "Now who's ambushing who?"

But he doesn't look angry or like I made him do something he didn't want to do. And he definitely *did* do something.

"She's suspicious," I hiss to Luke. "She's going on about how she didn't see us at Dynasty when she was there on Friday. Also, who's Court?"

I fold my arms across my chest.

Luke looks surprised. "Court?" he repeats. "How do you—"

"Apparently you've been speaking to her at all hours of the day and night." I try not to let it show how desperately I'm hoping he'll refute the claims, that he'll say Naomi misheard or something. *Something.*

He just pushes his hand through his hair and reaches around me for a cereal bowl.

I know I should drop it, but I can't. "How are we supposed to seem like a couple when you're having phone sex with some girl?"

Luke turns on me. "First of all, we were *not* having phone sex." An embarrassing sensation that feels a little like relief washes over me. "Second, I'll be more careful." He takes a step toward me, so only I can hear. "And third, you're welcome to fuck whoever you'd like. This is just for show, remember?"

His words make me feel like I've been slapped.

"You know, I liked you better when you weren't a giant asshole."

Luke narrows his eyes at me. "Did you?"

I can't answer him, so I turn away and go back to washing dishes.

10

THEN

"**When I finish** kicking your ass," Ro said, his eyes fixed on the tennis ball as it hit the edge of his racket frame over and over again, "what do you intend to reward me with? Lunch? A parade?"

His tennis racket was turned on its side, and he was essentially juggling the ball with it. It was a game we'd played since we were little, trying to see who could bounce the ball on the racket frame the longest.

I'd shown up at the club that day intent on hanging out with Rowan whether he liked it or not.

I ignored him and kept counting.

"One hundred thirty-nine. One hundred and forty. One hundred forty-one. *Yes!*" I cried as his ball spun away from him. "You're at one hundred and forty-one. *I'm* one hundred and forty-nine and undefeated, baby! So close and yet so far."

"My eyes got tired," Ro complained as I did my victory dance around him.

"A W is a W," I said, still flapping my arms around like a chicken.

"It's because you distracted me," Ro said, changing tactics and trying to blame his loss on me.

"I did not! Next time, maybe *don't* get cocky and try to talk, mkay?" I danced directly in front of him until he shoved me out of his way so he could walk back to the clubhouse.

"You're such a dork," he said.

"You love me," I said.

He came to a stop again and glared at me. "Are you *skipping*? It's just a fucking game."

"Then why are you so upset?" I asked.

The truth was, he had a right to be suspicious. I absolutely was ecstatic to marginally hang on to my victory with the racket frame game, but a lot of my happiness had to do with non-tennis things. His brother, to be specific. Being with Luke made me feel full and loved, like I knew exactly who I was and where I belonged. Like I would never again have to wonder about where I fit in this world.

In much the same way his family had when I was a kid, Luke was beginning to feel like home to me.

When we got into the air-conditioned lounge room, Ro plopped down in a chair and took a swig of a sports drink. He offered it to me, and I took a sip.

"I'm so glad we got to hang out. I've missed you," I said.

He nodded. "Feels like I haven't seen you in a minute."

"Well, you're so busy with practice," I said.

"I've always been busy with practice." The implication was that when he'd been busy with practice in the past, I'd come to the court and watch him play or come over to the house to hang out. Now, other things occupied my time. These things went unspoken between us, but I couldn't shake the feeling they were there, dangling like cobwebs, waiting to be acknowledged.

I fiddled with the sticker on the bottle. I wasn't going to apologize for having a life. Yet it felt like that was what Ro wanted — for me to apologize for having something that didn't include him, and somehow I knew that thing was Luke.

I opened my mouth to protest, but he spoke over me.

"Me and Cassie Clairburne are a thing."

"No!" I exclaimed. "But what about Eric?"

Ro shrugged. "Should have made his move sooner."

"Wow, so a *thing* thing or just hooking up?" I asked.

"What's the difference?"

"Well, Rowan, sometimes people like to have casual sex and mess around. Other times, they get into these things called committed relationships."

Ro muttered something under his breath.

"What?" I asked.

It sounded to me like he'd said *guess you're the expert now,* but he just shook his head.

"Well, congrats," I said then, but he just held his hand out for the drink. I'd never seen anyone announce a new relationship with such melancholia.

Ro stood up from the table. "I'm going to go and get changed."

"Ro, wait," I said. "Is everything okay?"

"Yeah, why?"

"You just don't seem like yourself. You've been so different since the summer."

"Because my mom is fucking dying, Jessi, and the only thing I can do is hit some balls across a net."

I flinched at his explosion.

"Maybe other people are able to go on their merry way and act like nothing is happening, but I am not, okay? I'm just not."

"That's not fair," I said, feeling anger rise within me. "I don't see anybody acting like nothing is happening or going on their 'merry way.' I'm over there how many days a week to check on her."

"Okay, and where the hell is my brother? Huh?" he spat. "He just packs his things and hightails it out of Dodge when she needs him the most, yet he's still the hero."

A door opened and shut down the hall.

"Keep your voice down," I told Rowan.

He was breathing hard, looking down at me like he'd run a marathon. "I'm just over this shit, you know?"

"I know," I said. "But I hope you get that getting wasted every night is doing nothing to help."

I'd told Luke I hadn't *seen* Ro wasted recently, but something made me suspect that meant very little. When Ro didn't say anything to refute this, I knew I'd guessed right.

"You're just giving her something more to worry about," I said.

Ro sank into the seat again. "I just wish I could *do* something. Why couldn't she need a kidney or something? I have that. I'd *give* her that."

I blinked back tears as I reached for Ro's wrist.

"She knows that. I know that," I told him.

"I come out here every day and I train. I go into the gym four times a week and do even more training, and I just don't know what the point of any of it is. I'm not saving lives. I'm not changing anything. What's the *point?*"

"Think about Roger and Serena and Rafa, all the people you grew up watching. Think about the way it made you feel when they won or lost. *That's* the point. If you care about something, it matters."

Ro swiped at his eyes. "I don't know."

"I do," I said. "Plus, if you quit after all the money your parents have put in, after all the matches you've made her watch, Mel will actually skin you alive."

He laughed. "I just don't see how anything is ever going to be okay when she's gone."

"I don't think it will be," I admitted. "Like, it's going to suck so much."

Just thinking about it—a world without the sound of Mel's voice, without her hugs, without her humor—got me choked up.

"We'll all just have to stick together," I said. "That's what will make her happy."

Ro stood and sniffed his shirt. "Better go change for real now."

"Me too," I said, standing. We walked together, but when it was time for him to turn left for the men's locker room, he didn't move. I stepped forward and wrapped my arms around his waist, even though he smelled of sweat.

He stood stiffly for a few seconds, and then his arms slid around me. We stood there for a long moment, our hearts beating in sync.

"I fucking miss you," Ro whispered into my hair before taking a step back and heading into the men's.

I stayed there, my chest aching with something heavy, and I blinked back tears.

That Ro was hurting wasn't a surprise, given everything that was happening with Mel. What was surprising was that it felt as if we were going through it separately, as if our paths had somehow diverged, no matter how much I tried to course-correct.

I always pictured Ro and me being friends until we were old and gray, watching tennis and sneaking red velvet cupcakes even when we technically shouldn't have them. I pictured us talking through the hard stuff, leaning on each other, physically and emotionally. But for some reason, Rowan seemed to feel that he had to shoulder all his grief on his own.

Why?

What had changed between us? And why did it feel, even when our bodies were pressed together in a hug, like we were existing on separate planes?

NOW

I don't know what to think.

When I come down the stairs on Monday morning before work, my mother is in our living room, talking to a man I've never seen before. He has reddish-brown hair and a goatee.

"Thank you so much for dropping in so early. I don't get off work until five, so it had to be this morning," she is saying.

Yesterday, the last time I saw my mother, she couldn't get out of bed, but today she looks put together and alert. Her hair is pulled into a tight bun, and she's wearing work clothes.

"Morning," I say, and she spins around to look at me.

"Oh hi, honey. This is Chase. He's going to be doing our repainting," Mom says.

"We're repainting?"

Mom frowns. "I was sure I mentioned that."

Chase gives me a nod of acknowledgment, and the two of them go back to discussing colors while I head into the kitchen to get some breakfast. I'm in there still, eating a banana, when Mom comes in.

"You look nice," I tell her, and she looks down at herself and smiles.

"Thank you."

Now that she's closer, I notice that she has small dark circles around her eyes and she looks tired, like she's not fully inhabiting the role of Mom 2.0 yet. Maybe more like Mom 1.5.

"Are you okay? After yesterday, I thought—" I'm used to us not acknowledging her dark days, but for some reason, I can't stop myself today.

"You thought things were back to the way they were?" she asks, and she looks sad. She reaches forward and touches my cheek. "I just had a bad day. Those are normal, but we're not going back there," she says. "I promise."

I'm surprised by the way my eyes fill at her words and even more surprised when I feel myself reaching forward and hugging her tightly. I want to tell her how happy I am to see her up and about today, how scared I was yesterday when I saw her in bed again, but the words won't come.

Somehow, though, from the way she squeezes me back, I think she knows.

I'm feeling good, happy even, when I get to work. But my mood takes a swift turn when I see Luke. He's chatting to Rouge and a couple of other leaders outside the art cabin, and he doesn't see me, but I feel my body going hot with rage even as I head in the opposite direction. The words he said in Mel's kitchen last night come storming back to me, and they infuriate me.

You're welcome to fuck whoever you'd like. This is just for show, remember?

As if I've let myself forget for even one second that we're pretending. As if *he* has let me forget it, with the way he barely looks at me when we're alone.

In the rec room, I noisily arrange chairs around the four round tables we're using for this morning's first activity.

"Is everything okay?" Willow asks me.

"Dandy," I say, and keep pulling plastic chairs off the stack and setting them down around the table.

"What's wrong? Is it Luke?" she asks, stopping in front of me. "What did he do?"

"Nothing," I say.

She narrows her eyes at me. "I thought we agreed no more lies."

My lips twitch with guilt. If Willow only knew all the things I haven't told her, she would be completely done with me. My not telling her about a stupid fight with my pretend boyfriend would be the least of her concerns.

"You're right. Sorry," I say.

"So what are we mad at him for?" she asks, hands on her hips.

"He just made this comment . . ." I look to Willow and see that she's waiting for me to continue. I can't think of anything to say on the spot, so I give her the version closest to the truth. "Like, he doesn't care what I do when we're not together."

I'm hoping it's ambiguous enough that she'll let it go, but Willow's smart, and her eyes widen. "You guys aren't exclusive?"

"Um," I say, wondering how I walked into this. "I don't really know."

"Is he seeing other people?"

I shrug.

"You have *got* to sit down and talk about it. But honestly that sounds like bullcrap to me."

"What does?"

"That he doesn't care what you do when you're not together," she says. "I've seen the way he looks at you. The day Eric was saying all that stuff about you, he looked like he was going to hop the table and smash his face in."

Oh, Willow. Sweet, sweet Willow.

"Obviously he opted for kissing the living daylights out of you instead," she says, smiling. "An unexpected choice, but since I'm pro kissing and anti punching, I wholeheartedly approve."

"There's an xothelodown saying there somewhere, isn't there?" I say. "Smash lips, not faces."

She laughs. "Not bad, not bad. Take anger, make love. See, it only works when it comes out naturally."

"No, that was actually pretty good," I say.

As our campers start arriving, I still think Willow is completely off about the way Luke feels about me, but our talk makes me feel better.

The day passes uneventfully until it's science time and we're in Luke's classroom.

The kids are in a particularly rowdy mood, so Willow and I are sitting with different groups of kids to try to limit the level of acting out. I've made a point of not making eye contact with Luke, not that he's looking at me.

Each table is creating a papier-mâché volcano in preparation for tomorrow's experiment. When Luke comes around to my table to see what the kids are doing, a kid named Kevin goes, "Hey, Duke? Is J.J. your girlfriend?"

"Kevin, that's so not appropriate," I say right away.

"We saw you kissing in the cafeteria," Patrick, Kevin's wingman, pipes up.

My face burns, and I pointedly do not look at Luke.

Then Kevin is singing, "'Duke and J.J. sitting in a tree, K-I-S-S-I-N-G.'"

"Kevin, you're asking for a time-out right now," I say. How the hell did I end up back in third grade? "Is that what you want?"

"But *are* you his girlfriend?" Kevin asks. At this point I am exasperated, but Luke stoops down to his level and says, "Depends why you're asking, Kev. If it's so that you can keep singing, then it's none of your business. If it's so you can ask Jessi for her number, then yes, she is most definitely my girlfriend."

Patrick laughs, but Kevin says, "Why do you call her Jessi?"

I don't hear what Luke says, because at the table behind him, Willow is grinning maniacally and mouthing, *I told you.* I roll my eyes. As if what Luke says to a nine-year-old is of any importance when we're lying to pretty much everybody we know.

Later, at lunch, Luke slides into the seat beside me.

"Hey," he says.

"Hey," I say coolly before going back to listening to something Rouge and Willow are discussing.

Luke's arm falls around my shoulder, and as his fingers make circles on my arm, I try to ignore the feeling of his touch on my bare skin. Embarrassingly, goose bumps prickle all the way down to my elbow, and I'm hoping he doesn't notice.

"Hey, Jessi?" Willow says, and I startle at the sound of her voice. I guess I wasn't doing that good a job of listening to their conversation. In fact, Rouge seems to have moved on completely to talking to the person beside her.

"So I meant to tell you . . . Brett is coming over to my house tomorrow," she whispers to me.

One of my eyebrows skitters up. "You told your parents?"

She shakes her head. "No. But I agreed he could come over — under . . . duress." Her face flushes, and I laugh.

"Is that what they're calling it these days?"

"You don't work at All Saints on Tuesday nights, do you?" she asks.

I shake my head. "Why?"

"I was hoping you might be able to come too?" she says. "That way, my parents just think I'm having a bunch of friends over and not A Friend."

"Okay," I say.

"Luke, you could come too," Willow says now, which is the first time I realize he's listening to our conversation. "You both could."

I shoot Willow daggers with my eyes, trying to convey the fact that Luke and I are still not on good terms. She pretends she can't read my expression.

"I'd be down," Luke says, and I look at him, surprised. He'd be *down?* To hang out with work people outside of work and have to continue our façade? "We'll be there."

"Perfect." She claps her hands. "We'll have the pool all to ourselves, and *Eric* won't be there."

I know she's alluding to the terrible party at Bailey's a few weeks ago, and it's definitely a relief to hear it will be just the four of us. If Luke and I are going to have to keep up this charade outside of work and Mel's, the smaller our audience, the better.

We go back to talking about the activities we have scheduled for the rest of the day.

When lunch is done, I push off from the table, wriggling my body out from under Luke's arm. I'm almost out of the cafeteria when I notice that he's on my tail. I keep up the pace, walking faster, until he has no choice but to jog to catch up with me.

"Hey," he says.

"Do you need something?" I ask.

He rubs the back of his neck. "I'm sorry," he says. "I was a jackass yesterday."

"Gee, you don't say."

"Honestly, I thought you'd be happy to hear that you could still hook up with Eric or whoever you want."

I start walking again, my blood boiling.

"Shit. Sorry," he says, grabbing my arm to stop me. "Look, it's weird, okay? This whole thing is weird. I don't *know* how to do this."

I don't know whether he means he doesn't know how to be around me anymore or he doesn't know how to keep up the whole fake relationship thing.

"You could try not making idiotic comments, for one," I say, folding my arms across my chest.

He nods, runs his hand along his jaw.

"Also, you're not the one running the show. You don't get to tell people *we'll be there*."

"You already told Willow you would go."

"That was before *you* said you would. Maybe I changed my mind."

Luke's face is serious, but I recognize the twinkle in his eyes and I know he's trying not to laugh. Which makes me even more annoyed.

"You don't get to decide when we touch and when we kiss, when we hold hands and when we don't," I say.

"As I recall," Luke says now, his voice low, "you were the one who jumped me in the kitchen yesterday."

"That was one time," I say, my face warm. "Every other time, it's been you."

"So what you're saying is you want to be the one to touch me?" he asks.

I have no clue how this conversation got here, but I refuse to back down. "Maybe I do."

"So do it," he says, taking a step toward me. "Touch me."

I swallow over the lump in my throat. "I don't mean right now."

"I know. Whenever you want," he says. His eyes are intense, as if he's saying one thing but meaning another.

"Fine," I say.

"So, truce?" he asks, holding out his hand.

I hesitate for a second and then put my hand in his. "Truce."

11

THEN

It felt Like some sort of game.

The challenge of going from one mundane task to the next and the payoff of clearing that level. It wasn't a perfect analogy, but being with Luke felt a little bit like that. The weekdays were the tough part, the anxious, boring moments when I longed to be able to touch him or kiss him, to see his face outside of a palm-size screen. The weekends were the payoff for all the waiting.

The second weekend in October, for the fourth time in a row, Luke drove down again. I felt guilty thinking of all the quality bonding time he was missing with his fellow freshmen, all the social events at the start of a new year that he didn't get to be a part of. But I told myself that he would probably have made the trip every weekend anyway, to check on Mel. If anything, I was giving him something to look forward to, aside from watching his mother deteriorate a little every time he saw her. For the most part, Mel was still doing okay. She had lost a bunch of weight, and her skin looked sallow and pale all the time, but she kept reminding me whenever I worried that it was the treatment making her look sick, not the Big Bad itself. She could handle the treatment if it kept her around a little bit longer, she said.

After finishing his first midterm late on the Friday, Luke was scheduled to drive down super early on Saturday. He would get something like twenty hours at home before he had to turn around and drive back. It wasn't ideal, but it was better than not seeing him at all.

Ro, on the other hand, had a tournament an hour away in Millwood, and Mel was determined to go and watch him play, despite the fact that she'd had a bad week. "The season is almost over," she kept saying, but what she meant was that she'd have to wait a year to see another of his matches, and nobody knew if she had that kind of time. The doctors were hopeful, but not sure.

So, while Ro and Mel drove to Millwood, I turned up at Mel's house bright and early on Saturday morning to look after Sydney and wait for Luke. It was something ungodly, like five thirty a.m., when Mel hugged me goodbye and Ro jumped into the driver's seat. The tournament was one in which they would play multiple matches in one day until a winner was determined, so it would be late before they got back.

"Take care of my Sydney baby for me," Mel told me, and I promised I would.

After they were gone, Sydney and I made ourselves comfortable on the couch. Strictly speaking, the dog wasn't allowed on the furniture, but for years each of the Cohens had been making "exceptions" without telling the others. At this point Sydney had pretty much determined that it was her divine right to sit on the leather throne. I let her climb up beside me, my feet tucked under her furry belly, and turned on the TV. I meant to find something to watch until Luke got home, but within minutes I was yawning.

I woke up briefly to let the dog out and then woke up again hours later, when I felt someone tucking a strand of hair behind my ears. My blurry vision told me it was Luke, but even if it hadn't, I had developed a hyperawareness to his scent.

"Hi," I whispered groggily, my face still smashed against the couch in what I'm sure was a deeply attractive pose. "I meant to stay awake until you got here. Sorry."

"Don't apologize," he said, still leaning over me. "Did I ever tell you you're the cutest when you sleep?"

I gave a tired smile. "I don't think you've ever seen me sleep."

"Hmm," he said thoughtfully. "We have to do something about that."

Despite myself, my heart galloped in my chest.

"I need to go up and take a shower," Luke told me, still playing with my hair. "Want to come and hang out upstairs?"

"Yeah, okay," I said. I sat up and held my arms up over my head. Laughing, Luke helped me wrap my arms around his neck, and I wound my legs around his hips.

"Hi," he said when our cheeks were brushing.

"Hi." I kissed his cheek. "You're probably more tired than I am, and I'm making you carry me up the stairs."

"You're not *making* me do anything," he said.

Once we were upstairs, he pushed open the door of his room and tossed his backpack on the floor. Then he walked me over to the edge of his bed, where he gently let me down.

I tucked my feet under me, watching as he dug through his closet, his back to me.

"How was your trip?" I asked.

"Eh. Went by pretty fast actually," he said.

"What time is it?" I stifled another yawn.

"Eight thirty, I think?"

My mouth dropped open. "How the hell did you get here in two hours?"

"I left at like three. Thought it'd give me more time here."

I tried to seem as stern as possible. "Luke. There's no good reason to be driving when it's that dark out."

"Seeing you's a pretty good reason," he said, and all the sternness left me. I smiled at him, then yawned.

"You should get in," he said, pointing to the bed. "Promise it's clean."

Flurries swirled in my stomach. Luke was asking me to climb into his bed. Of course, he didn't intend to be in it at the same time, but that didn't matter.

Me in Luke's bed.

I stood up, went around to the side of his bed, and slipped under the covers, carefully lowering my head onto one of his pillows. He watched me the whole time, holding a change of clothes in his hands.

"Be right back," he said after a moment.

"Okay."

When I heard the door shut, I buried my face in his pillow, sighing. It smelled just like Luke. Clean and fresh, like boy and like home. Once again, I meant to wait up until he got back, but when I woke up again, he was fast asleep on his back beside me.

I stared at his profile, his long eyelashes, the strong set of his jaw. His perfect nose.

"I'm not as cute when I sleep," he muttered, covering his eyes with one of his arms. I shifted closer even though he was on top of the covers and I was underneath them.

"I'll be the judge of that," I said, running my finger along the contours of his face. I wanted so badly to kiss him, to bury myself in the space between his neck and shoulders. I wanted . . .

"Is Mel going to freak out?" I asked, imagining her walking in and finding us in bed together. For all the talk of how much she loved me, I suspected there was still a good chance she'd throw me out on my ass if she caught us in a compromising position.

"I'll stay over here. Or I can take the couch downstairs, if you're uncomfortable," he said, opening his eyes to look at me. His eyes were intense and worried, like maybe he thought his nearness was freaking me out.

"I'm not uncomfortable."

Uncomfortable was the last word I'd used to describe the sensations wreaking havoc on my heart and limbs and brain.

"I promise I won't touch you," he said, still looking at me.

It was the reason I loved Luke so much. He was always thoughtful and respectful and sincere, but at that exact moment I wasn't so sure respectful was what I wanted.

I reached over and traced the outline of his lips with my fingers. I watched as he swallowed, his Adam's apple bobbing.

We fell asleep that way, touching but not touching. Close but not close enough. I knew right then that I wanted to do everything with him, but it had been just a few weeks. This was only the beginning, and we still had so much time, so many more minutes and hours and days, so I closed my eyes and slept.

I'm lying next to Luke on Tuesday evening as the sun bounces off the roof of Willow's massive house. Her huge infinity pool glistens a few feet away. Luke and I lie on separate beach towels next to each other. Separated from us by a pair of lounge chairs, Willow and Brett are sitting on their own beach towels.

I close my eyes and try to enjoy the feeling of the warm air against my skin. I tell myself to relax, that everything is okay, but none of it feels true when Luke is close enough for me to feel the heat of his body. He is wearing nothing but a pair of swim shorts, and the sight of his chest sends me back months into the past, then years. When he was mine — and way back when it seemed like he never could be mine.

Somehow, now we seem closer to who we were when we were kids. When the only string holding us together was his brother and his mother. When I would try to think of excuses and reasons to talk to him — because I felt so sure that, without constant reminders of my presence, he would soon forget I existed.

"Tell me whenever you're ready to get in," Luke says, nodding toward the pool and drawing me out of my thoughts. I glance over at him, but he's staring up at the sky, dark sunglasses over his eyes.

I say nothing, and a few moments later he speaks again. "I called you."

"When?" I ask.

"That night. You asked whether I saw your messages after," he says. "Did you see mine before?"

My heart drops. I can't believe we're talking about this. That he's bringing up the night when everything changed.

"Only when I got home hours later."

He nods.

"Why?" I ask, but he doesn't answer. His question sounds random, but it tells me that he's still stuck in the past. Dreaming about it, reliving it, wanting it back, and wanting it as far away as possible. It tells me he's still sifting through all the details of that night, trying to find the exact moment before everything fell apart. The same thing I used to do for months after.

If only I'd never gone out that night.

No — if only I'd never kissed Luke the very first time.

If only I had never met Rowan.

If only I had stopped him . . .

If, if, if.

"Okay, rise and shine, sleepyheads," Willow says, coming over to us. "We're getting in the pool. Do you want to play volleyball?"

"Sure," I say, standing up too quickly.

"Us against you guys?" she asks.

Behind me, Luke is standing, pushing his sunglasses up on his head and brushing off his shorts.

"I don't know if they can handle our trash talk," Brett says, wrapping an arm around Willow's waist, and she giggles.

"We're both competitive. Like, supercompetitive," Willow says.

"If that's you trying to scare us, it's not working," Luke says as he dips a toe in the water.

Brett laughs. "Why do I get the sense *you* can handle our trash talk?"

"Hey, so can I!" I protest.

"It's true," Luke surprises me by saying. "She might seem all quiet and delicate, but Jessi's not afraid to get her hands dirty."

I run his comment through my mind, checking for any possible hidden meanings. When I find none, I say, "Thank you."

"You're welcome."

Which is the last thing I remember before his arms wrap around my waist and I'm fighting to stay afloat in Willow's pool.

"Luke!" I squeal, too shocked to form any other words. "You jerk!" I cry, but when I see him doubled over laughing, I can't help but grin too.

"Your face . . ." Brett says.

"Are you okay, Jessi?" Willow steps closer to the pool and calls over the sounds of Luke's and Brett's laughter.

"Barely," I say, which makes the boys laugh even harder.

"I'm so sorry," Willow says, shifting even closer to Brett. "It's just so *mean*—" On 'mean,' she shoves Brett with all her might, and then he's falling belly-first into the pool and sputtering. I can't help laughing too. The timing was perfect.

"That was deeply satisfying," she says. She holds out her hand to Luke, and they high-five.

"You *planned* that?" I ask.

"Yep," Luke says with a grin. It makes him look younger and mischievous, like someone else. Like Rowan.

My heart plummets, but before I have a chance to think anything else, Brett is coughing and flailing a few feet away from me. Luke's and Willow's laughter stops abruptly.

"I . . . can't . . . swim . . ." Brett pants between breaths.

Luke and Willow exchange a look.

"Are you serious, man?" Luke asks.

"Brett, you better not be lying," Willow says.

Sensing my cue, I say, "I don't think he is, you guys."

I start swimming toward Brett.

Within half a second Luke and Willow are both in the pool. Luke reaches him at the same time I do, but when he tries to lift him out of the water, Brett lunges and pushes Luke down. It's the perfect time to exact my revenge, so when Brett lets Luke go, I use all my force to push him back under.

Luke manages to writhe his way out from our grips, and then he's shaking out his wet hair, laughing a full belly laugh. I've heard it maybe three times in my life. Once, before Sydney was housetrained, she pooped in Ro's tennis shoe. When Rowan went to put it on, he squealed out a string of expletives that were totally inappropriate for a ten-year-old but completely hilarious. Another time was during a movie Mel took all three of us to. The third time was with me. I made him laugh with his whole being.

Now I just stand and watch, watch him being happy and carefree and fun. I always thought of Luke as serious, kind of high-minded, but it's not until I see him now that I remember he wasn't always like that. He used to *giggle* when we were younger. He used to love practical jokes and making fun of his younger brother. It was after his father left that he changed and became more conscientious and practical, more concerned for his mother and Ro than he was with friends or having fun, or even with school. He was happy when we were together. I know that with all my heart, but he was also always scared. Everything with Mel wouldn't have allowed anything else. It's nice to see him as he would have been if his father had never left, if his mother never got sick, if I'd never ruined everything.

While Brett splashes Willow, Luke swims over to me, his eyes still sparkling. "You enjoyed that, didn't you?"

I swallow over the lump in my throat. I want to tell him how much I love seeing him happy, how much I miss him, how sorry I am for everything. Instead I smile and say, "What can I say? Payback is a bitch."

We both float there for a second, treading water, and then he lifts his hand and moves a strand of hair away from my eyes.

"Thanks," I breathe.

He just looks at me.

His gaze is like the pull of gravity, strong and magnetic. His eyes slide all over my face, lingering at my lips.

My first thought is that Brett and Willow are preoccupied with themselves; he doesn't have to look at me like that.

My second is that I really, really want to kiss him.

So I do.

I close the distance between us, loop my arms around his neck, and press a kiss to his lips. He kisses me back, his tongue pushing my lips apart and sweeping over the inside of my lower lip. We drift until my back is against the edge of the pool, our bodies pressed against each other. His hands roam the bare skin of my side, my stomach, my thighs, while my hands are trapped against his chest. Everything feels familiar, but different and terrifying, like walking through the city you grew up in after a war.

When we finally break apart, Willow and Brett are lobbing a small beach ball back and forth and trying to seem busy.

"I keep forgetting we should be doing that," Luke says, his voice husky. He steals a look in their direction again. "Think they're buying everything?"

"Yeah," I whisper, my knees like jelly. "I think they are."

12

THEN

It was twenty-four hours after I spent the morning in Luke's bed, and Mel patted the side of her king-size bed, waiting for me to climb in next to her. A vague joke about bed-hopping between the Cohens crossed my mind and I smiled to myself. Mel adjusted the pillow behind her, and I was brought back to the present moment.

"I'm sorry you feel so gross," I told her. The tennis tournament in Millwood seemed to have taken everything out of her, but she got to witness Rowan win the whole thing, so she was adamant that she didn't regret going.

She gave a weak smile. "Thanks, Jessi-girl. The company's not so bad, though."

I leaned back against the headboard and watched her. Everything about her was tired, from her breathing to the skin under her eyes to the sound of her voice, but she seemed to feel that acknowledging it meant yielding to it.

"So," she said. "How are things going with my firstborn?'

I struggled to fight my grin, and Mel laughed.

"That good, huh?"

"Is it weird?" I asked, turning so I was facing her.

"You want me to be completely honest?" she asked, and I nodded.

"I'm not the least bit surprised. I saw it coming a mile away from both sides."

"Both sides?" I repeated. Okay, I had been more than obvious about my crush, but I wondered what hints Luke could possibly have given his mom that he had feelings for me.

"You know I'm a hopeless romantic, so it was hard not to try to play Cupid," she said. "But I tried as hard as I could to stay neutral, not to push or pull in any direction, and let you figure it out on your own . . . The thing I cared most about—the thing I *care* most about—is that you are safe and that nobody gets hurt."

We were silent for a moment, and then she said, "I'm glad you're happy."

"I am," I said. "I just feel like I don't see him enough."

Mel snorted. "When Gary and I started dating, I was off in Hungary on an exchange program and he was starting medical school in Michigan. There was no FaceTime, no WiFi. It was snail mail and calling collect in some kitschy European phone booth. That's what I call not seeing each other."

And look how that turned out, I thought but didn't say.

"There's something I've been meaning to talk to you about," she said now.

"Okay."

"I worry so much about what will happen to Luke and Rowan when I'm gone." Her voice was soft and sad in the dark room. "I worry about you, too."

"They'll be okay," I said over the lump in my throat. "We'll be okay."

It was a flat-out lie. How would we survive without Mel's advice, without her warmth and her baking and her unconditional love? The answer, I was afraid, was that we wouldn't. That somehow without her holding us together, we would crumble and fall apart.

"I worry about Luke," Mel said.

"Luke?" I repeated. "Ro has been kind of a mess."

"Isn't he always, though?" she whispered conspiratorially, and we laughed. "No, I absolutely worry about Ro, but Luke scares me. He bottles everything up and carries the world on his shoulders, and my fear is that one day it'll all suddenly get too much for him. Ro — he acts out and makes bad choices, but you always know how he feels. There are no secrets."

It was a complete one-eighty on the way I had been seeing things. As far as I was concerned, Ro was the one who seemed ready to explode at a moment's notice. Ro was liable to make bad decisions and date the wrong girls and lose the tennis scholarship he'd worked so hard for all his life. Luke was . . . Luke. Calm, collected, dependable. Sad for his mother, for sure. Afraid of losing her. But strong.

The realization that we couldn't both be right scared me. Either Mel — whose eyes always saw more than I imagined they could — was wrong, or I didn't know Luke as well as I thought I did.

"I wish they were closer to their father," Mel said now. "I think I made the mistake of letting my feelings about him trickle down to them. When it's just you, you forget sometimes that your kids are not your friends, they're not your therapist, not your doctor. They are just kids who will one day have their own view on the world, with or without your input."

Mel's words reminded me of what Luke had said a couple of

weeks earlier about the way his mother had handled the divorce. I cringed now at the way I'd defended her. My blind devotion to her hadn't allowed me to even consider that he might have been right. But now here she was saying the very same thing.

"Gary went to see Luke last week," I said, hoping that would make her feel better. I wondered belatedly whether Luke had mentioned it to his mom. Why couldn't I keep my mouth shut sometimes?

"I know," she said, to my relief. "He's so secretive, though. You ask him how it went, and all he'll say is 'Fine.'" Mel sighed. "I swear, I got a big mouth as compensation for the fact that I'd have two boys and they would never say a word to me."

I smiled at her. "They love you."

"I know that too," she said, looking at me with a serious expression. "I would never ask you to look after them — that would be so incredibly unfair to you."

"You know I will," I promised her.

She took one of my hands in hers, her palms slick with sweat. I worried that she was running a fever and putting on a brave front. "Thank you," she said. "The only thing I'll ask of you is the same thing I'm going to ask of them. That you three always remember that you're family. They're your people."

When a tear plopped down on our joined hands, I realized for the first time that I'd started to cry.

"Don't say that. You still have so much time left."

"Oh, I know," she said, rubbing my hand in an attempt to comfort me. "I'm not saying this for today or tomorrow. But whenever the time comes, I want you to have each other's backs."

My vision was now completely cloudy, but I could make out a trail of liquid on Mel's cheek. Or was it sweat? Would she let me take her temperature?

"Do you promise?" she asked me, and I nodded.

"I promise."

"Good girl," she sniffed. I snuggled closer to her, and she held my head to her chest and ran her hand over my hair the way she had when I was a little girl. My mother hugged me sometimes too, but her hugs were seconds long, quick and controlled, as if to remind me that I couldn't have her for too long. She belonged to something bigger and stronger than I am.

"Mel—" I said before I could stop myself. "Why did you . . . When we were kids, why did you choose me?"

I sat up so I could look at her.

"Well, first of all," she said, smiling, "it's cute that you think you're not a kid *now*."

I rolled my eyes but smiled too.

"Second, I didn't *choose* you." She said the word *choose* like there were quotation marks around it. "I mean, Ro was your doubles partner. You guys became best friends."

"I know, but like, how did you know that I needed . . . you?" My face heated as I said it. That was another of the few things Mel and I had never really talked about. The actual surrogacy, the way she had taken me in. As far as I was concerned, it had just happened. One day I wasn't part of the Cohen family; then one day I was. "Was it my clothes? Could you tell that my dad was clueless and didn't know how to take care of my hair?"

Mel laughed. "None of the above, actually," she said. After a moment her face sobered. "I don't really know what you're asking me, Jessi. I treated you like I'd have treated any of Ro's or Luke's friends, but from the beginning, you just . . . you fit.

"I don't know what that means," she continued. "Whether it was destiny, meant to be, or any of that stuff. I couldn't care less about the mechanics of the whole thing. I only know that whenever you were with us, it felt like you'd always been here, you know? Like you always would be."

I nodded, feeling my heart swell.

I'd always be a part of them.

What she was describing sounded a lot like what I'd always thought, what I'd hoped they felt too. It sounded like family.

"Love you, Jessi-girl," Mel said now, and hugged me again.

"Love you, too."

When I told Mel that her body felt warm and asked if she wanted me to call her doctor, she shook her head and insisted that she just needed to sleep.

I was back home, fast asleep in bed, when Ro called, his voice strangled and quiet, as he told me she was in the hospital.

NOW

I still feel a pinch of relief every time I walk into her house and find Mel sitting in the living room, smaller but alive. *She's still here,* a voice in my head says, but there's another voice, a quieter voice, that says she's not really. She's not the Mel I knew, and with every day that passes, she drifts further away from that person and becomes someone else.

"Jessi-girl," she says today as I come into the living room, and I'm hit with a wave of guilt.

Just because she looks different, it doesn't mean she isn't still Mel.

"Hi," I say, going around the couch to hug her. As I do, she throws a blanket over what looks like a pile of papers in her lap.

"What are you doing?" I ask, trying not to sound as hurt as I feel at her secrecy. She never used to hide stuff from me.

"Oh, just this and that," she says vaguely. "Luke's out for a run."

"That's okay," I say. "I'm here to see you."

She smiles at me. "Actually, I'm glad we have some time alone. There's a couple of things I wanted to talk to you about."

My heart sinks.

She knows.

She knows that Luke and I have been faking, that deep down he still secretly hates me, that deep down I still secretly hate myself. She knows what I did.

"What is it?" I ask.

"I still remember the talk we had up in my bedroom last year. Do you remember?"

"Of course," I say, not sure whether to be relieved about the direction this conversation is taking. I remember feeling that she loved me when she told me I had always just fit with them. I remember the courage and certainty it had given me for the next few weeks, foolishly believing that I wasn't a bomb waiting to detonate on everyone I loved.

"I know everything blew up in our faces after that," she says, using the perfect metaphor. "That you found it too hard to be around me and Luke anymore once Ro was gone."

I swallow over the lump in my throat. *Is that what she thinks?* That I found it too hard to be around them?

"I know how much you miss him."

"I do." Just saying so nearly makes me crumple with sadness after a year of not being able to talk about him with any of the people that matter most. I miss Ro so much every day, it's like a physical ache. I miss our shed meetings, miss hiding out with him in the dark. I miss the way he made me laugh, the way he frustrated me. I miss playing mixed doubles with him, even though I hated it. I miss eating cinnamon rolls with him, miss tracing the calluses on his palm to tell his fortune.

I miss my best friend with everything inside me.

"I hope you know I don't hold it against you," Mel says now, and for a second I think she means she doesn't blame me for what happened the night he died, but then I remember, *she doesn't know.*

I swallow. "Hold what against me?"

"Your staying away all this time. I'm just so relieved that you and Luke figured out a way to move forward."

I nod, unable to speak.

"I'm also still not asking you to look after him, because he's a big boy. He can look after himself," she says. "Not that anybody needs my permission or anything, but will you remind him that he's allowed to be happy?"

"How?" I ask.

Mel narrows her eyes at me. "I love you, but we're not discussing the methods you're going to use to keep my firstborn happy."

I give an embarrassed laugh. At least she hasn't figured out the truth.

"And you're allowed to be happy too, you know," she adds.

I can't meet her eye. "Thanks, Mel."

"No, don't 'thanks Mel' me," she says firmly. "I mean it."

She looks me dead in the eyes. "You and I are lucky that we found our people relatively early in life. Sure, shit happens. Gary turned out to be a cheating SOB, but he's still the reason I found two of my *actual* people—my two boys." Her voice breaks. "Naomi is my people, if there ever was a people."

I laugh.

"And Luke and Ro and I, we have always been your people. And we always will be. My big, dysfunctional blended family." She's joking, but it reminds me of what my mother said a couple of weeks ago, about the way her family refused to accept Dad because of the color of his skin. If Mel and Naomi and Ro and Luke and I could form our own little unit despite all our differences, how sad is it that my grandparents were willing to lose their only daughter rather than take in the person she loved?

"Did you know that Mom's parents cut her off because Dad is black?"

"No," she says. "How do you know that?"

I tell her everything my mother told me, and I tell her how it makes the story of us even more special.

"The story of us," Mel muses. "I like it. And you know, it doesn't have to have a tidy ending—hell, I was so looking forward to being a cranky bitch of an old lady."

"So like Naomi?" I offer, even though my eyes are welling now.

Mel throws her head back and laughs the way Luke did in the pool the other day — with what is left of her whole body. "I'm going to tell her you said that."

"Please don't," I say, only half joking.

"Anyway," Mel continues. "I don't even remember the point I was trying to make. Just that you and Luke, you'll be what's left of us soon. Love each other well, okay?"

I blink at her. How do I tell her that there *is* no love between Luke and me anymore? That I destroyed any chance of us ending up together, broke whatever chains used to bind us and made him "my people." How do I make her see that she was wrong about me all along? That I could never have fit with them, because it turned out I was jagged and misshapen, not made to fit anywhere.

"God, I feel like I've been on this endless farewell tour," Mel says, resting her head back against the couch. "One of those rock stars that make you feel nostalgic. You're sad the first time they announce they're leaving. Then you look up and they're still there, and they're *still* there —"

"Mel," I say, interrupting her. "I'm glad you're still here."

A wave of guilt hits me again over what I thought when I first walked in. That she is no longer who she used to be, but I was wrong. She is, in every way that matters. She is still vibrant, funny, beautiful Mel, and the Big Bad can never take that away from her.

I can't believe I stayed away so long. I can't . . . What if one day I had seen the obituaries and her name had been there? I would never have forgiven myself. Never.

I still can't forgive myself for everything I destroyed, but I remember what Mom told me that night: at least I'm here now. At least I get to see Mel again. Luke's idea sounded so ludicrous at first, but now I'm grateful that I agreed to go along with it.

It brought the three of us back together, if only superficially, one last time.

"I feel good today," Mel says out of nowhere now.

"Really?"

She nods. "Do you know what I feel like doing? Listening to some of the classics."

I grin at her. It's been so long since we sat around doing nothing but listening to her favorite jazz songs. Billie Holiday and Ella Fitzgerald. Duke Ellington and Louis Armstrong.

Even though most of the good songs are on my phone, I get up and turn on the old CD player.

Before I can sit down, though, Mel holds up her hands to me. I'm confused at first.

"Help me up!" she says over the sound of "Bugle Call Rag."

"Wait, but . . ." I panic as she attempts to pull herself into a standing position.

"It's criminal not to dance to this song," she says, pushing up weakly with her arms. Her blanket falls to a pool at her feet and the papers she'd hidden fall, too. I grab one of her hands to steady her, and then I bend down to pick up the stuff she's dropped.

I want to respect her privacy, but my curiosity gets the best of me and my eyes sweep over the page on the top.

It says in writing so jerky it's hard to read, "reading from Psalm 23—too cliché???"

I place the papers on the couch, stand, and offer Mel my second hand.

"Are you sure about this?" I ask her as she struggles to catch her breath. Just standing seems to have taken all her energy.

"I'm not going to break," she says, sounding like she very well could. So I hold her hands while we shake our hips and shimmy our shoulders and make faces at each other. My mind keeps going back to the piece of paper I found. It can mean only one thing: Mel is planning her funeral, and I want nothing more than to curl into a ball and cry. But she's counting on me, so I keep dancing and grinning like I have no cares in this world.

Before the end of the song, Mel shakes her head apologetically, and I know she needs to sit down again. I'm in the process of helping her onto the couch when I spot Luke standing in the doorway, his eyes wide and his shirt wet with sweat.

"That was the most fun I've had in forever," Mel says, laughing. I'm too aware of Luke's gaze on me as I readjust her blanket before sitting down beside her.

"Hey, Mom," he says, stepping out from the doorway. They chat about random things for a couple of minutes. I don't think I'm imagining that his gaze keeps coming back to me.

When I stand to leave a few minutes later, Luke says, "I'll walk you out. Be right back, Mom."

We go out through the front door and down the driveway in total silence. Finally, when I can't stand it anymore, I say, "She said she wanted to dance. It wasn't my idea."

"What?" he asks, looking distracted.

"She said it was criminal not to dance to that song."

"No," Luke says, shaking his head. "No, you don't have to explain."

"Oh." Of all the things I was expecting him to say, it was not that.

"Listen," he says, rubbing the back of his neck. "The one thing I've never doubted is how much you care about her. Never."

He meets my eye on the last word, and I feel like I'm drowning in the pool of his eyes.

"That's good. I . . . I'd never hurt her intentionally."

"I know," Luke says.

I slide in behind the wheel of my car, and Luke steps back so I can drive away. As I go, I hear his words again: *the one thing I've never doubted*.

And I'm glad he doesn't doubt that, but it confirms what he hasn't said this whole summer: that he doubts everything else that happened between us.

13

THEN

"How can you tell me not to come home? She's in the hospital," Luke said over the phone, and I imagined him tugging at his hair the way he used to do when we were little and he was stressed about something. "I can be there in six hours. Five, if I push it."

"Yeah, but the doctor said the fever's under control and she'll probably be able to go home tomorrow," I said. "Plus, you have like three midterms."

"Screw midterms," he said, and I wasn't used to the dark tone in his voice.

"Luke—" I said with a sigh.

"I should never have come here," he said. "I knew I shouldn't have, but she swore she'd be fine. And she said all that bullshit about wanting to see me live my life so she'd know I would be okay."

I stayed quiet so he could keep venting, but he was silent after a minute.

"I promise I'll call you if anything changes," I said.

"Even if it's bad?"

"Even if it's bad," I promised.

Mel ended up being in the hospital for two nights. Her treatment had weakened her immune system and she'd caught an infection, but by the time Naomi brought her home on Wednesday afternoon, there was a little more color in her cheeks.

Ro and I sat at attention in his room while Mel slept across the hall. Technically, Ro was pretending to play a game on his computer and I was pretending to do some history homework.

"What do you think happens to the house when she's gone?" Ro asked out of nowhere.

"Don't talk that way," I scolded him.

"Don't tell the truth?" he asked.

"We don't know what's going to happen. She could . . ." Get better? Outlive every known patient with her diagnosis? "She could still have a long time."

Ro made a noncommittal sound and went back to his game.

"I say, Luke gets the house," he said. "He's older, more responsible, all that good shit."

I swallowed. I didn't want to think of anyone divvying up any of Mel's possessions, but Ro was in the kind of mood where it was better to let him get everything off his mind.

"Maybe I get her car or something. She'll give you her whole music collection."

"Can we talk about something else?" Despite myself, I couldn't go on with this conversation.

Ro eyed me for a second, then, mercifully, went back to playing his game.

I couldn't concentrate, so I stared at the lineup of trophies that took up most of the space on his bookshelf. Where normal people (i.e., me, Luke, and basically everyone I knew) had books, Rowan just had a collection of silver declaring how good he was at the thing he loved best in the world. It must have been a pretty good feeling, I thought, to have that kind of validation. He would never say he was good enough, of course. He'd say he could always improve, his forehand could be better, his drop shots better executed, his serve faster, but even Ro knew he was pretty damn good at tennis.

"Been talking to my dad a bunch," he mumbled now, still focused on his computer screen.

"About?" He didn't hate his dad as much as Luke did, but he also never made much effort to have a relationship with him. In fact, for as long as I'd known him, he'd always seemed pretty much indifferent to his father. If there was such a thing as a mama's boy, Rowan was definitely it. Always had been.

"I keep waking up with my elbow all stiff," he said. "And it hurts like shit to hold stuff. Even like a glass."

My eyes widened. "Does your coach know?"

"No. You think I'm an idiot?"

"Does Mel?"

"No," he said. "And you better not tell her."

"But Ro, what if it's something serious?"

"It's fine," Ro insisted. "I've probably been training too much. I'll just lay off for a while."

"What did your dad say?"

He shrugged. "He wanted to refer me to this orthopedic surgeon, but I said no."

Rowan could be so freaking frustrating sometimes. "Why would you say that?"

"'Cause then it will be this big thing where Coach has to get involved and I can't travel to Florida for the last competition of the season next month. And then Illinois will have to be on notice that they might be getting damaged goods."

"Damaged goods?" I repeated, incredulous. "Injuries heal."

"Exactly. Don't need to get everyone all worked up."

I sighed. "I just hope you don't make it worse."

"I won't," he said. "Dad said to keep doing cold compresses, take Advil, and see how it goes."

After a moment he said, "I'll probably end up living with him and Vanessa after."

We had circled back to talking about Mel's death again. I hated the way it lingered, clouding the air constantly like a bad smell.

"You don't think he'd let you finish out the year here?" It was the first time I'd considered this. If Mel didn't last till next May, Ro might have to leave in the middle of senior year.

"Where would I stay?" he snorted. "With you?"

"You could," I said, but we both knew he couldn't. Right from the beginning of our friendship, everything that mattered had always happened at the Cohen house. We had playdates at Rowan's, ate at Rowan's, slept at Rowan's. My house was just this sinkhole full of dark energy. It stung that I knew I could never give Ro what his family had given me, that I could never take him in and take care of him.

"It'd only be for a few months," I said, trying to make us both feel better.

"Maybe I could stay at Eric's," Ro said, and I prayed that was the start of hope in his voice. "His sisters are hot as fuck, so it would be a win in more than one way."

I threw my pen at his head. It bounced off his temple, making a satisfying *thunk* before falling on the ground.

"Nice aim," Ro said.

"I try," I said, grinning. "So you're going to hook up with Cassie Clairburne *and* Eric's sisters? He'll kill you."

Ro gave a shit-eating grin. "He's already used to getting my sloppy seconds."

"Ew," I said.

"I meant he could have Cassie, not his sisters! What's your problem?" But he was still smiling.

"Cassie's not a thing that he can *have*," I said, sounding even to my own ears like his mother. "But I guess it's Rowan Cohen's world and we all just live in it."

"Bullshit," he said. "It's Luke Cohen's world and we all just live in it."

I frowned. "What does Luke have to do with anything?"

"Just stating facts," Ro said, returning to his game.

I rolled my eyes, too tired to try to decipher the latest grudge Ro apparently had with his brother. Ro had always been jealous of Luke, with good reason, since his older brother got the kind of grades Ro could only dream of and seemingly without having to try very hard for them. But then again, there was a bookshelf full of trophies boasting of Rowan's adequacy in other ways. As far as I could tell, he'd never had a bad day on the court. The irony was, while the two brothers were each convinced that the other one had an easier life, it was unbelievably clear to me that they both worked hard at what they loved. Sure, they were both born with gifts, but they'd worked to cultivate them. Why was it so difficult for them to acknowledge this? And why, in the past few months, had the gulf between them seemed to stretch further than ever?

"You're asking questions I can't answer," Ernie says stubbornly, leaning back in his rocking chair.

"You said you wanted me to fill out the crossword for you!"

"Yes, and I thought you'd think of the answers and then write them down," he says.

"Ernie," I sigh.

"Jessica," he echoes.

"My name's not Jessica. I told you." I remember the conversation I had with my mom about my name. "It almost was, though."

"Hmm," he says. "Never met a girl who was just Jessi before you."

"I'm one of a kind," I say, and wink at him.

He snorts. "You're just lucky you haven't met my granddaughter. She'd add a *ttifer* or *cules* to your name. Jessittifer. Jessicules."

I laugh. "Okay, so forget the crossword. Can we go for a walk today?"

"If you feel that I have not suffered enough in my eighty-some years, then yes, we can certainly go for a walk."

"Great," I say, clapping my hands. "It's gorgeous outside."

Ernie harrumphs as I grab his shoes from near the door. He leans forward to put them on, his hands shaking. I would offer to help, but he likes to do it himself. I drag his walker to him and he stands and follows me to the door.

As we walk down the hallway, we pass several other residents and some nurses, all of whom greet us enthusiastically, except for one short woman with white hair who glares at Ernie as she opens the door next to his.

"That's Clarisse," he whispers once she's gone into her unit and shut her door. "An angel on earth, that's for sure."

"I'd be cranky, too, if you kept me up all night with a tennis ball," I tell him, and he roars with laughter. Honestly, at this point, I think I'm just encouraging him.

Outside, we walk through the garden before finding a bench under the canopy of a leafy tree.

"See, isn't all this fresh air and sun worth the walk?"

"Eh. Unless we got a new sun in the past week, I already saw this one," he says grouchily.

Ernie says nothing for the next few minutes, so I let him enjoy the silence.

Finally I ask, "What are you thinking?"

"Trying to think if I can convince one of the grandkids to send us a fart machine," he says. "I think Clarisse would enjoy that one at lunch."

I shake my head. "Leave the poor woman alone."

Ernie smiles. "So, when are you leaving?"

"Leaving?" I ask. "I still have an hour with you!"

"No. I mean, for good."

I narrow my eyes at him. "Not for a long time." He signals for me to help him up, and I draw his walker close so he can use it to heave himself up. "If I didn't know better, I'd say you're eager to get rid of me."

"I just hate to see someone like you, with your whole future ahead of you, putting everything on hold to spend time with an old geezer like me. Don't you kids go to university anymore?"

"Some of us do."

"Will you?" he asks.

"Probably next year."

"Didn't you say you graduated? Why not this year?"

"I'm not ready," I say. "I'm not sure what I want to be."

"That's nonsense. Nobody becomes what they want to be," he says dismissively. "You just go out there, try not to face-plant, and hope nobody notices."

What if you already face-planted? I want to ask him. What if you're still on home base and you've already ruined the entire game? Then what?

"You'd make a fine nurse," he says. "But I wouldn't pursue anything that involves using words too often. Your performance on that crossword was abysmal."

I hold open the door and wait as he shuffles into the building. "I was only supposed to be writing what you told me to!"

"That's not how crosswords work," Ernie says, and I roll my eyes.

"Just don't wait too long," he says as we turn down the hall back to his unit, "to start trying to be what you want to be — or whatever nonsense you said.

"Eighty years flies by," he continues. "Except when you have hemorrhoids. Then it's like watching the goddamned concrete dry."

I giggle. "I hope I never find out."

"I wouldn't wish it on my worst enemy. Not even my brother, Gareth Richard Solomon IV, the unlucky son of a bitch."

We go on to discuss the fact that All Saints is taking Ernie and some other residents to a movie on Saturday afternoon, so I have that day off.

The rest of the night, while I'm volunteering at the club, and the next day at Camp MORE my mind keeps replaying Ernie's words. *Just don't wait too long.*

Eighty years flies by.

And some people don't even get eighty years. Some don't get fifty. Or eighteen.

But what if you've fucked up colossally and the universe isn't done punishing you? What if there is something fundamentally wrong, something inside you that chases people away and hurts those who stay? Is there any point in trying to do anything but burrow and wait until the world forgets who you are? Until *you* forget who you are?

I'm so distracted mulling this over in my mind that I'm powerless to do anything by the time things have gone spectacularly wrong.

"We could do Saturday morning," Willow is saying now. "Brett can pick you guys up and then we'll grab some coffee on our way out of town. I am *not* giving up both my bed and coffee."

"Your bed?" I repeat. We're on lunch duty today, so we're circling the cafeteria, keeping an eye on all fifty-something kids.

"I know, I know. You'll say we have sleeping bags, but a sleeping bag is not a bed," Willow says.

Now I'm completely confused. "What do you need sleeping bags for?"

"For camping! I knew you hadn't been paying attention," she says. "Where do you go in that head?"

To the past.

Always to that night.

"Who's going camping?"

Willow stops walking abruptly and sets her hands on her hips. "Okay, seriously?"

"I'm sorry. I've been spacing out all day."

"Yeah, I know you have," she says. "We're going camping. You, me, Luke, and Brett."

If she didn't look dead serious, I would be laughing.

"Uh, what gave you that idea?"

"The fact that Luke told Brett you would? Also, I've been talking about it all day, and all you've done is nod and agree. You're not going to back out, are you?"

"I was never *in*, Wills," I say. "Why the heck are you going camping?"

"For my vlog. Xothelodown does the woods."

I stifle a smile. "That sounds . . . interesting."

"My followers voted for it. Honestly, I'm a little terrified. You know what Brett is like: supermacho and nature-y and all that. If you don't come, I'm not sure I'll be coming back alive."

"Okay, supermacho and nature-y does not mean he's going to bury your body in the woods. Also, a getaway in the woods with just the two of you? That's so romantic."

Willow gives me a stern look. "If it's so romantic, why are you trying to get out of it?"

"Willow, I can't," I say firmly.

"On account of?" she prods.

"On account of . . ." I struggle to think of an excuse. I'm not even working this Saturday, thanks to Ernie's excursion. "I don't camp. Plus! I volunteer at the club on Saturday morning."

"We'll go after. Or I can talk to Daddy. We can totally get you out of it." *Shit, it's true.* Willow's father owns Tennis Win.

"Willow —" I say.

"Please. I will love you forever." She bats her eyelashes at me. "Plus, if you don't want to go, you have to take that up with your boyfriend, because he already said you would."

"Fine, I think I will. Take it up with him."

"Fine," Willow says.

When I stop by for dinner at Luke's house, I plan on confronting him, but he's on the phone as he opens the door.

Mel is in her room tonight. She's sitting in her wheelchair, a piece of paper in her hand, but it looks like she's struggling to hold the pen.

"Do you need me to write something for you?" I ask.

"Oh no. I'm fine," she says, smiling at me. She lets the pen drop in her lap. "Luke says you're going camping."

"I think maybe *he's* going camping. I'm not."

One of Mel's thin eyebrows skitters up. "Why not?"

"Because he signed us up for it without checking with me first. I'm busy on Saturday."

"Tsk, tsk," Mel says jokingly. "I thought I raised him better than that."

"Raised me better than what?" Luke asks, entering the room. I'm wearing a shirt that hangs off my shoulder, and I'm speechless when he leans down and kisses me there. "What did I do now?"

Even though I can still feel the shadow of his lips on my skin, I fold my arms across my chest. "Why did you tell Willow and Brett we'd go camping?"

"Oh . . . that," he says.

"Yes, that." I sit on the edge of Mel's bed. "I thought we talked about you not running the show."

Though we try to keep up a happy front in his mother's presence at all times, I'm feeling so pissed that I can't contain myself. Besides, happy couples fight all the time.

Luke's eyebrows raise in surprise, but his eyes are twinkling, as if he's enjoying this.

"Is something funny to you?" I ask.

"You're just so damn cute when you're mad," he says, and a lump lodges in my throat. Is it just me or is he getting better and better at this acting-in-love thing? He almost sounds like . . . he almost sounds like my Luke, the person I used to know.

"What can I do to make it up to you?" he asks, still looking at me like he's trying not to laugh.

"Tell them we're not going. I volunteer at the club on Saturdays. Also, we really shouldn't leave Mel by her—"

"Oh, hell to the no!" Mel exclaims. "You are not using me to get out of anything."

"We're not *using* you," I amend quickly.

"In fact, I'm kind of sick of having you two around all the time. You're like those horrible gnat things."

"Fruit flies?" I say, incredulous.

"Fruit flies!" she says. "You hover."

I'm genuinely hurt by this, and if Luke's face is any indication, so is he.

"We're around too much?" I ask.

"Way, way too much," she says. "Luke, the last time you were this annoying, you were two years old and trying to follow me everywhere, even when I went to pee. I'll survive for one night. If you're so worried, Naomi can stay over."

Luke is looking at her, his eyes narrowed. "Are you just trying to make us go?"

"Yes," Mel says. "I am just trying to make you go. I literally have no time to myself."

"You have all day when I'm at work," he says, still sounding wounded.

"But then Marilyn is around, and honestly it's exhausting."

"We're just worried about you," I say gently, touching her arm.

"I know, and God love you. But if you don't go on this camping trip, I'm going to throw myself in front of a moving vehicle."

"Mom—" Luke says.

"Obviously I *can't,*" Mel says. "But I can get creative, if it comes down to it."

I look at Luke and know we've lost; if Mel has her way, Luke and I are going camping.

14

THEN

"**Since when did** Mel get so manipulative?" I asked Luke, playing with a strand of his hair. We were in his car, his driver's seat inclined all the way back, as I straddled him. It was the most . . . confined space we'd ever been in together, and every part of my body was aware of it. So, apparently, was Luke's.

"Right?" he said, burying his face in the crook of my neck. "She thought if she told me to grab a box of doughnuts on my way into town—"

"And if she told me to get doughnuts on my way to visit her," I continued, "she would get double the doughnuts. Except, surprise, we actually talk."

"At least we're making her wait an appropriate length of time before giving them to her," he said.

"Yep," I said, though the truth was that the amount of time we were spending parked in front of my driveway had very little to do with punishing Mel and way more to do with rewarding ourselves for not having seen each other for the past week. Technically, Luke's being in town this weekend had more to do with seeing Mel after her stint in the hospital. He'd written his midterms and then driven down after his last class on Friday.

It was past eleven now, and his first stop had been to see me.

He raised his head from my neck now, his gaze intense, and I pressed my lips against his. The kiss started out tender and soft, but as the seconds passed, it grew more urgent. My hands dug through his hair as we kissed, our bodies pressed against each other, and his arms scalded the skin on my back and hips under my shirt.

I broke the kiss and breathed against his lips. "Have you ever . . ." My voice trailed off, but I knew he'd understand what I meant.

"No," he said, chasing my mouth with his. "But I've done other stuff."

I tried not to stiffen too obviously.

"With who?"

He stopped kissing me and looked up at me with heavy-lidded eyes. "Do you really want me to answer that?"

"It was that Meredith girl who used to be your lab partner, wasn't it?" I asked.

"Jess," Luke said, half sighing, but even in the dark, I could tell he was blushing.

Meredith was this petite, pixielike red-haired girl who used to come over to the Cohens' house and work on "bio lab" at least once a week when Luke was a junior and Ro and I were sophomores. Sometimes Luke went over and worked at her house. She had perfectly clear skin, claimed never to have had braces, and called herself a "flexitarian." She was also super nice, which was how I knew to be suspicious of her.

"Have you?" Luke asked now, making a trail of kisses down the side of my neck, past my collarbone, to the swell of my chest.

"You're my first real boyfriend. Obviously not," I said, still kind of put out over the Meredith thing.

"Nothing's *obvious* when you look like you do."

I was trying really hard to maintain a healthy level of annoyance —how dare Luke have done "other stuff" with a girl who wasn't me! And a flexitarian, of all people! —but he was making it really hard.

"Stop," I said.

"It's true."

"Well," he said, kissing the part of my shoulder where my collarbone met my arm, "we'll go slow and make everything count."

I readjusted my body against his and heard his sharp intake of breath. "Slow?" I said. "Are you sure that's what you want?" I was secretly delighted to have this much of an effect on him and even happier that his body was so quick to betray him. So I did it again.

"You're a monster, you know that?" he said, leaning back against the headrest for a second, but he was grinning from ear to ear. "I'll worry about . . . that. You, meanwhile, should have other concerns."

"Like?" I asked.

He leaned forward like he was going to kiss my temple when I felt his tongue dip into the top fold of my ear.

I gasped.

His laugh sent tingles through my ear and the rest of my body. And then he did it again and again.

A few minutes later I settled back into the passenger seat. We decided to wait a few more minutes to cool down before driving to Mel's house.

"I'd let you hold the doughnut box for cover," I teased, but

Luke said, "Mom's tearing into those doughnuts the minute she sees them."

"At least her appetite seems to be coming back," I said.

We were both quiet for a moment, staring out through the windshield at my garage door.

"I guess I'm getting a little taste of what it's been like for you, huh?" Luke said now, and I turned to look at him, confused. "Without your mom."

"Oh," I said. "It's not the same . . . She's still here."

"I don't know. It sucks when someone is here but not present. And honestly, your dad hasn't been much better."

An unexpected protectiveness came over me. "I think they're trying," I said.

Luke nodded, but I knew that he knew the truth. Nothing was changing with my mother or my family. Despite the brief moments when we almost connected, my parents remained as distant from me as they always had, and neither of them seemed to think it was a problem.

I thought he might start the car then and take us to Mel's, but he asked another question. "What do you guys do in the shed? You and Ro."

I glanced at him, surprised. It was pretty much the last question I'd imagined he'd ask.

I shrugged. "Talk."

"Just talk?" he repeated, and I frowned.

"What kind of question is that?"

"I don't know. Ro said it's like therapy or something, that he always feels better after he leaves."

"I do, too," I said. "It's basically just finding a dark place with your best friend and telling them everything you can't tell anyone else . . .

"That, and spiders," I added with a smile. "And earwigs. And house centipedes. Possibly vermin. Also cockroaches."

"You're not making it sound too enticing," Luke said, finally starting the car.

I grinned into the night. "It has its perks."

For the rest of the drive to the Cohen house, we talked about the lake shindig Ro was planning for his birthday next weekend. Or I did. Luke wasn't doing much talking.

Finally I said, "Are you planning to get here on the Friday or Saturday?"

Luke was hyperfocused on the road.

"Luke?"

"I don't think I'm coming," he said, and my mouth dropped open. "I've driven down here almost every weekend since school started, and it's taking its toll."

"I know," I said. "And I hate you driving so much every weekend. But this is Ro's birthday."

"He won't care if I'm there or not."

"Are you kidding me? Of course he'll care." I couldn't believe he was saying this. The three of us had celebrated every single birthday together since Ro and I were seven.

"What is with the two of you lately?" I asked.

Luke didn't answer, his jaw tight as he faced the road. If Mel had been healthy, she would have kicked their butts. As it was, I was going to have to do it on her behalf.

NOW

Exactly nothing is going my way.

To start with, my mom has bounced back from her dip a couple of weeks ago and Mom 2.0 has returned in full force. A really good thing — except suddenly she's refusing to let go of the idea of having Luke over for supper.

"Mom, it's awkward," I complain as I stuff a muffin in my face for breakfast on Friday morning. "Everything is still super new."

"How is it new when you dated last year?"

I remember the night last fall, while Mom and I cleaned out the fridge, when I told her that Luke and I were dating. It's still one of my favorite memories — just the two of us, talking boys and crushes over a glass of milk.

Her spiral a couple of weeks ago made me realize how much I've grown used to the idea of the new her. It's such a relief to have her happy and present that it makes me wonder what my life would have been like if I never had to know that another side of her existed. What if I had Mom 2.0 all my life? If it wasn't just her occasional moments of lucidity and my father's assurances that she loved me that I'd had to go on?

Maybe I'd never have gotten so close to the Cohens. Maybe I'd never have made such a mess of things. Maybe Rowan would still be alive.

I push these thoughts back and say, "Well, we just got back together."

"Maybe, but he's been in your life so long, I'd like to at least get to know him better. I feel like I hardly know him."

"Okay," I relent. "I'll ask him."

"That's all I want," she says, smiling.

So that's the first crappy part of my day. The second is getting out of this camping trip with Willow and Brett.

By the time Willow and I are setting up for our last Camp MORE day for the week, I've prepared a list of plausible excuses for why Luke and I shouldn't crash their couple's hangout.

A horrific case of food poisoning, for one.

Head lice, contracted from one of the many kids we work with daily. As lice are contagious, Luke could even have them, too, if he wants.

Pinkeye. Again, contracted from a student.

There are literally hundreds of ailments that could potentially keep us from going on this trip, but unfortunately, Willow has managed to figure me out over the few months she has known me.

"I hope you're ready for tomorrow!" she says brightly as we unstack chairs. "I don't care what deathly syndrome you suddenly contract, you're not getting out of it."

I open my mouth to protest, but she continues. "In fact, if you die, I will personally carry your deceased body and put it in the car with us." When I blink at her, she covers her mouth with her hand, surprised at her own words. "That took a dark turn."

"I just don't think it's a good idea."

She places her hands on her hips and looks me up and down. "Is there something you're not telling me?"

I avert my gaze. "What? No."

"Okay, so then what's the big deal about going away for *one night* with our boyfriends?" Her eyes widen, and she lowers her voice. "Are you guys, like, saving yourselves or something?"

"No! Oh my God," I say, my face burning. Unbidden, memories of kissing Luke's jaw, touching his chest, straddling him flash through my mind.

"Well, I don't know these things! And I wouldn't judge even if you were. More power to you. But it's literally the only thing I can think of that explains the way you're behaving."

"I'm not behaving any way," I insist.

"So let's just do it, okay? It will be so much fun."

She's still singing the same tune when Brett's Jeep pulls up in front of my house on Saturday morning. It's an insanely hot day, so I'm dressed in a pink tank top and a pair of shorts.

Brett jumps out and helps me stuff my things in the back, and then I climb in and face Luke, who is wearing the most amused expression on his face. Honestly, I kind of want to slap it.

"Morning," he says. His lips are almost brushing mine before I remember our audience. The audience we're not going to be able to shake for the next twenty-four hours. Freaking hell.

His lips linger on mine even a moment after the kiss is over, our faces pressed together, eyes evaluating each other. When Willow clears her throat, I jerk my head back.

"Okay, so as y'all know, this trip is for my vlog, so I'm going to be recording most of it," she says. "I know being on camera is not Jessi's favorite thing, but this is a special occasion. Are you guys willing to be in the video, or do I have to, like, spend forever editing out everything that has you in it and look like a friendless jerk?"

"Hey, I'll be in it," Brett says.

"My viewers already know you," Willow says, patting his knee. "I'm talking *other* friends."

Luke looks at me. "I'm in if you are."

Sure, make me look like the bad guy.

"Yeah, I'm not really comfortable being in it," I say.

Willow sighs.

"Why not?" Brett asks.

"All my fans are super nice," Willow says. "Not like those internet trolls you always see in the comments section."

"That's not it," I say.

"So what's the problem?" Willow asks.

I glare at her to convey that I do not appreciate them ganging up on me, but she blinks cluelessly at me. There's this vulnerability that comes with being on the other side of a camera. It feels like, through a lens, people get to see much more than they ordinarily can. More than *I* want them to see.

"I'm camera shy," I say.

"Bullshit," Luke says. Everybody turns to look him, and he shrugs. "I'm sorry, but bullshit."

"I'm *shy* shy," I say, making him the sole focus of my glaring now.

"Bullshit," he says again, looking me right in the eye.

"I'm in the witness protection program."

One corner of his lips twitches up in a smile. "Bull. Shit."

"Please, Jessi?" Willow says now. "Honestly, I'll edit you out as much as possible, but it's just much less work if I'm *allowed* to feature you a little bit."

Everyone is silent for a minute, watching me, and it's completely unfair the way all this is going. I know they're thinking I'm the most uptight person on the planet, and maybe I am, but . . .

"Fine," I say at last. "Literally as little of me as possible."

"Yay!" Willow squeals, and claps her hands together. Within seconds she's dug out her camera and is recording. Thankfully, Luke is the one directly behind her, not me.

"Hi, Lo Downers, it's me, Willow. So, thanks to you guys, I'm doing something I've never done before. I'm going camping!

"But I'm not going alone. I'm taking my friends . . . Luke." She swings the camera around to face him, and he gives it a dazzling smile. I'm shaking my head frantically at Willow — she never said anything about introductions — when she points the camera at me. I immediately stiffen and shoot the camera a helpless look. Completely charming.

Not.

"Jessi, say hi!" Willow says.

I give the camera a lame wave, and then, mercifully, she's turning it on Brett. "And you guys all know my hunny, Brett. Babe, say hi."

"Sup," Brett says, throwing up a peace sign. "Are we ready?"

"I think we are!" Willow says, and then Brett starts the car and pulls away from the curb.

NOW

I can't get comfortable, I can't relax when Willow's camera is rolling. She holds it up intermittently throughout our drive, vlogging on and off for the nearly four hours it takes us to reach the camping site. Luke and I sit in opposite corners of the back seat, but the space still feels small and claustrophobic. I spent so much time with Rowan growing up that I must have become desensitized to just how much space a Cohen boy takes up. Luke's legs are long, and even in the spacious back of Brett's Jeep, he manages to look cramped. I've obviously driven in his car several times since we started this whole dating ruse, but it's different being up front, with the center console between us. Back here, he is too easy to touch, and the air smells minty and clean, his patented smell.

When the car starts moving, Luke pulls out a paperback and begins to read. I'm glad, because I was worried we'd have to talk and act all loved up for the entire ride. I stare out the window at the landscape, the world of trees and asphalt whizzing by. After a while I'm lulled to sleep by the hum of the car's engine and the hypnotic scenery.

When I wake up, Brett has steered us off the road and onto a beaten path through the woods. We drive for a couple of miles before he stops at some indiscriminate location under a bunch of pine trees. How it differs from the other clusters of pine trees we passed, I'll never know.

"We're here!" Willow says excitedly, holding the camera at arm's length. We all climb out of the car, and she walks around, filming. "Look at these woods. They're so . . . natural. Very tall."

Brett snorts as Willow, having run out of descriptors for the outside world, turns back to human subjects.

"What did you guys do in the back the whole way?"

The camera pans between me and Luke before landing squarely on me. I wither under its gaze as it occurs to me that there's a good chance my nap has made me a disheveled, drooling mess. I'm going to kill Willow when she turns that thing off, but in the meantime, I scramble for something to say.

"Um . . ."

I startle as Luke's arm slides around my shoulder. "I read a little. Jess slept."

"Yep." I shoot him a grateful look, and he winks at me. I know he's just turning up the charm for the camera, but butterflies flutter hard inside my stomach.

The four of us spend the next few minutes picking a camping spot. By that I mean, Brett points out a particular section of ground and tells us it's "the one."

Naturally, Willow is still filming this, giving her viewers a play-by-play of everything as it happens.

"We have two tents that we're going to put up next to each other," she says. "Wish us luck — we have no idea what we're doing."

Brett sounds offended, saying, "Speak for yourself. My dad and I used to go camping all the time."

"But have you ever put up a tent?" Willow challenges.

"Sure," Brett says, sounding not entirely confident.

"By yourself?"

"I think so," he says.

Willow turns the camera on herself to give it a skeptical look. "Okay, Brett," she says.

As it turns out, Willow has a right to her skepticism. Brett has no idea what he's doing. It takes us three hours before we manage to get the tents upright. And surprisingly, it's Luke who saves us all in the end.

"Luke, tell us," Willow says, using a water bottle as a microphone as she pretends to interview him. "Where did you learn such mad skills?"

Luke laughs, totally at ease in front of the camera. Just the way his confidence as a teacher caught me off-guard, I'm surprised by how comfortable he is playing for Willow's audience. *Maybe he's just a good actor.*

The thought stabs me in the gut because it explains why it's been so easy for him to pretend to be with me these past few weeks. It's not because there's still some part of him that loves me . . . he's just good at pretending.

"I guess my dad . . . we went camping a few times when I was a kid. Must have picked up more from him than I thought." He says it jovially, like he's still acting, but he catches my eye at the last second. I'm sitting on a log close by, the sun beating down on my neck and shoulders, and I stare back at him. Only someone who knows him knows how Luke feels about his dad, knows how little he wants to have picked up from him.

It's as if, by finding my gaze, he's telling me something. As if he's acknowledging that he can't hide the whole truth from me. As if he's acknowledging that he doesn't really want to.

I glance away. It's entirely possible that I'm reading way too much into one look.

"So now that the tents are set up," Willow tells the camera, "we're going to go and explore for a bit. There's supposed to be a river not far off."

Brett sticks his head into the frame, saying, "I want to go for a swim."

Willow shakes her head, like he's crazy. "Is it safe to enter random bodies of water? Let us know in the comments."

"Hopefully we're still alive to read them," Brett says, then laughs at his own joke.

"Actually," Willow says, turning to Luke again, "Luke's helpful for a lot of things. He's also our science guy! Luke, is it safe to enter random bodies of water?"

Willow's camera follows Luke as he walks over to where I'm sitting and surprises me by pulling me up to my feet. "Depends on a lot of factors," he says, threading his fingers through mine. Again, I know it is just for show, but my traitorous heart gallops in my chest.

"My hands are all sweaty," I say, breaking contact with him to wipe my hands on my shorts. It's just an excuse to get myself under control, to remind my fingers that they are not all nerve endings made to react to one boy's touch. But I'm kind of hoping I've grossed him out enough that he will give up completely on holding hands.

He surprises me yet again by immediately taking my hand and entangling it in his.

My emotions are waging war inside me.

I know he's feeling confident in the entire act he has going on, but he doesn't have to be over-the-top affectionate. We could be one of those couples who aren't into PDA. Is he intentionally trying to remind me what I used to have, what I can never have again? Or is it possible that he's . . . not acting. That he's actually getting swept up in all this, that he still likes the feel of my hand in his as much as I like the feel of his in mine.

I stare at his profile as the four of us start to walk, but his face gives me no answers.

So I do something incredibly stupid. I decide to go with it, to imagine just for today that Luke really is my boyfriend. That I love him and he loves me. The first part isn't at all hard to do, but I pretend the second part is true too.

As we walk hand in hand, I let my body relax, let my hips settle close to his as the four of us go exploring through the woods. It feels a little like a dream, being this close to Luke again. I feel happy and peaceful, even though our hands are sticky with sweat and there's moisture on every inch of my skin.

"We *would* choose the hottest day of the year to come camping," I tell Luke. We're hanging back as Willow and Brett lead the way, taking footage of our walk and surroundings and the web of trees that form our sky.

"As I'm sure you'll be reminding me from now until eternity," Luke says in a low voice that makes tingles spread throughout my body, and I can hear the sound of a smile in his words. "Only some of us *chose* to be here."

As I'm sure you'll be reminding me from now until eternity.

The word *eternity* echoes through my mind, and God, I wish we had that long. If not the me and Luke from last summer, then at least the me and Luke of right this moment. This moment where we're pretending our mistakes didn't happen, that nothing is broken between us.

"At least you're acknowledging that you dragged me here," I say, playing along.

"I could never make you do anything. That was more my problem."

I frown up at him, and we stop walking for a second. "What's that supposed to mean?"

"I don't know. I guess they call it being whipped. I would have done anything for you," he says, so close his lips brush my ear.

When he says those words, I actually hate myself. For having that—a place to belong, the thing I most wanted in the world—and losing it. For having *him* and losing him.

"Lovebirds, you're falling behind!" Willow says, the camera trained toward us again, and we jump apart like we've been caught doing something bad. Behind the camera, Willow grins mischievously at me, but I ignore her.

Luke and I hurry to catch up, and we've just reached them when a loud wail cuts through the air.

"What the heck?" Willow says, looking at the rest of us frantically. "Is that a coyote?"

"Nah, babe. It's some kind of bird," Brett says, but Willow looks to Luke for confirmation.

"He's right. Sounds like a bird of some kind."

Willow resumes walking but gives the rest of us a stern look. "I swear to God, if I get mauled by a coyote, I will come back and haunt whichever of y'all survive."

The three of us burst out laughing.

"Wills, has anyone told you that you have kind of a dark side?" I ask.

"Right?" Brett exclaims. "Thank you, Jessi! I tell her that all the time. She looks so sweet and innocent . . ."

Willow makes him change course with just a glance.

"Which—er—she is," Brett finishes, making Luke and me laugh.

All in all, it's a pretty perfect day. We find the river, and Brett is the only one brave enough to wade into it. We keep hiking through the trees and get lost on the way back to our tents, but none of us is really worried. Luke and I act light and happy and in love. I even start to get used to Willow's camera. I decide the best approach is to act silly on film. That feels safer, more likable than broken and tired and sad.

So every time Willow's third eye pans to me, I ham it up. I do a little jig with Brett when we realize we're headed in the right direction back to the tents. When Willow tells me to do something interesting, I play peekaboo with the camera behind some trees, then spin around under the canopy of leaves with my arms outstretched and my face pointing skyward.

And soon I actually start to *feel* like I'm the girl I'm pretending to be. I start to feel happy and free, like a whole other Jessi. The entire time, Luke watches me with this small amused smile on his face, and it occurs to me that we never really had a chance to hang out with friends when we were together, because he was away at college. Maybe, with other people around, people other than his family, I'm different from what he thought I was. Or maybe, just for a minute, he sees the Jessi I'm trying to be. Someone other than the girl who destroyed his family, who ruined his life, who broke his heart.

15

NOW

So it turns out the alternate spelling of my name is h-y-p-o-c-r-i-t-e. I'm constantly telling Ernie to go outside and breathe in the fresh air, and I rarely do it myself.

I'd forgotten what it felt like to genuinely smile. To not spend each moment at attention, waiting for the universe to inflict every big blow I deserve. Which isn't to say that I've stopped deserving it. But for the first time in nearly a year, my life isn't a series of Befores and Afters, of Thens and Nows. It's just now. This moment with Willow and Brett and Luke. Sure, a lot of it is a façade.

Willow and Brett don't know the truth about me. And Luke, who does, secretly hates me for it.

Brett and I have just gotten a fire going while Willow and Luke went back to the car to get our food for the night.

"Nice fire," Luke tells us. "Should keep those grizzlies away."

"Are there seriously grizzlies?" Willow asks with a modicum of panic in her voice. For the first time today, her camera is not in sight.

I swat Luke's arm. "He thinks he's being funny."

"Well, if there're coyotes," he says, "there could be grizzlies. There could pretty much be anything out here. Loch Ness monsters. Dinosaurs. Mammoths."

243

Willow shoots Brett a worried look, saying, "I literally told you to pick the safest place for this trip."

"Willow, he's joking," I say, putting an arm around her shoulder.

Luke looks contrite. "Sorry. Jessi's right. I'm an idiot."

Willow whacks Luke's shoulder and sits down in front of the fire.

We eat a sautéed dinner that Willow found out how to make on the internet. She's brought precooked sausage, peppers, and onions dipped in olive oil and wrapped in foil. We heat it in the foil over the fire and then eat.

Dessert is roasted marshmallows.

"I feel like we should take turns around the fire and tell secrets," Willow says.

Brett groans. "Really?"

"I'll start," Willow says. "I still really miss Texas, but I'm kind of starting to like it here. Not *here* here," she amends. "But like, Winchester here. You know what I mean. Too bad we're all leaving in a few weeks. Most of us, anyway."

Luke follows her pointed gaze to me, but he doesn't say anything.

When no one jumps in to share any secrets, Willow continues, "Also I like who I am now way more than I used to."

"You were always gorgeous, babe," Brett says. "I've seen photos from when you were little."

"Oh, well I *have* always been decent-looking," Willow admits.

"Gorgeous," Brett and I say at the same time.

"Fine," she says with a grin. "Your words. But I was also such a huge mess. I hated my body, my hair, my face."

"That's ridiculous," Brett says.

"I used to look in the mirror and I'd see a beast," she says. "But then my aunt died in this plane crash, and it just basically woke me up. It sounds cliché, but I realized that none of the stuff I hated about myself mattered, like in the grand scheme of things. And yeah, makeup, cute clothes, that stuff is nice, and some days it makes me feel better, but it's not what helped me. What helped was realizing that I'm honestly not even interested in being perfect-looking, if that's the entire point of me. I can be beautiful *and*—" She smiles. "I still hate my troll feet, but the rest of me is okay."

"You're amazing," I say, giving Willow a side hug. She hugs me back.

When Willow first told me she'd undergone a glow-up, I thought it was all about new clothes and some expensive makeover. I wish I could come near the vicinity of being okay with myself. I wish it even felt like a possibility.

We are silent for a moment, and then Luke surprises us by speaking next. Maybe he surprises himself most of all. "My mom's sick," he said. "And I'm a fucking coward who ran away so I wouldn't have to watch her die."

He stares into the fire as he speaks. Luke is beside me, and I know Willow and Brett expect me to put my arms around him and comfort him, like a good girlfriend. But I can't pretend right now. He's forcing himself to tell the truth. The least I can do is let him, without draping myself all over him and making him pretend to want or need my comfort.

Willow reaches across me, though, and rubs his knee. "God, I'm sorry, Luke. That really sucks."

"Yeah, man. I can't imagine," Brett says.

I'm the only one who says nothing, not sure whether it's the smoke from the fire or my tears that are making the world blur.

"Well, my truth just makes me sound like a douche now," Brett says. "I was going to say that I'm concerned about not getting a soccer scholarship for school or some shit. I'm sorry. I haven't had anybody die."

It's kind of dark, but it breaks the somber mood, and we all laugh.

I wrack my brain for something to say, something that doesn't make me feel exposed. "I guess I've never told anyone that I know the words to every song on the country station."

Bullshit.

I hear the words in Luke's voice.

The silence following my "admission" is excruciatingly loud, and I feel Luke's eyes on the side of my face.

"Well, we should probably all go to bed," Willow says. "So, should we sleep in our pairs, or do we do girls together, boys together?"

She shoots me what I'm sure she believes is a subtle look, still not convinced that Luke and I aren't "saving ourselves."

"Pairs," Luke says, standing and dusting off his shorts.

Brett starts putting out the fire.

"Alrighty then," Willow says, shooting me another nonsubtle look. I flush. "Y'all have a good night."

She pulls me into a long hug before she follows Brett into one of the tents. "I'm so glad you came."

For some reason, the gentleness in her voice makes me want to cry. "I'm glad I came, too," I admit.

Luke heads into the other tent, bending to fit in, and I follow

246

after him. My body feels warm at the thought of spending the night in such close proximity with him. Why did he say we should sleep in pairs? He clearly thought it would help us keep up appearances. But maybe I'm the idiot for denying Willow's celibacy theory.

It is still so hot out that Luke lies on top of his sleeping bag instead of going into it. He doesn't bother getting changed, so I figure I shouldn't either. I have a cotton tank top and sleep shorts that would be more breathable than my denim shorts, but no way am I stripping off in front of him if he's not doing the same.

I putter around aimlessly for a while, zipping and unzipping my backpack, checking my cell phone even though we all lost service a good hour before we reached our camping spot. If there truly were grizzlies or coyotes out here, we would totally be done for.

When I can't invent any more reasons to not do so, I lie on my sleeping bag, overly aware of Luke's body just a few inches from my own. We're both on our backs, staring up at the dark canvas, and by the sound of his breath, I know he's not sleeping.

My mind goes back to the fire just now and the things he said. I know he didn't say those things for my benefit, and he sure as hell doesn't want me to comment on it, but I can't help it. I have to.

"You didn't run away," I say, and my voice comes out hoarse and quiet.

So much time passes that I don't expect him to respond, but he does.

"I did," he says simply.

"Mel asked you to go. You did it for her."

"Maybe that's what I told myself." His voice is as soft as mine. "It let me sleep at night. But you think I wasn't relieved to be out of there? For my biggest worry to be making it to a lecture on time or my roommate snoring too loudly or hooking up with girls?"

My heart stops.

Luke clears his throat. "After you."

I believe him that it was only after, but I can't decide why he said it at all. Is he trying to hurt me or just tell me the truth? Is he *always* trying to hurt me?

"You're an asshole," I say, my voice still a whisper. He doesn't apologize or take it back or defend himself.

"You're not going to State in September?" he asks now.

"Not this year."

"Why not?"

Because my life doesn't get to start yet. Because I haven't figured out a way to escape being me. "Not sure what I want to do," I say.

I don't want to talk about this, and I'm more confused than ever about what Luke meant about running away, so I go back to that.

"If you ran away, you wouldn't have come home so often. You wouldn't even be home now."

"Assholes still have consciences," he says. "When Ro . . . After he . . ."

He can't say the word, and I swallow.

"After Ro, I stayed home till January," Luke says. "Mom was getting sicker and sicker, and I knew I shouldn't go back, but I did. Made up some bullshit about not wanting to lose my scholarship. It was just too fucking miserable in that house."

"That's not your fault."

Luke sounds a little bit angry when he speaks next. "Why are you so set on making excuses for me? You're so obsessed with thinking the best about the three of us. Me and Mom and Ro."

I flinch at his words.

Then he adds, "That's one of the things I loved about you."

Love.

We never used that word when we were together, but it was always there, this warm, bubbling lava underneath everything else.

And he said *loved,* because this isn't October anymore. And there were girls after me. And the only way he can make himself pretend to like me is by pretending to love me.

"When the semester finished, I signed up for more classes to make up for the courses I didn't finish first term. Instead of coming home in May, I dragged it out to the end of June. When I was literally out of excuses, when she could barely stand anymore, that's when I came back."

His voice is thick with anger and self-loathing.

"I didn't go to see her at all," I say now.

"She's not your mother." The words should sting, but they only sound like the echo of Rowan's words to me a year ago.

"She's still one of the most important people to me," I say.

"You thought she knew," he says, and we both know what he means. *She should know,* a voice in my head says.

"I should still have gone," I say. "I should have let her hate me as much as she wanted."

Luke turns so he's on his side, facing me. "Tell me about the guy you're always sneaking off to see."

I nearly choke on my own saliva. "What?"

I can hear the smile in Luke's voice. "Willow told me when we went to get the stuff from the car that you're in love with this old guy."

"Ernie?" I half laugh, half cough.

"He even has a cool name."

I roll my eyes in the dark, but I'm smiling too. "He's the best. He's hilarious and cranky and mischievous. Totally old people goals. You'd love him."

When Luke shifts closer, I realize I've been whispering and he's probably having trouble hearing me. Except now he's whispering too. "Like you do?"

"Are you seriously jealous of an eighty-seven-year-old?"

"Depends if you're in love with him. Old habits die hard, I guess."

I know he's only teasing, but a tingle of pleasure runs through me. Maybe there's a part of him that doesn't completely hate me.

Feeling brave, I take a chance and shift closer to him. Our heads are so close now, they're almost touching. I can just make out his eyes in the dark.

"If I was in love with him, I don't see how it would be any of your business. I'm allowed to fuck whoever I want, right?"

It's out without my permission.

Luke doesn't say anything, and the word diarrhea just keeps coming: "Just like you and *Court?*"

"What does she have to do with anything?" he asks.

"You tell me."

"She's a friend," he says. "From school."

"Sounds lovely."

"Why do you hate all my lab partners?" he asks. "First, Meredith. Now Courtney."

Wonderful. Her parents bothered to give her a full first name, unlike mine.

But what I say is, "I never told you I hated Meredith."

"But you got all stiff and pouty the day we talked about her."

"I never got pouty," I say, indignant. "I can't believe you even remember that."

I can't believe that any of what we were before still registers in his mind. The us of now is a pile of ashes, burnt remains so unrecognizable it's hard to say what either of us used to be.

Luke shifts his face forward until his lips rest against mine. "I remember everything," he says, and it reminds me of earlier today, when he said he'd have done anything for me. I shut my eyes and wait for him to kiss me, but he doesn't. His lips just stay against mine, not moving.

What does he want?

And then I remember something: I started this.

When Mel said she wanted to be happy and grateful and well-dressed and brave, I adopted her mantra. I stopped letting every second pass me by, and I took the first step and kissed Luke.

But that was last year.

What do I want now?

Before I know it, my body answers for me and I'm climbing on top of Luke in the dark of our tent. Our kisses are frantic and breathless, searching and desperate. Our hands are trying to do too much at once. Luke's hand is in my hair and under my shirt and on the curve of my butt. I lose my hand in his curls, in a fistful of his shirt, then under his shirt.

"What? What do you want?" he asks, stilling my restless hands as if his own are any better. My lips are too busy to respond, so I answer by tugging on his shirt. He tears away from me for a second to lift it over his head. My fingers map the terrain of his chest, his abs, his bellybutton.

He makes a sound in the back of his throat when I bite his bottom lip.

Luke's hands search until they find the button of my shorts. He works it open and slips one finger under the waistband of my underwear.

A bloodcurdling scream makes us freeze. We are still pressed against each other, hearts beating wildly, fingers caught in awkward places, when we hear Willow's voice.

"BRETT, WHY WOULD YOU DO THAT?"

"Shh," Brett says. "I'm sorry. I didn't know you'd freak!"

"I thought you were a freaking bear!"

We hear a hand making hard contact with flesh.

"You're such a jerk."

"Sorry, babe."

"We probably woke them up. Sorry, guys, if you're awake," Willow says. "Brett is just an idiot."

Luke and I find each other's eyes in the dark.

For a moment, outside the cloudy frenzy and the want, we are who we are again. Two broken, angry, tired souls whose love destroyed more than it fixed.

What do I want now?

I want to be more than a mistake, I want to be better, I want to love someone I haven't already lost.

Without a word, I roll off his body, bring my knees up to my chest, and turn so that my back is to him.

It takes ages before I fall asleep.

When I wake up, Luke's body is curved around mine, his front around my back.

NOW

The ride home is quiet and feels much longer than the ride to the camping site. Willow records on and off as we drive. I listen to music with my earphones in, and Luke buries his head in a book again. We are having trouble making eye contact this morning, but for once, it's not because of what I've done. It's what *we* did, or almost did.

When Brett pulls up in front of my house, Luke gives me a demure kiss on the corner of my lips. It's almost . . . shy.

"See you guys on Monday," I call to Willow and Brett. I feel Luke's gaze on me as I walk up my driveway, but I don't look back.

Inside, my parents are settled in front of the TV on our new sofa set.

"How was it?" Mom asks.

"Good."

"How far up north were you?"

I'm really not feeling like discussing the specifics of the trip, but they seem genuinely curious. It's new for me to get to debrief with my parents after any kind of outing or novel experience, and, I don't know, it makes me feel like a little kid—eager to tell my parents

about my field trip, what we saw and what we did and how I'm dif
ferent because of it. So I sit down on the couch and talk for a few
minutes, telling them about where we hiked and the trouble we had
with the tents and how crazy hot it was. I obviously leave out the part
about jumping Luke's bones last night, even though it's the part most
fresh in my mind. When I stand to head upstairs, Mom stands, too,
and throws her arms around me.

"I'm glad you're back. The house is lonely without you," she says.

It's lonely without *you,* I almost say, but decide to hug her back
and breathe in her flowery perfume.

"Oh, I almost forgot!" Mom says when we break apart. "Did you
ask Luke about dinner?"

Shit.

"Not yet."

"If you don't want him to spend time with us, you can just be
honest with me," Mom says, her voice drenched in hurt.

"No, I'm sorry," I say quickly. "I just keep forgetting to ask. I'll
ask him now."

I take my stuff upstairs, flop onto my bed, and close my eyes,
trying to regroup. I replay all of yesterday in my mind. The hand-
holding, the easiness, the truce. Then last night, wanting so badly to
lose myself in Luke but knowing it would only be temporary. That,
come morning, I would still be the person who destroyed everything
and he would still be yet another person I had driven away.

The next time I open my eyes, my room is dark and shadowy.
In a panic, I run through all the things I might have missed, things I
might be late for.

School? Nope.

Volunteering at the club? No. Willow sorted that out with her dad.

Work with Ernie? No. I'm seeing him four days this coming week to make up for not visiting him yesterday.

Camp MORE? No. Not a weekday.

I cycle through the panic once more to be certain I'm not forgetting anything, and finally I start to breathe again. Is it possible I literally have nothing to do for the rest of the day?

There was a time, even past the first few weeks of summer, when it didn't feel like I was doing enough. When I still had too much time to wrestle with my thoughts and memories, my Befores and Afters. Sundays, the least busy days on my calendar, used to be lessons in torture. But today, for once, I'm happy to break with routine, to not have anything pressing on my back.

Well, except for the dinner thing I promised Mom I'd ask Luke about.

I stand and stretch, turn on the lights in my dark room, and grab my phone so I can text him.

I'm shocked that it's not even that late — only eight p.m.

I'm even more shocked to see that I have not one, but three texts from Luke.

I feel a well of anxiety as my thumb hovers over the phone. What if something happened to Mel while we were gone? What if she's in the hospital again — or worse?

We should never have gone on that trip.

For so many reasons, but especially this.

My hands clammy with sweat, I force myself to open the first message.

At three, probably only an hour after they dropped me off at home, he wrote: **Hey.**

That's it. Hey.

Then, thirty minutes later, another text.

Come over?

And only about ten minutes ago, he added, **Mom wants to see you.**

Is she ok? I write back.

He answers almost immediately. **Hey. Yeah, she's fine.**

Then a second later: **Are you?**

I settle back on my bed. **Yeah, I'm good. Why?**

Didn't hear from you.

Just fell asleep, I write.

Okay, he texts back.

So Mel wants me to come over?

Only if you want to.

I'm not entirely sure I want to see Luke again today, so soon after our camping trip, but how can I say no to Mel?

I hop in the shower, wash my hair, and break out one of the summery dresses I haven't had much time to wear. I hear Mom humming in my parents' bedroom. I stick my head in the doorway and tell her I'm popping over to the Cohen house.

"I thought you'd have a quiet night at home for a change," she says.

"I'm just going to see—"

"Melanie. I know," she says, looking up from the magazine she's reading in bed. Everything from the mattress to the bed frame has been replaced in the past couple of weeks. "But you just got home.

You've worked all week, and you're over there so much to begin with. I thought we were past you spending every waking minute in that house."

My head spins in confusion. "Mel wants to see me."

"I think she understands your having a life that includes more than just her."

I stare at my mother, trying to figure out what's going on. There's a strange bitterness in her voice, like I'm doing something wrong by spending all this time with Mel.

"I'll be back soon," I assure her, and shut the door before she can offer any more resistance.

The whole way I'm driving to Mel and Luke's, I can't get the weirdness of my mother's reaction out of my mind. Mel is dying. Mom knows this; she knows I didn't see Mel at all after Ro died, and she knows how guilty that makes me feel. She should get why spending time with Mel is a priority for me.

As a kid, one of my favorite things to do was imagine that Mel was my mother. I imagined having her flowing black hair, her raspy voice, her double-jointed elbows. This was something I told no one, but now, for the first time, I wonder if my mother knew. I wonder if some days, in the dark of her room, she was thinking about the secrets I'd told Mel, thinking that it was Mel's phone voice I imitated, Mel's clothes I played dress-up in, the sight of Mel's tears and not her own that could make me dissolve into a puddle.

The thought of this — the possibility that my closeness with Mel might bother my mother — floors me. For most of my life, it felt like she hardly even noticed it.

"What's wrong?" is the first thing Luke says when he opens the door for me.

I shake my head, trying to snap out of my daze. "Just something with my mom."

One of his brows skirts up. "Another bad spell?"

"Not exactly," I say, but don't elaborate. I slide past him into the foyer and then go into the living room.

"Hey, Mel! Sorry I didn't come sooner. I wiped out after our trip."

Mel gives me a puzzled look. "Come sooner?"

"Yeah, you wanted to see me?" I throw Luke a worried look, but his face is impassive. Is Mel starting to lose her memory?

"You said Jessi knows how to make your red velvet cupcakes, remember?" he says.

"Hmm . . . but that was days ago," Mel says. "Or maybe I'm losing track of time. It all kind of blends together after a while."

"That's okay," I say. I glance at Luke again, but he doesn't seem worried, so I try not to be either. "You want me to whip up some cupcakes?"

"If you're up for it, that would be amazing. Though I have to be honest, I might take one bite and not be able to get down any more. And it won't be because of your baking."

I laugh. "You have too much confidence in me."

"No. You have too little confidence in you," she insists.

"I really have never attempted it without you, Mel," I tell her now.

"Well, if Luke brings my wheelchair out from the guest room, maybe I can come and offer you some moral support."

"I'd love that," I say.

Baking means I'm spending at least a good hour here, probably longer. I know Mom wants me back home right away, but there's finally something I can do for Mel, even though it's small, and I'm not leaving until I finish.

While I'm in the kitchen finding Mel's recipe book and pulling out ingredients, Luke wheels Mel in to a spot beside the counter.

Mel is still insisting that her presence is not needed. "I'll eat whatever you make," she says. "I'm already on death's door. What's the worst that can happen?"

"Mom," Luke sighs.

Mel motions for him to bend down in front of her. She holds his face in her palms and says, "At some point it's okay to laugh about it."

I see Luke swallow, and I can tell he's trying hard to fight tears.

He straightens and turns to me. "What do you need me to do?"

"You wanna help?" I ask, surprised.

"Of course he's going to help," Mel says. "Honestly, if I didn't think he would accidentally poison us all, I'd have gotten *him* to make the cupcakes."

Luke rolls his eyes good-naturedly and comes to stand next to me, looking expectant.

"Oh, um, okay," I say, then glance away from him as, unbidden, a memory of his hands all over my body flashes through my mind. "Do you wanna beat the butter and sugar?"

"Sure."

I'm clumsy at first, distracted, and still replaying last night in my head way too much. But before long, we fall into a rhythm of mixing and beating, then spooning batter and cleaning up.

Luke insists on washing up because he feels his contribution has been "minimal," so I plop down on the counter and talk to Mel the way I did so many times when I was growing up, the way I always wished I could with Mom. We talk about my jobs, about Sydney and the videos her new family has sent Mel. We talk movies and books and music. The only difference is that tonight Luke is listening in. I wonder what he thinks, whether he's silently judging me. Whether he feels like I'm monopolizing his time with his mother, the way Rowan seemed to sometimes.

We pull the cupcakes out of the oven, let them cool down, and get started on the frosting. Mel doesn't believe in making cake out of the box, but she's all for buying premade frosting. Luke and I stand side by side as we slather the cupcakes with an excess of vanilla cream cheese. Since neither of us is particularly gifted in the area of putting on frosting, we decide to have fun with it, trying to make patterns and write words.

"Mom, yours is gonna have your name on it," Luke tells Mel.

"What? I'm making Mel's!" I protest. "This one has been hers the whole time."

"Nope."

"Yes," I insist.

"Guys, there's enough of me to go around," Mel says.

"Let's offer both to her and see which one she wants," Luke suggests.

I hustle across the kitchen, and I've almost reached Mel when I feel myself being lifted from the ground and plopped back down a good five feet away from where I was.

"Hey!" I protest.

Luke laughs as he hurries toward Mel, who is laughing. I tug at the back of his shirt in an effort to stall him, but he outmaneuvers me and is soon holding his cupcake out to her. Scowling, I catch up and offer her my own.

"Sorry, baby, but Jessi's actually looks edible," Mel says.

"Wow, the truth comes out," Luke says. "All this time and she's still your favorite?" I'm relieved he didn't call me the chosen one.

"She didn't make me push for eleven hours."

I laugh and triumphantly present my cupcake to Mel. Luke hands her a spoon, and she takes a small bite. Now that I'm standing closer to her, I notice her pale color and the way her eyes seem weighted. She's more than exhausted, but she's putting up a brave front for us.

"You can have the rest tomorrow," I say with false brightness when it becomes apparent that she is not going to be able to swallow much more than that bite.

"Let me try Luke's," Mel says, and Luke hands her his cupcake.

"Both excellent," she says. "Almost as good as mine."

Luke laughs, and I try to be heartened by this. Maybe Mel's pallor is all in my head.

I go back to the counter to finish icing the rest of the cupcakes while Luke finishes cleaning up. When I'm done, I bite into what's left of the cupcake I gave Mel. I'm still eating when Luke joins me to eat the one he frosted.

"Good?" I ask as he takes his first bite.

"Mmhmm," he says.

"You know, you . . ." My voice trails off as he kisses the corner of my mouth, almost in the exact same spot where he kissed me this morning when they dropped me off after camping.

"You had some frosting," he says now as I try to hold on to any of my thoughts. I have no idea what I was about to say. At this point, I'm downright confused. Does he hate me or does he not? Is everything he does for the benefit of the people watching us, or is it possible there's something else?

"I think I'm going to turn in for the night," Mel says, distracting us from the staring contest we're having.

"I should get going, too," I say, because frankly I'm a little afraid to be alone with Luke right now. If last night (or the way every cell in my body jumped at his kiss just now) was any indication, I will not be able to keep my hands to myself. And we've already established that that is a bad thing.

Luke is apparently not going to make this any easier on me. "Mom, is it okay if I walk Jessi out? I'll come help you out after."

"Of course."

I walk over and kiss Mel's cheek.

"Love you, Jessi-girl," she says.

"Love you, too. Good night."

Luke and I are mostly silent as we walk to my car, my mind whirring with a hundred thoughts. In the end, they amount to this: *He loves me. He loves me not. He loves me. He loves me not.*

And then I remember my mom's constant reminders about asking him to dinner.

"What?" Luke asks. I guess my groan was audible.

"It's silly."

"So?" he says.

"So, you won't want to do it."

One of his eyebrows skirts up. "Do it? Do what?"

"Dinner with my family. My mom keeps telling me to ask you."

"Why wouldn't I want to do it?" he asks, and I seriously don't even know who I'm talking to. Luke doesn't mind having dinner at my house?

"It's more pretending," I say.

He shrugs. "Tell me when."

"Seriously?"

"Yeah. It's not a big deal."

I get the urge to throw my arms around him then, but I control myself. Maybe it's really not a big deal to him. After all, I've spent something like half my waking life in his family's presence. Surely he can spare one night to hang out with mine.

Even if we're significantly . . . less.

"Okay, cool," I say. "Thanks."

"You're welcome." He takes a step closer to me as we stand outside my car. For one second I think he's going to lean down and kiss me, but all he does is sweep a tendril of hair off my face.

"Night, Jessi."

"Good night, Luke."

16

NOW

It's Monday, the start of a new week, and things are already off to a strange start.

Willow and I are setting up for the day when Eric enters the rec room. I immediately go back to unstacking chairs, expecting him to ask Willow for whatever he needs. Instead, he stops in front of my stack of chairs.

"Do you need something?" I ask.

Behind him, Willow shoots me a look that says she has my back.

"Yeah. I actually thought we could talk," Eric says, scratching his head.

I blink at him. "You want to talk?" Is that code for something? Is this a setup?

"If you don't mind," he says, then throws Willow a look over his shoulder. "And could it be in private?"

Maybe it's the complete unexpectedness of the request, or maybe I'm just a tad curious to know what's going on, but I nod in the direction of the door, and we start toward it.

"I'm here if you need me!" Willow calls after me.

I give her a grateful smile, which gradually turns back into a frown once I'm outside the building with Eric.

"So the thing is . . ." Eric begins, his eyes darting all over the place, like he's looking for a way out. Which makes no sense, since he instigated this. "I know Ro considered you his best friend."

Not the words I'm expecting to hear.

I stiffen at the name.

"Hear me out," Eric says, sensing that my walls are up. "You were his best friend—but for me, he was mine." He looks down at the ground. "We were competitive, yeah, but in a good way. We made each other better."

"I'm glad to hear it," I say now. "Is there a point to this?"

"The point is, I always had his back. I still do, and for the longest time, I've thought that meant giving you shit for what happened."

He scuffs his shoe on the pavement. "Anyway, I'm sorry for that. It wasn't—isn't—my place. Ro wouldn't have wanted me to treat you like this."

"You don't know what Ro would have wanted—" I spit out, too late to catch myself. I hate when people speak for people who can't speak for themselves.

"I do know," Eric says without hesitation. "He'd do anything for you."

My stomach turns at those words, so similar to what Luke said to me on Saturday, and guilt is wrapping itself around my intestines like a noose. "Is this because of Luke? Is it because we're . . ."

Eric shakes his head. "I mean, kind of, but not really. I just started to wonder whether maybe what happened that night was more complicated than I thought. And really, even if it wasn't, he was still your best friend. He would kick my ass for being such a dick to you."

I force myself to keep an even expression, though my chest feels tight.

"So . . . I'm sorry," Eric says. "And that's it. That's all I wanted to say."

He looks like a weight has been lifted off his shoulders, but I feel like I'm carrying it now. It always made sense to me why Eric was so awful to me. He knew Ro better than almost anyone. He also knew more about that night than most people did. So why is he apologizing?

Everything he's thought about me for the past nine months is true. As much as it has hurt, there's almost been a tinge of relief, knowing that someone was saying what needed to be said.

"Thanks," I say belatedly. "That's . . . thanks."

He nods. "No problem."

"I better get back to work," I say, and he says something about doing the same, and then he's gone.

Back inside, Willow looks at me with expectant eyes. "Well?"

"He wanted to apologize," I say.

"That's great!"

"It's weird."

"No, it's great! It's about time. All those comments and just over some old middle-school grudge?"

"Yeah," I lie.

We don't have time to talk more about it before the first set of kids arrive. We welcome them and fall into our usual routine. At lunch, Luke sits next to me, his hand on my shoulder or back the whole time. I don't know what it says about us that it has become so easy, so natural to pretend. By day, we are Duke and J.J. By night, we're the old Luke and Jessi, but neither version of us is even close to the truth.

On Wednesday night, after spending a couple of hours after camp with Ernie, I'm in my room, rifling through my closet, trying to find something for tonight. I know it's just dinner, that it will only be my parents and Luke, who is used to seeing me sweaty, drab, and makeup-less in my Camp MORE uniform. Still, I can't get myself to not care.

It's all an act. He's only coming to keep up appearances, I tell myself over and over, but my brain is relentless. No matter how many times I tell myself to relax, I still find myself tapping my fingers on any available surface. It takes me five tries to decide on the off-the-shoulder shirt and black jeans. I paint my fingers and toenails. I'm wearing perfume, for God's sake.

"You look nice," Dad says when I enter the kitchen. He is chopping up ingredients for a salad, and Mom is pulling out garlic bread from the oven.

"Thanks," I say. "Do you need any help?"

"No. I think we've got everything," Mom says. "Just double-check that I put out enough glasses on the table."

I go to the dining room and have just finished surveying everything when the doorbell rings.

"I'll get it!" I call, and hurry for the door. Luke is standing there, one hand in his pocket, the other around a bouquet of roses. He looks good in his light blue button-down shirt and gray slacks, but his eyes keep jumping all over the place. Like he's nervous or something.

"Hey," I say, the butterflies in my stomach doing a weird dance when he finally meets my eye. "You look . . . dapper."

He raises one eyebrow. "You sound surprised."

I can hear my mom coming out from the kitchen, so I stand on my tiptoes and kiss his cheek in case we have an audience. I feel considerably less stupid for the perfume and five outfits when I catch the whiff of cologne on his neck. He must really be getting into character tonight.

"Well, you've met my parents," I say quietly, stepping back.

"Not as your boyfriend."

My heart beats faster in my chest. Nervousness turns to sadness as I think of what could have been. In another world, this could have been real. Luke and I could have been dating, and his coming over would have been a sign of Mom's progress and a reason to celebrate.

Luke steps inside and notices my bare feet. "Should I take my shoes off?"

I shake my head.

"You didn't have to get me flowers," I say, loud enough for Mom to hear as she approaches us.

"Hate to break it to you, but these are actually for your mom," Luke says, grinning. His smile gets bigger as Mom stops in the foyer and beams at him.

"Hi, Mrs. Rumfield."

"Oh, please. How many times do I have to tell you to call me Katherine?"

He hands her the rainbow roses and she draws the bouquet to her nose.

"Feels a little weird," he admits, rubbing the back of his neck. He seems less sure of what to do with himself now that the flowers are in Mom's hands.

"You're so respectful. This one is always 'Mel this', 'Mel that,'" Mom says, pointing at me.

My mouth drops open, and Luke winks at me.

"That's what she asked me to call her even when we were little," I protest. I know she's joking, but it feels like too much too soon.

If Mom had been around more during our childhood, maybe Luke would be fine calling her Katherine. The truth is, ever since her weird reaction to my going over to Mel's the other night, I haven't been quite sure what to make of anything where my mother is concerned.

Is she annoyed at me for spending so much time with the Cohens all these years? And how can she really blame me for that, when she and Dad were so absent?

"Luke. How are you, son?" Dad asks, meeting us in the dining room. Luke and Dad shake hands, and Dad immediately launches into an assault about school. Is Luke still majoring in biochem, does he want to get into a health profession, will he go to med school like his dad, etc., etc.

"Dad, he doesn't have to know that yet. He's only in his second year," I point out as I signal for Luke to sit in the chair next to mine.

"Yes, and it's important to think ahead," Dad says. "Otherwise you end up at the end of a long path and you still have no idea what you want to do." He is not so subtly referring to my college deferral.

"People don't have to figure out their whole lives right away, and Luke certainly doesn't have to," I say. For some reason I'm suddenly on edge. Maybe it's getting to me that we're playing Picture-Perfect Family tonight, acting like my parents were so concerned about my future career or *Luke's* future career prior to the arrival of Mom 2.0.

"It's okay, Jessi," Luke says, giving me a reassuring smile.

I try to tell from his face whether he really means it, but he gives me nothing. Everything that comes out of his mouth sounds sincere, and since it can't possibly be, I have no choice but to doubt everything he says.

"I think I eventually want to go to grad school, but I'm actually thinking about switching to an engineering major."

"Interesting," Dad says. "That's another good choice. Lots of job prospects."

Not that Luke owes me anything, but I wonder how I've managed to make it through countless hours by his side this summer without ever hearing about his new plan. That was something we talked about throughout the years, even before we ever dated. Luke always knew he was going to become some kind of scientist. At the start of last summer, when he was tutoring me, he told me he'd decided on bio-chem. It feels like losing something, no longer being able to follow the progression of his dreams the way I once did.

"I've heard so," Luke says now as we all sit down. "But to be honest, I feel like more and more these days you have to make your own way. It's not as simple as finding a major with good prospects. You need to be smart, willing to work hard, passionate, and brave enough to take chances, to do unexpected things."

"Amen to that," Dad says, nodding vigorously.

"Which is why I think Jessi will be just fine. She has all those things." My head snaps in Luke's direction, and he's already looking at me.

His defense of me almost sounds . . . genuine. He is completely killing it tonight. If I'm being honest, he has been killing it all along, selling our charade far better than I have.

Thank you, I say with my eyes.

He gives the slightest nod in response.

"Hmm," Dad says, far less enthusiastic about Luke's second point.

The next hour passes with more school and life talk and a whole lot of questions aimed at Luke, which he answers without flinching. I feel embarrassed and find myself thinking of all the ways I can apologize for my parents when this is over. They are so . . . not Mel. Instead of being easygoing and funny and warm, they are serious and overly earnest, trying to make cases for themselves as Good Parents, like they're trying to disprove anything contrary that I might have told Luke. And then the questions. My God. You'd think Luke was at an interview or something. But he's so good at fielding them that I start to wonder how many times he's met a girl's parents. He probably met Meredith's, since he went over to her house so many times, but who else has there been? Court? He said there were hookups in college. I wouldn't have expected those to involve any parental run-ins, but what do I know?

Luke leans over and whispers to me when my parents get up to grab dessert from the kitchen. "You look miserable."

"I am. This sucks."

He looks stricken. "Why? Am I doing something wrong?"

"What? No!" I insist. "It's . . . them. They're trying too hard, and . . ."

"They're great," Luke tells me, placing his hand on my knee and squeezing. Tingles spread all the way up my thigh, but I try to act normal.

"You're lying."

"I'm not," he says.

271

At the end of the night, when I walk him to his car, he's still sticking to his story.

"Listen, you're their only child. They want to make sure you don't end up with a deadbeat."

"They only started caring about that yesterday."

I'm surprised to hear the words leave my mouth, but before I can backtrack, Luke says, "That's what's bothering you, huh?"

"What?"

"Their . . . new interest."

I shrug. "It's nice that they care—it really is—I know lots of people have parents who suck, but it's also . . . new. I feel a bit like I'm in an alternate reality."

"I get it," Luke says, surprising me. "I'm glad they're here now, though. That counts for something."

"I know," I say, but I'm still uneasy about the whole night. It felt like all four of us, my parents especially, were acting. Like they were trying so hard to pretend the past never happened, trying to pretend things have always been this way.

Maybe that's what's bothering me—that we've never actually addressed it, this change. There was no moment when my mom sat me down and said *I'm feeling better* or *I'm sorry* or tried to explain about the past eighteen years. It feels like I'm the only one with any real memory of how things used to be.

"Well, thanks for coming and being such a good sport," I say now.

"If I'd been in Winchester when we . . . before," he says awkwardly, "I'd have come a lot sooner. I've always wanted to know your parents better."

"Well, now you know them," I say, trying to be comical.

"Maybe it would have helped solve some of the mystery."

"What mystery?" I ask, confused.

"You. You were this gorgeous, brilliant girl who just appeared in our lives one day. Out of nowhere."

I guffaw. "I was never a mystery."

"To us, you were."

Luke climbs into his car then and drives away, but I'm still going over his last words.

To us, you were.

Who is us?

Him? Mel? Rowan?

For some reason it feels like he meant Ro and him, and I wonder now if they used to talk about me when I went home at night. What they thought about me.

I always thought I was such an open book, perhaps a little too open. I wonder what Luke could possibly have wanted to know about me that he didn't.

And why didn't he just ask when we got together?

Maybe he didn't have enough time.

Or maybe, as perfect as everything seemed to me at the time, there were still some parts of me that he was afraid to know.

17

When Willow and Brett ask me to come to the staff party on Friday night, my answer is "absolutely not." For one thing, it's at the lake. For another, it's a party.

"Oh, come on," Willow pleads. "The one at Bailey's house only sucked because of Eric, and Eric is a changed man now. You said it yourself."

"I don't believe I used those words."

"Close enough."

"I hate the lake," I tell them, glad that Luke isn't at our lunch table yet. The last thing I want is for him to hear this discussion.

"You don't have to swim in it," Brett says.

"It's still . . . the lake."

"Don't be a spoilsport," Willow says. "Everybody is going. Everyone except you."

"Luke isn't," I say.

"Do you and Luke *talk?*" Willow asks. "Because he said he would."

I blink at her, unable to believe my ears. "He said he would? Does he know which lake it is?"

Willow looks to Brett, who looks at me like I'm the dumbest person on the planet.

"On account of how it's the only lake in Winchester . . . yeah," he says.

"Oh."

"Ask him yourself," Willow says as someone slides into the chair beside me. When I look up at him but don't say anything, Willow asks, "Luke, did you say you'd go to the party tonight?"

"Yeah, why not?" he says.

Why not?

It's the place where everything fell apart, that's why not. But as I stare at him, he shrugs and goes on as if that place holds absolutely no meaning in his life. As he reaches for the ketchup across the table, he whispers to me, "It's just a place."

Except it's not just a place. It's *the* place.

Does it mean that little to him?

Did *us* mean that little to him?

"So, you're scared of the lake?" Brett asks, still confused.

"I guess," I say, not willing to go into detail.

"I'll protect you!" Willow promises, giving me a side hug.

"Be brave," Brett says. "If you don't go, you're giving it power over you. Plus, if you hate it, you can always leave."

Be brave.

The words catapult me back in time to the night I kissed Luke.

The night I made a commitment to myself to be happy and grateful and well-dressed and brave.

It was the beginning of the end of everything.

But it was also the beginning of everything.

That things turned shitty a few months later didn't negate the fact that I loved those words, that I wanted to live by them.

"I'll come for an hour," I say.

"Yay!" Willow says. "I was thinking of live streaming it. And since you were in the camping video, you can be in this one too!"

I give her a look.

"Or not," she says.

So just like that, I'm doing it. I'm going back to the place where everything changed.

Luke looks so completely unbothered that I feel a swell of rage at him, and that fuels my determination to go and show him how equally unbothered I am. Because that's what everything is between us, isn't it? A game. A farce.

On Friday night, Willow comes over to my house to get ready. She picks out a denim miniskirt for me and a flowy, thin-strapped polka-dotted monstrosity of a top that I never wear. It reminds me of the opened wings of a ladybug.

"Monstrosity?" she repeats, shocked. "Girl. No, this is perfect."

"It's so . . . hippie-ish."

"So? You can be hippie-ish. You can be anything for just one night."

She goes with a long maxi-dress herself and gives herself gorgeous beach curls. Then she does our makeup. By the time she's done, I look like a glamorous hippie version of myself and she looks like royalty from some sunny, exotic island. Because we live near each other and we got ready together, I drive us both to the lake. I'm also not planning on drinking, so I can be Willow's ride back.

As we pull up to the lake, there are more cars than I'd expected.

"I thought it was just for staff," I say.

"Maybe it snowballed," Willow says easily.

We park in a line of cars under some big leafy trees and make our way to the "beach" part of the lake. The music is relatively quiet, so we won't get a police visit, but people are laughing and talking and clearly having a good time. They are also decidedly not people from work, but I try not to dwell on that.

Besides, it's not the people who are the problem. It's the place. The memories it brings.

Before I can fall into a spiral, someone grabs my arm and I whirl around to find Luke, but I barely have time to say anything before his mouth is on mine. The kiss is wet and sloppy, and I step back from him.

"Are you drunk?" I say, with just a trace of hysteria in my voice.

"It's Friday!" Brett says, appearing out of nowhere, too, and putting his arms around Willow and then me. "Let the man relax a little."

So Brett is obviously also drunk.

I shrug him off and turn back to Luke, eyeing the can of beer in his hand. "How much have you had?"

Luke pushes his hand through his hair. "Didn't count," he says.

I drop my voice a little lower. "Did you drive here?"

"It's Friday. Let my man relax a little," Luke parrots.

First, what he said doesn't even make sense. Second, what the hell?

I look around, wanting to grab someone, to explain to them, but there's only one person in the world I would have grabbed if I ever found Luke drinking. And he's not here.

I try to get Willow's attention, but her camera is on and she's holding it toward her and Brett.

I want to grab them by the shirts and explain. *You don't understand. Luke doesn't drink.*

He hates the taste of beer. He doesn't like the way it makes him feel, the way it makes him lose control.

So what the hell happened before I got here?

I realize for the first time that apart from my crippling anxiety, I was kind of looking forward to tonight. Luke and I have had a string of good days, days where it didn't feel like we were hiding folds of hate under love. And now I feel all that shattering right before my eyes.

Brett is inviting Luke into the camera shot. I duck away from the three of them before I'm captured on film with people underage drinking. Not that I have any scholarships to worry about losing.

"Rumfield," someone says, giving me a nod as he walks past. Eric.

I grab his elbow. I'm that desperate.

He looks taken aback. "Whoa," he says.

I quickly let go. "Sorry. It's just . . . how long have you guys all been here? I thought it started at eight."

"A bunch of people went from work to Blueberry Diner for dinner; then they came here and started drinking, I guess," Eric says with a shrug.

"Luke?" I ask.

"I don't know," he says, following my gaze to where Luke and Brett are mugging for Willow's camera. "Kinda looks like it."

"He doesn't drink," I say now, trying not to sound like a concerned wifey or something. "I mean, usually."

"Yeah, I believe you," Eric says. "It's fine. He's just having a good time, but let's keep an eye on him, okay?"

The *let's* almost makes me cry.

It means I'm not alone in this, that I'm not crazy or overreacting. That I'm not reliving the worst night of my life.

"Okay," I say. "Yeah, let's do that."

"Want something to drink?" Eric asks. "I know where there's some unspiked punch."

"Where?" I ask.

"In my backpack. I brought my own, like a freaking kindergartener," he says, and I laugh. "I try not to overdo the booze thing too often anymore. Not this summer, anyway."

I remember the night when he humiliated me at Bailey's party. He wasn't drunk then? I don't know whether that makes it better or worse.

I glance over my shoulder to make sure Luke is still with Brett and Willow. At least Willow isn't drunk . . . yet. To my surprise, Luke is looking over here. When his attention drifts back to Willow again, I hurry to catch up with Eric.

"So what kind of punch?" I ask.

"It's made from the tears of infants and the sweat of old men."

I make a face.

"That was a joke. Meant to imply that I know you think I'm an asshole."

I give a reluctant laugh.

Eric stops under a tree and pulls out a backpack. He holds out a nearly full Gatorade bottle to me.

"*This* is your punch?"

"What, you thought I was at home mixing lemonade and shit?"

When I still don't take the bottle, he sighs. "I didn't poison it, Jessi. I'll prove it."

He opens the bottle and pours it into his mouth without letting it touch his lips.

"I think I'm good," I say.

"Come on!" he says. "It's a show of good faith between us. I'm done being a jerk, you're done believing I'm a jerk."

He pushes the bottle on me and I hold it over my mouth and drink. Someone bumps me from behind, and my next swig completely misses my open mouth and trickles down my shirt. "Shit," I say.

Eric coughs, holding his hand to his mouth to hide a laugh.

"Oh, screw you!" I say, handing him his bottle, but he's still laughing, so I start laughing too. "Now I have to walk around like this all n—"

I jump at a hand on my shoulder.

"I want you to be honest with me." It's a voice that sounds like Luke's but also so unlike it.

I turn around, and it's him, his eyes looking unfocused, a brand-new bottle in his hand.

"Hey—are you okay?" I ask, already feeling a knot of anxiety in the pit of my stomach.

"I just want one question. One simple question," he says.

His tone and the way he's looking at me are making me very uncomfortable. "Okay?"

"Did you fuck him?"

I freeze at his words, my heart plummeting to a pool at my feet. "Luke, you're drunk . . ."

"It's just a question. One question. He's always around you, and I knew something was going on. I always thought about it, but I told myself, no, she loves *you*."

"Luke—"

"—and then I see you with him."

Eric, who has been silent all this time, takes a step forward toward Luke. "Dude, it's not what you think. We were just talking."

"So — you did?" Luke completely ignores Eric as he looks at me. "That's a yes?"

I try to reach for Luke's arm, but he shrugs me off, and his voice gets louder. "It's a simple question. Did. You. Fuck. Him."

"Luke, stop it," I say, my eyes filling.

"Man, you're totally overreacting," Eric is saying. "I swear to God. We don't even talk, normally, but she was worried about you and —"

"Eric, shut the fuck up," Luke says, turning on Eric.

"Don't talk to him that way," I say. It's not Eric that he wants. He's not asking about Eric. None of this is about Eric.

Luke shoves a rough hand through his hair, and his voice is broken and swollen with alcohol and anger and tears and fear. "It's so simple. God, it's such an easy answer. But you did, you fucked my brother . . ."

"No, I didn't," I say, but my voice comes out tiny in the dark. Around us, a crowd is forming.

"I should have known," he says, his voice still threatening tears, though none are running down his cheek. Only mine. "You didn't want me. You wanted my family. Hell, maybe you didn't even want Ro, you —"

My hand on his cheek makes a terrible sound. Loud and hard, and my fingers are stinging so badly. "Fuck you," I say, and I'm surprised to hear myself speaking almost as loudly as he was.

He's staring at me with wide eyes, the imprint of my palm leaving a red mark on his face.

"Fuck you." I say it again, and then I'm pushing through the crowd, ignoring the sound of a girl calling my name. My eyes are blurring so hard I can barely find my car.

I knew it I knew it I knew it . . .

I should never have come tonight.

THEN

Luke and I had our very first fight over it. It was on Wednesday. He'd gone back on Sunday, and he was still refusing to drive down for Rowan's birthday on Friday.

"Why's it such a big deal to you if I come?" he'd asked over the phone that night.

"Are you serious?" I asked.

"Well, yeah."

"First, because I want to see you. Second, it's your brother's freaking birthday and you've never missed it before and you actually *have* the weekend off, but you're just not willing to come down. Because of some stupid ego trip you're on."

"I'm not on an ego trip."

"Could have fooled me," I said.

"You're being so unreasonable."

"No, *you* are."

In the end, he'd said something about how this was between him and Ro, and if his brother didn't care about him not being there, neither did he. I'd said fine and then I'd hung up.

The next day, Thursday, was the first day since our fro-yo date that we didn't speak once, either over the phone or even by text. I couldn't believe I was seeing this other side of Luke. He was so damn stubborn. *Insufferable* was the word, actually.

I'd spoken to Ro about it, and he'd just shrugged and said, "If Luke doesn't want to come, he doesn't have to."

I was certain he was putting on a brave face. I obviously didn't have siblings, but I knew I would care if they missed my birthday for reasons that were not totally unavoidable. I knew what it was like to have a family that was alive but not living. Here, but not present. Knew what it was like to feel like an afterthought to the people who were supposed to love you. And there were few things that sucked more.

The day of Ro's party, I'd spent the afternoon at Mel's house, where we piled the back of Ro's car with snacks, paper plates, napkins, and two foldout tables.

"There better not be any drinking," Mel warned, and Ro scoffed and acted like his mother was being ridiculous.

"I'm not an idiot," he said.

I suspected that he was bluffing and that someone (or several someones) was bound to show up with alcohol, but I would always be loyal to Rowan, so I said nothing to Mel.

At seven thirty, dressed in a pair of jeans, a nice top, and a bomber jacket, I jumped into Ro's car and waved at Mel and Naomi, who had come over for wine. Ro drove us to the lake.

It was kind of dumb to begin with. Having a party at the lake in October. It had been an unseasonably warm fall, and we didn't have to worry about snow or ice or anything yet, but it was still fall. When I pointed this out, Rowan shrugged and said he couldn't help when he was born.

When we arrived at the lake, we got to work setting up. My phone was in my jacket, which I'd thrown in a pile on the beach after realizing that Ro was right; it wasn't "that cold" yet. By eight, most of Ro's friends were starting to arrive. Cassie Clairburne greeted him with a passionate kiss, whispering something in his ear. She didn't acknowledge me as I continued setting up. For some reason, there had been this weird tension between me and Cassie since she and Ro started dating. Before they were together, we never really spoke to each other. And now that they were together . . . we never really spoke to each other. I didn't worry too much about it, though, since I suspected that their relationship had all the longevity of a juniors tennis match.

The party got underway, and music blasted out from Ro's speakers. Despite not being as cold as I'd expected, it was still October and mostly dark by six thirty.

For the first hour, I circled among different groups, chatting to people from different classes. I didn't know half as many people as Ro knew, and I certainly wouldn't consider them all "friends," but Rowan and I had never been the kind of best friends who always had to be joined at the hip. I was fine, drifting in and out of conversations, laughing with people I'd known since elementary school and people I hadn't. The whole thing was going pretty well.

Until I realized I couldn't find Rowan.

I shimmied through different clusters of people, looking for him. Thought about finding my jacket and grabbing my phone, but then I remembered that he'd asked me to put *his* phone in my second pocket while we unloaded the car. I grew more and more panicked as I searched. Especially when I saw Cassie sitting next to a lacrosse player who had his arm around her. Instead of feeling vindicated that I was probably right about her, I felt sorry for Ro and hoped he hadn't seen this.

I continued threading my way through the party, looking for Rowan. Since he certainly was not with Cassie, I knew the most likely person I'd find him with was Eric, so when I spotted Eric laughing with a group of girls I didn't know, my heart sank.

"Do you know where Ro is?" I asked him.

"No," he said. "I'm sure he's around somewhere."

Helpful, I thought. *And drunk.*

My biggest fear was that he had done something stupid and wandered into the water. He wasn't suicidal, but if there was a bad idea to be found, Rowan would find it. So I started walking, following the path around the lake until I saw a small figure several yards ahead. Just as I feared, I found him way down at the other end of the lake, his jeans rolled up as he stood in water up to the middle of his calves.

"Ro, are you insane?" I cried, running up to where he stood.

"You found me." He grinned at me like he'd won a bet with himself.

"Yeah. Because I thought, where's the stupidest possible place I could find him, and that's where I went."

I searched his face for signs that he was upset. Maybe he'd seen Cassie with that guy and decided to walk away.

But I saw no sign that he had.

He smiled at my comment and took a swig from the bottle in his hand.

"Thought you told Mel you weren't drinking."

"I didn't tell *Mel* anything," he argued.

"Okay. Well—come out. It's dark, and that water's looking freaking creepy."

He looked down at it as if noticing it for the first time.

"Why aren't you with your friends?" I asked. "Like, who throws a party and then runs away?"

"I'm not in the mood for company."

"Well, gee, could you have notified all these people before they came out?" I pointed to the other side of the lake. I was feeling increasingly annoyed that I'd spent all this time looking for him, and here he was, fine and totally unbothered about disappearing on me.

"Didn't know this would happen," he said.

I took a step closer to the water and saw his face more clearly. His eyes were unfocused, and he *was* upset. But for some reason, I didn't think it was about Cassie.

"What would happen?"

"Coach found out about my elbow."

"Oh, Ro, that sucks," I said, feeling a wave of sadness for him. Nothing upset Rowan more than not being able to play. "How?"

"I was in too much fucking pain to hit a damn ball today. That's how."

"Hopefully this will give you a chance to rest?" I ventured, trying to put a positive spin on it.

"I don't *want* to rest," he said, sounding petulant. "I want to play."

"You will play. Next season and in college and for the rest of your life."

He drank from his bottle and then appraised me, a twinkle in his eye. "Want to do something crazy with me?"

"Not really," I said.

"Come on, Jess," he said. "Please."

"What's the thing?"

"I want to get in the water."

"You *are* in the water," I pointed out.

"I want to get in properly. Like all the way."

"That's disgusting. You have no idea what's been in there or what *is* in there. And it's so dark. Ew. No way."

"I'll protect you. Nothing will happen to us," he said.

"No. Come out or I'm going to go and call Mel."

"Why are you like this?" Ro asked suddenly, glaring at me.

I glared back. "I'm not like anything."

"You're not *you*. You're not my best friend anymore."

The words caught me off-guard, and they stung. "Because I won't let you drink and go swimming in some disgusting lake in the middle of the night?"

"Because you're different," he said.

"Different than *what*, Ro?" I asked, exasperated. Were we really going to do this now? And what the hell did he mean? After all the ways *he* had changed over the past few months, he was accusing *me* of being different?

"Remember when we were kids and we'd play mixed together, and you'd call out 'mine' for every shot? And then Coach was like, 'Jessi, you have to let Rowan get the shots on his side of the court. When it's for him, say "yours."' But for like the next year, you wouldn't listen. You still called out 'mine' every single time, so I just started running for every shot, and sometimes we'd go for the same one and collide?"

Despite myself, I smiled. "Yeah, so?"

"So, you used to fight me, They called us water and oil."

"Because water and oil don't mix."

"They're just as strong as each other," Ro said. "They have an understanding."

I sighed. "If you're going to say that the understanding is that the water doesn't tell the oil's mom when the oil gets drunk, I'm not buying it."

"No," Ro said. "I'm going to say that my mom is fucking dying, I don't know where I'm going when she does, I can't play, and all I want is my best friend to get in the water and get drunk with me." He was full-on crying now. "That's all I want."

"It doesn't solve anything," I told him now, softly.

"For a minute it does," he said. "Please."

And because he was my best friend and everything was falling apart, because he said it would make things better for a minute, because we'd been drifting apart for months and it felt like maybe for one moment we could find each other again, I did what everything in my head was telling me not to.

"Turn around," I ordered.

He grinned through his tears and obeyed.

Unable to believe myself, I unzipped my jeans and climbed out of them. I discarded the tank top I was wearing and started toward the water.

Ro turned around when I was still only ankle-deep. I felt his eyes appraise my nearly naked body and I hugged my arms around my waist. I told myself I was pretty much in a bikini, underwear and a bra, but it did nothing to reduce the exposed feeling washing over me.

"It's so cold," I said, regretting this decision with every ounce of me but continuing forward. "What is even happening right now?"

"It's not that bad," he said. "You get used to it."

Rowan peeled off his shirt then and flung it toward the beach, but he missed, and it landed in the water. "Son of a——" he said, wading out to retrieve it. He kept going until he was on the beach, where he started to take off his jeans.

I looked away, my entire body suddenly feeling warm even though I was immersed in lake water up to my thighs in October.

Ro whooped now as he ran back into the lake, the bottle still in his hand. I tried not to look, but my eyes immediately went to the gray boxer briefs he was wearing. They left absolutely nothing to the imagination, and my neck went hot as I snatched my gaze away again.

"Give me that bottle," I said. "I need some liquid courage."

Smiling, Ro handed me the bottle. I grabbed it by the neck and took a long sip of something that burned the back of my throat. Together Ro and I waded deeper into the water.

"What if there's fish in here? Or flesh-eating bacteria?" I asked.

"Nah," he said. "I know a dude who swims here all the time. He's missing a few toes, but . . ."

I whacked his chest, and he laughed.

"I'm not going in any further," I said. I was about hip-high in the water now, while Ro was in up to his mid-thigh.

I took another drink, then handed the bottle to him.

"What do you want to do next year?" I asked. "Do you want to go to your dad's?"

"It doesn't matter what I want. It seems like everything I want exists just so someone else can have it. The crazy thing is I always thought you and I were different."

It felt like the alcohol was already making my mind cloudy.

"I literally have no idea what you're talking about," I said.

"Of course you don't," Rowan said in a voice that sounded strangely bitter.

"Am I supposed to?"

"I guess not. And yet you somehow manage to understand the complete lack of facial expression and the caveman grunts my brother makes."

That was definitely bitter. And completely out of line. "Don't talk about Luke that way."

"That's the thing," Ro said. "I don't *want* to talk about Luke at all. Not with you. Not after all this fucking time."

"Why are you yelling?"

"Because you don't get it!" he shouted. "And you don't get it because you don't want to."

I stayed quiet and watched as he got more and more worked up. "All these years. I'm the reason you *met* him. Me." He pointed at his chest.

"Ro —" I said, but no words followed.

"There's nothing about me you don't know. And there's nothing about you I don't know. Except that — oh wait, you're in love with my fucking brother."

"I didn't . . . I don't know everything about you," I said.

"Like what?" he spat. "Name one thing you don't know about me."

"Oh, I don't know," I said, feeling a fire start to burn inside me. "Why did you make me leave that night at your mom's?"

"I *told* you," he said.

"You said you didn't want me to see you cry. That's bullshit!" I yelled back, even though I had made my peace with the answer. It wasn't so much that I didn't believe it. But it didn't make any freaking sense. And it hurt.

Why would he ever, ever ask me to leave if I was truly family?

"Because, generally, *Jessi,*" he spat my name out like it was a bad word. "When you're in love with someone, you don't want them to see you bawling like a baby."

I opened and shut my mouth like a guppy.

I repeated the words in my head. *When you're in love with someone . . .*

"You're saying you love me?" I asked, so stunned I felt as if I had woken up in the wrong body. The wave of doubt he'd started in me about whether the Cohens really cared about me, the cloud of confusion my relationship with Ro had become—and all along it was because he *liked* me?

"I'm saying I love you," he said, looking me dead in the eye.

"But when . . . how . . . why didn't you say anything?" I stammered. "You're dating Cassie Clairburne."

"Because she'll look twice at me," he said. "Because she didn't find out everything about me and then decide I wasn't good enough."

"I did not say you weren't good enough."

"But you picked *him.*"

"It wasn't a choice, Ro! There *was* no choice." I was spitting the words out, but I didn't even care. "And quite frankly, it sounds like you only decided you liked me when I started dating Luke. Because you've always wanted what Luke has."

Ro laughed. "I've always wanted what Luke has?"

"All you ever talk about is how perfect Luke is, how your dad loves him because he's smart, how your mom loves him because he's kind. You have *always* wanted what Luke has."

He glared at me. "So what you're saying is you don't know me after all?"

"I don't know what I know," I said lamely, my voice less loud this time.

Rowan took a step toward me. "When you say there was no choice—" he said now. "Would it have changed anything if there was? If you saw a choice?"

I opened my mouth to speak, but no words came out.

Ro kept walking until he was right in front of me. "Yes or no?"

"Don't, Ro," I said, swallowing as he came even closer. "I'm with Luke."

"Tell me," he said, ignoring what I had said. "And I'll never ask you again."

"I . . . I don't kn—" I barely got the words out before he crushed his lips against mine.

Ten years.

Ten years and I had never considered—not even once—what it would be like to have Rowan's lips on mine, what it would be like for him to touch me, to want me.

Everything was different with Rowan. It wasn't as if Luke had never kissed me with passion, but with Ro, everything was passion. Everything was fire and ice. It was scalding, it was freezing. I wanted him to touch me and I wanted him to stop. I wanted his lips, his body, closer, but I wanted to be back at the other side of the lake, not knowing everything I now knew.

We were on our knees in the water, and his lips dropped to my neck and my chest. He pushed my knees apart so more of him could touch me.

And then everything stopped.

We heard voices on the beach and flew apart.

It was Eric and — somehow I knew instantly — Luke, who was staring into the water at us like we were strange, mythical creatures.

His name poured out from my mouth, the same mouth that had been kissing Ro seconds before, but he turned and started back up the path he and Eric had come down.

"Luke!" I raced out of the water and sprinted, but he wouldn't stop. I ran back to the beach for my clothes, then took off after him again, but by then all I saw were trees. Shadows and night.

Eric came up behind me then, and I screamed at him, "Where did he go?"

"He parked on the other side of the trees, and then we cut through . . ."

He was talking too slowly, and I took off running again.

"Jessi!" Ro called from somewhere behind me. "Jessi!"

His long legs soon caught up to mine. At some point he'd managed to put his jeans back on, but his shirt was still in his hands and he was dripping wet.

"Jessi, Jesus, slow down!" he said, grabbing my shoulder.

"What do you want?" I snapped at him. All I saw was red. Everything was red. I wanted to strangle him. I hated what we'd done. Hated that I'd played just as much of a part as he had.

He stared at me for one second, appraising me, as if he were figuring out something just by looking at me, figuring out everything.

"I'll go after him," he said suddenly, throwing his shirt on. "I'll tell him it was all me. I'll . . . I'll fix this."

"You can't fix this," I said, starting to cry.

"I can," he said. "I know I can. I'll take care of it."

He hesitated a moment, as if he had something to say, but I didn't want to hear it. I started walking again until Ro brushed past me and said, "I'll get my car and go after him. I'll go all the way to State if I have to."

Then he disappeared through the clearing, the details of his body so washed out by the darkness that soon he was a part of it.

I kept running through the trees until Eric caught up to me.

"He went back to his car. You can't catch him," he said, breathless, and I knew he was talking about Luke.

"Ro's driving after him. I'll go with him," I said.

"And what do you think will happen when both of you show up together? How do you think Luke's going to take that?"

"I don't care," I said.

"Just let Ro go," he said, touching my shoulder. "He knows what he's doing."

My lungs were burning, and I was still in my wet underwear, so I stopped.

I let him go.

18

NOW

I pull open the door of my car, collapse in the front seat, and cradle my head in my hands.

I knew this day would come.

I knew it I knew it I knew it

In one night, I single-handedly destroyed everything that was good in my life. Me and Rowan. Me and Luke. Worst of all, Mel's family. They were broken because of me.

Because I took and took and took.

I was seven and needed a friend, so I used Rowan. I needed a mother, so I latched on to Mel like she was the best thing that ever happened to me. It still wasn't enough, so I turned to Luke.

And I completely destroyed each and every one of their lives.

And everybody but Mel knew it.

Mel, who always saw me as better than I was.

Mel, who would never look at me again if she knew.

Love each other well, she said.

The thing I care most about is that you are safe and that nobody gets hurt, she said.

How could I tell her that I had broken every promise I made to her?

How could I tell her what I had done?

THEN

It was one a.m. and I was lying in my bed, eyes still swollen from all the tears I'd shed.

I gripped my phone like a lifeline, waiting for it to ring.

Rereading all the texts I'd missed from Luke while I was getting ready for the party with Ro.

J.J., I'm sorry for being such a dick.

I'll come tonight.

Are you mad at me?

Leaving now. So much traffic.

I'll probably get there toward the end, but better late than never, right?

I can't wait to see you.

We stopped at a very interesting place last time I was home. Can't wait to pick up where we left off. (You're in charge this time.)

Seeing his words made my heart hurt.

God, I hoped Ro was able to catch up with him. I hoped he was able to fix this.

If he couldn't, then I'd managed to destroy one of the very best things in my life.

My relationship with Luke played in my mind like a film. From the moment he'd called me beautiful at the Continental to later that night when I'd kissed him. The evening he'd shown up at my door weeks later and kissed me back. The morning we'd fallen asleep side by side in his bed.

I'd ruined everything.

I tried to squelch the voice that told me this was destined to happen, that from the start I hadn't belonged with the Cohens. Maybe there was something about me, or inside me, that did something to break the people I loved.

My parents had both been asleep when one of my friends from Spanish class dropped me off, so thankfully I hadn't had to deal with any questions about why I was crying or why my clothes were wet. Not that they would have really noticed even if they were awake, but still.

I'd had a shower and changed into my pajamas, but sleeping hadn't even occurred to me.

I couldn't sleep until I knew what was happening. If Luke and I were finished or if we still had a chance.

I knew Ro had said he'd handle it, but I couldn't stop myself from sending a couple of texts to Luke.

I'm sorry.

Please call me.

And then I'd set my phone beside me, watching it, waiting for it to ring.

When it finally did, when it vibrated on my bed, my heart nearly fell out of my chest.

It was happening. He was calling.

Except it wasn't Luke's name that appeared on my phone.

It was Mel's.

Mel.

I stared at it for a second.

Had things gotten so bad that Ro had to involve her? Was she calling to yell at me?

It was what I deserved, if she was. I braced myself for the impact her words would have on me.

Stay away from us, she might say.

I told you not to hurt him.

Look what you've done.

I took a deep breath and answered.

Mel's first words to me were "Tell me he's with you."

"What?" I said. Stupidly, my first thought was relief. Mel didn't sound angry. Maybe she didn't know —

"Tell me he's with you! Please! Just tell me he's with you!" Mel shouted into the phone. I felt confused, alarmed, as her hysteria registered for the first time.

I sat up in bed. "Mel, what are you talking about?"

"Ro. You drove together. You're always together, and now they're here and they're saying . . . they're saying . . ." Her words were barely making sense, and I heard a woman's voice in the background. Naomi's voice?

And then a male voice I couldn't place.

"Where are you?" Mel asked now. Her voice was shrill and desperate.

"I'm at home," I said, my heart starting to beat faster in my chest. Mel was never like this. Never. Not when Ro fell off his bike and broke his elbow when we were nine. Not even when Dr. Cohen admitted his affair to her. In one of our shed meetings, Ro had told me what he'd overheard that night. Mel's voice had been quiet and calm, a controlled sort of anger.

Something was very, very wrong.

"Okay, so is he with you? Is Rowan there? I tried telling them you'd be together. They're saying he cut through Freetown Road, that he was heading to the interstate. But he wouldn't be on the interstate. He's with you."

Her words were starting to sink in now. Rowan.

Not Luke, but Rowan.

Something had happened to Rowan.

Ro would have had to go on the interstate if he was going to State, if he was following Luke back to school.

My mouth was completely dry, my stomach churning.

"They said he didn't have his phone. That maybe he would have been able to call for help if he had it," she said. "But he wouldn't need to if he's with you."

I launched for my bomber jacket and checked the pockets. Both were empty.

I *had* had Ro's phone earlier tonight, but I'd lost it somewhere. Or maybe he'd taken it. Could he have gone back to the beach for it? He had to have.

Even as I thought through what Mel was saying, as I tried to rationalize and assure myself that Ro was all right, panic seared through every cell in my body and a low hum was building in my ears.

"Is he with you?" Mel asked again, desperate and frantic. "They're saying they found the Ford."

Who? I wanted to ask.

Who was *they?*

But I knew the answer without her explaining.

The police had found the Ford.

They'd found the Ford and Ro had been heading to the interstate and Mel was crying and I knew.

I knew what she wasn't saying. I knew.

"He's not with me," I choked out, and Mel let out a guttural sound I had never heard before and hoped never to hear again.

"No, not my baby!" she was shouting. "Not my baby. No."

It felt like claws digging into my chest, between my ribs, inside my lungs, hearing Mel like this. It felt like someone tearing the skin off my body, ripping it from the bone slowly. Agonizingly slowly.

Rowan.

That's all I could think.

Rowan.

"Mel!" I shouted into the phone, but she sounded far away now, like she'd dropped it and was screaming from across the room.

"No, no, no, no," she cried. She sounded like a wounded animal. She sounded . . .

No.

Not Rowan.

No. Her refrain became mine now, too.

No, no, no, no.

I held the phone to my ear, hoping someone would pick it up and say something else to me. Hoping it would be Ro, saying he'd just walked in and I'd never believe the way Mel was behaving.

I waited and waited and waited, listening to Mel wailing for so long that she stopped sounding human. She stopped sounding real.

There were voices, people consoling her. But none of them was Rowan.

By then I had started to shake, because I knew.

I knew.

He was gone.

My best friend was gone.

Because of me.

Everything was because of me.

19

NOW

I call in sick for everything I have on Saturday. I don't go to Tennis Win or go to see Ernie.

I just lie in bed, reliving everything. Reliving the way Luke looked at me that night — and last night. Reliving the way Ro had looked at me before he'd run after his brother. Reliving Mel's wails.

Reliving the funeral, the way I was sandwiched in the back between my parents, as if Rowan had been an acquaintance. The way my father rubbed my knee when I started to cry. The way Luke's gaze had caught mine, briefly, as Ro's family marched out of the church behind the body. And the way he'd looked away — as if he hadn't seen anyone he knew.

The numerous texts I sent to him:

I'm so so so sorry.

Please call me. Please just . . .

He didn't.

The next time I saw Eric, he snarled at me. "Slut," he whispered under his breath. He got louder each time he saw me, until he was walking around saying things about me to everyone we knew. I don't think he told them what he'd seen, what I'd done. In fact, most people probably figured something had happened between me and Eric.

Maybe I'd teased him and led him on, maybe I'd been with him and he'd found out I already had a boyfriend. I didn't give a damn what anyone said about me. I had worse things to say.

It's just after noon when my mom sticks her head in my door. "Is everything okay, honey?"

"It's fine."

"Okay, well, Luke's here to see you. Thought maybe that would cheer you up."

"No," I say.

"No?"

"Tell him I'm out."

"I'm not going to lie for you," Mom says sternly. She has been in full 2.0 mode the last twenty-four hours, popping into my room to check on me, trying to coax me out of bed. "If you're upset with him, tell him to his face."

"Fine," I say now, defiant. "Tell him whatever you want, but I'm not going down to see him."

"Can I send him up?"

"No."

She gives a long-suffering sigh, shuts the door, and goes down the stairs.

Sunday.

"Luke's here to see you."

"I told you . . ."

"I'm not going to lie for you, Jessi."

"Why not?"

"Because it's wrong, that's why."

"I don't care."

303

"I don't like your attitude," Mom says. "I'm bringing him in."

"No!" I jolt into a sitting position. "Please don't."

"It's your choice. You go out and speak to him, or I let him in. I don't understand why you would treat such a nice boy this way."

I press my lips together in anger but don't say anything as I crawl out of bed. Luke is not seeing the filth my room has accrued in the last twenty-four hours. I still have my dignity. Or some of it anyway, since I go down in the ratty pajamas I'm wearing. There's also the matter of my unkempt hair and the prominent hole in my right sock.

Luke is sitting in the living room, and he stands as I come down the stairs. I fold my arms across my chest.

"Hi," he says. "Should we maybe talk outside?"

When I don't answer, he leads the way. Once we're outside the front door, he pushes his hand through his hair.

"I shouldn't have . . . Friday night was . . . I'm an idiot," he says with a sigh. "I agreed to go to the lake because I thought I was ready. I thought I could do it—be back there again. But then, the closer it got to the time, I started freaking out and I ended up getting wasted."

"Anyway," he says now. "All that stuff I said . . . I'm sorry."

"Please don't lie to me," I say.

"Lie to you?" He sounds confused.

"You're not sorry. Those are things you've been wanting to say for nearly a year. Friday was the first day you were honest enough to say them."

He shakes his head. "That's not true."

"It is, Luke. I saw the way you looked at me at the funeral. I saw the way you looked at me when you first came back this summer."

"How do I look at you now?"

"Now?"

"Now," he says, taking a step toward me, and it's true. All the disgust from the start of the summer is gone. The Luke in front of me looks solemn and desperate. But why would he be anything but angry at me after everything I've done?

"At first it hurt to be near you, to even look at you," he admits. "But the last few weeks . . . I've been happier than I've been since Ro. I've been remembering all the good stuff, the happy stuff."

"So everything is just fine now?" I hiss, because I know it can't be true, and I want Luke to be honest with me, to be honest with himself.

"No, everything isn't *fine*, Jessi," he says, "but how do you explain the way it's felt to be us again?"

Us.

How do I explain the way it's felt to be us again?

The word makes my stomach flip, but all I do is shrug. "Maybe I get you off or something, so it makes it harder for you to be angry," I say.

"You *get me off*?" he repeats. "That's how you think I see you?"

"I killed your brother, Luke."

"You didn't kill . . ." He shakes his head, unable to look at me.

"I'm the reason he's dead," I say, and it's the first time I've been honest enough to say those words to anyone but myself. "I'm the reason you drove off, the reason he followed you, the reason he didn't have his phone. It's *me*, Luke. I did all this."

My voice breaks, and tears spill down my face.

He doesn't say anything. He can't even deny it.

"You didn't mean . . ." he begins, but I don't want to hear it.

"Tell me you haven't thought exactly that for the last nine months. Tell me you didn't — don't — hate me."

"I . . ." He can't get the words out.

"I'm not stupid, Luke. Maybe I don't share your genius IQ, but I'm not a fool. I know what you think of me. I know part of you bringing me back to Mel was so you could hurt me. You *want* me to watch her die. You think I deserve to, after everything I've done."

Luke just looks at me.

"Deny it," I say.

"Maybe I . . . at first, maybe that's what I wanted. But not anymore."

"Why not, Luke? I'm still the same person. I still destroyed everything. But we kissed, so everything's fine now? We both know that's not true."

"I'm not going to deny that I was angry," Luke says, his jaw tight, and I can tell that I've unleashed something in him. He's about to tell the truth. "I was, and I am. Because my younger brother is dead. He's gone, okay?"

His voice breaks and his eyes well. "When he died, we were fighting over a *girl*."

It stings the way he says it; I'm a girl. I'm any girl.

Not family, not one of their people, like Mel said a while ago.

Just a girl.

"He probably thought I hated him," Luke said. "And I did. For a minute, I really, really hated him. He took you from me. He was fucking you right under my nose."

"We never —"

"I thought you did. I see you in the water like that, what am I

306

supposed to think?" he says. "And things hadn't been bad with him for only that one night. They'd been bad for months, maybe even years, because of you.

"But then you and I happened. You kissed me, and I liked it. And you know what the worst thing is? I fucking knew it. I knew how he felt about you."

I blink at him.

No. That's not possible.

"Maybe I even knew before he did. Which is why that first night when you kissed me, I backed away. All that shit about trying to be a good guy? All a joke. I was the worst kind of person, and I knew it.

He looks at me. "But, God, I wanted to be with you. I couldn't stop thinking about you or dreaming about you. And eventually I broke. I had to come and find you."

I blink hard, not sure what to make of what I'm hearing.

"So when you say all this crap about how everything is your fault and you're the reason and . . ."

"I *am* the reason. You just said so yourself!"

"You're *a* reason. The other fucking reason," he shouts, "is me. I'm the reason he's dead."

I shake my head.

"You know it's true. I don't steal his girl? None of that shit happens. I'm not at his party, or I'm there on time unlike the selfish prick I am? None of that shit happens. I see him with you and accept that you were always his? None of that shit happens."

"I wasn't *his*," I say.

"Well, you sure as hell were never mine," he spits back.

"I was in love with you."

"Not enough."

It's not true. I was just stupid and tipsy and horny and flattered and caught off-guard and stupid and stupid. But I loved Luke. I always did.

"I'm sorry," I say now because I've never said it to his face. "It was the dumbest thing I've ever done. And I hate myself just as much as you hate me."

He doesn't deny that he hates me, that even the slightest bit of him hates me. "I could never hate you as much as I hate myself," he says.

He runs his hand through his hair and leans against the wall. We appraise each other for several seconds.

"So what now?" he says with a small, tired smile. "Now that we've yelled at each other in front of the whole neighborhood and any illusion of romance is ruined."

I hate that the answer is on the tip of my tongue. I hate that I know what to do.

"You go back to your life and I go back to mine."

"That's what you want?" he asks.

"That's what needs to happen. We've ruined everything. We *ruin* everything."

I say we, but I still mean *I*.

He just stares at me.

"What did Mel think was the reason I stopped visiting her?"

He brushes a hand over his face. "She said grief was hard to watch. That you couldn't stand to be there for her when you'd just lost your best friend. And she wasn't going to ask you to."

I swallow.

God. Mel.

Always thinking the best of me.

"I have to tell her the truth about that night."

"You don't have to."

"I want to," I say, even though I feel sick at the thought. I'm about to lose one of the best people that ever happened to me—because people do happen, the way natural disasters happen and sickness happens and death happens. They collide for reasons outside of anyone's control, and sometimes they love each other and there's no rhyme or reason to it. They are not flesh and blood, not required to care in any way for each other, but they do. They become each other's home.

I owe it to Mel, after everything, to tell her the truth about how her son died.

"You always had a hard time keeping things from her," Luke muses, rubbing his jaw.

"I used to feel like she just looked at me and knew. That she looked at people and saw everything true about them," I say. "But I think all that really happened was that I talked and she listened."

We are silent a moment, and then Luke says, "When do you want to tell her? Naomi and Bobby are having her stay over at their place tonight. To get her out of her usual environment. She's been going a little stir-crazy."

"Is she well enough for that?" I ask, worried.

"I hope so."

"Can I come over later? When she's out?"

"Uh . . . okay," Luke says, and I can tell he's confused.

"I won't tell her then, obviously," I say. "But there's one last thing I want to do for her."

Before I'm out of her life forever.

Before she never wants to see me again.

"Okay," Luke says.

20

Now that I'm in the Cohen house, my whole idea feels stupid and trite. I stand in the guest room that is now Mel's room and survey the bare walls, the hospital bed, the closet that is almost empty.

"What do you need me to do?" Luke asks, standing in the doorway. It's evening but still bright out, so light spills into the room.

"I'll need your muscles, if that's okay," I say.

He follows me back up the stairs to Mel's real room, the master bedroom she used to sleep in. It's a hundred times warmer than the guest room. The comforter is white, with splashes of colorful paint. There are pictures all over the room of Rowan, Luke, Sydney, Naomi, and even me. Pictures from Mel's time in Hungary during college. There are clothes she doesn't use anymore. A bunch of them are too big now, but I decide we'll take them anyway. Sometimes the most important thing about certain clothes isn't physically wearing them; it's seeing them and remembering who you were in them, where you wore them, who you kissed.

I know I'm shameless now in the white skinny jeans that I love, the ones I was wearing when I kissed Luke that first night. I saw him notice them when he opened the door for me tonight, his eyes roaming the length of me and then trying to act like he hadn't noticed. I didn't wear them for his reaction; I wore them because this weekend has been crappy and I felt like putting on jeans that reminded me of something good.

"Okay, so I don't know if this rug will fit in there," I tell Luke.

He does some mental math and decides it's worth a try. So we spend the next half hour shuffling this giant accent rug out from under Mel's old king-size bed, rolling it up, transporting it down the stairs, and lifting everything off the floor in the guest room to see if it will fit.

"It takes up nearly the whole room," I say, biting my lip as I try to figure out what to do. "Should we take it back upstairs?"

"Seriously? We could have made a trip to IKEA and been back by now," Luke complains, but I can tell he doesn't mind.

"The whole point is that it has to be stuff she owns that we bring in here," I say. "I just wish it fit."

He crouches down and starts to roll up the rug, when I change my mind again.

"Hold on, maybe we can make it work."

He sighs. "I'm guessing we should cross interior decorator off your future careers list?"

"Rude," I say as I lead the way back up the stairs to Mel's old room.

I pile her clothes into some plastic storage containers while Luke collects pictures and knickknacks from around her room. We don't take everything downstairs, but we try to take everything we know she likes or misses.

"Thanks for doing this," Luke says as he hangs up a picture of the three of them plus Sydney.

I shrug. "She'd do the same for me."

And it's true. She *did* do the same for me.

The point of this is to take this sterile room that represents her sickness and make it into home for her. Make it a place she enjoys coming to, where she feels like herself, where she has good memories. Just like she did for me.

It takes a couple of hours, but soon we are standing in a room that doesn't quite look like Mel's old room—it's certainly not as big—but isn't quite a dying woman's room either.

I take a moment to pretend to survey my handiwork, but really I'm saying goodbye to my memories of Mel. Her favorite brown sweater. Her purple house shoes. Her matching purple robe that is almost as ratty as the pajamas I was wearing when Luke came to visit me this morning.

After I come back tomorrow night to tell her the truth, Mel will never welcome me into this house again. I won't have a right to these memories, to her hospitality, to her love.

Luke is watching me look at the room, and he rubs his neck once he's caught. "We still have some cupcakes from last week," he says. "If you're up for it."

"I should probably get going," I say. Now that we're done with the masquerade, he doesn't have to pretend to be nice to me anymore. He doesn't have to treat me like someone who matters. Not like his girlfriend or his ex-girlfriend or his sister or his brother's best friend. I'm "a girl" as far as he is concerned. Or I should be, anyway.

"Mom's not holding down her end of things, in terms of eating them. I'm only one man," he says with a crooked smile.

"One," I concede. "I'll have one."

"Coming right up."

I follow him into the kitchen, my bag still on my shoulder, my keys in hand. I watch as he pulls out a full container of cupcakes.

"You weren't lying," I say as he offers me one, then pours us both glasses of lemonade.

He shakes his head and takes a bite. "It's pretty sad when you have nearly a dozen cupcakes in a house and no one to eat them."

I know it's not intentional on his part, but sadness creeps into the space between us. Once, these cupcakes wouldn't have lasted more than a day. Once, Ro and Mel and even Luke occupied space in this house. *I* occupied space in this house.

"J.J.——" Luke says, drawing me out of my thoughts. I startle, not just at the name, but at the way he says it. Like we are the old Luke and the old Jessi. He says it like it's the summer he loved me again, the best part of it and not the worst.

I don't know what he means to say, and I don't know if he does either.

Instead, our bodies are drawn toward each other, magnets that should repel but are attracting. He touches my hair, and I back up, running right into a wall. Luke closes the distance between us again, his hand finding my waist.

In my head, I'm arguing with him. I'm telling him that I don't belong here, in this house, with him. That I never did. I'm sliding away from his touch. I'm pulling my bag tighter over my shoulder and walking out of his house. In real life I am standing on my tiptoes, wrapping my arms around his neck, drawing him to me.

His lips are soft and gentle against mine. I kiss him back, unhurried and loving and sad. His lips taste like frosting and lemon, bittersweet, like the end of something.

We kiss and kiss against the kitchen wall for what feels like hours, and when we can't possibly kiss anymore, we kiss harder. My tongue claims every spot in his mouth and his hands are starting to roam, starting to burn my skin. When the strap of my bag falls off my shoulder, I let it. In fact, I drop my keys next to it.

After that, it's all over.

He presses me harder against the wall, and I let my feet leave the ground, let them wrap around his waist as he hoists me up. Then we're walking. He's kissing me and carrying me up the stairs.

I haven't been in his room in a year.

It is still not neat, still covered in books, and his bed is unmade. He kicks the door shut with his foot and carries me to the bed. I reach for him, impatient, and pull him down with me. I dig my fingers into his hair and he starts undoing the buttons of my blouse.

Then I'm in my bra and he reaches for the button of my jeans.

"I fucking love these jeans," he rasps.

I surprise him by going for his shorts first, unbuttoning, pulling down. He's on top of me, kissing me again, and it's unfair because his shirt is still on.

He laughs in the back of his throat at my frustration when I try and fail to get his shirt off.

"Want me to do it?"

"No," I say, so he lifts his arms over his head like an obedient child and I yank it up over his head. As soon as it's off, I paw at his chest, his abs, the happy trail going down from his bellybutton. As I'm doing that, he untangles his arms from me enough to reach into the drawer beside his bed for a small silver packet. Our hands and mouths are everywhere. It's a far cry from "I won't touch you" and the last time I was in this bed. I remember thinking that morning that I wanted to do everything with him, and tonight I do.

After, we lie there tangled up in each other. My head on his chest, his hands in my hair. I fall asleep to his heartbeat. Wake up again and he's still there, and it's dark out now, so we go back to the beginning and hold each other in the darkness.

I squint when he turns on the lamp, then shut my eyes against the light.

"Sorry." He plants a kiss on my forehead and gets out of bed. When I hear his footsteps again, I force my lazy eyes open.

He smiles at me as he slips back under the sheets, and he's wearing his glasses. I haven't seen them in so many years, and I don't know why it makes my eyes start to water. Maybe because it takes me back to a time when everything was simpler, when I thought we — Mel, Luke, Ro, and I — would have a happy ending.

"Are you okay?" he whispers as he pulls me to him again. I nod, but he must feel the tears on his bare chest.

In the morning, just enough light streams in through the crack in the curtain. Luke is fast asleep still, the sheets tangled up somewhere around his legs.

I get dressed quietly, make my way downstairs, and find my keys and bag in the kitchen.

I think about leaving a note, but I don't know what else to say.

We said everything last night and yesterday morning when he came to see me.

It's just after five when I step out the front door.

I walk out of Mel's house, knowing that everything will be different the next time I'm here.

NOW

I've barely entered my house when a door shuts and then my mom is hurrying down the stairs.

"Jessi?" she says, as if she's expecting someone else.

"Hey, Mom," I say, not meeting her eyes. I don't know how other kids feel when they're doing the walk of shame, but I feel like she can see everything scrawled all over my skin.

"You cannot be serious," she says, looking me up and down. I check my body for any inadvertent markings, any words, giveaways. As far as I can see, the only signs of where I've been are my bed-tousled hair, my swollen kissing lips, and yesterday's clothes. "You told me you were going to see Luke last night, you don't answer any of my calls, and you just never come home?"

"I'm home now," I say sheepishly.

"No, you're home *the next day*. At five in the morning. Jessi, this isn't like you."

Guilt spreads like fire over my body. "I'm really sor——" I start to say, but my mother speaks over me, her voice growing louder.

"*Five a.m.*, Jessi," she hisses.

I open my mouth to speak again, but she keeps talking. "You might be eighteen, but as long as you live under our roof, you do not get to stay out at all hours, doing God knows what with whoever you like."

"I was with Luke——" I begin.

"I don't care who you were with. I don't know what other people's rules are, but in this house we have a curfew."

I realize there's no point in trying to defend myself. She won't let me speak. Her hands are on her hips as she scowls at me, and despite the fact that she has a point, my remorse begins to morph into frustration.

As she continues her speech, I try to push back the memories of Luke and what we did, how desperately I want to be back in my own bed, reliving each moment. Reliving the warmth and peace I felt in his arms, and the cold and vulnerable feeling that remains in its place. Does Luke feel the same way?

"Jessi," Mom says, and my attention snaps back to her. "Your father and I raised you to be more responsible than this."

I feel myself flinch. Did she just say that?

To be more responsible than what exactly?

And she raised me?

She raised me.

Something inside me snaps.

"I can't do this right now," I say, heading for the stairs.

"I'm talking to you!"

"And I'm walking away!" I shout back. "Because you know what? You do not get to show up on the scene eighteen years late and start telling me what to do. You do not get to decide when to start giving a fuck."

Her eyes widen. "How dare you—"

"How dare I what? Tell the truth? Call you out for something you couldn't control?" I seethe. "I'm not calling you out for being sick, Mom. I get it. I'm sorry having me made things so bad for you."

"It's more complicated than that."

"Well, let me make it more simple. You do not get to have a kid and then opt out of her life. And if there's no opt-out, there sure as hell is no opt-in option."

"What's going on?" Dad's voice comes from the top of the stairs.

"I tried my best," Mom says, and she's crying now.

"So did I. I found homes in other places, with other people."

"Mel," she says. Not a question, just one accusing word. It's the first time I know for sure that it bothered her how much time I spent at the Cohen house. Somehow it still hadn't been enough to wake my mother up to fight for me. She is here now, apparently; what pisses me off is that she's acting like she never left.

"Yes, *Mel*," I spit. My voice trembles like I'm about to cry, which just makes me angrier. "She's been more of a mother to me than you ever were."

"Jessi!" Dad calls sternly from halfway down the stairs. "Stop that right now."

I laugh. "What is it with people who never gave a fuck about my life caring all of a sudden?"

"I always cared," Mom says teary. "I loved you. You knew that."

"Did I?" I ask. "What did you ever do to show me that? What did you ever *do?*"

I'm surprised at myself, the way my voice is rising, the way I'm spitting my words. I never thought we would talk about all of this. How do you condense eighteen years into one conversation?

"I kept going." Mom's voice is small. "I woke up every day, and I kept going.

She shakes her head. "I know now that I should have gotten help sooner. I was so stubborn, and I hate myself for it every day, but my family . . . you have to understand that being depressed wasn't considered a sickness, just a weakness. I thought I could fight it on my own."

"That's what you call fighting it?" I ask. "Being in bed for most of my life?"

Mom gives Dad a desperate look. "I made a lot of mistakes, Jessi. But I'm trying to right them now. I know you can see how far I've come the last few months. It's a work in progress, but I'm doing better. Everything is going to be different now."

"It's too late." I hear myself saying as I back up, starting up the stairs past my father.

"Can't we talk about this?" Mom asks, her voice breaking.

But it's too late for that, too. We didn't talk for the past seventeen years. We didn't talk one year ago, when Mom started treatment and tiny changes started happening. We didn't talk when she was back in bed a few weeks ago. We *never* talk. Why start now?

I break into a run down the hall until I reach my room.

I slam my door and then bury myself in my bed.

Tears come unbidden, for everything I've lost and everything I never had. Two families. Two homes. Two brothers. My best friends. Mel.

I've lost it all, and the saddest part is, I'm still not sure if they were ever mine to begin with.

I sniff my clothes, hoping they still have Luke's scent that I love so much. But I smell nothing; it's all me.

21

Willow's lips form a long, thin line when I arrive at work.

"I'm sorry I didn't get to call you back," I say, remembering the three missed calls from her that I have on my phone.

"That's okay," she says coldly. "I guess you were busy."

"I was. Luke and I worked all day yesterday on this surprise . . ."

Willow holds up her hand to stop me. "Honestly, it's fine, Jessi. You don't need to tell me. You don't need to tell me anything about your life."

I'm surprised at the bitter tone in her voice. I know I should have called her after Friday night at the lake, but I was kind of preoccupied with other stuff.

"Wills, come on," I say, reaching for her shoulder.

She shrugs off my touch. "No, *you* come on. I came here to this town and I wanted to be your friend. I told you about my channel. At camping, I told you about my issues from before . . . And honestly, let's talk about camping. Luke told us about his mom. You told me you like *country songs*," she hisses. "Country songs."

"I do," I say lamely.

"Well, whoop-de-doo," she says. "So does everyone in Texas, where I came from. Tell me something that freaking matters."

I'm not sure if she's actually asking me to tell her now, and then the moment passes, and she's looking even more pissed than she was a minute ago.

"Um . . ."

"Just forget it, Jessi," she says. "College is a couple weeks away. I'll make friends there. I'll be fine."

She starts to walk away before she turns back. "Honestly, it's you I feel sorry for. You push everyone away. You act like you have some kind of plague. You think no one will like you if you tell the truth, but it's only because *you* don't like you. And I hate to break it to you, but you're only one person. You do not get the final say on everyone's opinion of you."

"Willow, I'm sorry," I say, feeling like I'm about to cry. "I really didn't mean to hurt you."

"Luke had a brother?" she asks.

I nod hopefully, thinking maybe she's forgiven me enough to want to know details now.

"And he died?"

I nod again.

"And that's why Eric hates you? Not because of some childhood grudge, but because of whatever happened," she says.

"Yeah. I mean, I think we're fine now, but . . ."

"Wow," Willow says, shaking her head in disbelief. "Eric told me all that. I really should thank you for something."

Hope springs eternal, and my eyes light up again. "What?"

"I realized because of you how completely awful it is to be lied to. If you love someone, you tell them the truth. Everything else is an excuse," she says. "So I told my dad about my channel, and about Brett, and about not wanting to major in business."

"And?" I ask.

"I'll tell my friends in college what he had to say. I have no interest in telling you anything more about myself."

Her words feel like a physical slap. Two of our campers arrive at exactly that moment. Willow busies herself setting up, leaving me to approach them, welling eyes and all.

"Hey, Kelsie, Lydia," I say. "How was your weekend?"

They launch into a story about their Slip 'N Slide, and I nod and try to seem like I'm listening.

Getting to lunch is more of the same, and it's excruciating. The whole thing with Willow hasn't given me enough time to worry about seeing Luke after the weekend, and a sick feeling falls over me as we walk over to the science station. Except it's Sunshine there, not Luke. Maybe, after the way I left him, the thought of seeing me today was too much and he decided to take a sick day. I would probably have done the same.

At lunch, I check my phone and nearly have a heart attack.

I have nine missed calls.

Five from Naomi.

Three from Mom.

One from Dad.

No, I think.

No no no no.

Willow's walking past me in the locker room, about to go out to the cafeteria, but she stops when she sees the expression on my face.

"What's wrong?" she asks, despite herself.

I can't speak. I just show her my call log.

"I don't get it," she says. "Who's Naomi?"

"Luke's mom's best friend. I think . . . I think . . ." The room is spinning around me, and suddenly it makes sense why Luke is not here today.

No no no no.

Willow looks stricken, but she quickly schools her face. "Did anyone leave a message?"

When I shake my head, she says, "Okay, so we don't know for sure. Maybe there's another emergency. Maybe . . ." She seems to reconsider putting any other potential emergencies in my head.

"Let's just sit down and call someone. It's probably nothing," she says.

But it's not.

It's not nothing.

I know it the way I knew what had happened to Ro.

Still, I nod, and my shaking fingers touch Naomi's name on my screen.

After the fight with my mother, the last thing I want is to hear it from either of my parents. Besides, they won't know as much as Naomi knows.

As the phone rings, I start to tell myself that Willow's right. It could be a million other emergencies. I mean, Mel is the most likely one, but it might not be *the* one. She might have another infection. Maybe she's in the hospital.

Maybe it's good news.

"Jessi?" I can tell from Naomi's stuffy voice that it's not good news. I look at Willow, but she just nods encouragingly.

"I saw you called."

She's not dead she's not dead she's not dead

"Mel's unconscious."

She's not dead.

She's not dead.

"Okay, so what do we do? Is there a drug or a surgery . . ."

"Honey, they're not expecting her to wake up," Naomi says now. "You probably wanna come and say goodbye."

22

I want to tell Mel . . .

That Naomi called me honey.

I want to tell Mel that I never got over her oldest son.

I want to tell Mel that I lied to her, that *we* lied to her.

I want to tell Mel that she saved me, that she cared about me when it seemed like nobody else did.

I want to tell her that I'm sorry. There's a whole list of things I'm sorry for, and I'd start at the beginning and go through it.

I'm sorry that the day we met, when she put me and Ro in the minivan and drove us to her house for our first playdate, I purposely spilled the root beer she bought me, because I think root beer tastes like toes.

I'm sorry that a couple of years later, when my dad took me to the clinic because our babysitter canceled, I saw Dr. Cohen walk by the store window, laughing with a blond woman, and I never told anyone. I thought she was beautiful, and I'm sorry for that, too.

There's so much that I want to tell Mel, but when I sit down beside her and hold her hand, all I do is cry.

Cry, whisper "I love you I love you," and choke on the rest of my words.

23

Mel dies two days later in the middle of the night in the guest room of her house. Her nurse is just outside the room, but she's not in a hospital and there are no doctors around. When she was still well enough, she'd made specific arrangements so she could die in her own house.

I'm asleep at home, my home, and I'm tossing and turning, the way I have been since she went into a coma, but I don't feel anything. I don't feel a jolt or an earthquake or an absence in the world. Maybe that's because I felt the jolt the day she told us that her doctor suspected something but it was probably nothing. Maybe I felt the earthquake on the day she told Ro and Luke and Naomi the news, but not me, because I was not family and Ro didn't want me to see him cry. And maybe the absence has been there, growing deeper and deeper every day with each piece of her that was stolen by the Big Bad.

Maybe, maybe not.

Dr. Cohen flies back for her funeral, which Naomi says would irritate Mel, but at least he doesn't bring his new wife, which Naomi says would make Mel die all over again.

I'm glad, though, that he's here for Luke. Luke, who no longer has any other family in the world but the father he hates so much. Luke, who I hurt over and over and over again, who I haven't spoken to since the first night I came to visit Mel after she came home from the hospital. He was in the living room, talking with Bobby, Naomi's husband, and he said "hey" when I walked in and I said "hey," and that was it.

The second night when I came, he was upstairs on the phone. Probably with Courtney. And I hate that I'm petty enough to think that even now. He deserves someone who didn't break his heart, who didn't let his brother drive drunk, who didn't leave his bed in the middle of the night.

The funeral is beautiful. Naomi asks me if I'd like to say a few words, but I refuse. Then she asks me to choose one of Mel's favorite jazz songs for the ceremony. Apparently Mel said in her instructions that I would "know."

I don't know, but I pick "Detour Ahead" by Ella Fitzgerald, and I hope that's okay.

Naomi makes me and my parents sit two seats behind the family row. I've refused to sit any closer. When my mother takes my hand and leads me into the church, I let her. The day Mel passed away, my mother was at my side constantly, running her hands through my hair and asking if I needed anything. I wanted to repeat what I'd said to her — that it was too late, it was already so, so late, but I didn't have the energy for words. And anyway, I no longer know if it is true.

Luke is a pallbearer.

Again, Luke is a pallbearer.

He walks with his head down, takes long, sad steps that look all wrong on him.

The pastor reads from Psalm 23. I guess Mel decided it wasn't too cliché after all.

I cry through the whole ceremony and all through the ride back to Mel's for the wake.

I almost throw up when I step into the house.

It smells like baked goods and food, and it sounds like conversation and life, and it makes me realize that for the last few months the Cohen house smelled and sounded like death and loneliness.

When my parents get caught up talking to one of Mel's neighbors, I can't take it. I can't take the past tense or the sadness, the way they sum her up in simple words.

A "good" lady. A "brave" battle. A "strong" spirit. A "wonderful" mom.

No no no no.

I see his head moving above everyone else's, watch as he says something to his father, and Dr. Cohen pats him on the back and moves aside so Luke can go. Luke starts up the stairs, and before I can stop myself, I'm following after him, squeezing through people's circles.

I watch him from the second step, see the way he exhales and lets his head fall before pushing into the bathroom he and Rowan shared. I pad upstairs behind him, knowing I should let him grieve in peace, knowing I've done enough damage, but needing to be near him.

I knock once on the door.

"Just a minute," he calls back over the sound of running water, and even with a door between us, he sounds broken and lost and afraid.

A couple of seconds later, the door swings open. Luke's face is wet, like he just washed it.

"Sorry, there's a . . ." His voice trails off as he sees me. He just stands there, lets me slip around him into the bathroom.

He shuts the door and looks at me.

I walk back toward him and throw my arms around him. I feel him shaking in my arms and then I'm crying and it's hard to say who is holding who up. All I want is to make this better for him, so I kiss the side of his jaw. He turns so his lips are facing me, and I kiss them too. He kisses me back, and our mouths taste like tears and grief and anger. He presses my back against the vanity, and I untuck his dress shirt from his slacks. His kisses grow wild now and desperate, and he hikes up the skirt of my new black dress. I match his desperation and undo his fly. He reaches above us and opens a medicine cabinet, pulls a box from it and a foil packet. As we get louder, I reach back behind me to open the tap, letting the water drown us out. We hold tight to each other and kiss and cry and fill each other for as long as we can. We stay that way, breathless, for several minutes after, and then he lets go and starts to get dressed again. I watch him, my dress still up around my stomach.

He doesn't say anything before he leaves the room, but he looks back once, and our eyes hold.

When he's gone, I slide down to the floor, pull my knees up to my chest, and sob.

24

Luke doesn't come back to work.

My mom says she heard from the neighbor at Mel's wake that he's
spending the next few weeks at his dad's.

I haven't seen him since that day in the bathroom.

On my first day back at work (a week after Mel's funeral), I arrive
early to set up. As soon as Willow sees me, she hurries over and gives
me a hug.

The day I found out about Mel's coma, Willow was the one to
drive me home. I think she's forgiven me already, but I want her to
know that everything I didn't tell her was about me and my shame
and my guilt. It wasn't about not trusting her or not wanting to be
her friend.

She nods. "I get it. I'm sorry everything sucks so much right now."

I swallow to keep from crying. "Can I tell you about them?" I ask.
"The Cohens?"

"All of them?" Willow asks.

"All of them," I say.

She nods.

So I do.

When I enter Ernie's unit after two weeks away, he heaves a huge
sigh of resignation. "I thought you'd finally heard me and left while
you were ahead."

"I told you it's not happening," I say, trying my best to be as lively as possible.

"So what happened to you then? Jail time? Food poisoning?"

I laugh. "Food poisoning for two weeks?"

He cuts me with a withering look, as if I don't even know the things he has seen.

I sit down next to his rocking chair, and he says, "Well, what's the story? Someone break your heart?"

I shake my head. "Someone died."

"Sorry," Ernie says, sounding sincere for possibly the first time since I've met him.

"Thanks. It was a long time coming." I add the disclaimer because I've spent the last week trying to numb my pain by telling myself that I knew this was coming. And yet everything still hurts.

"Doesn't make it any better," he says. "Hell, I've been dying for eighty-seven years and I'm still no good at it."

I smile. "That's a good thing, Ernie."

He harrumphs. "You missed a lot while you were gone," he says.

"Tell me," I say.

"The granddaughter sent me this watch thing. Except it doesn't tell the time. It's blasting music, showing pictures. It's terrible." He pulls it out from his pocket and shows me.

"Ernie, this is really cool. It's the latest fashion."

"Why does a wrinkled potato like me need the latest fashion?"

"You can talk to your great-grandkids with it, you can turn on your music without having to get up and go to your speaker. So many cool things. I'm going to show you how to use it, okay?"

Ernie seems skeptical, but he patiently sits through our tutorial.

Thirty minutes later he knows how to check and respond to messages and also to check the time, which he claims is the only thing he really needs it for.

"Now I can text you, and you can text me back," I tell Ernie.

"If I have something to say to you, I'll say it when you're here. Unless you've wised up and decided to stop coming after all."

"No, I have not," I say firmly. "And you better respond to my texts. It's rude not to."

He mutters something under his breath.

"What was that?" I ask.

"I'm saying maybe my brother got the better end of the deal, not having to deal with this nonsense. Gareth Richard Solomon IV, the lucky son of a bitch."

I try not to laugh.

"I haven't told you the best news," Ernie says now, after we've put the watch away for the day. "Clarisse has asked to be moved from next door. Says living beside me has been a nightmare, worse than all her previous marriages combined."

He slaps his thigh as he roars with laughter, but I only shake my head.

"She seems like a nice lady. Maybe the two of you could have been friends if you'd been kinder to her."

"Oh, come on," Ernie says. "What's the point of making it this far in life if I can't have a little fun every now and again?"

"Kimberley said she would send the fart machine," he continues now. "So whoever the next goddamned sucker is, he's in for something special. I give him a month."

Maybe I've fallen out of the rhythm, being away from Ernie for a couple of weeks, but instead of laughing with him the way I might have, I just feel sad. Why is he so determined to keep everyone away? He chases off all his neighbors, tells me repeatedly not to come back, and acts for his family like he doesn't care if they visit or not.

He's never denied what he's doing, either. He straight up told me weeks ago that he wants me to go before I get sick of him. And maybe I should be the one who's worried about him getting sick of me, but I'm all he has, and I care about him. If Mel taught me anything, it's that being all someone has and caring about them counts for a lot.

"You know there's nothing you can do to chase me away, right?" I tell him now, but he just snorts.

At the end of my two hours with him, I squeeze his arm. "I'll see you in a couple of days, Ernie."

He doesn't say anything as he watches me go.

Over the next few weeks I fall back into a rhythm. Camp, Ernie, tennis lessons. In the last week of August, Willow's dad calls me into his office at Tennis Win and asks if I'm interested in a paid part-time coaching position. I'd pretty much be doing the same hours, but I'd be paid for it. It's basically a no-brainer. Except it's not why I started volunteering at the club. First, they lost an instructor when they lost Ro. Second, I wanted to make someone love tennis as much as Ro did. He never got to come back to Winchester and become head coach, the way he always said he would if he didn't make it as a pro or when his tennis career was over.

So I thank Mr. Hastings for the offer and say I'd rather keep volunteering. He looks at me like I've sprouted a second head.

"I'm essentially offering to pay you for exactly what you're already doing," he says.

"I know. I just don't feel comfortable taking it," I say. "This is my way to . . . give back."

He stares at me for a second, then shakes his head. "All right. Let me know if you change your mind."

I promise I will, but I know I won't.

The next day, Diana calls me into her office to talk to me. In my mind, because the meeting with Mr. Hastings was a "good" thing, this meeting with my boss has to be a bad thing. It's the only way the universe maintains its balance.

"You wanted to see me?" I say, sticking my head into her office.

"Yes. Come and have a seat," she says, motioning to the empty chair on the opposite side of her desk. "So—all of us here at Camp MORE have been so impressed by your work over the summer. Now that camp is ending, most of your fellow leaders are going back to school or college, but I understand you'll be in Winchester for another year?"

I nod.

"Great. Before you commit to something else, I wanted to talk to you and see if you would be willing to be part of the team that runs our day programs during the school year."

"Really?" I ask.

She smiles at me. "Really."

I take the job. I'm not stupid enough to think I don't need some sort of job for the next year, and this is different from the tennis thing. Plus, this would be forty hours a week, and between my other job with Ernie and continuing to volunteer, almost every hour in my day will be accounted for.

The last day of camp is full of tearful goodbyes, full of hugs and colorful drawings offered as gifts from the kids. I'm sad the summer's over, but I'm sad in general, so I barely feel anything.

On Sunday, two days after the end of camp, I stand in Willow's driveway and hug her before her parents take her to the airport.

"Everyone remembers my best friend Jessi from the camping video, right?" she asks, pointing the camera at me. I try not to stiffen or act like a weirdo. "Well, she's here saying goodbye now. She brought me these Red Vines and a gorgeous new camera bag that I can't wait to start using."

She puts her arm around me and pulls me into the frame with her. "I'm so sad, I don't wanna leave anymore."

"You'll love Houston," I say, a lump forming in my throat as I realize I am losing my last friend.

"Probably," she says. "But it won't have you or Brett."

She's sniffling suddenly, and then her camera goes down and we're hugging.

"Ugh, I'm ruining my makeup," she says.

"No, you're fine," I say, wiping some mascara off her cheek.

"Did Brett tell you he's coming to visit me next weekend?"

I shake my head.

"That's making me feel a little better. I'm also excited for us to no longer be under the watchful eye of the parental units," she whispers. Her parents are puttering around inside, but they do not need to hear this.

"Aren't you still recording?" I ask, and I laugh as Willow says an uncharacteristic curse word before turning the camera off.

"Promise to keep me up to date on any Luke developments," she says. She is still hopeful that Luke and I will get back together, even though I've told her we haven't spoken since the wake.

"There won't be any, but okay."

"Be nice to yourself," she says now, throwing her arms around me one more time. A few minutes later I walk back to my car, wave one more time at Willow, and drive home.

25

Mom 2.0 calls a family meeting a couple of days after Willow leaves, and four days after Camp MORE ends. I've been part of several Cohen family meetings, where they discussed things like chores and the dog not being allowed on the furniture and other random things families argue over.

Naturally, my family has never had one of these. At least they've never had one involving me. For all I know, my parents have had dozens of them in the past.

I flop down on the couch after dinner, wary and unsure of what to expect. If I'm being honest, I'm also feeling slightly defensive. After all, we've never talked about the fight we had the day I came home from Luke's at five in the morning. When Mel died, my parents acted as if I hadn't said any of the things I'd said, and we all sort of went back to our version of normal.

Strangely, even though my mother called the meeting, she looks nervous, too. In the last couple of months I've started to notice that her eyes blink fast when she's anxious about something. It's such a tiny thing, a random detail anyone could miss, but all it does is remind me of how much I don't know about her. How little time I've spent with my own mother.

Dad sits beside Mom on the loveseat and looks at her, letting her take the lead.

"I'm sure we all remember the incident from a couple of weeks ago," she begins now, looking pointedly at me. I fold my arms across my chest, bracing myself. I know I should feel bad for going off on them like that, but to be honest, I don't really regret anything I said. And I'm not sure I can offer a convincing apology, if that's what this meeting is about.

Since Mel's death, I've felt numb. Distant from everything and everyone. Like I'm on an island by myself. One without touch or sound or sensation of any kind. I feel . . . mute.

"It was pretty . . . unpleasant," Mom says now. "Which is why I want to apologize."

Her words draw me back to this moment, and I'm not entirely sure I heard right. "Apologize?" I repeat.

Mom nods. "I owe you an apology for the past eighteen years, but for that morning too. Jessi, I know how much it hurt you, my being so absent from your life for so many years." She blinks hard now, and I see her eyes welling with tears. "It's the thing I regret most in the world — the thing I'll always regret, to have wasted so much time."

"You were sick," I say, feeling guilty. It's true that she was clearly not well, and my words during that argument weren't very understanding.

"I know I was," Mom says, "but I was also so stubborn and hard-headed." She looks at Dad, then back at me. "Honey, how much do you know about our lives before we had you?"

I shrug. "I know you met in grad school, that you traveled a bunch before you opened EyeCon. That you were happy." My eyes drift to the pictures mounted on the walls, most of them pictures of my parents before me or pictures of me alone, growing up. We don't have a lot of family pictures of the three of us.

"We *were* happy," Dad says now. "But we also overcame a lot."

"Mom's family?" I guess, and my mother nods.

"I told you a while ago how they felt about your father and our marriage."

"They had a lot of outdated views," Dad says. "I wish we'd told you about it sooner, but we thought we were making it easier for you, keeping you from the ugliness of that, letting you grow up to see that people of different colors can love each other. Because they *can*."

He looks at Mom as he says it, and for all the things I've doubted in my life — whether my mother loved me, whether the Cohens saw me as one of their own, whether I could ever truly belong anywhere — that was the one thing I've never doubted: how much they loved each other.

"Another of their outdated beliefs was about mental health," Mom continues. "You didn't treat depression in my family; you ignored it or rose above it."

"I owe you an apology, too," Dad says. "Because I let my own pride get in the way. You see, soon after your mother had you, I knew she was sick. It was like night and day how different she was. She lost her appetite, her drive, her joy."

I swallow. This part I know all too well.

"After the first couple of months I started pushing for her to get help, but she was so resistant. I tried to get her into therapy, tried to get her to see a bunch of doctors, but she wouldn't do it. And she started to resent me for it, to pull away from me. I couldn't bear the

thought of losing her, so I . . . I stopped pushing so hard. And this —
the way she was — became our norm. I convinced myself that as long
as she wasn't in crisis, I didn't need to worry. I told myself, *she still
makes it to work most days. She's not suicidal. She just needs rest and time."*

The familiar refrain from my childhood makes my head spin.

"It obviously didn't help," I say, surprised to hear the anger in my
voice.

"I know," Dad says. "I still brought it up sometimes, tried to talk
her into seeing different doctors, discussing treatment options."

"I wasn't . . . ready," Mom says. "Most days I could convince
myself that I was just tired, just overwhelmed, but on the days when
I could admit that something was wrong, I bullied myself into believing I was weak, that I should be able to snap out of it. You don't know
how much you internalize from the family you're born into."

It reminds me of what Luke said while we were camping over
the summer. About how he'd learned things from his father he didn't
know he had. My mind flits to him briefly and I wonder how he's
doing, how he's coping without Mel, whether he thinks of me.

"Like your father said," Mom continues, "I wasn't suicidal. I was
mostly functional. I just wasn't happy or present, and that didn't
sound sick to me. It sounded like something I should be able to fix on
my own . . .

"It was the day Mel was diagnosed, when I saw what it did to you,
that something changed. I didn't make the jump to getting help right
away — that came a few months later. But seeing you that day . . .
you were so heartbroken at the thought of losing Mel, and I realized
you wouldn't have anything to grieve if you ever lost me, your own
mother. Because I hadn't been there for you. I hadn't . . ."

She's crying too hard now to keep speaking, and Dad rubs her knee.

"You got help because of me?" I am incredulous. "Even though I was the reason you were sick to begin with?"

My parents exchange a look.

"Jessi, you were *not* the reason your mother was sick," Dad says firmly. "Yes, her issues started postpartum, but that's biological, neurochemical, nothing to do with you."

Mom crosses the room and takes my face in her hands, her hands that are warm for the first time that I can remember.

"You were the bright spot in my life, the thing that kept me going," she says, tears still streaming down her face. "I loved you. I *love* you."

I broke you, I think, but as if she can read my thoughts, Mom shakes her head.

"Don't you ever believe anything else," she says, her hands still cupping my face.

My eyes are filling, and I blink hard and fast.

"You said something the other morning — that it was too late," Dad says now. "Too late for us to change how things are in this family, but I think your mother's progress the last few months shows that it's never too late. That there's always hope . . . as long as you're willing to try."

It's similar to the conversation Mom and I had at the start of the summer about me being back in Mel's life despite all the time that had passed.

Mom lets go of my face and sits down on the couch beside me, reaching for my hand like she's afraid to let me go.

"I guess that's what we want you to think about," she says. "If you're willing to give us—this family—another chance. We've failed you, and we might not deserve it, but we're asking for it."

I've waited all my life to hear this. Literally, all my life. Even now, when I'm eighteen and old enough that my family should matter less, it still makes my heart beat faster. Still makes me wonder if there's a chance that everything *can* get better. But then I remember how much time has passed, and I remember that Mel is gone, and Luke and Ro and Sydney. I remember that the pillars of my life for so long have crumbled, and I don't know if I have the energy to try to rebuild it.

"Just think about it," Mom says now.

Right in this moment, her eyes don't have the determination and fervor of Mom 2.0. But neither do they have the sad, vacant look of the mother I've known for eighteen years. They look desperate and present and a little bit hopeful. The strangest thing, though, is that they also look the slightest bit familiar. Like the woman in the pictures from when my parents were newlyweds and traveling around the world. They look like someone who's slowly coming back from the dead.

"Think about it," Dad echoes, so I promise them I will.

26

When I wake up the next morning to a ringing phone and see Naomi's name on my screen, my first reaction is panic. I reach for it, chest tight, and answer.

"Jessi," Naomi says. "Where do you live?"

"Me?"

"No, the pope," she says impatiently. "What's your address? I have something for you."

"Oh . . . um, okay," I say. I tell her my address, and when she says she'll be over in half an hour, I climb out of bed and try to make myself presentable.

True to her word, the doorbell rings exactly twenty-nine minutes after she called. My parents are both working today, and my new gig at the community center doesn't start till next week. Quite frankly, I'm prepared for this week to be a bitch.

What I'm not prepared for is the big brown box Naomi hands me when I answer the door.

"These are for you," she says in lieu of a greeting. It is reassuring in a strange way to have the curt Naomi back. The one who doesn't call me honey or give me pitying looks. The one who is too much of a hard-ass to cry even if she's hurting just as much as I am.

Naomi pushes past me and leads the way into the living room, so I guess this isn't a quick visit.

The box is taped up, and I set it down on the ottoman in the living room. "Can I open it?"

"I don't care what you do with it," she says.

I go to the kitchen and come back with a knife. When I rip the box open, I gasp. It's full of Mel's whole musical collection.

"I can't take this," I say.

"Why not?"

"It's Mel's," I say.

"Does it look like Mel is enjoying its full benefits at the moment?" she asks. "She told me to give it to you. Don't make me have to drive around trying to find some place to donate it."

"I . . . okay," I say. "Thank you."

Naomi sits on our brand-new gray sofa. She pets it, as if she can tell it's new. "This is nice."

"My mom will be happy to hear you said that."

"How's she doing?" Naomi asks, surprising me. "Your mom."

I shrug, remembering the talk we had last night, the things my parents told me that I never knew. "I guess she still has good days and bad days, but mostly she's doing okay."

She nods. "Mel was worried about you," she says.

"Because of my mom?" I ask, wondering if there is a connection to our previous topic.

"Honestly I don't know why. Maybe because, if she allowed herself to admit it, she'd have seen that you and Luke were acting like a couple of novices in drama school."

"I . . ." I open and shut my mouth. "I don't know what you mean."

"Something was up with you two," Naomi says. "I knew it from the moment I laid eyes on you after all those months."

"We were newly back together," I lie.

Naomi waves her hand, like she's not interested in the details. "Mel didn't want to ask questions, because she didn't want to know. She wanted to believe that you two were happy and that you would take care of each other, but I think in her heart of hearts she knew something was off."

"Is he . . . is Luke okay?" I ask now. "Have you talked to him?"

She nods. "As okay as can be expected. It's been a rough year."

I don't say anything.

"I think he's heading back to school this semester," she continues. "It's soon, but you know that's his bread and butter. When you lose everything that feels like home, you go to the next best thing."

I nod, staring down at the carpet. I feel like she's summed up my life in a nutshell.

"Anyway," Naomi says, looking me up and down. "What do you do with yourself these days?"

"I'm working," I say. "Not right now, obviously," I add, feeling self-conscious about my ragged pajamas.

"Mmhmm," she says. "Still not done punishing yourself?"

I appraise her with wide eyes. "What?"

"Punishing yourself," she repeats, like I'm hard of hearing. "The seventeen jobs, the no friends, not going to school, giving up on Luke, all of it."

I blink at her. "I have friends." I sound ridiculous, like I'm two years old, but what the hell is she even talking about? She knows nothing about my life. She's not Mel. We've barely ever talked.

"Then why are you acting this way?"

"I'm not acting any way," I say, feeling my blood get warm. "Naomi, I think maybe you should go."

She completely ignores me. "I don't need to know all the details to know that you're punishing yourself."

I can't believe how completely obnoxious she's being. I open my mouth to tell her just that, but what comes out is, "You don't know what you're talking about. You don't know everything I've done."

"What did you do, kill someone?" she asks mockingly, and my skin stings with anger, my throat closing up.

I don't say anything.

"Whatever you've done . . . if it's a crime, turn yourself in to the police. If it's not a crime, say sorry and move on."

I can't believe she said that. She doesn't even know . . . she has no idea.

"I can't just *move on*," I say.

"Why not?"

"Because I can't undo it. He's gone and he's not coming back."

Naomi's eyes soften, and I think she realizes for the first time that I'm talking about Rowan. "You didn't kill him."

"I didn't stop him."

"You didn't heal Mel either," Naomi says. "Because you *couldn't*. No one could."

"I could have stopped Rowan," I say, and my eyes are spilling over.

"You didn't put him in that car. You didn't get him drunk. That boy . . . that boy did a damn stupid thing." Her voice is breaking now. "He did plenty of stupid things. Remember when he showed up drunk at the Continental?"

348

"He was struggling because of Mel's diagnosis," I say, swiping a hand over my eyes.

"We all were," Naomi says. "There's no point in badmouthing him now, even though I have Things to say. Do you know Mel blamed herself, too? For not being stricter, for not paying more attention, for letting him have that party at the lake."

"It wasn't her fault."

"Or maybe it was, a little bit," Naomi says, and I can't believe she's saying that. "Maybe it was your fault a little bit, too. But you've *paid* for it, and you'll pay for it for the rest of your life, because he's gone."

I'm bawling my eyes out now, crying so hard it's difficult to breathe. "I just want to go back to that night."

"You can't. All you can do is go forward."

"I'm trying," I say. "I'm trying to be better."

"The only way to be better is *to be better*," Naomi says, and I wonder when she dispensed with being Mel's irritable best friend and turned into a life coach. "Making life miserable for yourself isn't changing anything. It's not even being a martyr. It's being stupid."

I keep struggling for breath.

Naomi continues, "I mean, your refusing to go to school . . . If you don't want to go to college, don't go. But if you do, why are you here?"

"I don't know what I want to do."

"Bullshit," she says. "You're afraid to make another mistake. But guess what? You're going to make plenty more. Those plaid pants are a mistake."

She points at my old pajamas, and I almost—almost smile.

"I think something's wrong with me," I blurt out instead, and Naomi raises an eyebrow. "There's something about me. I can't make the people I love stay."

"Neither can I," she says.

"No, it's . . . me," I wheeze out. I'm crying so heavily that every time I open my mouth, I taste salt water. "It's my Big Bad. I chase people away or destroy them or something."

She gives a dismissive wave of her hands. "Oh, not that nonsense."

"Mel said everyone has one."

"Mel also said John Travolta would marry her someday. I'm telling you—it's in her high school yearbook."

At first I think she doesn't get it, so I start to explain. How for so long I have believed this horrible thing about my life—that just by being born, I stole the light from my mother's eyes. I tell her about my father, how he chased after Mom and constantly left me. How I didn't just lose the entire Cohen family—I obliterated them.

I did that.

Hurt Luke. Got Ro killed. Abandoned Mel. Hurt Luke again.

"That's not a Big Bad," Naomi says. "That's called life. Shit happens."

She narrows her eyes and leans forward so she's looking me right in the eye. "Listen to me," she says slowly. "I can't make people I love stay either."

It's the second time she's said it, but the first time it makes sense to me.

That maybe it's not me, or whatever is inside me, that drives away and destroys and ends things. Maybe things happen just because, and maybe it has nothing to do with me.

Except that doesn't bring anybody back. It doesn't change any of what has happened.

"I don't know what to do anymore. They're all gone. All three of them are gone."

"Maybe," she says, "but maybe not."

At first I think she means that Luke is still alive, but then she says, "Personally, I see Mel all around me every day. I hear her voice. I hear her favorite songs. And Ro—I can't get through a tennis match without thinking of him."

"Me, too," I admit.

"I can't get through a tennis match at all," Naomi amends now. "I like gymnastics. Every other sport is unbearable."

I choke out a laugh. Then I sober up again. "Mel would never forgive me if she knew the truth about what I did."

"Oh because there was other stuff she never forgave you for when she was alive?"

"I never did anything this bad."

Naomi rolls her eyes. "She loved you like her own child, and you know that."

"But I *wasn't* her child."

"And she still loved you," she argues. "Maybe you're right and Mel wouldn't have forgiven you, but so what? Who was she, God? She wasn't a saint. You don't need her blessing on every single area of your life. She was just a woman."

"She was Mel," I say.

Naomi sighs, like I'm not getting her point. "Yes, that was her name," she says. "And she was just a woman, but she loved you."

Naomi stands then, as if her work is done, as if there's nothing more she can say that will penetrate my thick head, and maybe she's right.

I still want Mel's forgiveness.

I still want her approval and her love and the way she made me feel at home. I don't know if anybody else will ever make me feel like that again.

Still, I cross the living room floor and hug Naomi tight, the way Mel and I used to hug. She stiffens and awkwardly pats my back.

"Thank you," I say.

After Naomi leaves, I come back to the living room, ball up on the couch, and cry. I cry for the people I love and for the people I lost. I cry for the mother who wouldn't wake up and for the one who never will again. I cry because of that night, and because of all the horrible things I still think and believe about myself as a result of it.

I don't know if I will ever be okay with me, the way Willow learned to be okay with herself. The way Mel was okay with herself.

But I decide right here and now that I have to try.

I have to try, because hating myself didn't save Ro's life or Mel's. It didn't give me Luke, and it didn't change the past.

I choose a random CD from the box Naomi brought over and stick it into the old stereo system in our living room.

Ella's beautiful voice fills the room. For a moment, I am seven and nine and thirteen, dancing in the Cohen living room with Mel. We are twirling and shimmying and laughing, okay and hopeful and alive. Then I am eighteen, alone in my living room. Not yet okay and not exactly hopeful, but completely alive.

It's not everything, but it's a start.

27

MARCH

Snow crunches beneath my boots as I walk across campus. It's a cloudy day, a film of gray covering the sky. I've just gotten out of my anatomy class when I feel my phone vibrate with a text. It's from Willow, telling me that she is going home for spring break.

What about you? she asks. **Or are you doing a crazy Mexico trip with all your new friends?**

I smile as I text back. **No Mexico trip. I'm probably coming home.**

She writes back almost immediately. **Yay!!!!**

While I have my phone out, I decide to take a selfie and send it to Ernie. I know it will piss him off. He hates getting pictures on his watch. But I figure if he gets to troll people constantly, I should get to troll him occasionally.

I've also texted or called him every couple of weeks since I've been at State. When I told him in December that I was leaving in January to go to school, he'd done his whole "yep, told you you'd get sick of me" bit, but I could tell he was hurt. I promised to keep in touch and make him get good use out of that watch.

"I already get good use out of it!" he said. "I check the time!"

"Now we can also check in on each other."

He harrumphed and changed the subject.

I find a tree that is stripped nude by winter but has wild, tangled branches that should make a nice background. Then I drop my backpack on the ground, hold my phone up, and smile for the camera.

"Thought you were camera shy." I nearly drop my phone at the sound. "Or is it *shy* shy?"

I turn and find Luke standing behind me, looking awkward and beautiful and here.

"Sorry if this is weird," he says when I haven't spoken. "I was on my way to class, and I thought I saw someone who looked like you, so I turned around and . . ." He runs his hand over his jaw. "Yeah—out loud, it's all coming out much creepier than it seemed in my head."

"No. It's not weird," I lie.

"I didn't know you were . . . here. I thought you said in September."

"I changed my mind. I started in January." I can see the wheels turning in his mind. If we've been on the same campus for three months, how have we managed to avoid each other all this time? The truth is, I've seen him, in the distance, walking with friends. One time he was nursing a cup of coffee over his laptop in the library. When you know to look for someone, it's much easier to spot them than when you don't know they're even in the same town.

"Oh," Luke says, and I can't tell whether he's hurt or surprised or relieved that I didn't text or call him and say I was here.

"Well," he says. "It's good to see you. You look great."

"You too," I say, a lump forming in my throat again at our stilted conversation. It's the conversation of two strangers who don't know anything about each other. Or maybe it's the conversation of two people who know too much about each other and have run out of things to say.

"I better get to class," Luke says, and starts to go. I raise one hand in a wave and turn my attention back to my phone screen, trying not to spiral over this one meaningless meeting.

I've just sent the selfie to Ernie when I hear Luke's voice again. "Actually," he says, "I'm not really . . . it feels weird to see you and then just go to class."

My face warms, even though there is absolutely nothing embarrassing about what he just said. "Yeah, for me too," I admit.

He rubs the back of his neck. "There's this great fro-yo place not far off campus," he says. "I mean, if you want. No pressure."

I swallow. "Sure."

We make small talk as we walk to Luke's car in the parking lot of his residence complex. He tells me he's changed his major to engineering, and I tell him I'm trying out nursing, but I don't know if it will stick.

"You'd be a great nurse. You're good at taking care of people," he says.

I inwardly flinch at the irony. I didn't take care of Luke, not while we were dating, not when Ro died, and not when Mel did. If anything, I've always been great at being taken care of. Especially by the Cohens.

When we reach Luke's car, he puts our backpacks in his trunk. I climb into the passenger seat and he jumps in on the driver's side.

A few minutes later we're at the fro-yo store. I order first and quickly pay for my own yogurt so we don't have a whole "who's paying" thing, and Luke doesn't say anything.

We settle at a table near the window. It's a little cold for frozen dessert, but this whole encounter with Luke plus the indoor heating at Yo Yo Fro-Yo is making me sweat. I peel off my jacket, hang it on the back of my chair, and then tug down the long sleeve of my shirt as quickly as possible.

Except I'm not quick enough.

Luke leans forward across the table. "You got a tattoo?"

"Yeah. It's nothing—just some words."

"Can I see?" he asks, reaching out his hand and carefully pushing the sleeve back up my arm. I feel all kinds of lightheaded at his touch and exposed by the quiet way he studies the words that cover the dip between my arm and elbow.

Happy, grateful, well-dressed, brave, alive, the words say.

I see Luke swallow as he keeps staring at them.

"I just always loved it ever since she said it that night," I say, rushing to explain. "It's not like I think I have the right to her words or anything like that. I just never forgot it, and I always thought . . ."

"It's nice," Luke says, retracting his hand and digging his spoon into his cup of yogurt. "She'd have loved it."

I don't know what to say, so I say nothing.

"When'd you get it?" he asks.

"October," I say. He glances up at me then, meets my eye.

October, which used to be the worst month of our lives, before August was. Or maybe it was still October.

"I like it a lot," he says. "You added an extra word, though."

I'm surprised that he noticed. I mean, duh, he was there when Mel said it. I just didn't think it made as profound an impact on anyone else as it did on me.

"Yeah," I say. When I got those words put on my arm, I thought a lot about Mel, but I also thought about me. I thought about the way I'd felt about myself the last year, like I belonged nowhere, like I would never be able to hold on to everyone I loved.

Ever since the talk with my parents, things had gotten better between us, but that didn't mean everything was always great. This new family that had meetings and laughed together and hung out still felt shaky.

But as the artist started to draw those words on in black ink, I'd decided something: it didn't matter whether my family broke again or whether it didn't. It didn't matter whether I had ever been an official member of the Cohen family or whether I hadn't. Not because they stopped mattering to me. If anything, they mattered more to me than ever, because I knew now that we *had* been family, we had chosen each other, and that was a special kind of beautiful.

But I also wanted something I could hold on to, a sense of belonging that never went away.

Maybe those words — the things I chose to believe about myself and the things I aspired to be — could be the space I carved for myself in this world, a place I could come back to over and over again, and it would always be there because it was inside me.

I say none of this out loud, and Luke and I are back to eating silently. When we're done, we walk back out to his car. He looks like he's deep in thought, and when we climb in, he doesn't start the car.

He runs his hand through his hair. "I'm going to be really bad at this," he says. "Seeing you, then going back to pretending not to know that you're here."

"I'll keep my distance," I promise, but he shakes his head.

"That's not what I mean," he says. "Or, rather, I don't know what I mean, but I don't want us to be strangers."

I blink at him. "Let's not be, then."

"I'm not promising I can be your friend." He doesn't look at me as he speaks—as if he's just made an awful confession.

I'm confused. Does he want me to change schools? Because that's kind of ridiculous. It's not like I followed him here. This is the best school in our state.

"I don't know what you want me to say," I say now.

"Maybe let's not say anything," he says. "No promises, but no bullshitting either."

I frown. "I don't get—"

"I want to know you," he says. "But not as Mel's son or Ro's brother or an ex or a coworker."

"That's pretty much all the titles."

He gives me a crooked smile. "So let's figure out what's left," he says.

I think about saying no.

For all the usual excuses.

We don't work.

We made mistakes.

I fucked everything up.

I don't deserve to be happy.

But I stop myself and recite the words I got inked on my skin just for moments like this. For moments that matter.

Mel's words, which would have been with me forever even if I hadn't gotten the tattoo.

Happy, grateful, well-dressed, brave. Alive.

I am all those things, and I don't know if there's room for Luke Cohen somewhere in there, but I'm willing to find out.

ACKNOWLEDGMENTS

Thank you to my wonderful editor, Emilia Rhodes, for making this book shine. Working with you has been such a pleasure!

Thank you to my amazing agent, Suzie Townsend, for championing each and every one of my books. Your passion and insight are unmatched.

Thank you to everyone at HMH who has had a hand in making this into a real live book, especially Mary Claire Cruz, who designed my beautiful cover, Helen Seachrist, Elizabeth Agyemang, Nadia Almahdi, and John Sellers. Thank you also to everyone at Team New Leaf, especially Dani Segelbaum and Pouya Shahbazian.

Thank you to my family and my friends who are family. Ruthie, for reading every draft and loving all my characters as much as I do. Esther and Grace, thank you for wanting to shout from the rooftops. Bek, for always remembering the length of forever. Cassie, thank you for teaching me to find my light! I'm still quite bad at it, but oh well!

Infinite thanks to the "dream team": Josh Woods, Karen Ng, Lydia Adebiyi, Nora Van Beek, Devin Bouchard, and Ife Hunter.

And last but not least, thank you to everyone who has read, reviewed, or shared my books. I am beyond grateful!

"Okay," I say.

He grins, starts the car, and looks over at me.

Before I know it, one hand is on my cheek, gently brushing hair off my face.

"Where's home, J.J.?" he asks me.

"I'll show you."

Find Your Story

HMH teen

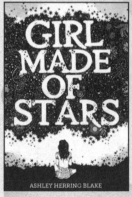